THE ULYSSES THEME

THE
ULYSSES THEME

*A Study in the Adaptability
of a Traditional Hero*

By W. B. STANFORD

BASIL BLACKWELL
OXFORD
1954

Printed in Great Britain for Basil Blackwell & Mott, Limited
by A. R. Mowbray & Co. Limited in the City of Oxford
and bound at the Kemp Hall Bindery

PREFACE

BEING curious to know why some modern variations on the Ulysses theme—Dante's, Tennyson's, and Joyce's, for example —differed so much from the classical prototypes, I looked for some comprehensive study of the tradition and found none. The Greek and Roman periods had been summarily surveyed in two German encyclopaedias and in a series of articles by an Italian scholar. There were many scattered essays and monographs on special phases of the classical and vernacular traditions. But no one, apparently, had tried to trace the development of the theme continuously from ancient to modern times. So it seemed worth while as a sequel to editing Homer's *Odyssey* to undertake this study of Ulysses's strangely varied wanderings in European literature.

Some explanations are due. Readers primarily interested in the classical period must be warned that my interpretation of Homer's Ulysses is based on a belief in the artistic unity of the *Iliad* and *Odyssey* as we now have them. This hypothesis, of course, begs a big question. But, whatever may be said against it on scholastic grounds, it at least has the support of almost every creative writer who has written on the Ulysses theme; and I found nothing in my further studies of Homer's characterization to make me disbelieve it: on the contrary the portraiture of Ulysses in each poem seemed more and more to reveal a unity of conception. It remains open for someone else to write another book based on the assumption of several Homers and more than one 'Homeric' Ulysses.

To readers more interested in the modern tradition I owe an apology for the comparative brevity of the later chapters. I originally planned a second volume for the post-classical period, but eventually ('let the cobbler get back to his last') decided against it. So, instead of trying to cover the modern ground as fully as the classical, I have offered an outline of what seemed to be the most characteristic developments in the Western traditions. Some details have been published in earlier articles, as cited later. If through ignorance or misjudgement I have omitted any major modern variations on the classical themes, I can only apologize, warning the reader that my knowledge of the post-classical period is mostly that of an inquisitive amateur.

I am grateful to many friends for help in collecting material and in preparing the work for publication. Most of these are named in the footnotes. Here I should like to express my special thanks to: Dr. M. H. A. L. H. van der Valk who suggested improvements in the chapters on the Greek epic and elsewhere; Mr. George Savidis to whom I owe most of my information about the modern Greek contributions to the tradition; Mr. and Mrs. J. V. Luce who made many helpful suggestions on the earlier drafts; Dr. W. H. Porter, whose discerning sense of style and fitness has prevented many lapses; the Rev. C. W. C. Quin who helped with criticism and encouragement; and especially to my wife who spared herself no effort in emending and checking every page of the successive typescripts and proofs. Finally I should like to thank Mr. Basil Blackwell for having so readily undertaken to publish this rather experimental book.

W. B. STANFORD.

9 TRINITY COLLEGE,
    DUBLIN.
July 1954.

CONTENTS

MODERN VARIATIONS ON THE CLASSICAL THEMES

x *Contents*

THE ULYSSES THEME

CHAPTER I

THE ADAPTABILITY OF MYTHICAL FIGURES

'WE have been too early acquainted with the poetical heroes to expect any pleasure from their revival; to show them as they already have been shown, is to disgust by repetition; to give them new qualities or new adventures, is to offend by violating received notions'. So Samuel Johnson wrote in criticism of a contemporary play about Ulysses.[1] He voiced the prevailing view of the early eighteenth century in England. But the literary theory and practice of other epochs has generally been against his opinion on this matter. Keats seems to have spoken more truly for the majority of authors and readers, ancient and modern, when in welcoming Dante's addition to the Ulysses myth he remarked: 'We ought to be glad to have more news of Ulysses than we looked for'.[2]

It is surprising that a critic so well read as Johnson ignored the obvious lesson of the European literary tradition, that authors—and often the most imaginative of authors—have constantly used the classical legends and the 'poetical heroes' as foundations for their work. If he had paused to test his remark he might have remembered that Sophocles and Euripides, Ovid and Seneca, Lydgate and Caxton, Shakespeare and Racine, Calderon and Metastasio, to mention only a few, had thought it worth while to attempt new portraits of Ulysses. Apparently Johnson's veneration for Homer—combined perhaps with the over-strict classicism of the Augustan Age in England—led him astray in this.

Yet Johnson's aphorism, though its basic assumption was not universally true, did indicate a dilemma that faces every creative author—as distinct from a historian or an interpretative critic—who chooses to revive some mythical figure, like Œdipus, or Agamemnon, or Ulysses, in a work of imaginative fiction. On the one hand audiences and readers demand some novelty of style or invention; and a creative writer by his own nature will be averse from mere repetition. On the other hand, if an adaptor of the familiar legends goes too far in inventing new qualities or new adventures for the poetical heroes, or presents them in too revolutionary a style, he certainly is in danger of offending his audience. This will be illustrated in many controversies about new versions of the Ulysses theme to be described in the following chapters. The scandal caused by the untraditional elements in Joyce's *Ulysses* was typical of its kind. Johnson rightly saw that mere repetition or extreme innovation would cause any revival of ancient legends to lose popular support. But he did not see that between these extremes lay a wide field for literary manoeuvre. Nor did he see that some versions of ancient mythology might shock contemporaries 'by violating received notions' and yet be welcomed by later generations.

Ulysses has not, of course, been the only mythical figure to be the subject of frequent literary revivals. Most of the more celebrated heroes of Greek mythology have been presented in modern dress from time to time. Some of them have continued to be popular chiefly as types—Achilles as the high-spirited warrior, Agamemnon as the haughty king, Nestor as the sagacious greybeard. Others have served as symbols for special periods of European history. Prometheus appealed particularly to the age of revolution, as the works of Byron, Shelley, and Beethoven, testify. Œdipus has a contemporary significance for psychological writers. A third group of mythical heroes has become fossilized in proverbs or mere fables— Hercules and Tantalus, for example. But whether with proverbial, or symbolical, or personal, significance the early heroes of Greece have always remained part of the living population of European literature. And a few more recent figures, most notably Faust and Don Juan,[3] have joined them as character-images capable of constant revival and re-interpretation.

Before considering Ulysses's special qualities as a traditional hero, it may be well to glance at the normal causes of variation in the development of a heroic theme. The demand of audiences, and the desire of authors, for originality provide the main motive for introducing novel features. But other factors are likely to influence each writer who undertakes to produce a new portrait of a well-known mythical hero. These will now be briefly considered.

To begin with, when an author decides to rehandle traditional material he must obviously acquire some basic information about the tradition. But he may approach it in various ways and with various abilities. He may, like Keats, be satisfied to rely on some mythological handbook; or, like James Joyce, he may try to survey the whole development of the legend. Here, if the author is over-scrupulous, he will often run into perplexing contradictions, as the

Ulysses tradition fully illustrates. Who was Ulysses's father, Laertes or Sisyphus? Was he faithful to Penelope after his return to Ithaca? Where and how did he die? The tradition speaks with conflicting voices on many fundamental matters of this kind. Is one to trust Homer or Dictys, Philostratus or Dares? Every writer who goes deeply into the development of almost any complex myth will meet contradictions and confusions of this kind.

Fortunately, however, for creative literature a professional writer rarely has time or patience to sift a complex tradition in its entirety. He will usually rely on some fragmentary information and invent the rest. Here chance may cause a revolution. If Dante had known the *Odyssey* he might not have conceived his epoch-making portrait of Ulysses in the *Inferno*. If James Joyce had not first met Ulysses in Charles Lamb's *Adventures of Ulysses* he might never have become aware of modern symbolisms in Ulysses. One cannot equate any particular author's knowledge of a myth with the total bulk of information available, and one cannot assume that an author's method of gathering and arranging his material is the same as a scholar's. Accident, ignorance, misunderstanding, or carelessness—fatal faults in a work of scholarship—may lead a creative author to valid new conceptions of the traditional myths.

Another source of variation in the tradition arises when a myth becomes internationally popular. Linguistic factors will then begin to affect it. A modern writer on the subject of Ulysses or of any ancient Greek hero has to reckon with a body of myth extending through all the vernacular languages of Europe. Even if he learns each of these languages for himself, when he comes to present his own portrait of the hero he will sometimes meet nuances of thought which cannot be precisely rendered in the language he proposes to use. St. Basil of Cappadocia rejoiced, it is said, because his native Cappadocian tongue was too crude to express some of the abstruser Greek heresies. But interpreters of the classical Ulysses myth often have special reason to grieve that so many nuances of Ulysses's character cannot be quite satisfactorily translated. What word outside Greek can express the subtleties of *polytropos*, or of *sophos*, for example?[4] Even the Greeks themselves disputed about these. The fact that Ulysses was one of the most typically Greek of the Greeks made the link between his nature and his native language almost indissoluble at times.

Yet in this, too, deficiencies and perplexities which have been the despair of scholars have not deterred creative writers. Sometimes ignorance has helped rather than hindered mythopoeic genius. If Shakespeare had known more Latin and Greek he might have produced something like William Gager's painstaking *Ulysses redux* instead of his magnificent *Troilus and Cressida*. If Garnier and Racine had known less of Euripides and Seneca, their portraits of Ulysses might have been more lively. Ignorance, in fact, is often the mother of imagination.

Another source of variation in a myth is the natural tendency of authors to assimilate old material to contemporary fashions and customs. Just as painters of Biblical themes in the freer epochs of European art generally presented their patriarchs and apostles in modern dress, so successive writers have dressed Ulysses as an Achaean warrior, a Roman legate, a medieval knight-at-arms, an Elizabethan councillor, a Spanish hidalgo, and so on to the Edwardian Dubliner of Joyce's *Ulysses*. And many other mythical heroes have had the same experience.

Such changes in costume hardly deserve further attention here. But historical assimilation may plainly go beyond this. By adapting not merely the outward appearance but also the manners and inner qualities of his hero to contemporary standards an author may radically alter his traditional nature. A Ulysses set in an environment of post-Reformation intrigue or of twentieth-century eroticism is bound to act more or less differently from a Ulysses in archaic Greece or imperial Rome, simply on the principle of *autres temps autres manières*. The following chapters will produce many examples of this ethical assimilation to contemporary conditions. Turn by turn this man of many turns, as Homer calls him in the first line of the *Odyssey*, will appear as a sixth-century opportunist, a fifth-century sophist or demagogue, a fourth-century Stoic: in the middle ages he will become a bold baron or a learned clerk or a pre-Columbian explorer, in the seventeenth century a prince or a politician, in the eighteenth a *philosophe* or a Primal Man, in the nineteenth a Byronic wanderer or a disillusioned aesthete, in the twentieth a proto-Fascist or a humble citizen of a modern Megalopolis. Some of these metamorphoses—there were many others—had no permanent effect on the main tradition. But others, as will appear, made a lasting contribution to the myth.

Problems of morality must also arise in the development of a myth through many centuries; and the traditional morals of a heroic figure are likely to be given different complexions by successive moralistic writers. Thus Fénelon will present Ulysses's notoriously flexible attitude to truth as a form of prudence suitable to French monarchs; but Benoit de Sainte Maure and the other writers on the Troy Romance will bluntly characterize him as an unparalleled liar. Theognis will recommend Ulysses's clever opportunism and ethical adaptability; Pindar will denounce it. Homer admires Ulyssean wiliness; Virgil seems to detest it. Rapin finds him an entirely despicable character; Ascham, following Horace and the Stoics, considers him a noble example of manly virtue. Sometimes these divergencies are caused by propagandist motives; sometimes they derive from deep personal feelings. But, whatever their cause, one must be prepared in advance for some remarkable differences of opinion on the moral worth of Ulysses. No other classical hero has been the subject of so much moralistic controversy.

A simpler cause of change in traditional material lies in the writer's technical intentions. This will be stronger or weaker according as the writer values the formal aspects of his work. But every writer must to some extent shape his traditional material to the conventions and exigencies of the genre he chooses as the medium of his work—heroic, tragic, idyllic, romantic, satiric, or whatever it may be. If he is writing a comedy he will tend to exaggerate Ulysses's vigorous appetite into gluttony, or will dwell on the ludicrous aspects of his hiding in the Wooden Horse or hanging under Polyphemus's ram. Melodrama will demand a villain, lyric verse a man of sentiment, burlesque a coward. Romantic writers have emphasized a Don Juanesque element in Ulysses's dealings with Circe, Calypso, and Nausicaa. Tragic writers have rejected the happy ending to his life implied by Homer, preferring later stories of patricide or poisoning.

Similarly if a writer is mainly interested in Ulysses, or any other traditional hero, as a means of propaganda, he will study the tradition like an advocate to find grounds for justifying or discrediting both the hero and the cause for which he is being conscripted. This is the reason why Ulysses will appear in the sixteenth century as a model for Protestant Englishmen; in the seventeenth first as a specimen of Calvinistic malevolence and then as a pattern for Spanish Counter-reformation gallants; in the twentieth as a prototype of a much maligned English Prime Minister. From the sixth century B.C. downwards the Ulysses tradition is continually bedevilled by propagandist interests of this kind.

Another source of variation in the tradition need only be mentioned here: it will be considered more fully in a concluding chapter. This consists in each creative author's personal reaction to the traditional personality of a mythical hero, the give and take between his own temperament and the figure which he has discovered in the earlier tradition. At times this sympathy or antipathy has been the controlling factor in the production of new portraits of Ulysses. It is to be seen clearly, and confessedly, at work in the case of Goethe, Tennyson, and d'Annunzio. Their reaction to the character-image of Ulysses went far beyond mere interest. It became a matter of self-identification, until for a while each saw himself as Ulysses and Ulysses as himself. In this intensely personal experience both the writer himself and his chosen hero-symbol may be drastically changed. For the writer it can be a means of self-discovery, self-encouragement, and self-realization. For the mythical hero who is the partner of this imaginative empathy, the effect may be an entirely new mutation in his evolution. When an author's thoughts and feelings merge into the traditional symbol, his imagination can make a sudden mythopoeic leap beyond the slow tide of normal literary development: then, quite unpredictably, a new conception of an ancient hero, a new major figure in the annals of European literature, may spring into life.

These factors will to some extent affect every creative writer when he begins to compose a new portrait of a traditional hero: the effect of the tradition, the problems of translation, the tendency to historical assimilation, the variation in moral standards, the exigencies of the chosen genre, and each author's personal reaction to the personality of the mythical figure. Others could be added, but these seem to be the main influences. They explain most of the vicissitudes in every popular hero's literary evolution, King Arthur's and Don Juan's as much as Jason's or Orpheus's. But why, then, has Ulysses had a much more varied career than any mythical hero, ancient or modern, if his character has merely responded to similar formative influences? A detailed answer to this question will be offered in the rest of this book. But it may be well to outline a fundamental distinction in advance.

Despite the many factors which tend to alter or supplement the qualities and adventures of a mythical hero, his evolution will depend primarily on his archetypal nature, the nature, that is, of his earliest definitive portrait. If the archetypal hero is of the simpler straightforward kind like Ajax, or Agamemnon, or Jason, or if his exploits are limited in range and nature, he will obviously offer less scope for adaptation than a more complex and wider-ranging hero. Of the Homeric heroes, and, indeed, of all the heroes of Greek and

Roman mythology, Ulysses was by far the most complex in character and exploits. His adventures in the *Odyssey* brought him beyond the limits of the known world into unexplored regions of mystery and magic. His character was both more varied and more ambiguous than the character of any figure in Greek mythology or history until Archilochus. And, most significant of all for the possibility of later adaptations of his myth, one of his chief qualities, as Homer portrayed him, was adaptability.

One feature of Ulysses's personality in the Homeric poems will need special emphasis. This is the inherent ethical ambiguity of his distinctive characteristic among the Homeric heroes—which is intelligence. Intelligence, as Homer indicates, is a neutral quality. It may take the form of low and selfish cunning or of exalted, altruistic wisdom. Between these two poles, firmly established in the archetypal Homeric myth, Ulysses's character vacillated throughout the whole tradition.

Intelligence may also take another form, which in turn contains an ethical ambiguity. The complement to the practical application of intelligence is intellectual curiosity, the desire for further knowledge without which an active mind tends to become sterile. But this desire for knowledge may grow into a dangerous obsession, overpowering considerations of prudence and safety. Dante was the first to emphasize the dangerous quality of Ulysses's craving for new discoveries and fresh experiences. But Homer, who so often planted seminal ideas in his poems without cultivating them further, had already suggested this second dimension of ambiguity in the Ulyssean kind of intelligence.

The archetypal Ulysses, then, offered a wider foundation for later development than any other figure of Greek mythology, thanks to Homer's far-reaching conception of his character and exploits. On this foundation almost all the subsequent myth was directly built. For a while, it is true, Homer's account of Ulysses was discredited by certain plausible impostures, as will be described later. But these impostures were themselves the result of a violent reaction to the fundamentally Homeric tradition; and they have had little influence on the modern myth. One may say with confidence that every major contribution to the Ulysses theme within the last four hundred years has been derived directly or indirectly from the *Iliad* and the *Odyssey*. It may be well, then, as an introduction to recent as well as to ancient versions of the tradition to spend some time in considering the complex nature of Homer's most versatile and most adaptable hero.

B

CHAPTER II

THE GRANDSON OF AUTOLYCUS

A S far as extant literature goes the story of Ulysses begins in the Iliad and the Odyssey. Earlier records have not revealed any definite references to it, as yet.[1] But Ulysses was apparently not Homer's own invention, and Homer never suggests it. On the contrary he makes it clear by implication that Ulysses was already a familiar figure when he began to write about him. Ulysses appears in both poems without any preliminary introductions; incidents in his career which lie outside the main story of the Iliad and Odyssey are alluded to casually, as if on the understanding that everyone knew their main features; and Ulysses's stock epithets[2] imply that at least some of his characteristics were proverbial before Homer adopted him as his chief hero.

This is not conclusive evidence. One cannot be quite certain when a sophisticated writer like Homer endows one of his characters with a traditional background that this is not simply a device for enhancing the prestige of a newcomer. There are, however, other indications that Ulysses was not Homer's own invention. First, there is the extraordinary variation in the spelling of his name.[3] In Greek alone there are twelve variations ranging from Odysseus to Oulixes. No other mythological name shows anything like the same variety. If these mutations are to be explained in terms of normal linguistic processes, the main variants must have emerged long before Homer's time. On the other hand there may originally have been two separate figures, one called something like Odysseus, the other something like Ulixes, who were combined into one complex personality.[4] But this still implies the existence of a Ulysses-figure before Homer, for it is unlikely that post-Homeric writers would have introduced the name Ulixes and its cognates to describe a hero invented and originally named Odysseus by Homer. Purely literary creations like Falstaff, Don Quixote, and Pickwick generally retain, more or less, the names given to them by their creators, no matter how far their legend travels. It seems, then, that whether linguistic mutation or mythological syncretism was the cause of the variations in Ulysses's name, the Ulysses–Odysseus figure was older than Homer.

Secondly, some at least of the motifs in Homer's account of Ulysses seem to have been taken from older sources. To mention only the most remarkable example: over two hundred and twenty versions of the Cyclops incident have been collected[5] from sources extending from India to Ireland. Many of these probably derive directly or indirectly from Homer's narrative. But some seem to incorporate older elements; and some have been found in regions where Homeric influence is improbable. The probability is that this part, at least, of the *Odyssey* goes back to a pre-Homeric source, though it is an open question whether its original hero was actually named Ulysses or Odysseus.

These internal and external indications of earlier origins have prompted many theories on the nature of the pre-Homeric Ulysses. They are mainly historical, religious, or anthropological. Obviously the primeval Ulysses may have been a historical person, a prince of Ithaca endowed with unusual mental ability and renowned for adventurous sea voyages, as Homer asserts; or else an Egyptian trader, or a captain in some Minoan fleet.[6] Or else, as other scholars suggest, he may have been a pre-Greek sea-god (whence the enmity of his Olympian successor, Poseidon), or a solar divinity, or a year-daimon. Anthropologists have dwelt on certain primitive-looking features in his myth, finding traces of a bear or horse fetish, or a Wolf Dietrich, in his description.[7] These far-reaching theories undoubtedly explain some details in Homer's narrative, and it may be that at an early stage in the evolution of the pre-Homeric Ulysses myth elements of this kind were incorporated into it. But since the fully developed personality of Ulysses as portrayed by Homer seems to owe little to remote divine or bestial origins, they will not be studied further here. Historical explanations could, on the other hand, be more helpful in explaining Ulysses's status in Homer. But in fact there is no genuine documentary evidence for the prototypal Ulysses outside Homer. Until there is, it will remain impossible to determine precisely what is fact and what fiction in the Homeric poems.[8]

Nor can the archaeologists, who have done so much to illuminate the physical background of life in archaic Greece, contribute much in the present study, unless by unearthing some pre-Homeric literary records of Ulysses. Even if they could entirely reconstruct the buildings, furniture, ships, and weapons of Mycenean Ithaca and Troy, it would not go very far to explain the character of a hero specially renowned for rising above his environment. Materialistic explanations of character are least applicable to a personality so resourceful and unconventional, who, besides, spent nine years of his life in fabulous regions beyond the reach of map or spade.

Another approach to the problem of Ulysses's origins bears more directly on his psychological complexities. Folklorists have pointed out that almost every cycle of folk-tales contains a figure of notorious cleverness, a Sly Boots or Wily Lad,[9] whose cunning deceits delight their hearers and infuriate their victims—like the German Tyl Eulenspiegel, the Irish Manannan Mac Lir, and the Polynesian Maui-of-a-thousand-tricks.[10] If it could be established that Homer's Odysseus was partly derived from such a figure, many unusual features both in Homer's version and in the later tradition would be explained. Undoubtedly some of Odysseus's ruses, especially as described in the *Odyssey* and in the Epic Cycle, deviate from the normal conventions of heroic conduct, suggesting, rather, the more plebeian atmosphere of folk-tales. At times, too, especially in the *Iliad*, one finds traces of something like a conflict between the diverse genres of epic poetry and folk-tale in Homer's characterization of Odysseus.

A general consideration supports this view that Ulysses originated in folk-tales. As has been noted, a Wily Lad is to be expected in every elaborate cycle of primitive legends. Greek mythology offers no strong alternative to Ulysses in this rôle. Sisyphus and Palamedes are shadowy figures in comparison. Possibly some folk figures of this kind were eclipsed by Homer's supremely wily hero and thus lost to later memory. But it seems more likely that Homer developed the outstanding Wily Lad into the more sophisticated personality of his Odysseus. If this is what Homer did, one cannot expect so reticent an artist to state his debt to tradition explicitly. One may, however, expect him to leave some clue to his hero's origins: and so he does.

Quite late in the *Odyssey* (19, 393 ff.) Homer finds it necessary to explain how Odysseus got the tell-tale scar on his leg. He was wounded as a boy, Homer relates, during a boar-hunt when he was spending a holiday with his grandfather Autolycus. The reference to Autolycus leads to a brief account of an earlier incident. Autolycus had arrived in Ithaca just after Odysseus had been born. The nurse in charge of the newborn baby tactfully waited until the old man had eaten his supper. Then, placing the baby on his knees, she asked him to name it. She hinted that some name meaning 'Child of Prayer' would be suitable for a first-born son. Autolycus was

apparently in sardonic mood. Ignoring the hint, he decided to give
the child a name that would commemorate his own experience in
life. 'Because I got odium upon myself before coming here', he
said, 'odium from many . . ., let the child's name be Odysseus to
signify this'.[11] The pun, as events showed later, was prophetic as
well as commemorative. Odysseus was to suffer much from the
odium of gods, men, and moralists, both in his Homeric career and
in the later tradition.

Homer explains the reason for Autolycus's unpopularity: he
excelled all men in deceptions and fallacious oaths. This dubious
talent had been conferred on him by the god Hermes, whose favour
Autolycus had won with acceptable gifts. The reference to Hermes
as a trickster's patron is significant.[12] Homer never emphasizes this
aspect of his divinity elsewhere. But the post-Homeric *Hymn to
Hermes* dwells on his knavishness with all the relish of a folk-tale,
and it is generally believed to be a primitive trait. If so, Homer's
reference to it here may be taken as another indication of folklore
influence in the story of Odysseus.[13]

Autolycus's ability as 'a snapper up of unconsidered trifles' is
mentioned once again by Homer, in the introduction to the story of
the tricking of Dolon by Odysseus in *Iliad* Ten. There quite casually
Homer remarks that the curiously designed felt cap, ornamented
with rows of boars' tusks, which Odysseus puts on for his night
raid had once been stolen by Autolycus. A difficulty arises in the
fact that Homer gives no hint here of any relationship between
Odysseus and Autolycus. Hence some have argued that the author
of the *Iliad* (or of the Doloneia in particular) did not know, or else
did not accept, the tradition that Odysseus was Autolycus's grandson. But two other explanations are possible. Homer may not have
troubled to emphasize a universally known fact: if an English
historian had to record that Henry VIII wore a helmet which
Henry VII had once confiscated he would not need to remind his
readers that these two were father and son. Or else a subtler reason
may have influenced Homer. He may have deliberately avoided
any reference to Odysseus's ancestry on the female side because it
would detract from Odysseus's prestige in the conventionally heroic
atmosphere of the *Iliad*.

The fact is that to have had a grandfather who enriched himself
by deceptions, semi-perjuries, and house-breaking, would be a
serious handicap for an enterprising hero in such an aristocratic and
conventional community as the High Command at Troy. Heroic

etiquette permitted piracy and the sacking of cities. One could even steal cattle in an open raid. But the knaveries that Autolycus practised were barred. In a strictly heroic environment a wise man would say as little as possible about such an ancestor. If his disreputable forebear was already known, he would do all in his power to prove he had not inherited any knavish propensities.

In contrast, Odysseus's ancestry on his father's side was respectable and undistinguished. Laertes, the conqueror of Ithaca, was the son of Arkeisios[14] who in turn was a son of Zeus. There was nothing here either to shame or to ennoble a conventional hero. All the peculiarity was on Odysseus's mother's side. In a sense, indeed, he was something of a half-breed—not in the racial or social sense, like the poet Archilochus, but as the grandson of a nobleman, on the one side, and of a professional trickster on the other. Since children often inherit features more markedly from their grandparents than from their parents, it is not surprising that this grandchild had an unusually complex personality.

If this interpretation of Odysseus's genealogy is correct, Homer's account of Autolycus's part in the naming of Odysseus is not merely a picturesque anecdote. From the point of view of the literary tradition it obliquely acknowledges a debt to folklore sources. From the point of view of Odysseus's characterization it indicates that he was not, so to speak, a self-made Wily One: on the contrary, wiliness was in his blood: he was doomed to cleverness at his birth. Further, from the point of view of his destiny, the name Odysseus, which Autolycus meant primarily as a memorial of his own unpopularity, had a significance for the whole of his grandson's literary career, not only in the Homeric poems but throughout the entire classical tradition. In every subsequent chapter of the present book the name 'Man of Odium'—whether the odium is deserved or undeserved—remains apt. Within three or four centuries from Homer's time, by the end of the fifth century B.C., Odysseus will have good cause to remember the etymology of his name. In a play by Sophocles he will bitterly exclaim 'Rightly am I called Odysseus, a name pregnant with harm: for many enemies have found me odious'.[15]

When one views Odysseus's conduct and reputation in the Homeric poems in the light of his Autolycan antecedents, some inconsistencies emerge at once. Anyone who expects to find Odysseus's proverbial wiliness prominently displayed in the *Iliad* will be disappointed. Apart from the deception of Dolon by a characteristically Autolycan piece of equivocation, and one deft, but apparently legitimate, trick in his wrestling match with Ajax, he never exploits a single ruse or deceit in the *Iliad*. On the contrary, his conduct is scrupulously honest and his words are studiously candid. If the *Iliad* were the only early record of Odysseus's career one would find it hard to understand how he had got his notoriety as a man of extreme wiliness. In contrast the *Odyssey* is a compendium of Ulyssean and Autolycan cunning. Odysseus's famous deceptions of the Cyclops and the Suitors, his ingenious stories and skilful manoeuvres when still disguised as a beggar in Ithaca, his masterly stratagem of the Trojan Horse (as related in passing by Helen and Demodocus), marked him out for posterity as the supreme man of wile in classical mythology.

Why this disparity between the two poems? Some have taken it as an indication of separate authorship, explaining the wiliness of Odysseus in the Doloneia as an 'Odyssean' addition to the original *Iliad*.[16] But, among other objections, this separatist view does not account for the consistency of Odysseus's reputation (as distinct from his conduct) in both poems. No effort is made in the *Iliad* to hide Odysseus's reputation for clever devices. Helen describes him (*Il.* 3, 202) as 'adept in all kinds of devices and toil'. The Trojan Sokos addresses him (*Il.* 11, 430) as 'much renowned Odysseus, insatiable in devices and toil'. These terms express precisely the same attitude to Odysseus's cleverness as one finds in the *Odyssey*: thus Nestor remarks to Telemachus (*Od.* 3, 121–2) 'Your father, the glorious Odysseus, used to be far outstanding in all kinds of devices', and Odysseus describes himself to the Phaeacians (*Od.* 9, 19–20) as 'minded by all men for my devices'. In every case the speaker's tone is not derogatory, the word used for 'devices', *doloi*, being neutral in force. To become derogatory it needs a pejorative epithet.[17] The significant fact is that Odysseus's wiliness is admitted, though not illustrated, as freely in the *Iliad* as in the *Odyssey*.

In view of this consistency in Odysseus's reputation in the two poems, theories of separate authorship will not simplify matters as far as the Ulysses tradition is concerned. Some other explanation of the differences between Odysseus's conduct in each poem must be found. The simplest is to say that the disparity is entirely caused by changes in his environment. In the *Iliad* Odysseus lives among open friends and open enemies. All are heroes together, honourable men and aristocrats, trained up to a definite code of etiquette in war and peace. In most of the *Odyssey*, on the contrary, Odysseus is generally either alone or else accompanied only by some panicky followers, and goes among monsters, magicians, and usurpers. No etiquette or convention prescribes any safe rule of conduct in such circumstances. Odysseus needs every atom of his inherited cunning merely to survive. Or one can put this disparity of environment in other terms: the genre of the *Odyssey* is much nearer to folklore and *Märchen* than to heroic epic and provides a more congenial atmosphere for Odysseus's Autolycan talents.

This is the simplest explanation for the contrast between Odysseus's candour in the *Iliad* and his deceitfulness in the *Odyssey*. Granted that Odysseus was naturally inclined to craftiness, Homer simply tailored his hero's coat of many colours to suit the conventional uniform of an Achaean warrior-prince. Or else he deliberately made the Iliadic hero into a greater rascal to suit the atmosphere of the *Odyssey*. But a subtler intention is possible. Perhaps in presenting the contrast between Odysseus's reputation for 'devices' and his scrupulously straightforward conduct in the *Iliad* the poet intended his hearers to enjoy the spectacle of a wily, sensitive, and self-controlled man disciplining his personality to fit into a rigid code of heroic conduct. According to this view, Odysseus's conduct in the *Iliad* was not prefabricated in the heroic mould by Homer for the community of Achaean aristocrats at Troy. One is intended instead to see him as a man consciously controlling his unusual versatility and flexibility in an uneasy environment, moving with alert circumspection among people of different heredity and outlook, like an Irish chieftain at the court of Elizabeth I or the Jewish hero of Joyce's *Ulysses* at Dublin High School. In such circumstances a person of prudence—especially if, like Odysseus, he has a dubious ancestry and comes from a remote and inglorious island— would be specially careful to conform to local etiquette. He is a marked man. Any individualism on his part will confirm the suspicion that he is an outsider; any ingenuity will prove he is a twister, any over-cleverness that he is a cad. Perhaps some curious references to Odysseus in the *Iliad* can be best understood in this light.

Early in the *Iliad* (3, 216–20) the Trojan prince Antenor describes his impression of Odysseus when he came on the first embassy to Troy to demand Helen back, before the outbreak of war (the subject of a notable play by Giraudoux to be discussed in Chapter XIV). Antenor recalls how Odysseus used to adopt (Homer

employs a tense denoting habitual action) an odd-looking pose
before he began to speak. He would stand with his eyes fixed on
the ground, holding the orator's staff in a rigid grip, 'as if he were
a man without any wits'. Why this ungainly stance for such an
accomplished orator?[18] An ancient commentator reasonably
explains it as a method of avoiding suspicion. Odysseus, knowing
or guessing that his reputation for cleverness had already reached
the Trojans, wished to avoid giving an initial impression of self-
assurance or artfulness, just as Antony in Shakespeare's *Julius Caesar*
insists that he is 'no orator'. As Aeschylus's Prometheus remarks,
'It is most advantageous for a shrewd man to seem like a fool'.
Through neglect of this prudent policy Antiphon suffered from a
reputation for over-cleverness in fifth-century Athens; and Lloyd
George lost more than he gained by being known as the Welsh
Wizard. One can study a clever man's reaction to this nemesis in
Hazlitt's essay on *The disadvantages of intellectual superiority*.

Odysseus's conduct before and after his Autolycan treatment of
Dolon in Book Ten provides another example of deliberate self-
restraint. It will be remembered how Dolon, son of Eumedes, set
out by night from the Trojan camp to spy on the Greeks; was
waylaid by Odysseus and Diomedes; was tricked by Odysseus's
ambiguous words into believing that his life would be spared if he
told them everything; and was immediately killed by Diomedes
without any demur by Odysseus. The ethics of the ruthless deed
do not concern us at the moment: Homer emphasizes that Athene,
at any rate, entirely approved. It may be noted in passing that when
Odysseus finally persuades Dolon to give his information, he smiles
his only recorded smile in the *Iliad*. There is irony, too, in Dolon's
name—'Wily-man, son of Good-planner'; for this Wilyman was
doomed to meet a wilier man in the grandson of that Autolycus
whose name Homer had mentioned (perhaps with studied casual-
ness) shortly before.

Elsewhere in this incident Odysseus displays his usual prudence
and resourcefulness. It is he who takes all the wiser precautions
while Diomedes performs the more spectacular deeds of valour.
The whole exploit was one of Odysseus's bravest achievements.
Yet—and this is the cogent point for the present argument—
Odysseus shows most unusual modesty in deprecating all praise in
connection with it.

This note of modesty is struck at the beginning of the incident.
It will be remembered how six of the chief Achaean heroes were

eager to be Diomedes's partner in the night raid. The choice was
left to Diomedes. He did not hesitate, exclaiming

> How can I doubt, while great Ulysses stands
> To lend his counsels and assist our hands?
> A chief, whose safety is Minerva's care;
> So famed, so dreadful, in the works of war:
> Bless'd in his conduct, I no aid require;
> Wisdom like his might pass through flames of fire.
>
> (Pope's version)

(Dante will add a grim irony to this last phrase in his description of
the twin flame containing Diomedes and Ulysses in the Inferno.)
Odysseus meets this tribute brusquely, almost gruffly: 'Do not
praise me or blame me much, son of Tydeus. You are speaking
among Greeks who know the facts. Let us be going.' This is more
the tone of one of Hemingway's characters than of Homer's vainglorious heroes. Yet, as though Homer did not want the difference
to be missed, Odysseus's modesty is emphasized again after the two
heroes have returned from their triumph. When Nestor hails him
with delight at the success, Odysseus ascribes all the glory to Athene
and Diomedes. He says nothing of his own prudence and cunning,
though in fact he had directed the whole action after the encounter
with Dolon.

A similar desire to avoid special praise for cleverness may have
prompted Odysseus to another effort in self-restraint which comes
later in the *Iliad*. It is surprising that Odysseus, despite his versatility
in athletics, competed in only two contests at the funeral games of
Patroclus. First he virtually won the wrestling bout[19] against Ajax,
but did not protest when Achilles appeased his irascible opponent
by announcing a draw. Then he competed in the foot-race and
won it, by Athene's help, to the indignation of another hero. But
he took no part in the archery contest, though with his degree of
skill he would have had a strong chance of winning.[20] The reason
for this may be that Homer wished to vary the contestants (though
Ajax competed in three events), or else that he did not wish to
emphasize Odysseus's skill in the obsolescent and apparently
despised technique of archery. But it makes for greater psychological interest if one takes it that Odysseus thought it best to avoid
any suggestion of being too grasping, especially after his deft
overthrow of the popular Ajax and his victory in the foot-race by
sheer favouritism on Athene's part. It might have gratified him

personally to win more prizes, but it would have increased the number of defeated rivals to dislike him.

These three incidents are obviously insufficient to prove the theory that Homer intended his hearers to see Odysseus in the *Iliad* as a man consciously striving to avoid giving offence and to avoid Autolycan odium. The alternative possibility, that Homer simply chose to eliminate unheroic deceits from Odysseus's Iliadic career, may still be preferred. But if one turns to consider the other side of the picture, his reputation among his fellow heroes, some confirmation of the subtler intention can be found. Had Homer's purpose been simply to bowdlerize Odysseus's character by omitting all Autolycan elements in his career and reputation, then he would hardly have included the two curious and significant remarks in the first part of the *Iliad* which must now be considered. Both remarks were passed in moments of great emotional stress, and both seem to reveal a deeply-felt prejudice against Odysseus. They are significant for the later tradition as well as for Odysseus's Homeric career, for they foreshadow the denunciations which Pindar, Euripides, Virgil, Rapin, and many others, will heap on him later.

As has already been noted the general—one might almost say the official—attitude of Homer's Iliadic figures towards Odysseus's 'devices' was tolerant or indulgent. There is no hint of blame in the remarks of Nestor, Helen, and Socus, quoted above. They were apparently willing to assume that Odysseus's cleverness was of the good kind, used *pro bono publico* and without Autolycan self-seeking. (This attitude will be further illustrated in connection with Athene's friendly patronage in the next chapter.) But this general courtesy and tolerance is violated by two prime movers in the *Iliad*. Here the nemesis of Odysseus's Autolycan heredity seems to reveal itself more clearly.

In the fourth book of the *Iliad* Agamemnon, enraged at the wounding of Menelaus, decides that he must rouse all the Greek host to drastic action against the Trojans. As he passes from leader to leader his impatience and arrogance increase. By the time he comes to Odysseus he is ready to abuse anyone on the slightest pretext. Because Odysseus is not already in action (he had not yet heard the battle-cry), Agamemnon addresses him abruptly as 'Thou who art adept in evil devices, thou of the artfully greedy heart'.[21] Two points are significant in this: a pejorative epithet is attached to the neutral term 'devices', and emphasis is laid on Odysseus's greedy artfulness. The combined phrases form a painfully exact definition of Autolycanism. It was a peculiarly indiscreet and intemperate outburst on Agamemnon's part, especially after Odysseus's valuable services to the Greek cause in handling the crisis caused by Agamemnon's own folly in Book Two. Agamemnon does, indeed, try to laugh it off later with a politic smile and a patronizing phrase, after Odysseus has made a spirited retort. The impression is given that Agamemnon with characteristic tactlessness has expressed one of those secret prejudices that a king should never utter in public.

The second incident is not so explicit; but it seems to imply a similar undercurrent of feeling. In the embassy of Odysseus, Ajax, and Phoenix, to Achilles in *Iliad* Nine, Odysseus makes a strongly-worded plea to the wrathful hero to help the weakening Greeks. Odysseus studiously avoids all trace of ruse or deceit in what he says. He speaks candidly and freely, though his arguments are chosen and marshalled with superb skill. Yet somehow Achilles seems to feel that the many-wiled Ithacan is trying to out-manoeuvre him. He exclaims: 'Zeus-born son of Laertes resourceful Odysseus, I am going to tell you quite directly what I intend to do. That will stop you people from sitting round and cooing at me. *For the man who hides his thoughts in his heart and speaks a different word is as hateful to me as the gates of Hell.*'[22] Some have explained this outburst as simply an introduction to Achilles's own frankness. But it seems too violently phrased for that. More likely those ancient commentators are right who take it as an oblique criticism of Ulyssean wiles. Achilles was too much of a gentleman, and liked Odysseus too much, to charge him openly with deceitfulness. But, like the Achilles of Shakespeare's *Troilus and Cressida*, he is both sensitive and touchy.[23] He suspects Ulyssean wile whether it is there or not. Out of good manners he expresses his suspicions as a general criticism. Yet the Autolycan cap fitted one member of his audience too well for anyone to be in doubt about its owner.

'Hateful as the gates of Hell', 'adept in evil devices', 'of the artfully greedy heart'—in these three phrases one can see how deeply the conventional hero hated Autolycanism. For a moment the veneer of politeness and tolerance is broken by deep emotional stress, and the deep-seated suspicions and prejudices and dislikes break out. Elsewhere the relations between Odysseus and the other heroes are quite normal. This is as one would expect from those archaic equivalents of officers and gentlemen. They would normally treat even a rather dubious member of their High Command with ordinary courtesy as long as he behaved himself as an officer and a gentleman should, or as long as no sudden flaring up of emotion dislocated their decorum.

On the other hand, if Homer, as has been suggested, intended us to see Odysseus as a man in a constant state of ethical tension with the other more conventional heroes, he could have chosen other ways of revealing the undercurrents of feeling involved in his situation. He could have shown Odysseus as unintentionally making a false move, or else as becoming overwrought by the psychological strain and complaining about the hidden prejudices of his co-heroes. But that would have been uncharacteristic of Odysseus as the patient, much-enduring man. Instead, if the theory presented here is correct, Homer chose to let the hidden tensions be revealed like this from the other side, by Agamemnon and Achilles.

It would seem, then, from two aspects of Odysseus's career in the *Iliad*—both from the unusual restraints which Odysseus imposed on himself and from these sudden outbursts by Agamemnon and Achilles—that Homer did intend his audiences to be conscious of Autolycan influence, both positive and negative, in Odysseus's conduct at Troy. Below the surface of heroic etiquette the poet occasionally allows us to see glimpses of Autolycan odium in the other heroes' attitudes to Odysseus's conduct, character, and prestige. In the later tradition—in Euripides's *Iphigeneia at Aulis*, for example—these latent tensions become open. Then Agamemnon and Menelaus will discuss their dislike of Odysseus without any scruples of loyalty towards a comrade in arms.

One would not expect to find any such attitude to Odysseus's many ruses and deceits in the *Odyssey*. They are performed without any inhibiting respect for conventional heroic etiquette, since there Odysseus is moving in the freer air of fairy-tale and romance. But another question now arises. What did Homer and his audiences think of Odysseus's wiliness in general? Did they agree with Autolycus or with Achilles? Moral values are involved here, and there is always danger of anachronistic thinking in matters of this kind. It may be well, then, to set the problem in a wider framework for a moment.

It will be convenient to adopt a classification made by the medieval schoolmen. They divided falsehoods and deceits into three main kinds. The first and most venial are those which are told primarily for entertainment, in a joke, novel, poem, or the like. None but the most austere moralists condemn these. As Aristotle remarks in his *Poetics*, 'When telling a tale all men add something to it, because it increases the pleasure'. Perhaps with the mischievous intention of shocking any strict Platonists in his audience he adds, 'Homer has outstandingly taught the other poets to tell lies in the right way'. It is significant that although Plato and Hesiod before him were hostile to these poetic fictions, yet they themselves freely used myths to symbolize truth. Shelley in his *Defence of Poetry* has superbly championed the deeper truths that such mythopoeic fictions often embody.

Odysseus's fictitious autobiographies in the second half of the *Odyssey* belong mainly to this class. True, he does not wear a poet's uniform and so has no acknowledged poetic licence there. But he does wear a beggar's rags, and anyone who expects to hear gospel truth from a beggar on his rounds is innocent indeed.[24] One need hardly delay to weigh the minute scruples of moral turpitude which might be extracted from Odysseus's deceits of this kind. By an irony of fate some recent scholars have claimed that these palpable fictions give a 'truer' account of Odysseus's wanderings after the Trojan War than that given in *Odyssey* 9–12. Such are the complexities that arise when one tries to distinguish between myth and fact in creative literature.

Lies of the second kind are those told to avoid a greater evil, as in reply to a homicidal maniac asking for information that would lead to murder. A good example of this well-meaning type is the lie which Hypermnestra, that *nobilis virgo, splendide mendax*, as Horace calls her, told her father in order to save her husband's life. History and mythology abound in noble lies of this kind. When, as with Hypermnestra, they involve the grave peril of their users one can hardly deny their heroism. Where they spring from an honest desire to help others, one must at least admire their motive. But, as stricter moralists rightly warn, they are often double-edged weapons, often wounding the good cause they are intended to serve, and establishing a dangerous lubricity. Few ancient moralists, however, condemned them entirely. Even the more religious writers admitted their usefulness. Pindar, very censorious of deviations from candour and honesty in others (including Odysseus) piously bowdlerized the divine myths to fit his sense of propriety. Plato, so eager to censor the 'lies' of the poets, allows Socrates in the *Republic* to condone the 'medicinal lie' which helps friends and hinders enemies and to permit a 'bold fiction' in the interests of the State (just as Euripides in the *Bacchae* represents Cadmus as advising his grandson to 'tell a fine lie' to enhance the family's honour). In the

Old Testament Abraham, Sarah, Jacob, Esau, as well as the arch-angel Raphael, tell lies that can only be justified as well-meaning. The New Testament prescribed stricter standards.

Many of Odysseus's falsehoods[25] in the *Odyssey* belong to this second kind. His intention is generally to save himself and his comrades from death, or else to avoid plunging his comrades into despair by telling them the whole truth. Once he told a notably chivalrous lie, when King Alcinous asked (*Od.* 7, 299–301) if his daughter had been guilty of some discourtesy to him. In actual fact her decision to leave Odysseus behind her when she came to the city, in order to prevent malicious gossip, was entirely self-regarding and a clear breach of archaic etiquette. But Odysseus gallantly told her father that he had chosen to remain behind himself. Later, too, he tells Alcinous the kind of fib that many a guest must tell after dinner when he says that, if invited, he would gladly stay on in Phaeacia for a whole year (*Od.* 11, 356–61). The atmosphere here is that of a royal court, where indulgence is customarily given and taken for such insincerities. One cannot expect the strictness of a monastery or a philosophic school in an environment of that kind —though Plato, to do him justice, did keep to his principles at the court of the Sicilian tyrants. But Odysseus had never set himself up as moralist. Compared with the servile hypocrisies of later European courtiers his conduct in Phaeacia was remarkably frank and independent at times. He did not hesitate to rebuke one of the young Phaeacian aristocrats on a point of honour (*Od.* 8, 166 ff.), and there is no reticence about his firm rebuke to the defeatist Agamemnon of *Iliad* Fourteen.

The third kind of lie is condemned by all men of good will, ancient and modern—the malevolent lie, the crime described in the Decalogue as bearing false witness against one's neighbour. But the problem at once arises, who is my neighbour? According to the Christian ideal all one's fellow creatures are to be regarded as one's neighbours, deserving the same love that one gives to oneself. (But it would be mere cant to pretend that all professing Christians have observed this ideal fully in the more competitive spheres of life, in war, business, or politics.) The average man in early Greece restricted neighbourly duty much more narrowly. One was bound to deal truthfully with relatives, friends, and comrades. But to love one's enemy? Ridiculous. On the contrary, it was deemed a positive virtue to hate and harm him by every practicable means. There were, of course, certain acknowledged restraints—the laws in time of peace (but lawyers are ingenious), in war such sanctions as religion and custom prescribed. Apart from these, and the unwritten laws of decorum, the more one could deceive one's enemy the better. The moral Socrates, the strategical Polyaenus, the imperial Leo agree that lies and deceptions were permissible against avowed enemies.[26] If *caveat emptor* was an admitted principle of equity, how much more justifiable was *caveat hostis et inimicus*. It was not the saintliest way, but neither was it a dishonourable way. Dishonour only entered in when the malevolent lie was used against someone who believed that he was within the protection of neighbourly loyalty and piety.

In view of the many denunciations of Ulysses as a nefarious liar in the later tradition it must be emphasized that nowhere in the *Iliad* or in the *Odyssey* does he tell one of these unforgivable lies against a friend or colleague. His Homeric falsehoods and deceptions are all of the less harmful kinds[27]; or else, when intended to harm, they are aimed at enemies like the Trojan Dolon, the Cyclops, and the usurping Suitors. When Virgil and Dante denounced his stratagem of the Wooden Horse as a crime worthy of execration and even of everlasting punishment in Hell's flames, they were speaking more as Roman partisans of the Trojan cause than as impartial moralists. Neither in imperial Rome, nor in medieval Italy, any more than in Homer's Troad or modern Europe, has any military leader acted on the principle that the enemy must be told the truth, the whole truth, and nothing but the truth, about every manoeuvre. *Dolus an virtus, quis in hoste requirat?* It is unjust to heap special odium on Odysseus for stratagems and barbarities that have always been features of bitter warfare. Yet that is exactly what was done by Euripides and Virgil and many others in the post-Homeric tradition.

But what of Homer's own personal view of Odysseus's wiliness? It is recorded[28] that when James Joyce was asked to give an opinion on the moral worth of Ulysses he replied that he was 'a good man', *tout court*. Had Homer been asked to make any such judgment he would probably have refused on the grounds that he was a storyteller, not a moralist.[29] Yet, while he is not a moralist in the sense of one who feels it his duty to approve or condemn the actions of his fellow men, he is an ethical writer in so far as he does not shrink from revealing the results of intemperate or unprincipled conduct. One can see this in the consequences of Agamemnon's arrogance and Achilles's wrath—which is the theme of the *Iliad*—and one can see it in the effect of Odysseus's wiliness on his own personality in the *Odyssey*. Without preaching any sermon Homer does not fail to show that deceitfulness and falsehood are bound to impair a man's morale, no matter how he thinks he can keep them under control. Three times towards the end of Odysseus's Odyssean adventures, when Calypso, Ino, and Athene wished in turn to help him, Odysseus suspected treachery or trickery.[30] He who had deceived so many others found it hard to believe, after all his sufferings, that others were not always trying to deceive him. Similarly when he reached home and was well on the way to his final triumph, his distrust of Penelope passed the bounds of mere caution. Subsequently, too, when there was no danger involved, he thought fit to tell his aged father an elaborate lie before revealing himself. Homer does not point a denunciatory finger at these symptoms. He simply records them as illustrations of Odysseus's Autolycan tendencies and as traits of his complex personality. And none of the other persons involved seems to have been annoyed at Odysseus's suspicions: indeed, Calypso and Athene were merely amused, as a later chapter will describe.

Elsewhere Odysseus's distrustfulness had more serious consequences. It will be remembered how when Odysseus and his companions had put in at Aeolus's island, the King of the Winds had given them a bag containing all the adverse winds safely tied up out of their way. Then Odysseus himself steered the squadron for nine days and nights continuously homewards; at last Ithaca came in sight; exhausted by his long vigil, Odysseus thought it safe now to snatch some sleep; while he slept his companions opened the bag, thinking that it held some secret loot; the winds rushed out and swept the ships back to Aeolus; as a result of this folly, Odysseus's return was delayed for nine years, and his companions never returned. Homer adds a unique detail. Odysseus was so despondent at the escape of the winds that (for the only time in his Homeric career) he contemplated what amounted to suicide (*Od.* 10, 50 f.). Perhaps the audience was intended to recognize here, though Homer does not state it explicitly, Odysseus's remorseful realization of his personal responsibility for the disaster. In reporting the event to Aeolus he attributed it to 'our folly', while on other similar occasions (except the Cyclops incident) he blames his companions' folly alone. The fact was that if he had trusted them enough to tell them the contents of the bag, all would probably have gone well. But his regular policy was seldom to take them into his confidence,

c

rarely to tell them the whole truth, and never to take their advice. As a result they suspected that he was up to some Autolycan trick in not telling them what was in the bag. Their suspicion was entirely unfounded in this case—just as Achilles's suspicion that Odysseus was trying to outwit him in the Embassy incident had been unfounded. One may take it that Odysseus's personal failure on both occasions was due to the atmosphere of distrust that he tended, even when determined to be scrupulously honest, to bring with him.

The answer, then, to the problem of Homer's own attitude to Odysseus's Autolycan qualities—and presumably it corresponded to what he wished his audience to think—is that without condemning them on moral grounds, he plainly revealed their insidious effects on Odysseus's conduct and reputation. Artistically this heredity provided that touch of the tar-brush, that skeleton in the cupboard, which is so often to be found in the favourite characters of humanistic writers as well as in the most dynamic figures of history. Post-Homeric authors emphasized this less honourable element until Odysseus, deprived of Athene's guidance and control, became a villain *capable de tout*. But Homer implies that Athene's influence was stronger than Autolycus's, that this tendency to deceitfulness could be controlled by divine intervention—as the next chapter is intended to show.

CHAPTER III

THE FAVOURITE OF ATHENE

IN estimating the Autolycan element in Odysseus's career it was necessary to rely mainly on innuendoes and hints, as one would have expected in a rather disreputable matter of that kind. In contrast, Athene's influence is presented quite differently. Except when she has to take precautions to avoid Poseidon's anger, she always intervenes in Odysseus's affairs openly and unambiguously. Further, Homer arranged that she should decisively intervene in Odysseus's fortunes at the beginning, middle, and end of both his poems. By this, too, Homer may have intended to indicate a contrast with the influence of Autolycus, which is only casually mentioned towards the end of the *Odyssey*.

But when one considers Athene's relations with Odysseus in the *Iliad* and the *Odyssey* separately, once more a significant difference of attitude would appear to arise. Her frequent, almost continuous, interventions in the plot of the *Odyssey* are devoted exclusively to Odysseus's personal welfare. In the *Iliad* only five[1] of her personal interventions concern Odysseus, and only one of the five concerns his private interests. To judge simply from the number of her approaches to the heroes in general, Achilles and Diomedes would seem to have been more her favourites in the *Iliad*.[2]

This apparent difference can be accounted for without any assumption of different authorship for the two poems. The *Iliad* is primarily a saga of warriors, a poem of physical and psychological violence. Odysseus is never considered pre-eminent as a fighter in formal battles. Achilles, Ajax, Diomedes, and Hector, surpass him in this. Correspondingly, Athene's main purpose in the *Iliad* is a military one, to cause the destruction of Troy. She still hopes, apparently, that this can be achieved by main force. As a result, when Achilles sulks in his tent she employs the valiant Diomedes as her chief champion, not the resourceful Odysseus. His turn will come after the *Iliad's* story is done, when Achilles and Ajax are dead. Physical violence must first prove a failure before Odysseus's ruse of the Wooden Horse wins victory for the Greeks.

In the *Odyssey* the circumstances are entirely different. Athene has seen Troy destroyed with enough slaughter to satisfy even the most bloodthirsty warrior-goddess—and Odysseus has been its main vanquisher. Also by the time the poem begins Odysseus is the only champion of the Greeks who has not reached home. Thus physically and psychologically the way has been cleared for Athene to show special favour towards Odysseus throughout his homeward journey from Calypso's island.

Besides this a closer examination of her interventions in Odysseus's career in the *Iliad* suggests that before the end of the poem she had come to take a more than military interest in his personal qualities. This preparation, as it were, for their closer relationship in the *Odyssey* is not emphasized. Even if Homer had wished to emphasize it, he could hardly have done so without distracting attention from the poem's main theme—the wrath of Achilles and its disastrous consequences. It would be characteristic of his masterly economy that he should both postpone exploration of the subtler aspects of Athene's favour towards Odysseus until well into the *Odyssey*, and at the same time give some indication of its widening potentialities in the earlier poem. This he seems to have done. If the analysis that follows here is correct, Athene's three main approaches to Odysseus in the *Iliad* are not merely random manifestations of her anti-Trojan zeal, but carefully graduated stages in a planned development of their relationship. This, of course, assumes that, whoever their author, the two Homeric poems were, sooner or later, composed as complementary poems.

Before Athene intervened in Odysseus's Iliadic career he had played only a minor rôle. A few references had established him as an honoured but not a pre-eminent hero. He had been sent on the unenviable task of restoring Chryseis to her indignant father. The episode is passed over without *réclame*: everyone doubtless knew that Odysseus was good at this kind of negotiation. Some of the prouder heroes might have regarded it as little better than huckster-ing. But later, in Book Two, at Athene's prompting Odysseus takes the centre of the stage with a spectacular coup. Homer introduces it in a curious way. When Agamemnon's foolish ruse has precipi-tated the Greeks into a disorderly rush for the ships, Hera, always zealous for the Greek cause, orders Athene to go and restrain each warrior with her 'gentle (or acceptable) words'. Athene, instead of doing this herself, seeks out Odysseus, 'equal to Zeus in counsel', and tells him to restrain each warrior with *his* 'gentle words'. Odysseus obeys and with his gentle words (Homer repeats the phrase again) succeeds in checking the leaders from their flight (but he uses his staff and some most ungentle words on the common soldiers). How he then quelled the mutinous Thersites and won the army's good-humoured support, is one of the most celebrated incidents in European literature. His prompt actions and apt words became a model for later statesmen. His aphorism on the dangers of mob rule—

> Evil it is when many rule. Let there be one lord,
> One king, to whom it is granted by Zeus—

was cherished by political thinkers for over two thousand years.

In this way by Athene's favour Odysseus not merely became the pivot of the whole plot of the *Iliad* for a while, but also first entered the main stream of European literature as an outstanding figure in political thought. In other words the serviceable negotiator of Book One has been promoted for a while to be the saviour of the Greek cause and the proto-evangelist of hierarchical order in European thought. The significance of the repeated references to 'gentle words' will become clear later.

Athene again intervenes notably to help Odysseus in the Night Raid in Book Ten. Autolycan aspects of the outwitting of Dolon in this episode have already been mentioned. But Homer makes it clear that Athene's influence predominates. As the heroes set out (after a passing reference to Autolycus) Athene sends them a good omen. Odysseus prays in reply: 'Hear me, daughter of Zeus, who dost ever stand by me in all my toils—no movement of mine escapes thee³—now show me thy special love, Athene, and grant that we may return again with glory and great success....'. Diomedes prays to her as well (for she had befriended his father, Tydeus, in the famous attack on Thebes), but he prays only for his own safety, while Odysseus had prayed for them both. After the killing of Dolon, Odysseus has no compunction in dedicating his armour to her with a pious prayer. When danger threatens later, it is Athene who warns the heroes to withdraw. Nestor clearly recognizes the benefits of her protection when the two heroes have returned in triumph. The episode ends with a picture of both heroes pouring a grateful libation to her. Homer could hardly have made her pervading influence plainer.

In this and in the Thersites incident Athene's main purpose is to promote the victory of the Greeks. Odysseus and Diomedes are employed as the best instruments⁴ for her partisan policy. But Homer is not just playing a *Kriegspiel* with brightly coloured puppets. In the second incident he allows us to see more of Odysseus's personality, as distinct from the public talents displayed in the Thersites affair. Odysseus's unusual modesty[5] both before and after the sortie has been explained in the previous chapter as a symptom of his constant effort to avoid Autolycan odium. That is its negative aspect. But seen in the light of Athene's influence a complementary reason emerges. It may be that Homer also wishes us to see how Odysseus, once he was conscious of Athene's special favour, was less susceptible to the normal heroic craving for public approval. Knowing now that he has won divine favour, he finds satisfaction in the action itself. He is eager to get to work without any flourish of trumpets, and when his work has been well done, to go to rest without such fulsome congratulations as Nestor offers. There is a foreshadowing here, too, of that spirit of *Non nobis, Domine, sed nomini tuo*, which becomes apparent towards the end of the *Odyssey*. In the later tradition this refusal to exult in his successes will turn to cynicism (as in the prologue to Euripides's *Philoctetes*) and disillusion (as in the epilogue to Plato's *Republic*); but there is no trace of these sophistications here.

The other notable feature of Odysseus's conduct in the Doloneia is his piety.[6] This is frequently emphasized elsewhere. Here Homer makes him unusually scrupulous. He calls on Athene three times with marked devotion and reverence—at the outset of the enterprise, after his first success, and when he has safely returned. Even in times of greatest stress in the *Odyssey* he is never as devout as this. Some modern readers may find this piety revolting in a man who had no qualms about deceiving a helpless enemy with a deliberate equivocation. But clearly Homer did not intend his hearers to feel any such revulsion.

Thus Athene's first intervention in Odysseus's Iliadic career resulted in a display of his superb skill in handling a major political crisis. Her second displayed his modesty and piety as well as his resourcefulness in a perilous, uncertain task. In both Odysseus serves as a means of advancing the Greek victory which Athene so ardently desires. In her third intervention at the Funeral Games he receives his reward in a personal and special way.

The circumstances are these. In the preceding wrestling match with Telamonian Ajax Odysseus had deftly tripped him and won a fall. After a second indecisive bout Achilles, perhaps fearing Ajax's quick temper, had intervened and proclaimed a draw. Odysseus did not protest though he had reason for feeling aggrieved. Next came the foot-race. Normally Odysseus with his unusually short legs would have had very little chance of winning this, especially against Locrian Ajax, the swiftest of the Achaeans. However, he got off to a quick start and doggedly kept close behind Ajax until the last lap. Then just before the final sprint Odysseus prayed Athene to come to his aid. She had previously intervened to help Diomedes to win the chariot race. Now she gives strength to Odysseus's limbs and makes Ajax stumble ignominiously. Odysseus wins the cup. The last we hear of him (and of Athene) in the *Iliad* is Ajax's[7] angry remark: 'Confound it, the goddess baulked my running, she who—and before this, too—stands by Odysseus and helps him like a mother'.

The words form an apt epilogue to Athene's care for Odysseus in the *Iliad*, and an apt prologue to her closer relationship with him in the *Odyssey*. It is hardly unreasonable to discern a careful arrangement here. Odysseus has advanced in the *Iliad* from being Athene's effective agent to being her special protégé. In the two earlier incidents she gave scope and assistance to his natural gifts of prudence, courage, versatility, and endurance. In the third she gives him supernatural strength to overcome his physical defects. Homer leaves it open to his audience to conclude that under such influence a grandson of Autolycus could become, if not a conventional hero, at least something nobler than a traditional Wily Lad. Yet it is significant, too, in view of Autolycus's reason for naming his grandson, that the last reference to Odysseus in the *Iliad* is an expression of odium at his success.

Troy has fallen before the *Odyssey* begins, so that Athene no longer has a military reason for prompting and guiding Odysseus. If Homer had regarded Odysseus's relationship with Athene in the *Iliad* as being simply that between an agent and his director, he would probably have let the relationship lapse or become merely vestigial in the *Odyssey*. Athene had paid off Odysseus, so to speak, in the Funeral Games: he could now find his own way home. But Homer chose differently. He decided, instead, to intensify the relation between goddess and hero, and to transform Athene's military motives into motives of personal sympathy and affection. The implication of the words 'like a mother'[8] at the end of her interventions on Odysseus's behalf in the *Iliad* become fully explicit before the *Odyssey* is concluded.

It is unnecessary to analyse all Athene's efforts for Odysseus's welfare in the *Odyssey*. She sets the plot in movement by persuading

Zeus to allow his return when the angry Poseidon is away in
foreign parts. As soon as he has passed out of the sphere of fairyland
by reaching Phaeacia, she is constantly at hand to guide, prompt,
and help him. After this Homer apparently felt that such a special
personal relationship between a divinity and a mortal needed a
special explanation. In other cases of the kind the motive was
generally either erotic passion (as with Aphrodite and Anchises) or
some definite practical purpose. Athene had neither motive for
favouring Odysseus in the *Odyssey*.

Homer devotes a whole scene to the answer. It occurs when
Athene and Odysseus meet openly and undisguised for the first
time in the *Odyssey*. Odysseus has just returned to Ithaca. Athene
approaches him (*Od.* 13, 221 ff.) in the form of a young shepherd.
In answer to his question she tells him that he is in Ithaca. He at
once becomes wary, 'loyal as ever to his own crafty nature'. He
pretends that he is a Cretan refugee, and extemporizes a fictitious
story. Athene listens with amusement. She smiles, puts her hand
on him in a gesture of friendly intimacy, and abandons her disguise.
'What a cunning knave it would take', she exclaims, 'to beat you
at your tricks! Even a god would be hard put to it. And so my
stubborn friend, Odysseus the arch-deceiver, with his craving for
intrigue, does not propose even in his own country to drop his sharp
practice and the lying tales that he loves from the bottom of his
heart. But no more of this: we are both adepts in chicane. For in
the world of men you have no rival as a statesman and an orator,
while I am pre-eminent among the gods for invention and resource.'
She goes on to refer to her constant protection of Odysseus and to
advise him about his further trials.

Odysseus replies with some annoyance. He complains that
Athene has neglected him during his sea voyages. He feels uneasy
and suspicious. Has he really reached Ithaca, or is Athene merely
mocking him? Athene's reply contains the kernel of the whole
scene: 'How like you to be so wary! And that is why I cannot
desert you in your misfortunes: *you are so civilized, so intelligent, so
self-possessed.*'⁹

The scene in general is full of sophisticated charm: it has been
well compared¹⁰ with the conversations of Benedick and Beatrice in
Much ado about nothing. Nowhere else in early classical literature can
one find such a graceful portrait of two wits, male and female,
exchanging banter and reproaches without malice or scorn in this
free and easy style. But Homer would hardly have composed the

scene for its charm alone. Its supple, effortless style carries the clue to the whole Odyssean relationship of Athene and Odysseus. She cannot desert him in his misfortunes because, cunning as he is, he is also 'civilized, intelligent, and self-possessed'. The Greek terms used are complex and deserve closer analysis.

The first epithet, *epētes*, is used only once elsewhere by Homer. When Amphinomos, the only likeable person among the Suitors, speaks kindly and compassionately to Odysseus in his beggar's disguise, Odysseus uses the same word in saying that he seems like a 'civilized' man. It implies[11] personal attentiveness, kindness, and gentleness, in contrast with boorishness and selfish indifference to other people's feelings—a quality closely akin to that philosophic gentleness which Plato praises in his *Republic*. Athene was specially fitted to appreciate it in Odysseus for she herself had this gift, as Hera made clear in requesting her to check the Greek retreat in *Iliad* 2, 165—'You go and restrain each man with your *gentle* words'. Hence, perhaps, her indignation when, pleading again for Odysseus's home-coming at the second council of the gods in the *Odyssey* (5, 8–10), she bitterly exclaims 'Let there be no more deliberate gentleness and mildness among reigning kings, and no more justice; let them ever be harsh and lawless instead; since no one among the people that Odysseus once ruled as mildly as a father now remembers him'. One is reminded of Antony's speech to the Roman plebs:

> When that the poor have cried, Caesar hath wept.

And it is significant that the first entrance of Odysseus into the main narrative of the *Odyssey* reveals him weeping tenderly for his home. Has Homer designed this to offset stories of Odysseus's callousness at the sack of Troy, obliquely making Antony's point?—

> Ambition should be made of sterner stuff.

Yet Euripides will say he was ambitious. . . .

Others besides Athene found gentleness[12] in Odysseus. When he met the ghost of his mother Anticleia in the Land of Shades she told him that the cause of her death had been her yearning for his thoughtfulness and kindness (*Od.* 11, 202–3). There are further tributes in the *Odyssey* from relatives, subjects, and servants, to this mildness and kindness of his.[13] 'He was as kindly as a father.' Among the other Homeric heroes notably Hector (and to some degree his father Priam) had this endearing gift of civilized gentleness in thought, word, and deed; and it was the loss of this that Helen lamented most at Hector's death (*Il.* 24, 770–2). In a world of heroic violence women would naturally appreciate this quality more than men. The cruder hero might despise it as weak and effeminate, for as Socrates insists (*Republic* 2, 375B), these high-spirited natures are apt to be savage with one another and everyone else. But, as Socrates adds, the ideal guardians of the commonwealth ought to be dangerous to their enemies and gentle to their friends, like a well-trained dog; and further, 'he who is likely to be gentle with his friends and acquaintances must by nature be a lover of wisdom or knowledge'.[14]

'Dangerous to enemies and gentle to friends, like a well-trained dog.' One may note in passing that Odysseus had good reason to weep when he saw his dog Argos[15] lying neglected and verminous while the Suitors roistered in his halls. But the main point is that to an ancient Greek Odysseus's civilized gentleness to friends was not incompatible either ethically or psychologically with his savage ferocity towards his faithless servants and towards even the best of the Suitors. As far as archaic ethics was concerned, usurpers and traitors were beyond the pale of kindness. And psychologically, allowance must be made for a much greater emotional resilience than can be expected in a modern 'civilized' hero. One must not be surprised at the contrast between Odysseus's tearfulness[16] and his fierceness, nor be shocked that the preliminaries to Odysseus's tender recognition scene with Penelope are the ghastly massacre of the Suitors and the barbarous hanging of the disloyal maidservants. There is no schizophrenia here. One can find the same combination of sensibility and ferocity, of gentle courtesy and daemonic energy in Renaissance men like Raleigh or Essex, half pirate, half courtier, as well versed in Castiglione's *Courtier* and Spenser's *Faerie Queene* as in the latest type of thumb-screw. One should judge this aspect of Odysseus's character more in terms of the *Duchess of Malfi* than of *Westward Ho*.[17]

The second word used by Athene, *anchinoos*, is not found again in Greek literature until Plato. Aristotle (*Nicomachean Ethics* 1142b, 2 ff.) explains it as a kind of 'skill in hitting the mark' which is quick in action and not dependent on logical thought. This meaning suits the Homeric context well. It implies a quality approximating to what is called feminine intuition, that gift of instantaneous insight into the essence of a complex matter, which both ignores and baffles logical analysis. Here, perhaps, is the secret of Odysseus's unusual promptness in action. Joined to his more masculine ability to work out careful plans, it made a formidable combination (as in

Aeschylus's Clytaemnestra). But it is not entirely clear just how it differs from Autolycan shrewdness; it is perhaps a purer, more spontaneous quality.

The third term, *echephron*, is much commoner, but with one exception Homer always applies it elsewhere to Penelope, the exception being when Achilles uses it of a man who is faithful to one woman.[18] It is often rendered as 'sensible, discreet', but this hardly gives the right emphasis. Literally 'mind-restraining' or 'thought-controlling', it describes a self-possessed person who does not allow his impulses and thoughts to lead to wrong words or actions. Thus Penelope never allowed any thought of marrying another man—a natural thought for a woman uncertain of her husband's fate for nine years, and surrounded by many insistent wooers—to make her abandon her love for Odysseus. She is 'self-possessed' in this—the opposite of fickle, or flighty. It is in many ways the highest form of self-control. Homer doubtless intended it as a special tribute to Penelope when he gave her almost a monopoly of the epithet in his poems. By making Athene use it to describe Odysseus here he may have intended to imply that the marriage of Odysseus and Penelope was such a marriage of true minds as Shakespeare's sonnet describes—

> Love is not love
> Which alters when it alteration finds,
> Or bends with the remover to remove.

This self-possession could go further than this. In a negative sense it implied keeping one's own counsel. Where other heroes like Agamemnon and Achilles and Ajax, or other figures of Autolycan propensities like Thersites and the Cyclops, would blurt out their least prudent thoughts, Odysseus rarely spoke an unconsidered word even under the strongest provocation. It did not always take the form of mere silence. It consisted rather in saying just as much as the present purpose warranted, and no more. When necessary Odysseus could be as brutally frank to Agamemnon as to Thersites. On other occasions he would mix frank criticism with his characteristic courtesy of manner so that the listener could neither evade the indictment nor take offence at it. This form of restraint was the most typical of his better nature through the whole tradition. One finds him using it in Shakespeare's *Troilus and Cressida* and Giraudoux's *La guerre de Troie n'aura pas lieu*, as effectively as in the *Iliad* or *Odyssey*. One of its finest examples in the Homeric poems comes when an insolent young Phaeacian prince taunts Odysseus with

looking less like an athlete than a trader. Odysseus's reply has won
a just tribute from that past-master of public oratory, W. E. Gladstone,[19] as teaching 'more than any composition with which I am
acquainted, up to what a point emotion, sarcasm, and indignation
can be carried without any loss of self-command'. A comparison
with the interchanges between Achilles and Agamemnon in the
first book of the *Iliad*, where self-interest, passion, and indignation
are in complete control, would show how much this Ulyssean
moderation differs from normal heroic conduct.

The most remarkable example of this kind of restraint (though
here its motive is less politic and more philosophic) comes at the
climax of Odysseus's career as a Homeric hero, the supreme triumph
of his valour, patience, and wiliness—the slaughter of the Suitors.
Their corpses now lie in heaps on the floor, a hundred and eight
killed by one hero helped only by his son and two servants. This,
if ever, is the time for Odysseus to boast and exult, and for Homer
to write a triumphal song equal to those of Moses and Deborah
after the defeat of the enemies of the Lord. But that is not Homer's,
or Odysseus's, way. Instead, when Eurycleia is about to raise a cry
of triumph, Odysseus prevents her: 'Rejoice only in your heart,
woman, and restrain yourself; raise no triumphal shout. It is wrong
to boast[20] over slain men. It was destiny and their own stubborn
deeds that laid these men low. They showed no reverence for
mankind, good or bad, whoever came to them. Therefore by their
own wanton folly they met a shameful fate.' This is a remarkably
dispassionate pronouncement for a Homeric hero in his moment of
success. It contrasts vividly with the vaunts of victorious champions
in the *Iliad*.[21] Odysseus completely ignores his own achievement.
He sees himself only as the instrument of destiny in punishing
harshness, inhumanity, and folly. It is partly the feeling of *Non
nobis, Domine*; but there is a difference. The emphasis here is less
theistic than humanistic: men reap what they sow. Zeus himself
had preached on the same text in the opening scene of the Odyssey:
'How men blame the gods for their ills, when in fact it is by their
own folly that they get woes beyond measure !' In so far as Homer
has any moral message in the *Iliad* and the *Odyssey* it comes to this:
only by Ulyssean self-control and moderation can men achieve
victory in life. In contrast the wrathful, vainglorious Achilles, the
arrogant, grasping Agamemnon, the headstrong Ajax, the self-
centred, unscrupulous Autolycus, paid their penalties.

For a moment here Odysseus touches on the deeper meaning of

life's suffering, and seems to speak for Homer himself. As the ancient commentators noticed, Odysseus was the first Greek to adopt the principle of 'Nothing in excess', which with its complementary principle of 'Know thyself' produced so much of what was best in Greek thought and art. He knew how easy it is to fall into excess and thence into destruction. He emphasizes this in his speech to the best of the Suitors, Amphinomus, who had spoken a kind word to him in his beggar's disguise (*Od.* 18, 125 ff.). Odysseus, as has been noted, recognized his courtesy and tried obliquely to warn him of the impending slaughter. There is nothing feebler in the world, he told him, than mankind. In his days of manly strength he thinks that he will never come to harm; but when the gods decide to change his fortune, willy-nilly he goes astray and suffers for it. (An unexpectedly Autolycan note is then struck for a moment in this moral and friendly discourse: Odysseus untruly states that he, in his beggar's misery, is himself an example of the miseries caused by foolish and unrestrained conduct.) The general tone of melancholy[22] and the suggestion that at times men are little more than the playthings of the gods reveal the darker side of an attempt to combine theism with even the most exalted utilitarianism. Generally Odysseus was too much involved in practical difficulties to have time to make philosophical pronouncements like these. By making Odysseus utter them here Homer gives a sombre depth to his hero's mind, even if he is partly using Odysseus to express his own view of life. Later writers on the Ulysses theme will explore this philosophic quality more thoroughly.

It seems, then, that Athene's favour for Odysseus depended partly on his value as an instrument for overthrowing Troy, partly on an affection for his personal qualities. It is the second motive that was unique. The only other relationship between a divinity and a hero which approached its intimacy and mutual understanding was that between Achilles and Thetis. But they were son and mother. Athene had no formal reason for picking out Odysseus as her favourite. Further, as the remarkable scene in *Odyssey* Thirteen reveals, her affection is for the whole of his complex personality. She recognizes his Autolycan qualities—his inveterate scheming, his deluding ways, and his wily words—with a genial tolerance because she, too, is 'an adept in chicane'. But what she admires most is his civilized courtesy and gentleness, his keen-wittedness, his firm self-possession. There is a steady deepening in their relations from the time when she gives Odysseus his first great opportunity in the *Iliad* until the end of his Homeric career. Significantly in the last scene of the *Odyssey* it is she who *restrains* both Odysseus and the hostile Ithacans and makes peace between them.

What did Homer mean by this continuous guidance and protection? Some may say, Nothing: the goddess is simply that part of Homer's divine machinery which manipulates the fortunes of Odysseus: Homer is a story-teller, not an allegorist. Certainly Homer is primarily a story-teller. But one has only to compare his poems with other heroic stories like the Burnt Njal Saga or the Nibelungenlied to see how much more he is than a mere chronicler or tale-teller. He is intensely interested in human personality and in the human qualities of his gods. The subtleties of the dialogue between Athene and Odysseus after his arrival at Ithaca would be entirely pointless, if Athene's function was simply to expedite the plot of the *Odyssey*. The physical events described in the *Odyssey* are not, as Homer makes clear in the first line, its subject. Its subject is 'the man of many turns', just as the subject of the *Iliad* is not primarily the siege of Troy or the exploits of the heroes, but 'the destructive wrath of Achilles'.

If, then, Athene is not simply a piece of divine machinery to keep his plots moving (an anachronistic emphasis on 'plot' has done much harm to Homeric studies), what is her significance? Can one detect the poet's own attitude to Odysseus behind her special patronage? Homer's artistic self-effacement prevents any certain answer here. One can only guess, and many guesses are possible. The favourite interpretation in antiquity was allegorical and moralistic. Athene, it was believed, was intended by Homer to represent the power of divine wisdom to guide and control men's lives. One can see this allegorical method confidently at work in the *Homeric Allegories* of Heracleitos (of the first century A.D.: formerly confused with fourth-century Heracleides Ponticus). He exploits it ingeniously. According to him Athene represented the power of divine wisdom, guiding and controlling men's lives. Thus when she seizes Achilles by the hair of the head to restrain him from attacking Agamemnon (*Iliad* 1, 197), it is taken as an allegorical representation of the fact that the reasoning faculty, through which the divine wisdom works, is situated in the head (hence, too, the birth of Athene from the head of Zeus). Her relationship with Odysseus is to be explained in the same way, he thinks. He makes the striking claim that Plato (whose hostility to Homer he energetically denounces) derived his tripartite division of the soul from Homer. If one elaborates a little on this last suggestion a neat equation can be framed to explain the problems of Homer's Odysseus. The Autolycan element in his character could be identified with the appetitive faculty in Plato's division, for, as Socrates explains (*Republic* 581A), 'if we were to say that the loves and pleasures of this . . . part were concerned with gain, we should then be able to fall back on a single notion, and might truly and intelligibly describe this part of the soul as loving gain or money'. (Autolycus, it will be remembered, devoted his wiles to cheating people for his own advantage.) Secondly, what one might call the Laertes element, that is, the conventional heroic qualities of Odysseus's environment, would then be represented by Plato's 'spirited element', which is 'set on ruling and conquering and getting fame'. Then, thirdly, Athene must stand for Plato's third principle, the rational element, controlling the dark horse of Autolycan self-seeking and the white steed of heroic spirit, like the charioteer in the *Phaedrus* myth. But Homer was hardly so good a Platonist as that.

Allegorical interpretations held the field in Homeric studies for over two thousand years, and they still pervade many discussions on Homer's meaning. The chief objection to them in the case of Athene is that they ignore the harsher features in Homer's characterization of the goddess and depend on categories of thought not to be found in the Homeric poems. In the *Iliad* Athene is far from being the urbane goddess of wisdom and industry who presided over the civilization of fifth-century Athens. She is essentially a partisan warrior-goddess intent on the destruction of Troy. When necessary she can be ruthlessly treacherous and deceitful. Her deception of Hector in his last encounter with Achilles is as brutal a piece of primitive partisanship as one can find anywhere in literature, inconceivable in a personification of divine wisdom. Secondly, the later moralists' conception of virtue and truth was not Homer's; and Homer never remotely suggests that Athene's ultimate purpose was to make Odysseus virtuous, good, or truthful in any sense. Nor did she favour him because he was specially righteous in his behaviour. No: she chose Odysseus first because he was the sharpest instrument for the overthrow of Troy, and secondly because she liked his personal qualities and had a fellow-feeling for his wiliness.

Yet somehow one is reluctant to abandon the moralistic interpretation entirely, at any rate in its less fantastic forms. It is so much a part of the European literary tradition—Heracleitus Ponticus was a favourite author in post-Renaissance times—that Homer would seem impoverished by its rejection. Perhaps it is reasonable to hold that, though Homer was not deliberately inculcating such consciously moral lessons, he did at times write more moralistically than he realized.[23] This is, after all, the characteristic quality of transcendent genius, to give beyond its conscious powers.

But allegorical and moralistic interpretations are generally out of fashion among contemporary scholars. Some prefer to explain Athene's favour for Odysseus in terms of early religious cults. It might, for example, have originated in her early function as the protectress of the Mycenaean kings[24] (though this would not explain her special interest in Odysseus), or else from her rôle as Goddess of the Palace[25] (so that she would be zealous to secure the safe homecoming of a pious prince like Odysseus). Theories of this kind can illuminate the historical background to the Homeric poems, and they support the view that Athene's patronage of Odysseus was not an invention of Homer. But they fail to throw any light on the subtler and more personal relationship between the goddess and the hero. Another theory is based on the hypothesis that the early Greek divinities can be separated into Olympian and chthonic powers.[26] Athene, it is suggested, represents the Olympian influence on Odysseus's career: Hermes (being the father of Autolycus according to post-Homeric sources) represents the chthonic influence. Odysseus's nature is 'polarized' between these two antipodal powers. This explanation presents an attractively clear schematization of the two main external forces on Odysseus's evolution, the hereditary influence of his maternal ancestry and the supernatural aid of Athene. But one may doubt whether so humanistic an author as Homer would be satisfied with a strictly theological rationale of this kind. Besides, despite the efforts of contemporary writers to keep terms like 'chthonic' from acquiring moral values, it seems a fundamental instinct of human nature, ancient and modern, to identify qualities like 'dark', 'underground', with cruelty, and evil, and 'bright', 'heavenly', with kindness and goodness—which leads one back to a moralistic interpretation.

One could also explain Athene's rôle in terms of literary genre. In the previous chapter it was suggested that Autolycus represents a folk element in the Odysseus myth. Athene, as Homer portrays her, belongs to the loftier style of the epic. Her constant surveillance of Odysseus's career, especially in the *Odyssey*, does in a sense run parallel with Homer's constant efforts to prevent his princely hero from degenerating into a mere Wily Lad. But this can hardly be more than an incidental, perhaps only an accidental, parallelism. His Athene is much more than a Muse, and it would be perverse, indeed, to try to find anything like a primeval Battle of the Books in his poems. Yet, it is not altogether impossible that tellers of folk-tales in Homer's time may have felt indignant at the slenderness of Autolycus's rôle in Homer's version of Odysseus's story, and may have seen Athene as a personification of the more sophisticated literature that would soon eclipse their art.

These moralistic, religious, and literary interpretations seem too rigid and limited to account for the fullness of Homer's comprehensive humanism. Homer is supremely interested in persons, both as individuals and in society. Everything in his poems is subordinated to the interests and fortunes of human beings. One fundamental problem seems to have challenged Homer as it challenged every great humanistic writer after him, the problem of human suffering. The conventions of the epic style prescribed an atmosphere of violence and suffering. Ostensibly an epic poet had to glorify war and slaughter, if he was to use the genre at all. Yet again and again Homer implies that he hated the effects of war and deplored the destructiveness of heroic passion and heroic folly. Whether Homer was in advance of his own time (as distinct from the Heroic Age) in this or was simply voicing a general reaction from archaic violence, one cannot tell. But undeniably there is a great difference between his attitude towards death and destruction and that implied in the early sagas of Western Europe.

It may be, then, that Homer used the Athene-Odysseus relationship to express his humaner instincts, his desire for a less violent order of society, within the militaristic conventions of the early epic. Odysseus had two supreme qualities, intelligence and gentleness. Intelligence *per se* is ambiguous. In an Autolycus it becomes greedy, selfish, and odious. But used to promote the common good of society it becomes the chief instrument of civilization. One cannot, indeed, say that the use Athene makes of Odysseus's intelligence is unreservedly public-spirited. Her favour is limited to the Greeks. Yet despite this partisanship, if one compares Odysseus's conduct under her guidance with the self-centred policy of an Autolycus there is some ethical progress here. Under Athene's influence Odysseus's cleverness is used *pro bono nostro* not merely *pro bono meo*. The highest use of intelligence—for the good of all mankind—had still long to wait for its fulfilment.

Thus one of the two qualities that Athene fostered in Odysseus

D

was the power of applying his hereditary intelligence to public service, through his innate self-restraint and patience. In this way she made him supremely serviceable for destroying Troy. Agamemnon's arrogance, Achilles's pride, Ajax's stolidity, Menelaus's lack of drive, rendered these loftier chieftains inadequate for her purpose. Here Athene seems to express Homer's own view of human society. The only kind of man that one can trust to bring a complex crisis to a safe conclusion is a man like Odysseus. Passionate heroism, glorious as it is, disrupts society and causes senseless destruction.

But what then does Homer intend by Athene's special liking for Odysseus's other outstanding quality, his gentleness and courtesy? Perhaps he implies something like this: intelligence, even when superbly under control and unselfishly directed to the public interest, is not enough to redeem a man or a society from knavery or savagery. Or, to look at it from the point of view of reputation rather than conduct, mere intelligence may win admiration but it will never win affection. Some warmer quality is needed. Homer's own poems illustrate this well; Virgil's even better. What eventually wins the reader's heart is not the impressive intellectual qualities of their style and design, but their pervading compassionateness, even tenderness, for suffering humanity. The quality that Athene admires in Odysseus is not so profoundly humane as this. But, whether one uses the terms 'civilized', or 'gentle', or 'courteous', for it, it does sometimes reach out towards that deeper compassion, as one sees in Odysseus's speech to Amphinomus. It is certainly an advance on the selfish indifference of an Autolycus or the angry arrogance of an Agamemnon.

Odysseus is not, indeed, the only Homeric hero to possess this quality of civilized gentleness. Nestor, with all his senile failings, is intuitively gentle: so is Menelaus.[27] It is significant that these two with Odysseus are the only Greeks whom Homer portrays safe and happy at home again after the war. One other courteous and gentle knight had to die at the hands of a hero of the more primitive type. This was Hector. But Homer, perhaps, meant to imply that gentleness alone is not enough, either. One must be clever as well, clever enough not to fight an irresistible foe and not to let an Athene lure one to death. More probably, however, the reason was that, being a Trojan in a saga of Greek prowess, Hector had to die. He and his equally courteous and gentle father, Priam, are the two most tragic figures in the *Iliad*—civilized men doomed to fight and die in a barbaric conflict. (Shakespeare in his *Troilus and Cressida* makes much of this.) Inescapably, Homer implies, in a world of hostile Greek and Trojan warriors there must be Andromaches who mourn gentle husbands, besides Penelopes who rejoice at their return. In the conventional framework of heroic poetry there must always be undeserving losers like Hector as well as deserving winners like Odysseus. Homer accepts this as an essential condition both of his literary genre and of all militaristic societies—but not without compassion.

Perhaps this is what Homer mainly meant or felt in his account of Athene's relations with Odysseus. As has been emphasized, it is not a static relationship. It grows and becomes more personal up to its psychological climax when Odysseus first sets foot on Ithaca again. What would be more natural than that this development expressed a development in the poet's own mind as he composed the poems? It would be a remarkable and unusual phenomenon for a poet to retain exactly the same conception of his chief hero in the course of composing nearly thirty thousand lines. Homer, as he described scene after scene of carnage and passion in the *Iliad*, may have felt a need for some symbol of faith in humanity, some hope of salvation from the Minotaur that lurks in the labyrinth of every man's dominant passion, if he was to escape despair. The final scene between Priam and Achilles in the *Iliad* provided one answer to the problem of pain and death. But its tragic resignation, for all its sombre magnificence, is desolate and hopeless. In contrast, the end of the *Odyssey*, with its promise of peace and reconciliation, is reassuring and confident. The pessimism of archaic heroism yields to confidence in an emergent humanism.[28]

Was this portrait of Odysseus and Athene drawn from contemporary figures and conditions known to Homer; or was it a prophetic anticipation of future trends in human destiny, like Dante's conception of Ulysses the explorer? Unfortunately the uncertainty of Homer's date, combined with ignorance about the personal qualities of people in archaic Greece, prevents any sure answer here. But it has always been a quality of poetic genius to discover potentialities in human nature as well as to describe its already active powers. It is possible that Homer in his development of Odysseus's personality, and especially in his development of Odysseus's relationship with Athene, saw qualities of the emergent Greek genius which were not yet established in contemporary society—in other words, that in Homer's Odysseus there is a foreshadowing of men like Solon, Peisistratus, Themistocles, and Pericles, who, under the aegis of a less vindictive Athene, established the foundations of European civilization.

If this suggestion is valid it is not simply another form of allegorical interpretation. Allegory implies telling a story with an intentional second meaning, or, from the interpreter's point of view, seeing two meanings in one narrative. The process described in the previous paragraph is not allegorical in this sense. It is better described as creative symbolism, by which an artist arrives at a deeper understanding of his subject (which for Homer was human nature) by thought and intuition. Homer's Odysseus and Athene are obviously not *both* themselves *and* figures of later Athenian civilization, even to the extent that Circe can be interpreted as being both an actual person and an emblem of sensuality. Odysseus and Athene as Homer presents them are not emblems of anything. They are essentially persons acting in and acting on human society. But in their mutual relationship, as it grew in his imagination, Homer may have seen potentialities that could raise humanity above both the selfish trickeries of an Autolycus and the insensate pride of the average Achaean hero.

CHAPTER IV

PERSONAL RELATIONSHIPS

THE *Iliad* says nothing of Odysseus's private life during the Trojan campaign. One sees Achilles in the privacy of his tent and alone on the seashore, Hector in affectionate conversation with his wife and son, and Paris in acrimonious dalliance with Helen. But all Odysseus's actions, speeches, and conversations take place in public—in the camp, on the battlefield, in the council chamber, on embassies. He does, it is true, converse alone with Diomedes on the Night Raid; but his remarks are strictly confined to military matters. There is no suggestion that either Diomedes or anyone else in the Greek camp at Troy was his intimate friend. There was no one, apparently, among his associates at Troy to whom he could open his heart and speak without suspicion or caution.[1] Achilles had his mother and Patroclus to comfort him in his troubles. Agamemnon and Menelaus shared the familiarity of brothers. But Odysseus kept his inner thoughts and feelings to himself. In the *Odyssey*, too, even among his shipmates Odysseus is a lonely figure, more like Captain Ahab in Melville's *Moby Dick* than the genial prince that the Ithacans had known before the war.[2]

Homer suggests no reason for confining his account of Odysseus's Iliadic career to public activities and official relationships. Perhaps he simply decided to reserve the more intimate aspects of Odysseus's personal relationships for the *Odyssey* purely as a matter of poetic economy. But there may have been a less mechanical reason. A marked degree of separateness, and often even of loneliness, is the common fate of those gifted like Odysseus with an abnormal degree of intelligence and subtlety. Friendship is naturally difficult with a person of this calibre. The razor-edge of his mind and speech, however well controlled, will be widely feared. The psychological ambiguities and complexities of his character will seem to offer no firm foundation for loyalty or confidence. The fact that he does not seem to suffer from any of the more amiable weaknesses of human nature will thwart feelings of sympathy and affection. His general efficiency and success in whatever he undertakes will give an impression of inhumanity and self-sufficiency. And when these qualities are tainted with a reputation for deceitfulness and trickery, the obstacles to any sincere friendship become almost insuperable. This may have been what Homer intended to indicate by Odysseus's aloofness among his associates at Troy and his companions at sea.

This intention would also explain why Odysseus's relations with his family in Ithaca, as well as with the Phaeacians, Calypso, and Circe, were, in contrast, so easy and genial. His family knew him well enough not to mistrust his subtlety; the Phaeacians did not know his common reputation until he had won their friendship and respect; the amorous goddesses, being divine like his patron Athene, had no reason to fear his wiles; and, besides, the element of competition, which was constantly present in his dealings with the honour-loving heroes at Troy and the gain-loving companions of his voyages, would not affect his associations with close relatives, strangers, and divinities.

Whatever the reason for Odysseus's complete lack of intimate relationships among his comrades at arms, Homer with characteristic deftness hints early in the *Iliad* that it was not due to any incapacity for affection on Odysseus's part. Twice[3] under stress of strong emotion (in rebuking Thersites and in expostulating against Agamemnon's outrageous charges) Odysseus speaks of himself, in a unique expression, as the father of Telemachus, as if this were the title nearest to his heart. Similarly his love of home is obliquely expressed in his speech to the Greek host after the discomfiture of Thersites. No wonder, he says, that there is some disaffection among them, 'for any man who stays away even one month from his wife is grieved . . . and we have been away for nine years'.[4] Here Odysseus speaks from his own heart, though with an admirable avoidance of egotism.

In contrast with Homer's silence on Odysseus's personal relationships in the *Iliad*, one finds them revealed very fully and variously in the *Odyssey*. A striking feature is that so many of them are with women. The post-Homeric tradition emphasized different aspects of these relationships according as literary fashions changed. Within more recent times writers under the influence of the romantic revival have tended to dwell more on his adventures with Circe, Calypso, and Nausicaa, than on his affection for his wife, parents, and son, as later chapters will show. Some have thought fit to present him as a primeval Don Juan or a primitive Byron. Others, following the fashion of the last three decades, have portrayed him as a man obsessed with sordid eroticism. Scholars and moralists, though naturally less extravagant, have noticed apparent inconsistencies between Odysseus's love for Penelope and his relationships with the women he met on his Odyssean wanderings.[5] This involves problems of fundamental importance for the development of the whole tradition, and it will be well to consider them in the full Homeric perspective here.

Justice demands that Odysseus's liaisons with Circe and Calypso should, like his wiliness, be viewed in the light of the customs of his time. On the one hand the Heroic Age was strictly monogamous; and Homer generally portrays the relationships between husbands and wives as affectionate, honourable, and equal. He offers little precedent for such a subordination of wives to husbands as one finds in later Greek epochs. A wife had to be wooed and won by a formal courtship and generous gifts. After marriage the wife organized and ruled the household, the husband looked after the estate and public affairs. In society they conversed, argued, or agreed, as equals. Homer does not hesitate at times to present women as more perceptive and intelligent than men. Arete is cleverer than Alcinous, Helen than Menelaus, Clytaemnestra (in a brutal way) than Agamemnon. In fact there have been few periods of European literature when women have been portrayed with such a frank appraisal as in the *Iliad* and *Odyssey*. Homer presents them without adulation or contempt, without romanticism or mysticism, simply as another kind of human being who is in some ways stronger and in some ways weaker than men.

On the other hand women suffered from one grave injustice in the heroic age. Concubinage, even open concubinage, was permitted to husbands but not to wives.[6] Yet here, too, Homer may have introduced a refinement. He implies that happily married men avoided the practice. During the Trojan campaign Menelaus and Odysseus had no concubines,[7] in contrast with the unhappy Agamemnon and Achilles. But Homer makes it clear that husbands might have other motives for avoiding concubinage. In the first book of the *Odyssey* he mentions the fact that Laertes bought Eurycleia for a large price and honoured her like a true wife in his house, but avoided cohabiting with her 'because he feared the anger of his wife'. The implication is that while concubinage was the usual custom Anticleia was a formidable wife, as the daughter of Autolycus might well have been. Laertes's motive for abstinence was fear. Menelaus's was his lasting infatuation for Helen. Odysseus's was, most likely, affection mixed with prudence. Without his being either afraid of Penelope or infatuated with her, his

affection for her merged in his desire to preserve the unity of his
home, and his faithfulness was doubly secure.

How, then, can Odysseus's liaisons with Circe and Calypso be
reconciled with this fidelity? And how can they be reconciled with
the later view of Stoics and Christians that Odysseus's conduct in
the *Odyssey* provided a pattern of virtue and wisdom? Why, too,
did Penelope, who had herself remained strictly chaste for almost
twenty years, refrain from reproaching Odysseus when he told her
about Circe and Calypso? Circumstances alter cases: it will be well
first to consider the circumstances.

At first sight Calypso and Circe seem to have much in common;
both are described as 'beautiful-haired, dread, vocal' goddesses; both
reside in magically beautiful lands; and both, having received
Odysseus into their homes when he is in need of peace and rest,
hold him in their sway for a long while. But when Homer has
developed the characterization of each and has painted in the details
of their environment, a strong contrast emerges, a contrast as
between darkness and light, between prototypes of the *femme fatale*
of sadistic romance and of the gentle Solveig of Ibsen's *Peer Gynt*.

Circe is the first woman Odysseus meets on his wanderings. He
arrives at her country after a series of disasters which have shattered
the morale of his few remaining companions. Homer warns his
audience by a genealogical clue to expect something sinister in what
follows. He describes Circe as a sister of the darkly malevolent
Aietes, King of Colchis (and thereby an aunt of the baneful enchantress Medea). But she is also the daughter of the lifegiving Sun.
Odysseus himself does not know about this significant ancestry until
later. But a note of sinister magic is felt as soon as the Companions
see her palace, where it lies in the heart of a thick wood, patrolled
by wolves and lions. In subsequent descriptions Homer builds up
a brilliant contrast between the general atmosphere of luxurious
beauty in Circe's palace and the latent horror of her enchantments.
She is no Gothic witch-hag scrabbling among cats and bats in a
murky hut, but a luminous daemonic creature combining two
equally dangerous but quite dissimilar personalities. As the sister
of Aietes she turns men into swine; as a daughter of the Sun she
delights them with every sensuous joy. It was left to later allegorists
to assert that these were two ways of saying the same thing: the
sensual man is the swinish man. The Cynics, always jealous for the
good name of the lower animals, argued that perhaps the pigs were
the happier of the two.[8]

The story of how Odysseus, forewarned by Hermes and protected by the plant called Moly, overcame Circe and rescued his companions needs no re-telling. A few details are significant for the present study. When Circe's potion has failed to work and Odysseus threatens her with his drawn sword, she falls at his feet in amazement and fear. Then, recognizing him as the hero, whose coming had been predicted to her by Hermes, she at once invites him to her couch 'so that by loving they may have trust in each other'. The abruptness of her invitation—though it may be due partly to the condensed style of these folk-tale episodes in Odysseus's wanderings —might well have surprised even the alert Odysseus if Hermes had not already prophesied it. Odysseus, following Hermes's advice, and his own instincts of prudence, makes Circe swear an oath not to harm him when he is unarmed, and accedes to her request. Later a feast is brought to them. But Odysseus cannot eat for thinking of his companions in the pigsties. Circe assumes that he is thinking of his own safety and reminds him of her oath. This is characteristic of her *égoïsme à deux*. It never occurs to her that anything outside his own personal welfare (which she now identifies with her own) can concern him. Odysseus's reply contains a mild rebuke: 'What decent man could bear to feast before freeing and seeing his comrades?' Circe promptly goes and transforms them back into younger and handsomer men than they were before. When they and Odysseus burst into loud lamentations together she ('even she', as Homer puts it) feels an altruistic emotion for the first time and pities them. Then, having realized the deep bond of loyalty that unites Odysseus with his crew, she invites him to bring the others from his ship so that they may all stay and recuperate with her for a while. Madame Wolf has become a Florence Nightingale, it seems.

The result of Circe's new policy of kindness towards Odysseus and his companions was that very soon Odysseus fell completely under her sway. A year passed before any move was made to continue their voyage home. In the end it was the Companions who had to approach Odysseus and remind him of his destiny. Their words suggest a mixture of bewilderment and diffidence.[9] Having heard them, Odysseus neither apologizes nor procrastinates. That evening he abjectly beseeches Circe to fulfil her promise to send him on his way home. She makes no effort to detain him against his will. She simply warns him of further perils on his homeward journey.

Two features of this are noteworthy. First there is the complete reversal of Odysseus's mastery of Circe. He who a year ago had brought her as a suppliant to his knees is now humbly supplicating her help. Secondly there is the complete absence of affection in their last words together. Here the contrast with Calypso is most marked. Circe, even when she has adopted a policy of winning by kindness, instead of subduing by witchcraft, shows none of Calypso's warm affectionateness. Though capable of pity and eager for physical love with a hero, she is primarily a dispassionate enchantress intent on having her own way—*la belle dame sans merci*. She is not, indeed, the vampirish monster of nineteenth-century sensationalism; but there is something inhuman and predatory in her. Perhaps once more this is because Homer had not completely assimilated a traditional figure to his more humanistic style, so that the abruptness of her actions are more those of a marionette than of a fully developed character. But, taken in its general context, her conduct has a sinister automaton-like effect, quite unlike Calypso's manner. She never entirely steps out of that world of fairytale which in such an alarming way anticipates the robot-like figures of modern scientific fiction.

In contrast with Circe's nonchalance in parting with Odysseus once his comrades had re-awakened his desire to return to Ithaca, Calypso does all she can to keep him for ever. Homer records nothing about the first seven years of Odysseus's life with her, except that when he was shipwrecked on her shore she 'received him with loving kindness, and tended him, and said that she would make him immortally youthful', and that afterwards she had always treated him 'like a god'. After his visit to the Land of Ghosts and his encounters with Scylla, Charybdis, and the Cattle of the Sun, Calypso's gentle kindness and the languorous, relaxing beauty of her island must have come to him like balm from Gilead. But at the very beginning of the *Odyssey* Homer takes care to show that Calypso's attentions did not succeed in killing Odysseus's desire for home. Athene emphasizes this in her first speech to Zeus in Book One:

> But grief and rage alternate wound my breast
> For brave Ulysses, still by fate oppress'd.
> Amidst an isle, around whose rocky shore
> The forests murmur, and the surges roar,
> The blameless hero from his wish'd for home
> A goddess guards in her enchanted dome.
> Atlas her sire. . . .

By his fair daughter is the chief confined
Who soothes to dear delight his anxious mind:
Successless all her soft caresses prove,
To banish from his breast his country's love;
To see the smoke from his loved palace rise,
While the dear isle in distant prospect lies
With what contentment would he close his eyes!

(Pope's amplified version)

Similarly when Odysseus first appears personally in the narrative, in Book Five, he is sitting on a headland with his eyes full of tears, gazing across the sea. Every day, we are told, he used to leave Calypso's cave to haunt the rocky promontories, sobbing and groaning in agonies of home-sickness, his spirit wasting away with yearning for home. It is clear that Homer wished none of his hearers to be in doubt on this point. He tells how at night Odysseus would indeed sleep beside the nymph, but only—cruel phrase—unwillingly and perforce.[10] Yet Calypso even in her parting scenes with this reluctant consort never expresses any bitterness or anger. The most she allows herself is a touch of scorn at his refusal to accept her offer of immortal youth. Even when she smiles to see how characteristically he distrusts the news of his release, she takes away the sting with an affectionate touch of her hand.

Unlike Circe, Calypso uses all the wisdom and prescience of a minor divinity to study Odysseus's thoughts and inclinations. She fully understands his yearnings for home and his eagerness to escape from his exile with her. Yet she continues to hope until the end that he may change his mind. When Hermes comes at the bidding of Zeus (prompted by Athene) and tells her that she must send Odysseus away, she is angry with what she considers a typical example of Olympian envy and spite. She makes a last effort to persuade him to stay. After a lavish banquet, she warns Odysseus of the trials he must undergo even when he has returned to Ithaca, and suggests that he would be much wiser to accept her offer of immortal life in Ogygia with her. She reminds him that, after all, Penelope is only a mortal woman whose beauty cannot compare with a goddess's. (Behind her words, as Odysseus realizes, stands the spectre, so much dreaded by the Greeks, of feeble, ugly old age.) But she fails to persuade him. He admits that Penelope cannot compete with her in beauty (just as barren Ithaca, Homer implies, could not rival the violet-strewn meadows of Ogygia where 'even a god would find wonder and delight'). Yet, no matter what

troubles await him, he wants to go home. He says nothing about
love or affection, but simply insists that home is best. Calypso
knows that she is defeated. After Odysseus has built his boat she
dresses herself in a beautifully perfumed robe—Homer deftly
suggests a variety of fragrances in Ogygia—sees to his provisions
for the voyage, arranges for a 'warm and harmless breeze' to waft
him away, watches him as he joyfully spreads his sails for home . . .
and turns back, alone, to her cave.

Why did she fail to hold Odysseus? Apart from the technical
reason that the plot of the *Odyssey* demanded Odysseus's return to
Ithaca, Odysseus's own nature precluded it. Homer always insisted
that Odysseus's love of home was his dominant desire, symbolized
in the much-borrowed image of 'the smoke rising up from his own
land'.[11] What was the essence of this devotion? A modern romantic
novelist might tend to concentrate it in an all-absorbing love for
Penelope. To an early classical writer this would seem little different
from infatuation and folly in an adult hero. As Homer saw it
Penelope was at the centre of Odysseus's affections partly because
of her own personal qualities but partly also because she stood for
the whole texture of Odysseus's normal life in Ithaca, the life which
he had been unwilling to leave when the call came to join the
expedition against Troy. It would be otiose guess-work to try to
mark a clear division between Odysseus's love for Penelope and his
love for his home and kingdom. In Calypso's Ogygia they were
part of one complex feeling in Odysseus's heart—his yearning for a
normal, natural, sociable life as husband, father, and king.[12]

Here one sees a radical contrast between Homer's conception of
Odysseus and that of many later writers on the Ulysses theme. The
movement of the *Odyssey* is essentially inwards, homewards, towards
normality. As conceived later by poets like Dante, Tennyson, and
Pascoli, Ulysses's urge is centrifugal, outwards towards the exotic
or abnormal. As Pascoli sees it, when Odysseus returns to Ithaca
he will be irresistibly drawn back to Calypso and to her mystical
island.[13] There at last, after many mysterious experiences in the
scenes of his Odyssean wanderings, he will find peace in the shadow
of her cloudlike hair and be blissfully absorbed into Nirvanic
annihilation.

This is, of course, mainly a fantasy of late nineteenth-century
aestheticism. But Pascoli's superbly evocative descriptions of
Calypso's island bring out a significant feature in Homer's narrative.
Homer's account of Ogygia, that flower-strewn, aromatic island,

does suggest something of the *dolce far niente*,[14] in implicit contrast with the rugged, harsh Ithaca which Odysseus so deeply loved. Modern attitudes must not be allowed to cause confusion here. The languorous life of the South Sea Islands, has attracted many Europeans in the last century—Gauguin, for example, to Tahiti, Stevenson to Samoa. But such a life of idle hedonism would never satisfy an early Greek, eager for action, society, and renown—least of all a hero so much endowed with practical ability as Odysseus. When Aristotle defined happiness as a manly (or 'virtuous') activity of the vital powers, he was echoing what Achilles had said to Odysseus in the Land of Ghosts: better to be the basest of farm labourers on earth than, without bodily strength and physical activity, to lord it over all the hosts of the dead. Calypso's mistake was to think that a man like Odysseus could ever be happy among the violets and the vines of Ogygia. Better, as he told her, the severest sufferings of war or sea-voyaging than that perfume-drugged lethargy, that voluptuous sloth, even with a goddess to love and tend him.

If these are true interpretations of Odysseus's relationships with Circe and Calypso, the answers to the questions posed earlier become clear. The reason why Homer, Penelope, and the moralists of the later tradition, did not think ill of Odysseus for these infidelities was primarily because in both cases Odysseus was not acting voluntarily. Both Circe and Calypso were demi-goddesses endowed with power to compel their will. Before Odysseus met Circe, Hermes had given him a specific command to grant her request to become her consort. With Calypso there was no direct command from Zeus,[15] but the circumstances were such as to overpower any man of classical antiquity, except perhaps Socrates. Besides, as Penelope would well know in those god-frequented times, to reject the advances of divinities was dangerous indeed. She would hardly have preferred him to be turned into a tree like Daphne or into an ineffectual prophet like Cassandra. Just what else Penelope may have thought in her heart Homer does not suggest. He is satisfied to make it clear that either through affection or through prudence she expressed no annoyance when Odysseus told her his story. The joy of their final re-union was left unclouded. Doubtless Homer intended his hearers to appreciate the contrast with Clytaemnestra's murderous reception of Agamemnon after his infidelities at Troy.[16]

But what of Nausicaa? One might have thought that inclinations to see Odysseus as a sentimental or Byronic amorist would have been checked by consideration of his behaviour with her in Phaeacia.

But it is not so. In late Victorian times a young poet, afterwards a distinguished Professor of Poetry,[17] went so far as to suggest that the happiest ending for Odysseus's life would be to return to Nausicaa and live happily ever after in Phaeacia; and more recently a generally sympathetic interpreter of the *Odyssey*,[18] while admitting that there is no real love story in Homer's account of the incident, has recorded his sadness at its absence. This demands some explanation.

Odysseus's first encounter with Nausicaa was perhaps the severest test of tact and resourcefulness in his whole career. He has been sleeping on the Phaeacian shore exhausted, foul, and naked, after his long ordeal at sea under Poseidon's wrath. His condition is much as it must have been when he was shipwrecked on Calypso's island —but Homer to avoid repetition did not describe that scene. There is, however, a psychological difference. Calypso was a mature and kindly goddess. Odysseus has now to deal with an inexperienced young girl. How will she react to the sight of a naked stranger when he appears suddenly beside her? It will need all Odysseus's adroitness to keep this situation in hand.

As soon as the ugly apparition is seen coming from the thicket, Nausicaa's handmaidens scatter in flight. But she herself, strengthened by Athene (just as it was by Athene's prompting that she had gone to this part of the seashore), stands her ground. Odysseus approaches her and speaks. His speech is very carefully phrased, and shows a remarkable delicacy of feeling. Perhaps Odysseus was helped by remembering that if Penelope had borne him a daughter before he had gone to Troy she would be about Nausicaa's age or a little older by now. Or perhaps, he remembered his own sister Ctimene when they were young together. So, at least, his gentle sensibility towards a young unmarried girl's feelings suggests.

He begins by expressing awe and admiration for her Artemis-like beauty (that is, slender, virginal, athletic, in contrast, it is implied, with the more voluptuous charms of Aphrodite). Then he blesses the father, mother, and brothers of such a maiden—how their hearts must be gladdened to see her gracefulness in the festive dances! (Odysseus has guessed that Nausicaa, like most girls of her age, likes dancing.) Happier still, he respectfully adds, the man who is to marry her. (A married girl would hardly have been playing like this with maidens on the seashore.) A deft comparison of her slender stature with a palm-tree at Delos enables him to imply that he himself is a man who goes on religious pilgrimages with a large retinue—no irreligious tramp, whatever his present appearance suggests. And he has suffered many woes (this to touch her tender heart); and more sufferings await him. This said, he appeals directly to her pity. She is the first fellow-creature that he has met and supplicated since his last shipwreck. Will she give him even a wrapping of her laundry to clothe himself in (he falls into a beggar's mock humility for a moment—a part he had played before at Troy and must play painfully soon again in Ithaca), and show him the way to the town? He ends with a wish that must have come from the heart of a man separated for so long from his own wife:

Then may the gods give you all that your heart is desiring,
Husband, and home. And the joy of united hearts may they grant you—
For what in all that Heaven can grant is better or stronger
Than when husband and wife in oneness of heart share their household together?

Nausicaa's first reply is what one would expect from a well-bred, brave, but naturally rather overwhelmed, girl in this unusual situation. It must have sounded prim at first in contrast with the kind of talk Odysseus had been used to for the last eighteen years among warriors, divinities, and monsters. She tells him that he doesn't look like an evil or foolish man. Why then has he suffered so much, if he did not deserve heaven's wrath?—a nice, but somewhat untimely theological question. But she has been well instructed. She knows the answer: Zeus sometimes apportions prosperity to evil men and misfortune to good men. Fortunately for the patience of Odysseus, she puts this very briefly and does not pause to discuss why Zeus is so arbitrary. She is a pious girl, but not inhumanly so. In her next words she promises the persuasive stranger all he has asked.

One need not examine the rest of the scene in detail, for its characterization is mainly devoted to Nausicaa, not to Odysseus. She has been criticized harshly for remarking to her attendants, after Odysseus had been miraculously beautified by Athene, that he looks like the kind of man she would like to marry.[19] But this is entirely in keeping with her naïve and frank nature, and it is addressed only to her intimate friends. There is obviously no deep personal emotion involved. Every day in the cinemas of our time adolescents say or think something like this about the handsomer actors and actresses on the screen. It is no more than a romanticized manner of expressing admiration. Here it is Homer's device for reminding us of Odysseus's personal attractiveness.

When Nausicaa has brought Odysseus safely to the town, she leaves him, and we see her only once again in the story. On the evening of the next day she meets Odysseus on his way to the banquet of the Phaeacians.[20] Both she and Odysseus are looking their best, Homer emphasizes. Odysseus has just been bathed and is wearing a fresh tunic and cloak; Nausicaa is 'endowed with beauty from the gods'. She speaks first: 'Farewell, stranger; and when you are in your native land see that you remember me, for it is to me that you owe the saving of your life'. Odysseus replies: 'Nausicaa, daughter of magnanimous Alcinous, may Zeus . . . grant that I reach home and see the day of my return! Then surely will I offer thanksgivings to you there as to a god, always, every day, as now: for it was you who gave me life, maiden.' That is all. Nausicaa is never mentioned again in Homer. There is no evidence that Odysseus kept his rather extravagant promise all his life. But it expressed his sincere gratitude and respect.

Some have found this brief parting scene disappointingly curt. 'Our heart is disappointed and defrauded of its dues.' The relationship, we are told, is 'like a musical phrase left incomplete'. In other words, if Nausicaa is a fairy princess, why does not Odysseus, the typical stranger-hero, become her lover?[21]

The answer, as elsewhere, is partly stylistic, partly ethical. The final purpose of the *Odyssey*, and of Odysseus within it, is the return and restoration of the prince of Ithaca. Nausicaa plays her minor part in advancing that purpose, and is then firmly bowed out both by Homer and Odysseus. Even if the composer of the *Odyssey* had been a woman (as Samuel Butler and an ancient critic believed), she would hardly have made it otherwise. The classical style demands strict subordination of the parts to the whole, of the episodes to the final purpose. And from the point of view of ethics Penelope would have had good reason to view any liaison between her husband and Nausicaa very differently from the Circe and Calypso incidents. There was no supernatural sanction on Nausicaa's side.

Suppose Odysseus and this *princesse lointaine* had become lovers, what would have been the likeliest result? Goethe,[22] with his profound insight into Homer's world, saw that any such relationship between the grizzled veteran and this unsophisticated girl would only bring tragedy to the weaker one. Homer or Goethe could have produced another Dido and Aeneas story here, if they had wished. But would it have pleased admirers of Nausicaa more than the idyll as it is now in the *Odyssey*? The other alternative—to imagine a starry-eyed Odysseus wandering blissfully hand in hand on the Phaeacian shore with his young bride Nausicaa happily ever after[23]—belongs to the world of Peter Pan, not of Homer or Goethe. Homer avoided both a tragic and a novelettish crisis, refusing to let an episode become a major theme. And at the same time he implied that Odysseus was neither a philandering Don Juan gathering rosebuds while he may, nor a home-forsaking Byron.

What of Penelope herself? The conventions of successive romantic eras in European literature, from the troubadours to the neo-Hellenists, have been hard on faithful Penelopes. It would take a whole volume to free her from the accumulated disparagements of centuries. The gravest injustice is to compare her, after nineteen years of anxious waiting, burdened with the cares of a young son and an unruly household, with the carefree Nausicaa, Circe, and Calypso, or with the petted and wayward Helen. A recent Swedish writer has solved this time-problem by portraying her on Odysseus's return as if she had not changed in looks or in mind since her bridal day in Lacedaemon twenty years ago. But Homer presents real men and women, not dream-fantasies. He does not hesitate to reveal the ravages of her long vigil.

For the first ten years, while Odysseus was still with the Achaean chieftains on the Trojan campaign, Penelope had simply to contend with her loneliness and the normal problems of a household whose master is absent. But when, after the sack of Troy, Odysseus failed to return in due time, her difficulties became much more severe. Then she had to cope with the obstreperous attentions of over a hundred lusty suitors insolently frequenting her house and devouring its substance; she had to manage disloyal servants; she had to control a vigorous and rather unsympathetic son in the uncertainties of his approaching manhood. It is hardly surprising, then, that when Odysseus returns in the twentieth year of her ordeal he finds her nerves frayed and her heart almost frozen with despair.[24]

Homer arranges for two major scenes between the long-separated husband and wife. In the first Odysseus is still disguised as a beggar, and Penelope does not recognize him. Yet, as has been recently argued, this scene acquires much greater dramatic and psychological force if it is understood that by the end of it Penelope has reached the point of feeling that this stranger may be, even must be, Odysseus at last.[25] According to this view Odysseus, too, knows that Penelope is by now almost convinced of his identity, but does not try to give her final proof until the Suitors have been killed. The situation,

E

then, in their first conversations will be like that in De la Mare's novel, *The return*, where a man comes back to his wife with his face completely changed by black magic (just as Odysseus has been transformed by Athene). During his first interview with his bewildered wife he thinks: 'She is pretending; she is trying me; she is feeling her way. . . she knows I *am* I, but hasn't the courage. . . .'. Odysseus is less detached, less self-conscious, and has more pity for his wife's sufferings than this modern schizophrene. But the two situations are fundamentally similar in their mixture of hope, fear, faith, and doubt.

Some aspects of Odysseus's conduct in the first scene[26] deserve special attention. He is reluctant at first to tell Penelope a flat lie in reply to her inquiry about who he is: on other occasions he is much readier with pseudo-autobiographies. Sometimes he speaks with a brusqueness one would expect more from a husband than from a beggar speaking to a queen. When Penelope shows deep emotion at his references to her missing lord, Odysseus has to hold his eyes 'as unflinching as horn or iron' to avoid weeping with her. Homer implies that it was one of the sternest tests of self-control that Odysseus had ever experienced. In fact he did begin to weep but hid his tears by a trick. But in this scene attention is mainly focused on Penelope, as she so fully deserves, and on the poignancy of her conflicting thoughts and feelings.

When, after the killing of the Suitors, Eurycleia goes to tell Penelope that Odysseus is home and has triumphed, Homer's skill in portraying personal feelings reaches its height. He refuses to rush to his climax, the recognition of husband and wife, as a cruder story-teller might have done. Instead, like an expert musician he increases the final effect by an unexpected diminuendo and by some wavering, indecisive modulations before the final diapason chords are struck. In the slowness of Penelope to accept the happy truth one sees the epic style at its best. At this level it rivals the finest achievements of dramatic art—in this tolerance of personal dubieties and uncertainties and hesitations and rebuffs, and in the ability to use them as elements in its full symphonic plan. In works of lesser genius, in the Ulysses tradition as well as outside it, one is often painfully conscious of a conflict between the exigencies of form and those of characterization. Here in *Odyssey* Twenty-three Homer unites form and content in a superb integration of art and life, so that one can say in the same breath 'How true' and 'How finely handled'. Perhaps some of Homer's original hearers were impatient, like Telemachus in the story, for the final re-union. But modern readers who are prepared to give Homer the freedom of technique that they give to contemporary writers will not complain.

Detailed analysis of the final recognition scene[27] would be out of place here. The texture of Homer's art is too closely woven to permit any effective substitute for itself. The feature most worthy of notice is Penelope's victory. Up to this point Odysseus had been very confident and very patient in accepting his wife's doubts and reservations about his identity. He had rebuked Telemachus for trying to hurry her into accepting him, and had left her alone for a while to make up her mind in her own way. Now he has returned again, cleansed from the gore of battle, finely clothed, and specially beautified by Athene. Certain that he is irresistible now, he addresses Penelope in almost the same chiding terms which Telemachus had used earlier. He is astonished at the unwomanlike hardness of her heart: surely no other wife would behave like this towards a long-lost husband. Penelope's reply shows that she is no more to be intimidated by her husband than by her son. 'I am equally surprised at you', she replies, 'and I am not the one who has got things out of proportion'. Then (after an ambiguous phrase which could imply that she no longer doubts his identity) she deftly springs her trap in an offhand remark about his special bed. Her implication that it can be moved from its place takes Odysseus completely aback—it 'pains his heart'. Revealing his deeper feelings spontaneously for the first time since his return home, 'he indignantly addresses his clever-witted wife'. Who has tampered with their unique bed, the finest product of his skill in carpentry? Penelope's purpose is achieved. She has deflated Odysseus's self-confidence, and she can be certain that he is really Odysseus—for when is a man more uniquely himself than in indignation and surprise at some interference with his special possessions?[28] Having triumphed, Penelope crowns her victory with complete surrender. Bursting into tears, she throws her arms about her husband, kisses him, and begs that he will not be angry with her. To Odysseus, as Homer says in a carefully chosen simile, this is like the sight of land to shipwrecked mariners. Though he has further trials to face before the *Odyssey* is completed—'Home is the sailor, home from sea'.

In these progressive stages of the final reconciliation of husband and wife Homer had three main problems. The first was to find adequate and convincing expression for the release of so much accumulated emotion. The second was to portray a Penelope

worthy of his Odysseus. Feminists may dislike this, but despite the
poet's admiration for feminine qualities it can hardly be denied that
Odysseus is the pivot of his poem. The third was to give a unique
and memorable quality to the final dénouement. Few who can read
Greek will deny his success in the first. For the second, even the
few illustrations given in this chapter should suffice to display how
well matched these two are in quick perception, intelligence,
caution, endurance, subtlety, affection, and deep emotion (which is
naturally less restrained in Penelope). Homer succeeds in the third
partly by superb constructional devices—carefully calculated
approaches and withdrawals, diminuendo and crescendo, as already
suggested—and partly by introducing an element of paradox,
noticed by an ancient commentator.[29] This last quality consists
mainly in Penelope's unpredictable changes of mood—pessimistic,
optimistic, sceptical, trusting, merry, sad. But the culmination
comes at the very end, when to Odysseus's surprise, as well as ours,
it is Penelope who plans and executes the final test of Odysseus's
identity. Once again Homer has paid a high tribute to woman's
intelligence. Already another woman, Eurycleia, had been quicker
than Odysseus had anticipated, when she perceived the scar and
immediately guessed who he was. But this had been accidental.
Penelope's triumph was planned and achieved by her own wit
alone.

Another aspect of their final recognition scene has been neglected.
Thanks to the poet's skill and Penelope's resourcefulness, Odysseus
is virtually compelled in the end to woo her again as he wooed her
some twenty years before in Sparta. He compliments her, chides
her, puzzles her, entertains her, flatters her, is patient with her, gives
her confidence, makes her doubtful; he exhibits his strength, his
feats of arms, his courage, his prudence, his resourcefulness, his
forbearance, his gentleness, his understanding; he boasts a little,
praises himself a good deal, smiles, sets his face like stone, is angry,
cajoles, bullies. And, most significantly for Penelope's status, it is
when he begins to bully and chide her that she trips him up and
outwits him. Yet—and this is her greatest moral triumph—once
she has got the effect she wanted by her subterfuge, instead of
boasting and making Odysseus admit that she can be cleverer than
he, when she likes, she simply yields.

There is something of the profoundest significance in this final
self-abandonment. As Eustathius, Bishop of Thessalonica (to whose
compilation of ancient commentaries these chapters owe much),

remarks, Penelope's problem about the stranger was really insoluble: for if the stranger was (as she feared) a god in the guise of her husband, what was to prevent him in his omniscience from knowing even the Secret of the Bed?[30] This is the kind of difficulty that belief in non-moral polymorphous divinities constantly creates in archaic literature, especially among a witty and logical prople like the Greeks. Homer makes Penelope solve it boldly by an act of intuitive faith. Intelligence cannot lead her the whole way. She must make a leap of faith—in this case to reject a hypothesis of divine action. So Penelope is more than just a clever, faithful wife. She personifies that universal affirmation, that spirit of self-abandoning surrender, which is woman's answer to man's negations and resistances to life. Her final submission to Odysseus is not a defeat. It is a paradoxical triumph of self-giving.

Homer says less about Odysseus's other family relationships. Two references in the *Iliad*, as already quoted, agree with many indications in the *Odyssey* in implying that Odysseus was proud of having a son and heir. But when he and Telemachus meet at last, and in their subsequent actions together, their conversations seem distinctly formal, almost hollow, compared with those between Odysseus and Penelope. This is another example of Homer's fidelity to life. Telemachus had been an infant in arms when Odysseus left for Troy: now he is a sensitive idealistic young man, like the young Apollo of Frances Cornford's epigram:

> Magnificently unprepared
> For the long littleness of life.

He and his father have almost nothing in common either in experience or in outlook. Though they share a strong sense of belonging to each other, this is still an entirely *a priori* bond of feeling—a cherished hypothesis without any empirical proof as yet. For nearly twenty years each has thought and wondered about the other. Now, when their hopes and anxieties are to be put to the touchstone of reality, what will the result be—love or hate? Odysseus with his knowledge of life, would be fully aware of the subtle tensions in a relationship like this. Telemachus, whose characteristic epithet in the *Odyssey* means 'well endowed with intelligence',[31] would intuitively apprehend them. That is why Homer keeps their relationship rather formal and rather guarded, though each is always ready to meet the other half-way, until the end of the *Odyssey*. It would have been false to equate so unsubstantial an

intimacy as this with the profound empirical understanding of husband and wife. Yet this father-son relationship is one of the deeper
elements in the Ulysses myth. Writers in the later tradition make
much of it.[32]

Odysseus's last re-union in the *Odyssey* is with his father Laertes.[33]
Homer enlists our sympathy for the old man's plight by first
revealing him as he works with his hoe among the briars of an
outlying farm. His tunic is patched and dirty. As protection against
the rending thorns he wears leggings and mittens on the limbs that
once had shone in heroic armour. His helmet is now a goatskin
cap. He is alone, bending low over his work. Odysseus sees all this
as he stands among the trees which Laertes had given him as a boy.
Naturally he weeps at the sight. But was it simply caution that
prompted him to postpone revealing his true identity at once, and
to 'test' his father with another fictitious tale? Homer in an introductory phrase[34] suggests something more, something that we can
hardly admire in Odysseus here—a touch of sly mockery. And,
indeed, Odysseus's first words do seem to show a trace of this:

> Old man, you have everything so tidy here that I can see there is little about
> gardening that you do not know. . . . On the other hand, I cannot help remarking,
> I hope without offence, that you don't look after yourself very well; in fact, what
> with your squalor and your wretched clothes, old age has hit you very hard. Yet
> it can't be on account of any laziness that your master neglects you, nor is there
> anything in your build and size to suggest the slave. . . .
>
> (Rieu's translation)

Odysseus goes on to spin out a rigmarole about this and that until
'a dark cloud of woe' covers Laertes. In an agony of grief the old
man fills his hands with dust from the ground and pours it in utter
despair down over his grey head. Then a sudden spasm of feeling
seizes Odysseus. To express its unusual force Homer uses a unique
phrase—'a pungent spirit thrust its way down his nostrils'. He leaps
forward, embraces his father, kisses him, and in broken phrases
reveals himself. Laertes demands proof of his identity, as well he
might after Odysseus's earlier conduct. He is easily convinced.
Embracing Odysseus in turn, he faints, overpowered by emotion,
in his arms.

The scene is full of deep psychological undercurrents: but, as
usual, Homer declines to explain them. It can only be a guess, to
be accepted or rebutted by each reader for himself as he reconsiders
the episode, that the poet is suggesting a latent father-son antagonism
here. (One does not need to discourse on Œdipus complexes to

admit the frequency of such a relationship, and there is nothing Œdipus-like in Odysseus.) Though the tradition never refers to any open conflict, Homer does imply, without explaining it, that Laertes had resigned from his kingship before Odysseus went to Troy. Since after twenty years Laertes was still vigorous enough to hoe a plantation (and in the final scene of the *Odyssey*, to don armour and, with Athene's help, to kill an enemy) this early abdication was curious. If he and his son, then perhaps about twenty-five, had reached a state of strong, but not ungovernable, antagonism, the action would be one of wise and generous policy on Laertes's part.

In contrast Odysseus's interview with the spirit of his mother Anticleia in the Land of Ghosts implies a deep and fully sympathetic relationship. Despite its brevity and its comparative unimportance in the development of the plot, the scene is one of the most memorable in the Homeric poems, and it was constantly imitated by later writers. Odysseus's primary purpose in visiting Ghost-land on Circe's instructions was to consult the spirit of the prophet Teiresias about his return to Ithaca. To his surprise the ghost of Elpenor, the Companion accidentally killed in Circe's palace, meets him first, and, after that, Anticleia's. At the sight of his mother's wraith Odysseus bursts into tears. He had not known that she was dead. Yet he does not allow her to come and drink the blood, despite his grief and wonder, until he has first interviewed Teiresias.

This is a shrewd touch of characterization. Homer makes it clear that Odysseus and his mother were most affectionately attached to each other. Yet here Odysseus purposefully—even callously, some may think—postpones all speech with her until his main purpose is achieved. He knows that the safety of both his comrades and himself depends on what Teiresias predicts. The common weal must take precedence over private affections: prudence must prevail over emotion. It is not an exclusively Ulyssean trait. For the same reason Agamemnon consented to the sacrifice of Iphigeneia, Brutus to the execution of his son. On the other hand Homer suggests nothing of the heartlessness of a Nero in Odysseus's action. Odysseus is never presented as an unfeeling or inconsiderate son, father, or husband. But at times he firmly chooses to set the *bonum publicum* above all personal ties. One sees a germ here, but only a germ, of his ruthlessness in the later tradition.

After Teiresias has given his prophecy and retired, Anticleia returns and is allowed to drink the blood. Her first inquiries are for her son. She says nothing of her own fate. Odysseus asks her what caused her death—was it a long or a brief illness?—and what about his father and son?—and what has his wife been thinking?—is she still faithfully looking after Telemachus and the royal possessions or has some noble Achaean married her? His mother with feminine understanding answers his last, but most important, question first[35]: he may rest assured, his wife is still faithful to him 'with enduring spirit, though the days and nights ever waste sorrowfully away for her in tears and grief'. His son is well and popular. But old Laertes is lonely, neglected, and unhappy on his country estate. (Here, too, Homer dwells on the misery of Laertes's condition.) Finally she tells the cause of her own death. It was not illness that laid her low, but yearning for him, her only son, for his thoughtfulness and for his kindly ways. Odysseus is too much moved to reply at once. He can only stretch out his arms to embrace her. But she is a ghost, and can no more be held than a shadow or a dream. Perplexed and distraught, he asks why she glides from his arms. She, always sorrier for him than for herself—'Alas, my child, unhappiest of mortals', she begins—tells him about the sad, disembodied state of the dead; says good-bye, and, thoughtful for others to the end, devotes her last words to his wife.

Though the scene is full of deep emotion, to deduce (in the manner of modern psycho-analysis) any abnormal relationship between Odysseus and his mother would be rash. The ghost of any other normally affectionate mother would hardly speak differently to her only son, unless he were unusually unlovable. Here Homer presents a typical scene in life—the devoted mother and the busy, rather self-centred, but not entirely inconsiderate or unaffectionate, son—endowing it with a pathos and nobility which the European literary tradition has never forgotten. But the contrast with the much less loving scene between Odysseus and his father may hint that a daughter of Autolycus would be better equipped to understand Odysseus's Autolycan characteristics than a man of more conventional origins like Laertes.

These relationships, with wife, child, parents, and goddesses (including Athene) were the most significant in Odysseus's life. Others Homer mentions more briefly. The noble swineherd Eumaeus obviously admired him with a genuine affection. It must have done much to restore Odysseus's confidence, after his return to Ithaca disguised as a beggar, to hear the warm tributes of that most gentlemanly of pig-keepers.[36] The same kind of loyal affection was more to be expected from Odysseus's old nurse Eurycleia, and

Homer does not leave any doubt that Odysseus received it. Some of Odysseus's subjects in Ithaca, too, speak warmly of his paternal benevolence and mildness. It is clear that, whatever his conduct was like at Troy, in his home and homeland he showed nothing of the machine-like disregard of personal feelings which the later tradition found in him.

A few passing incidents deserve some notice. The affability of Alcinous towards Odysseus as his unknown guest cannot be taken as significant. That genial old king seems to have been of the kind to welcome, like Nestor, any new victim for his garrulity. But he seems to have loved his daughter Nausicaa, so that his offer of her hand in marriage to Odysseus was a high tribute to Odysseus's personality—for Alcinous did not yet know the stranger's identity. Queen Arete is quite different. At first she maintains a strong reserve towards Odysseus, conceding nothing beyond her formal protection until over a day after his arrival. She lets Alcinous do all the talking, and is satisfied only to shoot a shrewd question at Odysseus, asking him where he got the clothes he was wearing.[37] (She had, of course, recognized them as some of those which Nausicaa had taken to wash.) After that she says nothing at all until late in the evening of the following day.

It does not seem to have been emphasized before that this is another example of Homer's consummate skill in blending formal construction with characterization. The situation is this: Odysseus has been describing his adventures in the Land of Shades. Is it too much, or too ungenerous, to suppose that while he told about his encounter with his mother's ghost, he was not unaware of the effect it might have on the listening Queen of the Phaeacians? Some (men more than women, perhaps) may be inclined to think this hypocritical and insincere. But the complexities of an artist's mind—and here, under Homer's hand, Odysseus is telling his story with superb rhetorical artistry—are not easily sorted into the simpler ethical categories. When an artist acts a part or heightens the emotion of a past incident he is not necessarily insincere or untrue to himself. Or, to put it specifically, if Odysseus deliberately emphasized or even amplified the emotional aspects of his interview with his mother, in order to present it as effectively as possible to Arete, we may condemn him as an untrustworthy witness, but not as an incompetent story-teller, or entertainer, or after-dinner speaker.

This opens up a psychological complication. It must not be allowed to lead too far from the subject in hand, but it cannot be

passed over entirely. In Books Nine to Twelve of the *Odyssey*
Homer ostensibly delegates his task as a story-teller to Odysseus.
Now comes the problem: does Homer intend us to understand that
Odysseus's narrative is factually as precise as it would have been
were Homer himself narrating it, or does he intend us to take it as
a Ulyssean (and sometimes even Autolycan) version of what 'really'
took place? To cut the knot it will be assumed that at least occasionally Homer allows Odysseus to adapt his narrative to suit his
Phaeacian audience. (And it may be observed that here Odysseus,
at the earliest stage of his literary career, speaks for Homer and takes
his place as a court entertainer. A later chapter will illustrate how
this relationship between the poet and his creation was made a
pretext for maligning them both.)

If Odysseus's purpose in describing the scene with Anticleia was
to win Arete's sympathy for a motherless wanderer, he did not let
his appeal to the feminine element in his audience end at that. As
his next experience he describes the celebrated pageant of beautiful
heroines. This has been impugned as a Boeotian accretion to the
original story. But its consequences can hardly be dismissed as
irrelevant to the general situation in Phaeacia. Immediately
Odysseus has finished his description of the famous women, he
breaks off his narrative, suggests it is time for sleep, expresses his
eagerness to begin his voyage to Ithaca, and then stops. It can hardly
be purely accidental that Arete is the first to break the charmed
silence in the shadowy hall, and that now for the first time she
expresses approval of him. Could this sudden decision have been
entirely independent of Odysseus's story about his mother and his
descriptions of the other women? Only if the poet of this episode
was indeed such a bungler as some critics would have him. It seems
more reasonable to accept the sequence as an intentional piece of
motivation. In any case, whether by luck or skill, Odysseus is the
gainer. He can reckon Arete now among his friends. His last
recorded words in Phaeacia are addressed to her.

Another significant interview with a woman is mentioned but
not described in the *Odyssey*. In Book Four, Helen tells Telemachus
how, when Odysseus ventured into Troy as a spy in a beggar's
disguise, she alone detected him. She had questioned him, and he
had tried to evade her inquiries with cunning. Then she insisted on
giving him a bath, which, naturally, spoilt his disguise. She assured
him with a strong oath that she would not reveal his identity until
he had safely returned to the Greek ships. Convinced of her good

faith, Odysseus told her all that she had been craving to know about 'the mind of the Achaeans'.

Homer merely sketches this scene in a few lines before continuing his main narrative. It is surprising that later writers did not make more of it. If one remembers that Helen was no hollow mask of feminine beauty, but, as Homer implies in this part of the *Odyssey*, a person of subtle intelligence and perceptiveness, an interview in such unusual circumstances between her and the cleverest of the Greeks stimulates the imagination. There is one unfortunate uncertainty in the Homeric context. Does Homer intend his readers to know that Odysseus had been among the suitors of Helen? If one could assume that this legend was already current in Homer's time and accepted (even though not mentioned) by him, the dramatic quality of this meeting would be greatly enhanced.

One general feature emerges from this study of Odysseus's more intimate personal relationships. He seems to have met none of the suspicion and distrust of his male associates among the women who knew him well. Their greater sympathy and tolerance cannot be explained entirely as a consequence of tenderer natures. Circe and Helen were hardly of that kind, or Athene either. It seems, rather, that Homer intended to imply a closer temperamental affinity between Odysseus and the women of the Heroic Age than between him and the more conventional warrior-heroes who felt uneasy and distrustful in his company. Not that there was any specifically feminine element in Odysseus's nature, but rather that he and Homer's women shared qualities not to be found in his male associates. Athene stated them clearly in the scene described in the last chapter. It was because of Odysseus's civilized gentleness, his intuitive intelligence, and his firm self-possession, that she would not 'leave him in misfortune'. In an age of violence and infidelity these were qualities that every sensible woman would value.

There was another reason. That Ulyssean versatility, which clashed with the more rigid standards of the typical hero, that power of changing one's manner to suit the occasion, would not antagonize or repel intelligent women; for what was it but a form of that feminine *varium et mutabile* quality which has so long irritated and baffled the more conventional of men?

CHAPTER V

THE UNTYPICAL HERO

THERE is nothing freakish about Odysseus's personality in the Homeric poems. In the *Iliad* Homer endows him with the normal qualities of an Achaean hero—princely birth, good physique, strength, skill in athletics and battle, courage, energy, and eloquence.[1] But in most of these Odysseus is surpassed or equalled by some of his colleagues at Troy. The Atreidae and Aeacids are of more illustrious lineage. Agamemnon and Menelaus are of more impressive stature. Achilles and Ajax surpass him in strength and force of arms. Diomedes is more gallant and dashing in battle. Even in oratory he is not unrivalled.

The fact is, of course, that Odysseus is not the chief hero of the *Iliad*. Achilles, and after him Ajax, Hector, Diomedes, and the Atreidae, are more prominent.[2] Not that the *Iliad* presents Odysseus as a minor hero: he has his triumphs in the council and in the assembly, on the field of battle and in the athletic contests. But his unique personality is not allowed to divert attention from the *Iliad's* main themes, the wrath of Achilles and the death of Hector. On the other hand, in the *Odyssey* he, 'the man of many turns', is the main theme, and his personal qualities become specially luminous against the sordidness of his environment, as he makes his way among foolish shipmates, ruthless monsters, and greedy usurpers. Yet here, too, Odysseus meets his equals at times. Eumaeus the swineherd shows a loyalty and gentle courtesy quite as fine as his, and Penelope is wily enough to outwit him in their final recognition scene.

By endowing Odysseus with a share of the normal heroic qualities Homer avoided any suggestion that he was an eccentric figure or a narrowly limited type. But at the same time Homer, especially in the *Iliad*, skilfully succeeded in distinguishing Odysseus by slight deviations from the norm in almost every heroic feature. In his ancestry there was the unique Autolycan element. In physique he had the unusually short legs and long torso described by Antenor and Helen in *Il.* 3, 190 ff. He reminded Helen of a sturdy ram, she said, as he marshalled the Achaean ranks. Any hint of the ludicrous in this comparison is removed by Antenor's subsequent description of Odysseus's imposing presence. But there is something a little unaristocratic, or at least non-Achaean, in this portrait, contrasting with the tall, long-limbed stature of the other heroes.[3] Napoleon would have looked like that beside Wellington; or Cuchulain, that 'short, dark man', among the taller champions of the Red Branch Knights. Possibly Homer meant to imply something more than a personal peculiarity here. It may be intended as an indication of some racial difference between Odysseus and the other Achaeans. Perhaps—but it is a pure guess—Homer regarded Odysseus as being partly a survival of the pre-Greek stock in Greece, an 'Aegean' or 'Mediterranean' type.[4] At any rate, the physical difference serves to mark Odysseus out as exceptional, without giving an impression of ugliness, oddity, or deformity.[5]

One finds the same distinction in a quite different kind of trait—in Odysseus's unusually frank and realistic remarks on the importance of food in human life. All the Homeric heroes were hearty eaters and drinkers. But, whether by accident or convention, none of them except Odysseus had anything notable to say about eating. Perhaps it was regarded as a plebeian subject, unfit for high-born Achaeans; or perhaps they simply were not interested in it as a subject for conversation. It was typical of the average Homeric hero that he was prepared on occasion to ignore the need for food, both for himself and for others. The contrast with Odysseus's attitude is well illustrated in a scene between him and Achilles in *Iliad* Nineteen. Achilles, now equipped with new armour and ready for battle, is impatient to launch a general attack against the Trojans to take vengeance for Patroclus's death. Odysseus objects. The Greek soldiers have been kept awake all night in lamenting Patroclus and in preparing his body for burial. The Trojans, on the contrary, have been able to enjoy a quiet supper and a night's rest. Odysseus, not being blinded by personal feeling like Achilles, knows that unless soldiers get a good meal first they will not be able to fight all day: even if they are eager to continue the battle, 'yet their limbs are treacherously weighed down as hunger and thirst overtake them, and their knees fail them as they go'. There is both compassionate understanding and Napoleonic common sense here: the spirit may be willing, but the flesh is weak; an army marches on its stomach. Odysseus adds some further remarks on the strengthening and cheering effect of food and wine, and ends by demanding that the army should have a full meal before being ordered to attack.

Achilles's reply to Odysseus's reasonable objection is characteristic:

'*You* go and busy yourselves with food: *I* shall not touch a morsel until Patroclus is avenged. And, let me tell you, if I were in supreme command, the whole army would have to fight fasting, too, till sunset. Then, with vengeance achieved, we should have a great supper.' What is one to call such arrogant confidence as this —with no thought of fatigue or death, no consideration for himself or for others? Is it heroic, or is it schoolboyish? Is it superb single-ness of purpose or callow rashness? Odysseus in his reply deftly and gently suggests that youthful heedlessness is partly, at least, to blame. Addressing Achilles with great deference as 'Much the mightiest of the Achaeans' he admits his own inferiority to him in martial valour. But he claims definite superiority in thinking things out. Then after an appeal to Achilles to listen patiently for a moment (Odysseus clearly wants to avoid provoking Achilles's wrath again in any way: but he insists on making his point about the need for food), he emphasizes the danger of fatigue in war, and mildly ridicules Achilles's notion that fasting is a good way for warriors to mourn those slain in battle. Bury the dead with pitiless heart, bewail them for a day, yes—but those who survive must eat to get energy for punishing the enemy. Odysseus is trying to persuade Achilles to eat with the others. If Achilles fights fasting against a well-fed Hector, even Achilles may be conquered. Odysseus's arguments fail, as in the Embassy scene, to overcome Achilles's passionate resolve. But, significantly, Athene intervenes later, at Zeus's request, and feeds Achilles with nectar and ambrosia 'so that', the poet remarks, 'joyless hunger should not reach his knees'. Thus obliquely Homer, Athene, and Zeus agree with Odysseus's advice.

But the typical Homeric hero would probably have admired Achilles's intransigence more than Odysseus's more practical policy. One does in fact find an indication elsewhere in the *Iliad* that Odysseus had already got a reputation for being too much interested in the pleasures of eating. In *Iliad* 4, 343–6, Agamemnon accuses Odysseus and the Athenian Menestheus of being quick to hear invitations to a feast, but slow to answer the call to arms. Odysseus emphatically denies any reluctance to join the fight, but he passes over the accusation of unusual alacrity in coming to feasts. Probably he thought it beneath contempt. Yet, as in Agamemnon's accom-panying accusation of evil deceitfulness, it may well be that Homer intends us to catch a glimpse here of a general tendency to regard Odysseus as rather more partial to good fare than a hero should have been.

This is uncertain. But there is no uncertainty about the attitude of post-Homeric writers. Attic comedians, fourth-century philosophers, Alexandrian critics, late classical chroniclers, agree in accusing Odysseus of greed and gluttony.[6] They based their slanders chiefly on some of his actions and remarks in the *Odyssey* which, considered out of their contexts, certainly do give a bad impression. Thus in *Od.* 6, 250, Odysseus eats 'greedily'. In *Od.* 7, 215–18 he asks Alcinous to let him go on with his supper without interruption, remarking that there is no more shameful compulsion than that of 'the abominable belly' which compels even a mourner to eat and forget his grief for a while. In *Od.* 9, 1 ff., after the Phaeacians have given him a splendid banquet, Odysseus pronounces that he knows of no more beautiful consummation in life than a feast with good food, good wine, good song, and general good cheer. Later, after his arrival in Ithaca, when still in his beggar's disguise, Odysseus returns to the theme of hunger and appetite. He tells Eumaeus that it is for the sake of 'the accursed belly' that vagabonds are compelled to suffer all the hardships of wandering from place to place (*Od.* 15, 344–5). Later he tells Eumaeus again (*Od.* 17, 286–9) that in his opinion it is impossible to conceal the 'accursed belly' when it is in its full fury: it brings many evils to men, and for its sake men sail the barren seas to attack their enemies. Soon afterwards (vv. 473–4) he attributes a violent assault by Antinous to the promptings of his 'baneful accursed belly'. In the following book he pretends that he wants to attack the rival beggar, Irus, at the behest of 'the evil-working belly' (18, 53–4), but repudiates a suggestion by a Suitor (18, 362–4) that he was good for nothing but gross eating (18, 376–81).

If one remembers that no other hero in the *Iliad*, nor any Homeric heroine in either poem, even uses the word for 'belly' and still less discusses its effects, it is clear that Odysseus is an untypical hero in this respect. And it is obvious how easy it was for comic writers to portray him as a glutton, courtly critics as a crudely indelicate eater, and philosophers as a confirmed voluptuary, by concentrating on a few passages out of their contexts. Thus Plato was shocked at Odysseus's praise of banquets, as being one of the finest 'consummations' in life.[7] But surely the effusive remarks of an after-dinner speaker at a royal banquet are not to be judged as a solemn philosophical pronouncement. Besides, should not Odysseus's more sober aphorisms on the harmful effects of appetite in human life be weighed against this? And should it not have been remembered to

Odysseus's credit how he had rejected the temptation of the Lotus-fruit and had resolutely held out against eating the Cattle of the Sun? When he eats 'greedily' after his reception in Alcinous's palace, should we not bear in mind that (apart from a snack from the remains of Nausicaa's picnic in Book Six) he had not eaten for three days and had suffered terrible physical and mental agonies in Poseidon's long storm?[8] Indeed, he had shown supreme self-control during his first supplication to Nausicaa: he had never mentioned food, but modestly asked only for a scrap of clothing and for information about the city. One almost loses patience with arm-chair critics who censure the conduct of a ravenous shipwrecked mariner for not conforming with the court etiquette of Alexandria or Versailles, and with moralists who demand the scruples of the confessional in the speeches of the banqueting-hall.

Odysseus's remarks on food in the second half of the *Odyssey* were less criticized, because he was obviously playing up to his rôle as a beggar in all of them. Further, as the Cynics noticed, he was a philosophical beggar. He showed that he understood the effects of appetite on men in general: how it drives men to war as well as to trade; how it moves the languid fingers of the courtier as well as the clutching fists of the starveling outcast. Yet he never suggested, as the more cynical Cynics did, that the belly was lord of all, and that he and his dog Argos were equally its slaves. He simply accepted it as one of the inescapable elemental forces in human life. Heroes like Agamemnon, Ajax, and Achilles, who had, as far as we know, never been compulsorily deprived of food in their lives, could nonchalantly disregard its demands. But Odysseus, by the time of his return to Ithaca, had become painfully familiar with the effects of involuntary hunger. Homer himself, if he was a bard wandering from audience to audience 'for the sake of the accursed belly', may well have made Odysseus his own spokesman here. He, too, if we can deduce his personal feelings from the vivid description of the blind bard Demodocus in *Od.* 8, 62 ff., appreciated the comfort of having a basket of food and a cup of wine within reach to take 'whenever his spirit prompted him'.

The contrast here between the conventional hero's insouciance, or reticence, on the subject of food and Odysseus's frequent attention to it is one of the best illustrations of Odysseus's unconventionality as a hero. But Homer, perhaps for fear that his less philosophical hearers might fail to appreciate this kind of example, also exemplified Odysseus's uniqueness in a small matter that all warriors would notice. It is frequently emphasized in the *Odyssey* (and also mentioned in *Iliad* Ten) that Odysseus had unusual skill as an archer. His triumph over the Suitors at the end of the *Odyssey* depended on this. But only a few, and those not the most illustrious, of the other heroes at Troy show any interest in the use of the bow. Indeed, there are some indications that archery was despised as plebeian or unmanly,[9] much as a medieval knight of the sword and lance scorned to assail another knight with arrows. Perhaps Odysseus was merely old fashioned in his military technique. Or perhaps it was because the plot of the *Odyssey* demanded a triumph by means of the bow. But the trait does also serve to distinguish him from the other chief heroes. Another feature is far more peculiar. It is twice mentioned in the *Odyssey* that Odysseus possessed, and so he presumably used, poisoned arrows.[10] This, however, like his Autolycan ancestry, is never referred to in the *Iliad*.

Though Odysseus's Homeric speeches were the admiration of every age of classical rhetoric, their excellence is not that of an orator among tongue-tied men. Oratory was a recognized part of heroic training. Thus in the Embassy scene Achilles's reply is fully as powerful and eloquent as Odysseus's pleadings. At times, too, Nestor's speeches in council are as wise and as cogent as Odysseus's. The difference is not one of skill. It lies more in the fact that, when the other heroes speak, their minds are obsessed with conventions and prerogatives or weakened by passion and self-concern. Achilles's wrath and Nestor's tendency to garrulous reminiscences tend to make their orations more effective as expressions of prejudices and personal feelings than as instruments of policy. In contrast, Odysseus's speeches are strictly functional,[11] as a rule. When he shows passion or introduces a personal touch it is almost always because it will help to achieve his aim—to quell Thersites and to rebuke the wavering Agamemnon or an insolent prince of Phaeacia. Those who consider passionate self-esteem an essential quality of the genuine heroic type may find this kind of self-possession mean or machiavellian. But, as Sophocles indicates in his *Ajax*, it is the faculty that maintains justice and humanity among passionate men.

Besides this functional difference between Odysseus's speeches and those of other heroes, Homer signalizes his oratory by a peculiar personal trait. In Antenor's speech, as already mentioned, there is a description of Odysseus's curious habitual pose before beginning an important speech. He would stand with his eyes fixed on the ground, his body and gestures stiff 'like an ignorant fellow's'. His

F

voice, Antenor adds, was of great power. But he seems to have controlled this Gladstonian organ with the deftness of a Disraeli: his words came smoothly, lightly, continuously, flake after flake like falling snow—perhaps in the quiet, level tone characteristic of adepts in the art of plausibility. The general effect, we are told, was overwhelming. Homer corroborates this impression in several scenes in the *Odyssey*, where he describes how Odysseus could hold an audience spellbound 'like a skilled bard'. Homer could hardly have paid a higher tribute to his oratory.[12] Once again he identifies Odysseus's powers with his own.

In the later tradition Odysseus was often accused of cowardice. The charge was based less on incidents mentioned by Homer than on others first recorded in the post-Homeric tradition, Odysseus's attempt to evade conscription, for example, and in later versions of his conduct with Palamedes and Philoctetes. There is nothing of that kind in the Homeric poems. But one ambiguous incident in *Iliad* Eight[13] left a shadow on his reputation for courage. The circumstances are these. A general rout of the Achaeans has begun. Agamemnon, the two Ajaxes, and Idomeneus retreat rapidly. Nestor is left behind in grave danger. Hector rushes forward to cut him down. Diomedes sees the danger and calls to Odysseus for help in rescuing the old king. 'But', Homer records, 'Odysseus did not hear (or listen to) his call, and sped on to the Achaean ships'. The crucial verb is capable of two interpretations. It was left open to Odysseus's defenders in post-Homeric controversies to argue that Odysseus had simply not heard Diomedes's cry in the confusion of the general retreat. But his detractors could take it as a deliberate ignoring of a comrade's cry for help. Homer's own intention is hidden in the ambiguity. However, no matter what he meant here, he soon makes it clear that none of his heroes attached any blame to Odysseus for his conduct. On the contrary, Odysseus's prestige is at its highest in the next three books.

If one considers the whole of Odysseus's career, a general accusation of cowardice is plainly absurd. In *Iliad* 11, 395 ff., he stands valorously alone against the whole Trojan host. His bravery in the Doloneia is incontestable. Similarly it took the highest courage to vanquish the Cyclops, to resist Scylla, to overthrow the horde of Suitors. Yet Homer does seem to hint occasionally, not at cowardice, but at a kind of tension between prudence and boldness. Thus in Odysseus's brief spell as supreme champion of the Greeks in *Iliad* Eleven, he pauses for a moment to wonder whether it would not be wiser to retreat with the rest. He immediately reminds himself of his heroic duty, and, with a touch of fatalism, unusual in him, fights on. There is obviously no cowardice in this. On the contrary, the man who fully foresees danger and then goes on to meet it is more truly courageous than an insensate Ajax or a furious Achilles. The best illustration of this tension between prudence and heroic valour is found in Odysseus's attempt to avoid conscription by feigning madness, to be discussed in a later chapter. Unfortunately it is not certain that Homer knew the legend.

A commentator on Euripides's version of the Cyclops incident has seen something of a Hamletesque figure in Odysseus as portrayed there. This was possible in the atmosphere of the late fifth century. But Homer's Odysseus is obviously no indecisive princeling sicklied o'er with the pale cast of thought. His decisive boldness is made clear both at the beginning of the *Iliad* in his handling of the Thersites affair, and at the outset of his Odyssean adventures when he sacks Ismarus like any Elizabethan buccaneer or Spanish conquistador. He is 'the great-hearted', 'the sacker of cities', as well as the prudent and resourceful Odysseus. Yet in both these bold deeds his prudence is not entirely in abeyance. While he faces Thersites uncompromisingly, he coaxes, amuses, and flatters the other Greeks. Again in the sack of Ismarus he orders a withdrawal as soon as a counter-attack seems likely. His comrades refuse, with disastrous results. Odysseus calls them 'great fools' for not obeying his prudent command. But when he first gave it, they, for their part, may well have thought his prudence was mere timidity.

The fact is that, even though no real cowardice was involved, Odysseus's gift for anticipating dangers and his readiness to avoid them when it best served his purpose, did separate him from the normal hero of his time. Whether one admires it or not, a certain mulish stubbornness in the manner of Ajax, a reckless *élan* like that of Diomedes, a readiness to let everything be turned upside down for the sake of some point of honour in the manner of Achilles, was more characteristic of the early heroic temperament than a prudent resourcefulness. When the typical hero found his path to fame and glory blocked, his instinct was to batter his own or someone else's head against the obstacle until something broke. The gentle Hector and the tough Ajax were alike in this intransigence. Odysseus was no less determined to gain his purpose; but he was far less intransigent. He was prepared to undermine an obstacle or to look for another path, to imitate the mole or the fox rather than the rhinoceros.

In the later tradition, admirers of the simpler, prouder kind of hero will despise this quality, calling it cowardly or opportunistic. Homer suggests no such disapproval. On the contrary the *Odyssey* implies that some such resourcefulness is necessary to overcome the trials of human life in general. Almost all Homer's more intransigent heroes die unhappily, Agamemnon murdered by his wife, Ajax killed by his own hand, Achilles slain by a cowardly arrow. Odysseus, like Nestor and Menelaus, returns home at last to live in peace and prosperity.

Odysseus was also the 'much-enduring' man. Among the other Homeric heroes only Nestor, whose life had extended over three normal generations, shared this epithet with him. Why? After all, many of the rest showed great endurance in battle. The answer seems to lie in a special implication in Homer's use of epithets in *poly-* meaning 'much'. As has been suggested elsewhere,[14] it seems to imply variety rather than degree, especially in its active compounds. The other heroes were 'much-enduring' in their own special forte, namely, fighting. But Odysseus and Nestor were men who had shown their endurance in an unusual variety of circumstances: Nestor because of his abnormally long life, Odysseus because of his enterprising nature. Here once again a clash between Odysseus's qualities and the typical heroic temperament emerges. Ajax or Achilles would never have been willing to undergo some of Odysseus's experiences—his three adventures in beggar's disguise, for instance, and his ignominious escape from the Cyclops's cave by hanging under a ram's belly (which was a kind of Trojan Horse stratagem in reverse). In the later tradition Odysseus is accused of ignobleness, even cowardice, for his readiness to employ disguise or stealth when necessary to achieve his purpose. Undoubtedly one can detect an element of Autolycanism here. But what was often forgotten was that these various examples of combined resourcefulness and endurance were generally used *pro bono publico*.

We shall see all this argued out in the later tradition. Here it need only be emphasized that without this quality Odysseus could never have been so serviceable to the Greek cause. This serviceability varied from such an ordinary task as that of pacifying the indignant Chryses in *Iliad* One to the final triumph of Ulyssean cleverness in the ruse of the Wooden Horse. But it is the common fate of serviceable men to be despised by their more self-centred associates.

All these deviations from the heroic norm are exemplified in the *Iliad* as well as in the *Odyssey*. The next quality to be considered has little or no scope in the restricted Iliadic *milieu*. It needs the more expansive background of the *Odyssey*. It is a quality that points away from the older Heroic Age with its code of static conventions and prerogatives, and on to a coming era, the era of Ionian exploration and speculation.[15] This is Odysseus's desire for fresh knowledge. Homer does not emphasize it. But it can be seen plainly at work in two of the most famous of Odysseus's Odyssean exploits. It becomes the master passion of his whole personality in the post-classical tradition, notably in Dante, Tennyson, Arturo Graf, and Kazantzakis.

This eagerness to learn more about God, man, and nature is the most characteristic feature of the whole Greek tradition. To quote a recent commentator[16] on Dante's conception of Ulysses:

To be a Greek was to seek to know; to know the primordial substance of matter, to know the meaning of number, to know the world as a rational whole. In no spirit of paradox one may say that Euclid is the most typical Greek: he would fain know to the bottom, and know as a rational system, the laws of the measurement of the earth. . . . No doubt the Greek genius means many things. To one school . . . it means an aesthetic ideal. . . . To others, however, it means an austere thing, which delights in logic and mathematics; which continually wondering and always inquisitive, is driven by its wonder into philosophy, and into inquiry about the why and wherefore, the whence and whither, of tragedy, of the State, indeed, of all things.

This eagerness to learn is not, of course, entirely a Greek quality. Every child, scholar, and scientist, shares it. But it can hardly be denied that the Greeks were endowed more richly with intellectual curiosity than any other ancient people. More conservative cultures like the Egyptian and the Roman judged the Greek spirit of experiment and inquiry either childlike or dangerous. But, for good and ill, it has been the strongest force in the development of modern European civilization and science.

Odysseus is alone among Homer's heroes in displaying this intellectual curiosity strongly. There is an obvious reason for this. A spirit of inquiry would naturally get more stimulus from the unexplored territories of Odysseus's fabulous wanderings than from the conventional environment of the *Iliad*. But it was hardly accidental that Odysseus should have had these special opportunities for acquiring fresh knowledge. To him that hath shall be given: adventures are to the adventurous. One may well doubt whether an Ajax or a Nestor would have shown as much alert curiosity even in the cave of the Cyclops or near the island of the Sirens if they had been there instead of Odysseus. Odysseus's personality and exploits are indivisible: he has curious adventures because he is Odysseus, and he is Odysseus because he has curious adventures. Set another hero in Circe's palace or in Phaeacia and you may have some story like *Innocents Abroad*, or a *Childe Harold's Pilgrimage*, or an *Aeneid*, but not an *Odyssey*.

Odysseus's desire to know is most clearly illustrated in the episodes with the Cyclops and the Sirens. He himself asserts that his original motive for landing on the Cyclops's island was to see whether its unknown inhabitants were 'violent, savage and lawless, or else hospitable men with god-fearing mind'—almost as if, in modern terms, he wanted to do some anthropological research. It is more the motive of a Malinowski approaching the Trobriand Islands,[17] than of a pirate or a conquistador. But his crew did not share this zeal for knowledge. When they entered the Cyclops's cave, the Companions felt a presentiment of danger and begged him to withdraw. Odysseus refused, still eager to see what the giant was like. In describing the consequences Odysseus admits his folly here in the strongest words of self-denunciation that he ever uses (*Od.* 9, 228–30). As a result of his imprudence six of his companions were eaten alive. It becomes clear later, in the Sirens incident, when Odysseus meets a similar temptation to dangerous knowledge, that he had learned a lesson from his rash curiosity, for he takes great care to prevent any danger to his companions from hearing their deadly song.

But Odysseus's motives in the Cyclops episode were not unmixed. He admits that his second reason for wanting to meet the ogre was a hope of extracting some guest-gifts from him—acquisitiveness as well as inquisitiveness. The post-Homeric tradition was inclined to censure Odysseus for unheroic cupidity here and elsewhere. But other Homeric heroes were quite as eager to receive gifts as he.[18] It was a normal part of heroic etiquette; and in general the Greeks always had a flair for trade as well as for science. Odysseus's fault lay not in his hope of getting gifts but in his allowing that hope (combined with curiosity) to endanger the lives of his companions. Homer left it to others to draw a moral.

But there is a deeper difficulty in this incident. To anyone who has followed Odysseus's career from the beginning of the *Iliad* up to his encounter with the Cyclops, Odysseus's general lack of prudence and self-control in it must seem quite uncharacteristic of his usual conduct, especially his foolhardy boastfulness[19] after his escape from the Cyclops's clutches (*Od.* 9, 490 ff.). By this last imprudence, despite his companions' entreaties, he nearly brought disaster on them all from the Monster's missiles. Perhaps the explanation is that this particular episode retains much of its pre-Homeric shape and ethos. It may have been fairly fully worked out before Homer incorporated it into his poem.[20] Its outline is almost pure folklore. Homer's additions seem to consist mainly of vivid descriptions of scenery and the motivation of Odysseus's conduct. In order to fit Odysseus into the traditional plot, and also in order to make him incur the wrath of Poseidon, Homer may have had to strain his own conception of Odysseus's character more than elsewhere. So while in one way the victory over the Cyclops was Odysseus's greatest Autolycan triumph—especially in the typically Autolycan equivocation of his No-man formula—it was also his greatest failure as the favourite of Athene. And, significantly, by provoking Poseidon's enmity it was the main cause of his losing Athene's personal protection for nine years. In other words, in this episode Odysseus relapses for a while nearer to his original character as the Wily Lad than anywhere else in the Homeric poems.

To return to Odysseus's intellectual curiosity: it is presented in a much purer light in his encounter with the Sirens. Here no greed for gain, or indifference to his companions' safety, intrudes. Circe (who in Athene's absence takes her place for a while in advising Odysseus) has warned Odysseus of the Sirens' fatal attractions, telling him of 'the great heap of men rotting on their bones' which lies in the flowery meadow beside them. Better not to hear their seductive song at all; but if he, Odysseus cannot resist a desire to hear it—and Circe knows Odysseus well enough to expect that he cannot resist it—he must fill his comrades' ears with wax and have himself bound tightly to the mast.

What happens in the actual encounter became one of the most famous stories in European literature and a rich source of allegorical and symbolical interpretations. Its significance for the present study lies in the nature of the Sirens' temptation. This was not based on any amorous enticements. Instead the Sirens offered information about the Trojan war and knowledge of 'whatever has happened on the wide, fertile earth'. To put it in modern jargon, the Sirens guaranteed to supply a global news-service[21] to their clients, an almost irresistible attraction to the typical Greek whose chief delight, as observed in the Acts of the Apostles (xvii. 21) was 'to tell or to hear some new thing'.

As Homer describes the incident, the attractions of the Sirens were primarily intellectual. Merely sensual pleasures would not, Homer implies (and Cicero[22] later insists), have allured him so strongly. He had resisted the temptation to taste of the fruit of the Lotus. But one must not overlook, with Cicero, the effect of their melodious song and their unrivalled voices. Music for the Greeks was the most moving of the arts. Besides, as Montaigne observes in his essay on *Glory*, there was a subtle touch of flattery in their first words:

> Deca vers nous, deca, O treslouable Ulysse,
> Et le plus grand honneur dont la Grece fleurisse.

And perhaps their subtlest flattery was in recognizing Odysseus's calibre at once and in appealing only to his intellect. If an Agamemnon or a Menelaus had been in his place, they might have changed their tune.

For some reason Odysseus's intellectual curiosity, as displayed in his encounter with the Sirens, was not much emphasized in the earlier classical tradition. Presumably so typical a quality of the early Greeks (as distinct from the Achaean heroes) was taken for granted. But the later allegorists, both pagan and Christian, made it a favourite theme for imaginative moralization, as will be described in a later chapter.

It might rashly be concluded from the preceding analysis that Homer's Odysseus was a man distracted by psychological conflicts and distressed by social tensions. The general impression derived from the Homeric poems suggests nothing of the kind. The inner and outer tensions are skilfully implied, but the total portrait is that of a man well integrated both in his own temperament and with his environment. As Athene emphasized, he was essentially 'self-possessed', fully able to control conflicting passions and motives. His psychological tensions never reach a breaking-point. They serve rather to give him his dynamic force. As a result his purposefulness is like an arrow shot from a well-strung bow, and his energy has the tirelessness of coiled springs. Resilience, elasticity, concentration, these are the qualities that maintain his temperamental balance. In contrast the Ajax-like hero was superficially firm and strong. His code of conduct and his heroic pride encased his heart like archaic armour. Once this psychological carapace was pierced by some violent shock the inner parts were as soft as any crustacean's. Odysseus's strength and self-possession did not depend on any outer armour. He could be as firm and enduring in the role of a beggar or in the cave of a Cyclops as in full battle-dress at Troy. This was the quality that the Cynic and Stoic philosophers were most to admire later.

Such was his inner harmony and strength. His conduct in matters of major importance shows a similar purposeful integrity. He had a remarkable power of taking the long view, of seeing actions in their widest context, of disciplining himself to the main purpose in hand.[23] Thus while other heroes at Troy are squabbling like children over questions of honour and precedence, Odysseus presses on steadily towards victory. And why? Not, Homer implies, for the sake of triumph and plunder, but in order to return to his beloved Ithaca as soon as possible. Here Odysseus's efforts for the Greek cause are integrated with his fundamental love of home; *pro bono publico* is ultimately *pro domo sua*. Similarly his loyalty to the Companions during the fabulous voyages, and his patience with their infuriating alternations of rashness and timidity, were part of the same enlightened egotism: he needed a crew to sail his ship home. His love for Penelope, too, was, as has been suggested already, not based entirely on *eros* or *agape*, but also contained that *philia*, that attachment to one's normal and natural social environment which underlies so much of Greek happiness. And his piety is the piety of one who wishes to keep on good terms with the gods.

Such mixed motives may seem impure or ignoble to those who take their ideals from self-sacrificing patriotism, or from self-effacing saintliness, or from self-forgetting romanticism. But these are post-Homeric concepts. Within the context of the Heroic Age and perhaps of the Homeric Age, too, this identification of one's own best interests with the general welfare of one's kith, kin, and comrades, with one's *philoi* in fact, was a saving grace for both the individual and society. All the Homeric heroes are egotists; but Odysseus's egotism has sent its roots out more widely into his personal environment than that of Agamemnon, Achilles, or Ajax.

One other aspect of Odysseus's Homeric character needs to be kept in mind at the last. In a way it is the most important of all for the development of the tradition. This is the fundamental ambiguity of his essential qualities. We have seen how prudence may decline towards timidity, tactfulness towards a blameworthy *suppressio veri*, serviceability towards servility, and so on. The ambiguity lies both in the qualities themselves and in the attitudes of others towards them. Throughout the later tradition this ambiguity in Odysseus's nature and in his reputation will vacillate between good and bad, between credit and infamy. Odysseus's personality and reputation at best are poised, as it were, on a narrow edge between Aristotelian faults of excess and deficiency. Poised between rashness and timorousness, he is prudently brave; poised between rudeness and obsequiousness he is 'civilized'; poised between stupidity and over-cleverness he, at his best, is wise.

Homer was large-minded enough to comprehend a unity in apparent diversity, a structural consistency within an external changefulness, in the character of Ulysses. But few later authors were as comprehending. Instead, in the post-Homeric tradition, Odysseus's complex personality becomes broken up into various simple types—the *politique*, the romantic amorist, the sophisticated villain, the sensualist, the philosophic traveller, and others. Not till James Joyce wrote his *Ulysses* was a successful effort made to recreate Homer's polytropic hero in full. Similarly after Homer judgments on Odysseus's ethical status became narrower and sharper. Moralists grew angry in disputing whether he was a 'good' man or not—good, that is to say, according to the varying principles of Athens, or Alexandria, or Rome, or Florence, or Versailles, or Madrid, or Weimar. Here is another long Odyssey for Odysseus to endure. But Homer, the unmoved mover in this chaotic cosmos of tradition, does not vex his own or his hero's mind with any such problems in split personality or ambivalent ethics. He is content to portray a man of many turns.

CHAPTER VI

DEVELOPMENTS IN THE EPIC CYCLE

THE group of post-Homeric poems loosely called the Epic Cycle influenced the later heroic tradition more variously, though as a rule more superficially, than the *Iliad* and *Odyssey*. All the cyclic poems were vaguely ascribed to 'Homer' until more enlightened critical methods established a difference in quality between works like the *Cypria* and the two genuine Homeric poems. But from early classical times both the *Iliad* and the *Odyssey* seem to have been treated with special veneration. As a result, writers were chary of trying to re-write Iliadic or Odyssean episodes, much as modern authors rarely try to improve on Shakespeare's handling of the Hamlet or Lear themes. The cyclic epics with their abundance of dramatic episodes and their wider chronological range provided a store of less highly finished material. Consequently it was from their chronicles that most of the more celebrated classical writings on the Troy tale in general and on Ulysses's career in particular, were derived. But in characterization, as distinct from plot and incident, Homer's influence appears to have long remained paramount, much as post-Shakesperean writers could hardly produce a play on the youth of Lear or the childhood of Hamlet without having Shakespeare's characters in mind.

Unfortunately almost all that is now known of the Epic Cycle consists of meagre summaries and a few short quotations. These give the impression that the poems dealt chiefly with vigorous action without giving much attention to personal motives and feelings.[1] Perhaps the complete poems were subtler; but in what follows here it will be assumed that they were not. A second difficulty is that it is uncertain how many of the events recorded in the Epic Cycle were known to Homer and his audiences (except in the few instances where Homer actually mentions them). Even when Homer mentions such incidents as the contest between Odysseus and Ajax for Achilles's armour one cannot always determine whether he had the same version as the cyclic writers in mind or not.[2] A full discussion of these difficulties would lead far from the Ulysses theme. But they cannot be entirely ignored.

In its entirety the Epic Cycle provided a full account of Greek mythology from the primal marriage of Heaven and Earth down to the deaths of the Greek heroes of the Trojan war. The Trojan cycle proper began with the quarrel of the gods and goddesses at the marriage feast of Peleus and Thetis and ended with the death of Odysseus and the marriage of his sons. Odysseus was first mentioned, if one can trust the surviving summary of the *Cypria*, in a curious and very characteristic incident. He had, it is implied,[3] been one of the unsuccessful suitors of Helen. Hence he was bound by the common oath which all her suitors had sworn in advance (at Odysseus's suggestion according to another early source) to fight for her chosen husband if his marital rights were interfered with. When Paris abducted Helen, then Menelaus, Nestor, and Palamedes (cleverest of the Argive Greeks) set out to recruit the confederate suitors for an expedition to bring her back. On their arrival in Ithaca, Odysseus, now happy in his marriage with Penelope,[4] pretended to be mad, in order to avoid conscription. Then Palamedes by a clever ruse, which endangered the life of Odysseus's infant son, exposed Odysseus's pretence. Odysseus had, reluctantly, to join the expedition. For once the grandson of Autolycus had been outwitted.

Here at the outset of the Cycle is a typically ambiguous action. What was its motive? Odysseus's enemies in the later tradition suggested cowardice, and gloated over the unheroic nature of his deceitful ruse. But his supporters could point to the fact that the valiant Achilles was equally slow to enlist (though he, it is true, was not bound by the oath of Helen's suitors). The best reason for Odysseus's reluctance to join the campaign is easily deduced: as Robert Bridges[5] makes Odysseus express it in answer to a direct charge of poltroonery:

> If I feigned
> 'Twas that I had a child and wife, whose ties
> Of tenderness I am not ashamed to own.

This, and not mere cowardice, is much the likeliest motive for the courageous Odysseus of the early epic tradition, though not, of course, for the despicable villain presented by later authors. Odysseus knew from the prophecy of Halitherses (*Od.* 2, 172 ff.) that if he joined the expedition to Troy he would be away from home for over nineteen years and would only return after much suffering and loss. It was only human, if not conventionally heroic, for him to try to avoid this long separation from the home he so deeply loved. Athene might well have condoned it as a symptom of his characteristic tenderness. It was very skilful of Palamedes to use Odysseus's love for his son as a means of unmasking his pretence.

Homer does not refer to this incident at all. Did he knowingly omit it, or was it a later accretion to the Ulysses myth? One can only guess. The fact that Homer does reveal, very casually, Odysseus's reluctance to join the Greek host against Troy[6] perhaps indicates that he knew the legend but deliberately gave no details of it, for the sake of Odysseus's prestige as a hero. Even if Odysseus's motives were love and affection there was a distinctly Autolycan element in his attempt to evade the consequences of an oath by a trick; and to try to avoid any opportunity of fighting was unheroic in the conventional sense. This aspect of the episode struck another writer on the Ulysses theme, James Joyce, when he himself was avoiding the war of 1914–18 in neutral Switzerland. Discussing Ulysses's career with a friend, he remarked: 'Don't forget that he was a war-dodger. He might never have taken up arms and gone to Troy, but the Greek recruiting sergeant was too clever for him'.[7] In Homer's time there was probably even less sympathy for neutralists than in Joyce's.

There was another reason why Homer should not refer to the incident—the perplexing figure of Palamedes,[8] Odysseus's rival in sagacity and resourcefulness. A wide field of speculation opens up here. According to the *Cypria*, Palamedes became the victim of the most shameful crime in Odysseus's early career, when Odysseus with the help of Diomedes successfully plotted his death later in the expedition. No details survive from this early version, except that Palamedes was drowned. Later accounts describe how Odysseus wove a diabolical net of circumstantial evidence to discredit Palamedes in the eyes of the Greek leaders. Even if one discounts these derogatory details, the fact remains that apparently Odysseus committed a murderous act of treachery against a companion in arms. Later writers constantly denounced him for it—Euripides, Virgil, Dictys of Crete, Tzetzes, the poets of the medieval Troy Romance, Vondel, and many more.

Nothing is known of the attitude of the author of the *Cypria* to this crime. He may not have considered it his duty to express any moral indignation at all. It was not unparalleled in the epic tradition: the murder of Iphitus by Heracles was no more venial. At best Odysseus's treachery could be viewed as a savage act of primitive vengeance on the man who had caused him to leave his beloved Ithaca. At worst its motives could be presented as envy and spite

against a rival Cunning Lad. It is, however, significant that Diomedes was an accomplice; and he on the whole was an honoured
hero. Perhaps a technical reason may also have been involved.
Shakespeare is said to have remarked that he had been compelled
to have Mercutio killed off in *Romeo and Juliet* because the strain of
keeping so exuberant a character alive would have been too exhaust-
ing. So the original conceivers of the Troy legend may have found
it necessary to eliminate one of the rival Wily Lads.

For the sake of Odysseus's good name Homer had good reason
to pass over this episode in silence, if he knew of it. As far as
Odysseus is concerned, whatever his motive and whatever the
details of his plot, it was by far the most culpable of his deceits, the
worst crime in his epic career. Other ruthless actions, like his
treatment of Philoctetes and the Trojan captives, had at least the
excuse of being *pro bono publico*. This, apparently, was a purely
selfish act of revenge. Such an assassination of a comrade in arms
was utterly foreign to the higher heroic code. (On the other hand
one cannot ignore the possibility that Palamedes really was a traitor
in the original legend.)

Another aspect of Odysseus's original reluctance to join the
Trojan campaign reveals a characteristic quality. As James Joyce
remarked in a continuation of the comment quoted above, 'But
once at the war the conscientious objector became a jusqu' auboutist.
When the others wanted to abandon the siege he insisted on staying
till Troy should fall.' This was always a Ulyssean trait, akin to the
firm-mindedness which Athene had admired. For good or ill, once
Odysseus undertook a task he carried it out, undeviatingly, even
ruthlessly. From the moment he left Ithaca his purpose was to
finish the campaign successfully, quickly, and conclusively. Many
of the other heroes give the impression of enjoying the war and its
diversions. Indeed, some of them had excellent reasons for not
wanting to hurry home. Odysseus never gives this impression,
either at Troy or on his Odyssean wanderings (except under Circe's
influence). He wished to end his absence from home quickly and
finally; or so, at least, all his actions suggest.

Other qualities of the Homeric Odysseus are illustrated in further
episodes in the Cycle, especially his outstanding ability in handling
difficult tasks. Some of these are also mentioned, but only cursorily,
in the *Iliad* and *Odyssey*—notably Odysseus's part in the preliminary
embassy to Troy (a favourite scene in the later tradition), the spying-
out of Troy by Odysseus in beggar's disguise,[9] and the famous

stratagem of the Wooden Horse. The first displayed his superb oratorical powers. The second two were more Autolycan and less conventionally heroic. Probably no other Homeric hero would have condescended to disguise himself in a beggar's rags even for the sake of winning the war. And, as Horace observed,[10] if Achilles had been alive he would scarcely have deigned to lurk with the other heroes inside a wooden box, completely at the mercy of their foes if they should be discovered too soon. Yet without the Wooden Horse Troy would not have been taken. Undignified or not, it was Odysseus's greatest military triumph.

Other exploits of Odysseus related in the Cycle are not mentioned in the *Iliad* or *Odyssey*—notably his part in the sacrifice of Iphigeneia at Aulis, in the affairs of Telephus and Philoctetes, in the stealing of the Palladium, and in the final treatment of the Trojan captives (which pained Euripides so much). Once again it is impossible to be certain if Homer knew of these incidents. As related by the cyclic writers there is nothing particularly depreciatory of Odysseus in them. The more odious features of Odysseus's conduct as emphasized in the later tradition are not found yet. Also, in every case Odysseus's actions are *pro bono publico*: the success of the expedition is at stake. Odysseus's killing of Hector's son, Astyanax,[11] for example, as narrated in the *Destruction of Troy*, was cruel; but (as Odysseus himself pleads in Seneca's *Troades* and elsewhere) it was necessary as a means of preventing a war of revenge. One may weep with Euripides at its inhumanity, but to spare Hector's son would have endangered the lives of every Greek hero's own son, Telemachus included. Besides, this slaying of all the males in a conquered city was frequent in primitive warfare, as the progress of God's Chosen People into the Promised Land abundantly illustrates.

The question arises whether any definite ethical attitude towards Odysseus can be safely deduced from the cyclic poems.[12] In the absence of any explicit comment by the authors themselves some scholars have argued (on the basis of Odysseus's conduct as recorded in the epitomes and fragments) that his reputation had declined from its Homeric level. They point to such incidents as the attempt to evade conscription, the killing of Palamedes, the stealing of the Palladium, and the slaying of Astyanax. The first two belong to the *Cypria*, and in view of the flagrancy of Palamedes's murder there, this poem, if any, is the most likely to have presented Odysseus in an unfavourable light. But there is no evidence that the author of the *Cypria* regarded Palamedes as being such a pure-souled martyr as the fifth-century writers held—a kind of Abel to Odysseus's Cain. He may, on the contrary, have admired Odysseus's triumphant wiliness and have justified it fully. The fact is that our information remains very meagre. In the other poems, so far as one can judge, Odysseus seems to have been largely the resourceful, eloquent, persuasive, public-spirited, courageous hero of the *Iliad* and *Odyssey*.

The one radical change from Homer's conception comes in the latest of the cyclic epics, the *Telegony* composed by an African Greek, Eugammon of Cyrene, in the sixth century B.C. This poem was written as a sequel to the *Odyssey* and is concerned with what happened to Odysseus and his family after his return to Ithaca. The details of Eugammon's narrative are uninspiring. What is significant is that he contradicts the impression left at the end of the *Odyssey* that Odysseus's worst sufferings were over once the Suitors were slain and peace had been proclaimed by Zeus and Athene. Eugammon substitutes a chronicle of infidelity and unrest leading finally to Odysseus's death at the hands of Telegonus, his son by Circe. Thus Odysseus's later destiny became tragic and unsettled instead of happy and tranquil. This change had a profound influence on the later tradition.

The *Odyssey* ends with a description of how Athene intervened to make peace between Odysseus and the angry relatives of the slaughtered Suitors. Homer does not then say, in the manner of a traditional fairy tale, 'And they lived happily ever after'. No typically Greek writer would make such an undiscriminating statement, and no Greek audience would expect it. As Homer knew, the gods give men two portions of woe for every one portion of joy. Yet the clear implication of the *Odyssey* is that Odysseus's wanderings are, with one remarkable exception, done and that he will now settle down to rule his island kingdom serenely to the end of his days.

Odysseus had never wished to leave home. His sole aim in the Trojan campaign was to finish it successfully as soon as possible. He had never wished to be a wanderer, or traveller, or explorer. The early Greeks had no romantic illusions about the delights of voyaging to unexplored regions across the seas. They travelled for war or piracy or trade, or else by compulsion; seldom, if ever, for choice. Odysseus remarked in a conversation in the second half of the *Odyssey*: 'There is nothing worse for mortal men than wandering',[13] and a similar attitude is often expressed elsewhere in the *Odyssey*. One must not let later developments colour the Homeric outlook here. Homer's Odysseus was not an inquiring tourist (like Herodotus or Pausanias) or a pious pilgrim, or an adventurous explorer, or a Byronic wanderer, or a happy-go-lucky vagabond like Lawrence Sterne. He cannot be equated with resolute seekers of promised lands like Aeneas or Moses, or with adventurous missionaries like Francis Xavier and Livingstone. These travelled under the guidance and favour of Heaven; but Odysseus's voyages were the result of divine anger. In this he is better compared with the Wandering Jew, the Flying Dutchman, and the Ancient Mariner.

This fundamental distinction will not, indeed, prevent later writers from converting Odysseus into each and all of these figures; and it cannot be denied that Homer does drop a seed of each as he speeds on with the major purpose of his *Odyssey*. Nor can it be denied that Odysseus, with typical adaptability, made the best of his enforced wanderings, even enjoying some of the new experiences and encounters. But he had always—except under Circe's supernatural influence—pressed on homewards. Ithaca was his Hesperia, his Land of Canaan. Even amid the delights of Calypso's flower-strewn isle, even after the nymph's offer of eternal youth, he had yearned with tears for his rugged homeland and his ageing wife. So in the last lines of the *Odyssey*, after twenty years of exile, Homer implied that he had won, by his courage and endurance and resourcefulness, the 'gentle death off the sea in sleek old age, with his people prosperous around him', that Teiresias had promised him.

But a mysterious uncertainty remained. When Odysseus had visited Teiresias in Hades during his fabulous wanderings, the prophet had prescribed how he should finally appease the wrathful Poseidon (*Od.* 11, 191 ff.). Once he had killed the Suitors and regained his kingdom he must take an oar and travel onwards till he came to a people who knew nothing of the salt sea, or ships, or oars. There he must plant his oar in the ground, offer a sacrifice to Poseidon, then return home and sacrifice hecatombs to all the gods. If these rites were duly performed, then, Teiresias predicted, eventually 'an ever so mild (or enfeebling) death' would come to him 'off the sea' and he would end his days 'in sleek old age with his people prosperous around him'.

Unhappily the Greek is ambiguous here, especially in the phrase for 'off the sea'. Some take it as a prophecy about the source of Odysseus's death (as in the post-Homeric legends of his death from a wound caused by a fish's spine, or from a warrior who came 'off the sea'); others as a prediction that Odysseus himself would be on

G

terra firma when death came to him, in other words that he would
not die the kind of death he had once so greatly feared, death at sea.
Where scholars cannot reach agreement creative writers are likely
to produce some surprising interpretations. From this one phrase
in Homer an astonishing wealth of imaginative detail evolved in the
later tradition.

Equally stimulating to the imagination of post-Homeric writers
was Teiresias's vague description of Odysseus's pilgrimage to that
unknown inland people. Homer apparently intended some kind of
expiation for Odysseus's offence in blinding Poseidon's son, the
Cyclops. But the fact that Homer left this journey still unfulfilled at
the end of the *Odyssey* offered scope for writing a sequel, especially
when Odysseus had told Penelope after their re-union that he would
see 'very many cities of men' on this journey (*Od.* 23, 267). Later
writers were not diffident in supplying details.

Once more one is faced with the fundamental problem of the
early Homeric and cyclic tradition. When Homer made these
references to Odysseus's journey inland was the story already well
known, or did he invent it himself as an off-hand way of ending
Poseidon's wrath? Further, what were the sources of Eugammon's
account of Odysseus's departure from Ithaca, his marriage with the
Queen of the Thesprotians, his return to Ithaca, and his death at the
hands of Telegonus, his son by Circe? Was all this based on pre-
Homeric tradition or was it Eugammon's own invention? No
certain answer is possible. On the whole, to judge from the meagre
summary now surviving, it seems more like the pedestrian work of
a sequel-writer, than the product of folk-lore or poetic imagination.[14]

Once Eugammon had opened the door to theories on the last
days of Odysseus, they multiplied rapidly.[15] In one version Odysseus
discovered after his return that Penelope had been unfaithful to him
(with Hermes or else with some, or all, of the Suitors), and went off
on his wanderings again to the mainland of Greece or to Etruria.
Another version had him finally transformed into a horse. In others
he was alleged to have had children by Circe and Calypso, and by
three other women whom he met in his later wanderings. One of
his sons by Circe, Latinus, was considered by some to have been
the eponymous ancestor of the Latin race—a source of much controversy, as will be discussed in chapter ten. The Mamilii of Rome
claimed to be his descendants through Telegonus the parricide; and
the Athenian orator Andocides traced his descent back to Telegonus
(who, according to this tradition, had eventually married Nausicaa).

It would not help the present study to dwell on the genealogical and geographical[16] details of this variegated tradition. We need only note how the high adventurousness of the *Odyssey* and the passionate heroics of the *Iliad* had degenerated into pedigrees and old wives' tales of adulteries and parricides. Yet this prolixity and confusion of legends about the final fate of Odysseus, together with the absence of any definite statement by Homer, was a source of notable developments in the vernacular tradition. By it Dante, Tennyson, Pascoli, Kazantzakis, and others, were given licence to use their imagination freely in devising the aptest end for the man of many turns; and they used their opportunity superbly. But it can hardly be too much emphasized that figures like Dante's doomed seeker after forbidden knowledge and Tennyson's Byronic victim of wanderlust are fundamentally different from Homer's Odysseus. They are outward bound, centrifugal, while in the *Odyssey* the force of Odysseus's heart and mind is essentially homeward bound, centripetal, towards Ithaca and Penelope.

CHAPTER VII

GROWING HOSTILITY

THE conventions of classical epic poetry precluded the poet from expressing his own personal feelings and opinions about the persons and deeds he described. It was different with the lyric poets. Personal opinions and feelings were generally the chief subject of their poems. Even when their theme was ostensibly heroic, as in Pindar's treatment of the heroic myths, the lyrists seldom showed the self-effacement of Homer and the cyclic writers. In their hands the myths became vehicles for expressing or symbolizing some personal mood or attitude.

As a result of this subjective attitude one finds few 'factual' additions to the exploits of Odysseus in lyric verse ancient or modern. Almost all that is new in the lyrists' contribution to the tradition derives from new emotional or psychological interpretations. The poet's problem no longer seems to be how he can improve and develop the traditional accounts of Odysseus and his deeds. Instead he asks 'What does Odysseus's personality and conduct mean to me personally?' The more moralistic lyrists then go on to decide whether he was a good man or not. In other words Odysseus, instead of sitting, as it were, for a carefully considered portrait by an objective artist like Homer, now finds himself under casual scrutiny by a highly emotional group of potential friends or enemies ready to idolize or execrate him as the impulse seizes them.

Unfortunately the references to Odysseus that survive in the fragments of the earliest Greek lyric poetry are scanty.[1] But there is enough, proportionately, to prove that Odysseus was not neglected after the decline of the epic style. Alcman, the first extant Greek writer after Homer and Hesiod to mention Odysseus by name, refers to his traditional endurance[2]—a quality that would naturally appeal to a Spartan audience even in the days when Sparta was not entirely militarized. Archilochus, himself a social half-breed and something of a misfit in aristocratic circles, seems to have found Odysseus a sympathetic figure.[3] He never refers to him directly, but he twice paraphrases Odysseus's famous refusal to gloat over the slaughtered Suitors, presumably finding in it an example that he would like to follow in his own verbal victories. In another fragment he tells how he hates a big, arrogant, carefully-dressed general, and likes a small, bandy-legged fellow with a sturdy stride and a bold heart. The description, except for the unheroic bandy legs, closely recalls the contrast in *Iliad* Three between the tall, lordly Agamemnon and the stocky, ram-like Odysseus. Elsewhere Archilochus admires endurance, writes of his own sufferings at sea, and prays for a 'sweet home-coming', in Odyssean language that suggests a close bond of sympathy between himself and Odysseus.[4]

Alcman and Archilochus wrote chiefly about aesthetic and personal matters. The succeeding century, the sixth, with its widespread political unrest, produced a series of politician-poets, beginning with Solon. Characteristically Odysseus was enlisted as a partisan in the conflicts—just as he was destined later to be involved in the controversies of post-reformation Western Europe. Theognis (or else a writer of his school), brooding over the defeat of the aristocrats in Megara, admired Odysseus's 'pitiless spirit'[5] as demonstrated in his revenge on the Suitors. Elsewhere in the same collection of poems—their authorship is disputed—one finds a remarkable eulogy on the value of chameleonic adaptability in social intercourse, which clearly alludes to the Homeric Odysseus. 'O heart', the poet exclaims,[6] 'present a different tinge of character to every friend, blending your mood with that of each. Emulate the complex (or crafty[7]) polypus that always takes the appearance of the adjacent rock. Cleverness is better than inflexibility.'

Here one recognizes a special aspect of Odysseus's traditional versatility and resourcefulness—the Pauline quality of being all things to all men. But as this poet phrases it, and in its wider context of political spite and rancour, the eulogy has a distinctly unpleasant flavour. Its tone is machiavellian, rather than Homeric or apostolic. Though Homer's Odysseus undoubtedly had these polychromatic qualities, he never boasted of them or made them the basis of his social life. Further, as has been seen, the Homeric Odysseus could show firm opposition at times towards even the most formidable personages. Yet undoubtedly we are faced here with one of the fundamental ambiguities in Odysseus's character. The border between adaptability and hypocrisy is easily crossed. Theognis had to make very little distortion to transform Odysseus's Homeric versatility into this despicable opportunism. Soon, when Pindar, Sophocles, and Euripides, reconsider the matter, Odysseus will pay dearly for Theognis's admiration.

The first direct attack on Odysseus's character in extant European literature is Pindar's.[8] In two odes (*Nemeans* 7 and 8) he denounces Odysseus's victory over Ajax in the contest for Achilles's arms, as an example of how a cunning plausible liar can overthrow a simple, splendid hero. The traditional background to this outburst needs to be considered before the effect of Pindar's denunciation can be fully appreciated.

The earliest full account of the contest between Odysseus and Ajax was that given in the *Aethiopis*; but this unfortunately is lost except for a summary and a few references. The episode lay outside the chronological scope of the *Iliad* and *Odyssey*, as it happened late in the Troy campaign. But it was clearly part of the tradition in Homer's time, and he refers to it in an impressive passage of *Odyssey* Eleven, when towards the end of Odysseus's visit to the Land of Ghosts he sees the shade of Ajax in company with Achilles and other heroes. Before relating this incident to the Phaeacians Odysseus expresses deep regret that his victory in the trial for the arms had caused Ajax to kill himself in outraged pride. 'Would that I had never won in such a contest', he exclaims, 'when as its result the earth now covers such a figure as Ajax who in stature and in action surpassed all other Greeks after the faultless Achilles!' Odysseus's regret here has every appearance of sincerity; and there was little to be gained (except, perhaps, credit for magnanimity) by showing sympathy for a dead Greek at the court of Alcinous in remote Phaeacia. The regretful tone is sustained through the whole of Odysseus's account of the incident.

Odysseus proceeds to describe how in the Land of Ghosts he addressed the shade of Ajax with 'honeyed words' (the Homeric phrase implies a desire to please rather than any ingratiating hypocrisy), choosing his terms with all the courtesy and restraint that he could command. He shows no trace of exultation or gloating over a defeated rival, a rival, too, whose attitude to him at Troy had never been very friendly. He begs Ajax to end his fatal wrath now that he is dead. (Here, of course, one sees the hopelessness of Odysseus's appeal to a temperament like Ajax's: the very fact that Odysseus speaks as the living victor to one who is dead and defeated, makes any overture of this kind seem bitterly patronizing.) He assures him that the Greeks had mourned his death as much as that of Achilles himself—such 'a tower of strength' did they feel they had lost in him. He adds the conventional, but not insincere, explanation of a good man's suffering—that it is not what he deserved, but simply the arbitrary will of Zeus. Finally he asks him to overcome his indignation and to hear him further. There is no suggestion of guile, or reason for it, here. Odysseus could no doubt easily afford to be magnanimous, since he had been the victor. But magnanimity towards a defeated competitor was exceptional in archaic Greece. It would have been more normal and natural for a hero to taunt his dead and helpless antagonist. Yet Odysseus characteristically refrains from any boasting or gloating. It is a foreshadowing, and very likely the source, of his magnanimous conduct in Sophocles's *Ajax*.

But overtures like this, as Odysseus would well know, leave one open to a humiliating reply—the snub direct, particularly when one addresses a person of nobler lineage and higher prestige than oneself. Ajax uses this last weapon of injured pride with superb effect. He disdains any reply. He simply turns away to join the other futile spirits of the dead in the dark inner lands, leaving Odysseus unanswered and ignored. *Seul le silence est grand.* . . .

As every sympathetic reader, ancient and modern, has appreciated, this is a scene unsurpassed in its sombre pathos—Roman rather than Greek in its majestic austerity. For a moment Ajax wins our admiration like a Cato or a Regulus. For a moment the flexibility of a Ulysses seems cheap and shoddy in the presence of this obdurate heroism. It is the last gesture in Homer of the older heroic style against the newer and more facile fashion. Like some obsolescent creature of the prehistoric world, a solitary mastodon or mammoth faced by a coaxing *homo pithecanthropus* eager to tame its rage, Ajax stalks scornfully and silently away. It is a poor poet who cannot respect a lost cause, who cannot venerate a doomed civilization. As Virgil with all his devotion to imperial Rome did not fail to bring out the pathos of the death of Carthaginian Dido, so Homer here, though his admiration and sympathy in general are for the agile Ulyssean Man, saluted the last of the titanic heroes.[9]

Dido at her death prayed for an avenger to scourge her Trojan deceiver. Pindar is Ajax's avenging Hasdrubal, Euripides his Hannibal, and between them they came close to ruining Odysseus's reputation for ever. There was nothing in the Homeric or cyclic accounts of the contest for the arms, as far as one can tell from the surviving fragments, to suggest that Odysseus won the prize undeservedly or by dishonest means. But Pindar makes both accusations unequivocally. Odysseus's victory, he asserts, was not due to an unbiased verdict by Athene and the Trojan captives,[10] but to a decision made by the Greek chieftains after the envious and unworthy Ithacan had won them over by guile. Pindar denounces this Ulyssean cunning as deplorable 'even in ancient times': it is 'a consort of coaxing words, a deviser of guile, an insinuator of mischievous calumnies, always attacking the illustrious and exalting the ignominious'. 'May I never', he exclaims, 'have a character like that, but walk in straightforward ways'.

The references are brief but they make Pindar's personal feelings very clear.[11] He admires the Ajax-type,[12] the frank, straightforward hero, and detests Odysseus as an envious, deceitful, slanderous knave. It is impossible, he holds, that an Ajax could have been defeated by an Odysseus on his merits. So he invents, apparently, the theory that Odysseus cheated in order to win. Homer's favourite hero has become Pindar's most hated villain. Why?

It seems to have been mainly a matter of temperament. By birth Pindar belonged to the Aeolic race.[13] By choice he admired and praised the austere Dorian style. As an Aeolic Theban he lived in an atmosphere hostile to the Attic-Ionic tradition with its mental and political dexterity. He studiously ignored the speculations of the Ionian philosophers, preferring to rely for his principles of life and conduct on the simple maxims of the older sages. Though probably an innovator in many matters of style, in ethical thought Pindar was an uncompromising conservative. It was natural that a poet of his tradition, training, and inclination, should prefer Ajax, the highborn prince of Doric Aegina, to the versatile grandson of Autolycus.

There may have been a purely personal motive as well. To judge from some passages in his odes Pindar was himself a victim of slanderers and malicious rivals, especially at the opulent court of the tyrant Hiero at Syracuse, a patron to be prized by professional poets. Significantly Pindar chose as a symbol of these crafty backbiters Ionian Archilochus, who, as has been mentioned, seems to have had much in common with Odysseus. It may well have been, then, that Pindar saw an emblem of himself in the noble figure of the defeated Ajax and an incarnation of his worst foes in the successful Odysseus —for Pindar eventually lost Hiero's favour. This personal identification combined with racial and cultural prejudices would go far to explain the vehemence of his denunciation of Odysseus. But it still remains surprising that he was capable of distorting Homer's account of the contest in order to stigmatize Ajax's enemy.[14]

Pindar represents the conservative and aristocratic tradition in early fifth-century Greece. Meanwhile the progressive left wing of

Greek thought was preparing the way for another line of attack on Odysseus's reputation. In earlier times the great prestige of Homer had probably helped to shield him from destructive criticism. But now, towards the end of the sixth century, Homer himself became a target for criticism, on the grounds that he had failed to tell the truth about nature and the gods.[15] This was not an entirely new development, though it did not become direct and formidable, so far as is now known, until the sixth century. At least a century earlier Pindar's fellow-countryman Hesiod had made an oblique attack on Homeric fictions in the opening lines of his *Theogony*. Without actually naming Homer he asserted that his own kind of poetry, theological and didactic, was true and useful, while Homer's poems were lies (the polite distinction between fiction and falsehood having not yet been established). It is significant that Hesiod chose to describe the poet's lies in a phrase[16] applied by Homer to Odysseus's personal skill in giving verisimilitude to his falsehoods: a subtle hearer might well have taken this as a hint that both the deceitful Odysseus and Homer, his creator, deserved the same condemnation. Whether these implications were consciously intended or not, the essential fact remains that here Hesiod began that tendency to disparage creative fictions which culminated in their condemnation as harmful and immoral in Plato's *Republic*. Naturally such an attitude was bound in the end to harm Odysseus's reputation as well as Homer's.

Hesiod's attack was only a passing blow. The ethical writers of the sixth century opened up a full campaign against Homer's delinquencies. At first Odysseus was not, it seems, directly involved, but his fate was foreshadowed. Thus when Pythagoras asserted that he had seen the soul of Homer hanging from a serpent-infested tree in Hades as a punishment for impiety, he anticipated Dante's vision of Ulysses in Hell some eighteen hundred years later. So, too, when Theagenes of Rhegium exploited the method of allegorical interpretation in defence of Homer's alleged errors and blasphemies, he prepared the way for some remarkable developments in the Ulysses tradition.

These and other critics of Homer, like Xenophanes and Heracleitus, were high-minded people eager to determine and maintain the truth about gods and men. The same cannot be said for many of the disparagers of Odysseus in the succeeding epoch, the Age of the Sophists. The Sophists were primarily interested in the technique of handling arguments, and not in philosophic truth. Though many of them were, no doubt, honourable, public-spirited men, yet, like some modern technologists, some of them seem to have been willing to perfect dangerous technical processes without any regard to their ultimate effect. In fact, what some of these Sophists effected by their verbal ingenuities was a kind of atomic fission in the previously permanent elements of the Greek ethical tradition.

Such men were bound to be interested in the ingenious Odysseus. On the whole they tended to depreciate him, influenced perhaps by the common tendency to be severest on others for one's own dearest faults. Two incidents in Odysseus's career became favourite subjects for their discussions, the murder of Palamedes and the defeat of Ajax.[17] Gorgias, most influential of the Sophists at Athens in the 420's, wrote a *Defence of Palamedes* in which Odysseus was roundly accused of envy, malpractice, and general knavery.[18] Socrates, when making his defence before the Athenian jurymen,[19] chose Palamedes as the prototype of his own impending martyrdom, the implication being that his accusers resembled the villainous and unscrupulous Odysseus. (Yet there was irony in the fact that Socrates was accused of corrupting the youth, much as Odysseus is portrayed as corrupting Neoptolemus in Sophocles's *Philoctetes*.) One gathers from other sources[20] that Palamedes had become a figure of deep emotional significance during this period. But the Athenian jurors apparently saw Socrates less as a Palamedes than as a sophistical Odysseus.

Controversy being the natural atmosphere of the sophistic movement, these attacks on Odysseus were bound to provoke some to defend him. Thus Alcidamas (who described the *Odyssey* as 'a beautiful mirror of human life'[21]) undertook to plead the case for Odysseus against Palamedes. Unfortunately the declamation now surviving is a feeble forgery,[22] and nothing is now authentically known of this attempt to clear Odysseus of his worst crime. Odysseus's second supporter in this period was a much more influential figure. He deserves careful consideration. It was mainly his doctrine that kept Odysseus's reputation from complete infamy in the later Latin and medieval periods when Homer's influence was weakest. This was Antisthenes, the vigorous-minded and outspoken forerunner of the Cynics, who with his forceful phrasing and ruggedly impressive character seems to have been something like the Samuel Johnson of late fifth-century Athens.

Antisthenes's views on Odysseus are known chiefly from two sources, his sophistic speeches on the contest between Ajax and

Odysseus and a notable reference in the Homeric scholia. The two short speeches are written to represent Ajax's claim and Odysseus's counter-claim to the Arms. Clearly Antisthenes's final intention was to show the much greater merit of Odysseus, from the point of view of a proto-Cynic. First Ajax disparages Odysseus in terms of conventional archaeo-heroic values. Odysseus prefers to act secretly; the true hero, like Ajax, scorns concealment for his actions. Odysseus would suffer any indignity to gain some end (witness his voluntary mutilations before his spying expedition into Troy); Ajax scorns all such debasements of heroic reputation. Odysseus was prepared to steal the Palladium from Athene's temple in Troy; how could such a sacrilegious wretch be worthy to win the supreme prize of valour? The criterion should be deeds, not words, military valour, not skill in arguments. And—a final touch of scorn—was it not a fact that Odysseus had been unwilling to join the expedition against Troy? What a contrast with Ajax, ever foremost in the fight!

The speech is arrogant, insensitive, and tactless. Ajax maladroitly implies that he thinks little of his judges, and lectures them on their proper attitude and duty. Antisthenes apparently intended his hearers to realize that Ajax was nobler in silence than in argument. Indeed, Ajax admits himself that he should not have spoken at all. No doubt his memorable silence in *Odyssey* Eleven was in the author's mind here.

Odysseus replies in a longer speech. He begins with a needlessly unconciliatory remark, more characteristic of the gruff Antisthenes than of Homer's hero. His claim to the armour is not, he says, directed against Ajax alone, but against all the listening heroes, 'Since I have done the expedition more good than all of you put together'. He proceeds to describe all that he alone had risked and suffered and achieved on behalf of the Greek cause. The aim of the war was not, he points out, simply to fight the Trojans: it was to capture Troy and regain Helen. The stealing of the Palladium was a necessary step towards that aim, since an oracle had predicted that Troy would remain uncaptured as long as it retained the fateful statue. If it is a fine deed to capture Troy, it was a fine deed to undertake this preliminary task. How then can the taking of the Palladium be denounced as sacrilege (if the end justifies the means)? Ajax's denunciations are simply proofs of his ignorance. Odysseus does not blame him for that: he sees that Ajax cannot help it, poor fellow.

Odysseus turns to the charge of cowardice. Ajax, he observes, may well prefer his own kind of heroism, the rashness of the warrior who rushes into battle like a wild boar. (Some day, Odysseus predicts, this unreasoning impetuosity of Ajax's will turn against himself in suicide.) And this great reputation for courage that Ajax so childishly exults in—is it not a fact that his armour is impenetrable so that he cannot be wounded? Odysseus contrasts his own form of courage—to be willing to go unarmed into the enemy's city, to be vigilant night and day for the sake of all the host, to be deterred by no apparent disgrace from doing his duty, to be constantly ready to fight against one or many, to venture on dangerous night expeditions when Ajax is snoring in his tent.

Some arguments on details follow. Finally Odysseus alleges that Ajax is ill—'diseased with envy and ignorance'. Ajax confuses brute strength with manly courage; he fails to distinguish between mere force and military skill. Odysseus ends with a prophecy that some day a poet skilled in discerning true manly worth will arise and portray him, Odysseus, as 'enduring, rich in counsel, resourceful, city-sacking' and single him out as the sole vanquisher of Troy. But the same discerning poet will compare Ajax to the stupid asses and oxen who let others harness and yoke them. This last touch is, of course, quite unfair to Homer's portrait of Ajax. It picks out two slightly unfavourable comparisons and ignores many tributes to him. But one may expect such sophistries in a sophistical discourse.

It would be injudicious in the present general survey to spend much time over these two brief speeches. In them, as a recent scholar[23] has shown in detail, Antisthenes is using a literary device to put out propaganda for his conception of the good man. Various commonplaces of Cynic doctrine can be seen in Odysseus's speech. Odysseus emphasizes his readiness to serve the common good, his individualism and self-sufficiency, his vigilance and 'gubernatorial' wisdom, his disregard of indignities and mutilations[24] which a conventional hero would think worse than death, his belief (shared by Socrates[25]) that the good man can suffer no true harm. The fact that Antisthenes chose Odysseus as the prototype of these Cynic, and in some respects Stoic, qualities greatly influenced the later tradition, both Christian and pagan.[26]

From another reference to Odysseus by Antisthenes one can see that the philosopher had to meet some further criticisms of Odysseus's ethics. A fundamental ambiguity in his character emerges in the first line of the *Odyssey*. When Homer said 'Tell me, Muse, of the *polytropic* man', what did he mean by the epithet?[27] Etymologically it suggests 'of many turns', but the ambiguity still remains. Apparently Odysseus's detractors in the late fifth century interpreted it pejoratively in an ethical sense as 'often changing one's character, hence unstable, unprincipled, unscrupulous'. In other words they saw in it much the chameleonic quality which Theognis had recommended: but they, being moralists and not embittered party politicians, condemned it.

Antisthenes rallied to Odysseus's defence. *Polytropos*, he argues, does not refer to character or ethics at all. It simply denotes Odysseus's skill in adapting his figures of speech ('tropes') to his hearers at any particular time. No reasonable moralist, much less a sophist, could find fault with versatility of that kind. Even the austere Pythagoras had recommended his disciples to speak in childlike terms to children, in womanlike terms to women, in governmental terms to governors, and in young men's language to young men.

The explanation is ingenious, and the effort to solve a notorious crux is noteworthy. But modern scholars[28] do not agree with either side in this controversy. It is now generally believed that by the epithet *polytropos* Homer meant 'one who has been turned in many ways, much-travelled, widely experienced', as is explained by the phrase that follows it—'who was driven very much from his course'. According to this view, Homer placed that epithet in the first line of the *Odyssey* to emphasize the poem's main theme; namely, Odysseus's many wanderings and adventures before he regained his kingdom. In other words, here, as already seen elsewhere, Homer's primary purpose is to tell a story: but yet here, too, as elsewhere, by a stroke of prophetic genius he used an epithet which would open up a wide field of ethical and psychological interpretation in the later Ulysses tradition. In the present chapter, however, the most significant fact is that the fifth-century controversialists seem to have ignored the simpler interpretation of *polytropos*. To such an extent had moral problems come to dominate the study of Homer in that period.

Antisthenes, then, like a good Cynic, chose Odysseus and Heracles as exemplars of the Natural Man, the Serviceable Man, the Individualistic Man, who in defiance of conventional heroic standards of conduct is able to endure toil and suffering in lonely enterprises to serve humanity. Ajax, he implies, stands for those stereotyped conventions and codes of etiquette which inhibit natural virtue.

Those who, like Ajax, sneer at voluntary self-abasement and at the willing acceptance of menial tasks are the enemies of the good life. They value the form above the substance, the letter above the spirit.[29] By this kind of argument, and by choosing Odysseus as an example of the wise man ready to undergo any humiliation for the sake of some high purpose, Antisthenes prepared the way for his acceptance by both Stoics and Christians.

But despite the support of men like Antisthenes and Alcidamas, general opinion seems to have been against Odysseus, as study of the dramatic poets will more clearly show. Not that all his actions and qualities were indiscriminately condemned. His more judicious critics, Socrates and Plato among them, gave him credit for at least some good qualities.[30] But if they and the whole body of well-informed Athenians of the late fifth century had been asked to vote for his condemnation or acquittal on the question of his moral worth, they would probably have condemned him. And, as will appear in the next chapter, Euripides would have served as leading counsel for the prosecution.

How could Homer's favourite hero have fallen so low? Why should the man whom later writers, like Horace and Ascham and Fénelon, regarded as a worthy example of virtuous living, be denounced as envious, treacherous, unscrupulous, and knavish? It is not a satisfactory answer to say that the Odysseus condemned by fifth-century writers was mainly the Odysseus of the Epic Cycle. Even if one were to admit that his portrait there was generally unfavourable, why should that side of Odysseus's character be emphasized and his Homeric virtues be minimized?

One can distinguish two general causes, apart from such personal reasons as have been suggested for Pindar's antipathy. The first is to be found in the stricter attitude to truth and morality which had emerged from the teachings of philosophers like Pythagoras and Xenophanes (and possibly from some Orphic sources). This would tend to deal hardly with flexible and variegated personalities like Odysseus, preferring 'pure' or 'simple' types like Palamedes, Ajax, and Heracles. Then when the methods of the Sophists became over-ingenious and unscrupulous, and were applied to base political ends, as happened towards the end of the fifth century, austerer moralists would see it as an additional reason for denouncing the Ulyssean type, whether he appeared in the shape of an aristocratic Alcibiades or of a plebeian Cleon.[31]

Here ethics merges in social history, and the second reason for

Odysseus's obloquy is to be found in the historical changes in the fortunes of Athens during the same period.[32] The death of Pericles in 429 B.C. had released a spate of competitive demagogy in which personal greed and chauvinistic imperialism were reconciled by impudent sophistries. As the Peloponnesian war dragged on, old standards of morality and humanity lapsed. The accepted meanings of honoured words were debased, as Thucydides describes, like the Athenian coinage. Revenge came to be regarded as a duty, ambition as the best motive, self-aggrandisement as the highest goal. The weak must go to the wall; the just argument must yield to the unjust; power must prevail over truth. When by the last decades of the century Athenian resourcefulness and intelligence had sunk so low as this, it is not surprising that the supremely resourceful and intelligent hero, the outstanding *homo politicus* of the archaic world, Odysseus, should become an object of detestation. The fact that he had been eminently successful in most of his career was now only an additional source of suspicion, for in Athens now political success had become almost synonymous with moral turpitude.

Besides this, as the ultimate defeat of Athens drew nearer in a series of disasters,[33] the Athenians had reason to sympathize with those who had suffered the horrors of defeat in the Trojan War. The slaughter of the Trojan warriors, 'old grandsire Priam' among them, the killing of Polyxena and Astyanax, the captivity of the Trojan women—all these had their contemporary parallels. And those who had suffered dishonour on the Greek side, Philoctetes, Palamedes, Ajax, and the rest, were seen to resemble many Athenian victims of militaristic intrigues. If Athenian morale was to survive the Spartan victory, a philosophy of defeat would have to be evolved. Symbols of success, like Odysseus or Menelaus, must be discredited.

It is impossible to determine just how far Athenian writers on the Ulysses theme were consciously affected by such historical influences as these. All one knows for certain is that by the end of the fifth century the Homeric lion was transformed into a machiavellian fox, and that this fox in turn had become the scapegoat of the Athenians. It was as if the Athenians felt that by tearing Odysseus to pieces they could purge away the curse of unscrupulous cleverness which had infected the heroism of their generation. As a result, one sees for the first time in their writings, and especially in the dramatic works to be considered in the next chapter, just how odious the grandson of Autolycus could be when deprived of Athene's favour.

CHAPTER VIII

THE STAGE VILLAIN

IN turning from the direct comments of the lyric poets and the philosophers to the dramatists' portraits of Odysseus, one again meets the problem of how far each author's personal feelings are involved in his creations. To put the problem specifically: when Sophocles presented Odysseus as a magnanimous peacemaker in *Ajax* and as a corrupt and contemptible sophist in *Philoctetes*, was this the result of some change in his personal attitude to Ulyssean cleverness? Or was it simply due to the technical reason that he wanted a hero in the first play and a villain in the second? Or was it due to a change in the moral climate during the long interval between the two plays, so that qualities which once had seemed admirable were later seen to be pernicious?

The same difficulty did not arise so acutely in discussing Homer's Odysseus, partly because so little is known about the ethical background to the *Iliad* and the *Odyssey*, and partly because epic poetry is a freer and more expansive medium than drama. The twelve thousand lines and upwards of an epic poem allow more room for cross-currents of thought, feeling, and motive, than the twelve hundred or so of a Greek tragedy. Epic figures have generally to undergo a certain amount of typing and simplification before they can be effective within the narrow and rather rigid limitations of the Greek theatre. Hamlets and Peer Gynts and Fausts are out of the question here. So one may expect that the drastic vicissitudes of Odysseus in Greek drama are sometimes, at least, due to technical exigencies, especially when one remembers the importance attached to the plot in classical dramaturgy. Aristotle may have been biased in rating dramatic characterization so low in his *Poetics*. But he would not have emphasized the value of the plot—the mathematics, so to speak, of the play—so strongly without justification. The Greek love of symmetrical form was influential here; and classical symmetry tended to minimize the abnormal and individualistic. A character so exceptional as that of Odysseus was likely to be specially affected by these assimilating and universalizing processes.

Odysseus plays no part in the seven extant plays of Aeschylus.

The only reference to him in *Agamemnon* is ambiguous.[1] But apparently he was a notable figure in at least seven of the lost works.[2] The surviving fragments and descriptions of these are too scanty to establish Aeschylus's general attitude with any certainty. It is known that in his version of the deceiving of Philoctetes Odysseus appeared as a cunning and sharp fellow, but free from any suggestion of undignified scheming or verbosity—in contrast with his knavishness in later plays on this theme[3]; his arguments and ruses, we are told, were not entirely unworthy of a Homeric hero—or, one may add, of Aeschylus's own magnanimous spirit. The few fragments of the play on the contest for the arms of Achilles suggest that Aeschylus sided with Pindar in preferring the blunt Ajax to the persuasive Ithacan. It is in this play that one finds the first reference to the legend that Odysseus's father was not the harmless Laertes but Sisyphus, that cunning and malevolent ruler of prehistoric Corinth. Whether Aeschylus invented this slander or not—and it is hardly what one would expect from him—it demonstrates the virulence of the hostility that had grown against Odysseus since Homer's time.[4] Sisyphus, according to tradition, had been cunning enough to outwit even Autolycus, and his general reputation was ugly. He was the sinister villain of early Greek mythology, while Autolycus was apparently more the cheerful rogue. If Sisyphus had really been Odysseus's father, Odysseus would have inherited a double portion of deceitfulness; and, since mythical genealogies are often symbolical rather than quasi-historical, this would have meant that he himself was doubly unscrupulous and vicious. It is uncertain whether Aeschylus meant his audience to accept the imputed parentage or not. But even to mention it would tend to smear Odysseus's character among more undiscerning members of the audience.

A fragment of another lost play, *The bone-gatherers*, describes how Odysseus suffered the foulest humiliation in the whole tradition. In the *Odyssey* he had had a foot-stool and a meat-bone thrown at him by arrogant Suitors, when he was still in beggar's disguise. But in Aeschylus's drama—a satyric play where one may expect some horse-play—a *pot de chambre* is emptied over his head with humiliating and ludicrous effect. Yet, with characteristic endurance, he suffered it without losing control of himself; and with characteristic self-detachment he was able to recount the details afterwards without excessive rancour or indignation. In another satyr play, *The ghost-raisers*, he had a similar but more disastrous fate: a heron flying overhead scatters ordure on his bald pate, causing his death by sepsis—a grotesque version of Teiresias's prophecy that he would die a death 'off the sea'.

These are mere details, and allowances must be made for the gross humour of satyric drama. But if Aeschylus had admired Odysseus, or if Odysseus had been a popular hero at the time, he would hardly have chosen him as a mark for such excremental humour as this. On general grounds it is probable that a man of Aeschylus's austere, conservative, and outspoken temperament would, like Pindar, have disliked the flexibilities of Odysseus, just as in contemporary politics his sympathies were against the crafty Themistocles and for the frank Aristides.

Odysseus's first appearance in extant Greek drama is in Sophocles's *Ajax*.[5] The opening scene soon shows that Sophocles has abandoned Homer's view of the relationship between Odysseus and Athene. They are no longer the 'cheerful conspirators' of the scene in *Odyssey* Thirteen. 'The badinage, the playful trickery, the comradeship in deception and revenge, have disappeared.'[6] Instead of arguing with a half sisterly, half motherly, patron, Odysseus is in 'the grip of a power which, while acting in his own interests . . . has no respect for his own plans and wishes whatsoever'. Indeed, some modern readers find Athene the chief villain of the play. There is a note of gloating in her description of how she drove Ajax, when he was furious at his defeat by Odysseus in the award of Achilles's arms, into homicidal mania. As soon as Odysseus sees Ajax's pitiable condition he compassionately reflects on the frailty of human fortunes—'What is man but an empty shape, a fleeting shadow?' But Athene brusquely checks him. She will have none of his indulgent sympathy. 'See that *you* never offend the gods or behave arrogantly in victory and prosperity: the gods love men of a restrained and balanced spirit, and hate the evil ones.'

The Sophoclean irony is surely intentional here. This is worse than Satan rebuking sin, when a vindictive goddess preaches moderation and restraint to the essentially moderate and restrained Odysseus. Without going further into the significance of Athene's rôle one can say that technically it serves to enhance the humanity and decency of Odysseus's attitude to his defeated rival. It is only when Athene leaves and Odysseus takes over the control of affairs that the imbroglio of passion and pride is cooled and purified.

Yet Odysseus's first appearances in the play are not prepossessing. He enters rather over-cautiously, almost like a second-rate sleuth in a detective story, peering anxiously at the tracks of his dangerous foe.[7] Athene watches him contemptuously for a while, and then remarks, 'Always at the same business, Odysseus, hunting about for some way of snatching at your enemies'. The echo of her banter in the *Odyssey* is unmistakable. But the tone is entirely different— patronizing and aloof. Yet Odysseus replies in terms of devoted affection and earnestly begs her help. Then Athene deliberately, almost sadistically, plays on his natural caution. Cruelly, despite Odysseus's pleading, she calls Ajax out. It can hardly be called cowardice that Odysseus wants to avoid this raving maniac with his tremendous strength. In general Sophocles's presentation of the scene (as distinct from Athene's attitude) is rather ignominious for Odysseus, if not explicitly discreditable. The Autolycan flavour is clearly distinguishable. And Athene's influence is no longer used, as in Homer, to help and encourage him.

Odysseus does not appear again until the closing scenes of the play. In the meantime his enemies have had ample opportunity to denounce him in Pindaric fashion. Ajax has called him 'that knavish fox'[8]. Ajax's friends in the chorus have accused him of whispered slanders against their hero, though in fact the alleged calumnies were no more than the truth about Ajax's misdeeds. A little later they refer to him as 'a scion of the prodigal line of Sisyphus'. Soon afterwards Ajax exclaims, 'You who see everything, you the un- failing instrument of every crime, you the dirtiest siftings of the host—how you are laughing with joy at this!' Ajax sees Odysseus only as a villain *capable de tout* (v. 445) with no redeeming feature whatever. He and the chorus (v. 954 ff.) assume that Odysseus's feeling can only be one of dark exultation over a defeated rival. In this they share Athene's opinion that gloating is natural and right for a triumphant hero. Homer's more civilized view is ignored.

Odysseus's justification comes in the last scenes. He enters again to find Ajax's half-brother, Teucer, and Agamemnon embroiled in a bitter dispute about the burial of the self-slain hero. Teucer insists on an honourable funeral, Agamemnon refuses it. The basis of the conflict closely resembles that between Antigone and Creon over the corpse of Polyneices. But here there is someone to effect a settle- ment. Odysseus voluntarily intervenes. He asks Agamemnon if he can speak to him as a personal friend. Agamemnon cordially agrees; but soon he is astonished to hear Odysseus plead for his defeated enemy. Agamemnon, too, believes in the heroic rule of kicking a foe when he is down. It is sheer madness, he holds, to respect an enemy's good qualities. Odysseus laconically remarks that he,

Odysseus, himself will be dead some day. This is simply a repetition of his earlier awareness of human mortality and helplessness. But Sophocles makes it the basis of an ingenious reversal in Agamemnon's attitude. The king interprets Odysseus's remark as being purely self-regarding,[9] as if Odysseus wished to ensure kind treatment for himself and his faults by being merciful towards Ajax's corpse now. Priding himself on his alertness in detecting Odysseus's true motive, as he thinks, he agrees as a personal favour to allow the burial. Odysseus with fine selflessness does not delay to repudiate the false imputation. It is a traditional feature of his dialectic that he readily accepts his opponents' assumptions, true or false, if they lead to the required conclusion. He accepts Agamemnon's unflattering kindness without demur. Ajax can now be buried as a hero. The chorus exclaim in admiration at Odysseus's innate wisdom (or cleverness—the inescapable ambiguity of this quality emerges again in the word *sophos*). Teucer has nothing but praise now for the 'noblest' Odysseus in comparison with 'that crazy general' Agamemnon. But Sophocles has reserved one further practical proof of Odysseus's restraint. When Odysseus modestly asks to be allowed to share in Ajax's funeral rights, Teucer courteously refuses. Odysseus quietly accepts his decision and withdraws. The play ends with preparations for the obsequies.

The impression left of Odysseus in the end is of a magnanimous, compassionate, modest hero, who retains both the tactfulness and the self-restraint of his Homeric archetype. If his appearance in the opening scenes of the play suggest his Autolycan nature, his conduct in the last scene is as noble as anything in his Homeric career. One could, of course, allege base motives for his generosity. One always can. But Sophocles seems to imply that Odysseus was genuinely sorry that his honourable victory in the award of Achilles's arms had destroyed a great-hearted hero, as Homer had already implied in the scene in *Odyssey* Eleven.

Many deeper meanings have been read into this profoundly moving, but rather loosely constructed, play, and there has been much dispute about the relative significance of Ajax's and Odysseus's rôles. One view insists that Sophocles's sympathy is emphatically with the suffering Ajax. In order to glorify Ajax, whose popular Athenian cult would be in the mind of everyone in the audience, Sophocles, it is suggested, accepted Pindar's view of Odysseus's baseness and trickery in the contest for the arms and showed how he was finally converted to admiration for Ajax. In other words, though Odysseus is obviously not the villain of the piece, his rôle approximates to that of 'the ranks of Tuscany' who in Macaulay's ballad can scarce forbear to cheer at Horatius's valour.[10]

At the other extreme is the theory that Odysseus is, morally at least, the hero of the play, symbolizing a philanthropic understanding of human destiny and a consciousness of the ultimate solidarity of men in face of the inevitable doom of death. In contrast Ajax is the 'hyperindividualist'. He accepts no limitation to his egoism. He is imprisoned in a dark tower of pride and passion. As long as he is alive, Odysseus, for the sake of humanity, must be his enemy. As soon as he is dead, Odysseus implements the loyalties of a common humanity in taking Ajax's part. Now Odysseus must fight and overcome the Ajax-like quality in Agamemnon. This, too, it is explained, is the reason why at the beginning of the play Athene so implacably hates Ajax: blind egoism is the worst of blasphemies. The moral of the play is that 'only the I which joins with the We can survive and perfect itself'. Another interpretation follows similar lines: Ajax symbolizes despair, the destructive principle in society; Odysseus represents the true solution of the drama of human life, the spirit of justice, understanding and reconciliation.[11]

One may doubt whether any such abstract meanings are intended in Sophocles's intensely human play. Like Homer's, Sophocles's aim is to portray, not to judge. It is not necessary to see Odysseus or Ajax as villain or saint here. If Sophocles intends any lesson it is probably what Ajax learned before his suicide: 'Shall we not somehow learn *sophrosyne* (i.e. balance and moderation in thought and deed)? Late in life have I come to recognize that enemies may soon become friends and friends enemies—and this prescribes restraint'. Ajax learned his lesson in the bitterness of defeat, *de profundis*. Odysseus, in contrast, learned it in victory, as few men do. Ajax's reason is a brutally realistic one: Odysseus's is humanely philosophical—the transience and unpredictability of human fortunes. But fundamentally they are similar. In so far as *sophrosyne* is the most typical quality of all Sophocles's thought and work, both Ajax and Odysseus speak with his voice in this. But in so far as Sophocles apparently learned his *sophrosyne* in a career of unrivalled success, Odysseus's tolerant, level-headed, sane self-restraint is closer to his own view of life than Ajax's pessimism.

One problem remains. Why, then, did Sophocles not make Odysseus's appearance in the first scene more honourable? Perhaps it was a concession to popular anti-Odyssean prejudice. If the

majority of his audience held Pindar's and Aeschylus's views on the
villainy of Odysseus, Sophocles would have caused an initial
antagonism if he had introduced a nobler figure at the beginning.
But by making his Athene so savagely vindictive he gave Odysseus
an early opportunity to reveal his humanity, so that his moral
triumph in the last scene would not seem to be unmotivated. In the
end it becomes clear that nobility is not a monopoly of either the
old-fashioned, or of the new-fashioned, hero. As Homer had shown,
there is more than one kind of heroism: there is the stubborn heroism
of an Ajax and there is the more supple heroism of an Odysseus.[12]

Some forty years later Sophocles wrote his *Philoctetes* (about
408 B.C.). There is no ambiguity about the ethics of Odysseus's
conduct here.[13] From beginning to end he is undoubtedly the
villain, though opinions may vary about the degree of his villainy.
Each development in the play reveals a fresh depravity in his
character. First we see him showing a caution near to cowardice
(as in the first scene of *Ajax*), when instead of going himself to spy
out Philoctetes's condition he sends Neoptolemus on the perilous
task. Then he methodically sets about corrupting his generous
young companion.[14] Addressing him first as 'Son of Achilles', he
appeals to his loyalty. He knows how eagerly a well-bred youth
wishes to conform to the adult code of honour, especially when he
is succeeding such an honoured father as Achilles. (Similarly, but
not quite for the same reason, in *Iliad* Nine, Odysseus had dwelt on
Achilles's father, Peleus, when he was endeavouring to rouse Achilles
from his dishonourable lethargy.) Neoptolemus knows that such
an exhortation usually precedes a command and simply replies
'What is your bidding?' The gist of Odysseus's answer is that
Neoptolemus must deceive Philoctetes by a tissue of lies into
surrendering his fateful bow. His last words are as Satanically
demoralizing as anything in European literature: 'I well know that
you are not apt by nature to speak or plan evil things. But be
bold, for victory is a sweet prize to get. *We shall be honest men later
on.* Lend yourself to me for just one day of shamelessness. Afterwards be called the most reverent of men.'

This is the authentic voice of the primeval tempter. Neoptolemus
soon yields to it. Odysseus accepts his consent with a cynical
remark: he, too, when young, thought that physical force could
rule the world; now, disillusioned, he knows how much men's
actions are controlled by words. To Neoptolemus's inquiry whether
Odysseus does not consider lies ugly and shameful, he answers 'Not

if they save the situation', and 'Whenever your action wins gain it is inept to hold back'. Odysseus promises Neoptolemus a double prize for his part in the deceit—a reputation for both valour and wisdom. The Greek here is skilfully chosen to express a wide range of nuance. For again *sophos* could mean 'clever, skilled in technique' as well as 'wise', and *agathos* implies moral goodness as well as martial valour (which was its older, heroic sense), not to mention many other intermediate shades of meaning in these elastic words. Nothing could be more cynical than Odysseus's use of words applicable to lofty wisdom and ethical goodness in such a context of corruption and deceit. But the naïve Neoptolemus is persuaded, and after some further instructions goes out on his dishonourable task.

The sequel is familiar: how Neoptolemus told his lying tale,[15] won Philoctetes's confidence, got possession of the bow; then in an eleventh-hour conversion repudiated all Odysseus's deceits, sided with Philoctetes, and showed the honourable spirit of Achilles his father. Odysseus's efforts to persuade and threaten him into completing his task fail. The last we see of Odysseus is in retreat from Philoctetes's menacing bow. The hint of cowardice is strengthened by the fact that shortly beforehand he had shrunk from a duel with Neoptolemus, at which Neoptolemus had sarcastically remarked 'You showed your self-control', ironically using a form of the word *sophrosyne*, the term used for the quality that Odysseus had so creditably displayed in *Ajax*.[16] Perhaps one may detect some bitterness in the heart of the aged poet here. Sophocles was eighty-seven now and in his later life he had seen what havoc political sophistry could make in a city like Athens. He had seen the distortion of honourable words to serve ambitious and corrupt ends which Thucydides so vividly describes in his history.[17] The gold coinage of language had been debased to worthless gilt. Even his cherished *sophrosyne*, as Neoptolemus sardonically implies, could be applied to pusillanimous discretion.

Various incidental remarks in the play help to vilify Odysseus. He does not care what infamies are spoken of him provided he wins his case (vv. 64–6, 607). He had, indeed, already shown this attitude in his argument with Agamemnon in *Ajax*. But the comparison only illustrates how a difference of context can alter ethical values. There his motive was honourable and his disregard of Agamemnon's uncomplimentary deduction admirable. Here we detest both the motive and the means. Similarly Philoctetes describes him (vv.

633–4) as one who would say or do anything to achieve his ends. The resolute purposefulness, so impressive when applied to honourable tasks, becomes abominable when directed against a weak and suffering comrade-in-arms like Philoctetes. One deft Sophoclean touch shows how much Odysseus has degenerated from his Iliadic stature: when Philoctetes describes Odysseus, as he conceives him, to Neoptolemus, the naïve young hero thinks that he is referring to Thersites.

It has been recognized from early times[18] that here Odysseus represents one of the worst products of the fifth-century sophistic movement—the quibbling, unscrupulous, corrupt, ambitious, self-seeking sophist, rejoicing to make the worse argument appear the better, delighting to corrupt the youth of Athens with insidious arts. His temptation of the young Neoptolemus is a classical example of mental seduction. Sophocles remained optimistic enough to represent it as having failed in the end, when Neoptolemus saw the full implications of Philoctetes's attitude. Cleverness, it is shown, does not always prevail. The heroic ideals of youth are sometimes strong enough to overcome the subtlest dialectic. It is Heracles, symbol of the older type of enduring hero, who speaks the play's final message: 'Show reverence to the gods'.

One plea can be made in justification of Odysseus's conduct: he is acting *pro bono publico*. The bow of Philoctetes is necessary for the conquest of Troy. But it is not implied that the bow could not have been procured by more honourable means. Besides, when Odysseus talks of victory here he obviously values his own personal success as much as the success of the Greek campaign, in a manner that contrasts strongly with his Homeric quality of sinking his own interests in the common cause. As Sophocles presents his motives they are more akin to that subtle interplay of personal ambition and patriotic policy which is always so potent to corrupt the more intelligent politician. With enough ingenious self-justification a political sophist like this can complacently bring himself to abandon every decent scruple, until even the fact that a man is maimed, deserted, agonized, despairing, and a comrade-in-arms, like Philoctetes, will count for nothing, if he owns something worth taking.

If one asks why Sophocles chose Odysseus for this despicable rôle after his noble conduct in *Ajax*, the most probable answer is simply that it served his dramatic purpose to do so. Sophocles was primarily a superb technician in the dramatic art, less of a preacher than Aeschylus, less of a propagandist than Euripides. The fact that in terms of real life it was hardly conceivable for the same man to act so inconsistently would not deter him. In *Philoctetes* he wanted a villain whose resemblance to contemporary sophists would arrest the audience. The Autolycan side of Odysseus, as exaggerated by Pindar and his successors, provided this. So he used it for a powerful, though rather melodramatic, conflict between a clever villain, a suffering martyr, and an ingenuous noble youth. Historical developments in Athens had obviously prepared the way for this, and Sophocles may have had some personal feelings in the matter. But the technical reason is enough to explain all. The honour of merely mythological heroes could not be allowed to stand in the way of a prize-winning play. Indeed, in some ways Sophocles is handling Odysseus here with the same purposeful skill as Odysseus used in handling Neoptolemus, making the better character appear the worse.[19]

Odysseus does not actually appear on the scene for long in any of Euripides's tragedies. But his single appearance in *Hecuba* is unforgettably detestable and he lurks in the background of *Troades* and *Iphigeneia at Aulis* as a sinister, malign influence. (His part in *The Cyclops*[20] and *Rhesus*,[21] if this play is by Euripides, need not be discussed in detail here: both plays are closely derived from Homeric episodes, and have had little influence on the main Ulysses tradition.) As it happened, *Hecuba* became one of the most popular of Euripides's plays in later times, much to Odysseus's disadvantage. Seneca strengthened its influence by conflating it with Euripides's *Troades* in his own *Troades*. Similarly Odysseus's part in the Iphigeneia play was much imitated by French neo-classical dramatists like Rotrou and Racine, with varying degrees of emphasis on his culpability.

Hecuba (produced about 424 B.C.) presents an Odysseus without a redeeming feature. Troy has fallen. According to custom all the adult Trojan males have been slaughtered. The fate of the women and children has now to be determined. The ghost of Achilles has demanded the sacrifice of Polyxena, daughter of Hecuba. Here Euripides chooses to lay the whole blame for her death on Odysseus. The cyclic *Destruction of Troy*, as far as is known, did not implicate Odysseus at all. Possibly Stesichorus—if one can rely on the testimony of the Tabula Iliaca—had involved Odysseus with Neoptolemus and Calchas in the sacrifice. But Euripides makes him bear the whole odium for it. The other Greeks are represented as merciful and compassionate in comparison.

Before Odysseus enters the chorus of captive women describes him as 'that shifty-minded, popularity-seeking, smooth-spoken prater' (v. 13). It is true that the speakers are Trojans, naturally biased against their conqueror. But Euripides's sympathy is clearly on their side and their view, like that of most tragic choruses, may be taken as expressing a widely-held opinion. It would be hard for anyone to win popular approval after such an introduction, and Euripides gives Odysseus no chance to do so. After a highly emotional scene between Hecuba and her daughter, designed to enlist the audience's sympathy on their side, Odysseus enters. Euripides makes him perform the duties normally assigned to a herald, in order to emphasize his harshness. His announcement of Polyxena's doom is brutally laconic. Hecuba appeals to him for mercy. She has reason, she thinks, to hope for special consideration. She reminds him how, when he came into Troy disguised as a beggar, she detected him and spared him. Odysseus admits that the recollection touches him deeply, and acknowledges his debt of gratitude. Hecuba reminds him of his promises to repay her as soon as he could. Now is his opportunity to show his sincerity. Odysseus cynically dismisses those promises as 'speeches devised to avoid death'.[22] At this Hecuba breaks into a scathing denunciation of demagogues who will promise anything to win political advantages, creatures careless of all debts of gratitude and ruthless towards their friends as occasion demands. Here, in other words, Odysseus meets the full tide of Autolycan odium, the furious hatred of a victim of deceptive promises. But we must be on our guard. It may be Euripides who is the deceiver here.

No doubt many simple, kindly Athenians gnashed their teeth at Odysseus's villainous ingratitude, as Hecuba described it. But some of Euripides's more critical hearers may well have asked two pertinent questions. What is the authority for this touching story of Hecuba's kind-heartedness? And what has Odysseus's conduct here to do with political demagogy? Homer had, indeed, related how Helen had encountered Odysseus on his spying expedition into Troy, and had seen through his disguise and treated him kindly. But there is no suggestion in extant earlier Greek literature—though the possibility of some now lost source cannot be excluded—that Hecuba knew anything about it. Besides, if one thinks for a moment and does not let emotion cloud one's critical faculties, does it not imply an entirely improbable situation—that the queen of a be-leaguered city should spare the most dangerous of its enemies when

she has caught him spying? In contrast Helen's help was natural.
She was a Greek, and apparently tired of Troy and Paris by then.
But would all Odysseus's proverbial skill in pleading have persuaded
Hecuba to let him return unscathed with his valuable information
to the Greek camp? It would have been a flagrant betrayal of all
she held dear.[23]

A second consideration is equally damaging to Euripides's carefully contrived villainization of Odysseus. The charge of being a
typical demagogue had been already made against him by Pindar.
In fact there is no justification for it in his Homeric or cyclic career
as we now know it, as the ancient commentators on Homer emphasized. Pindar and Euripides simply chose to distort his character to
make him a whipping-boy for contemporary politicians. Euripides's
presentation here is good theatre, and well calculated to inflame
hostility against Odysseus. But it hardly stands closer examination.

When Hecuba turns again from denunciation to pleading,
Odysseus replies coldly. First he formally discharges his debt of
gratitude to Hecuba by saying that he will keep her personally from
all harm. But Euripides makes it sound more like a politician
wriggling out of a commitment than anything else. Then Odysseus
argues about public as distinct from private debts of gratitude: every
political body must honour its benefactors, especially after their
death, if it hopes to promote loyalty and public spirit. The ghost of
the greatest Greek champion demands the sacrifice of Polyxena. To
refuse it would be both ungrateful and politically inexpedient. 'I
myself', Odysseus adds, 'would be content with few possessions in
this life, provided that my tomb was duly honoured after my
death'. This personal touch closely resembles his remark to Agamemnon in *Ajax*. Uncertainty of dating precludes any deductions
about priority. But the difference of context creates a marked
difference in tone. In *Ajax* Odysseus refers to his own mortality out
of sympathy with a defeated foe. Here in *Hecuba* he refers to his
own ambition to have an honoured grave as part of his argument
in favour of sacrificing Polyxena, and as a statement of personal
agreement with a general principle of political expediency.

His last arguments to Hecuba are frankly chauvinistic. Greek
women have lost many relatives in this war: why should not some
Trojan women suffer now? Blood is thicker than water. If the
Trojans wish, like barbarians, to make no difference between
kindred and enemies and neglect the honour of their illustrious
dead—so much the better for the more pious Greeks. Euripides,

the humanitarian, is, of course, speaking with fierce sarcasm here. He means that if the barbarians are those who refuse to exclude foreigners and strangers from their compassion, then let us turn to those barbarians for hope of a kinder world—as, in fact, he himself did when he left Athens for the court of Archelaus in Macedonia later. Like St. Paul, he turned to the Gentiles.

After Odysseus's callous speech Hecuba makes a last effort. Remembering that he, too, has children, she tells her daughter Polyxena to throw herself at his feet and appeal to his feelings as a father. At this Odysseus draws in his hand and turns away his face, either through a momentary flicker of emotion or else simply to avoid her ritual gestures of supplication, or for both reasons. Later Hecuba offers to die in Polyxena's place. Odysseus insists that this is not what the ghost of Achilles desires. He remains silent while the mother and daughter tearfully part. Then he silently leads the victim away for sacrifice. This is the last that is seen of him in the play.

Apart from the explicit denunciations by the Trojan women who naturally detest Odysseus, Euripides's own dislike of him in this play[24] can hardly be disputed. Euripides visualizes him as the extreme type of chauvinistic and militaristic power-politician, correct as any Nazi Gauleiter and as impervious to personal or emotional appeals. Odysseus has not even the excuse of anger, envy, or vengefulness here, as he had in the Palamedes incident. It is his sheer inhumanity that repels us, and his ability to believe that political loyalty can justify murder. Most sinister of all in the light of recent events in Europe is his convenient doctrine that to class a people as 'barbarians' is a valid reason for treating them as beasts.

Odysseus does not appear personally in Euripides's *Troades* (415 B.C.) but his malign influence pervades the play. It was he, according to Euripides's version, who inexorably urged the death of Astyanax, which is the essence of the tragedy. When Hecuba hears that she is to become his slave she describes him (vv. 281 ff.) as the 'abominable, treacherous, justice-fighting, law-breaking monster with a two-ply tongue'. Cassandra gains some comfort in predicting (vv. 431 ff.) the sufferings of his Odyssean wanderings. The titles of two other plays in this trilogy, *Palamedes* and *Sisyphus*, suggest further antipathy to him.[26]

In Euripides's last play, the *Iphigeneia at Aulis*, Odysseus once more suffers from the principle *les absents ont toujours tort*. He does not come on the scene, but Menelaus and Agamemnon discuss him privately (vv. 522 ff.). They suspect that if they refuse to sacrifice Iphigeneia, he will denounce them to the army to gain popular influence, for nature has made 'that seed of Sisyphus' ever quick to change and to side with the mob.[27] 'Yes', Menelaus replies, 'he is possessed by ambition, that potent curse'. Later in the play (vv. 1362 ff.) it is alleged that Odysseus was ready to compel Iphigeneia's sacrifice by force of arms if necessary. An impartial observer might have pointed out that the expedition was doomed to failure unless the sacrifice took place, and that Odysseus could have been acting purely for the sake of a Greek victory at Troy. But the Atreidae imply, as does Achilles later (vv. 1362–4), that he is exploiting the situation in his own interests. Odysseus is given no opportunity of defending himself.

The theme of selfish ambition was also dominant, apparently, in Euripides's lost *Philoctetes*. In the opening scene Odysseus soliloquizes on the hardships of a career of self-advancement, wondering whether he can really be so intelligent in being prepared to suffer so many trials and dangers for the sake of reputation. Would it not be wiser to live a quiet life free from troubles and business instead of spending himself like this? Then, Miltonically, he reflects, that fame is the spur to greater deeds. With a touch of cynicism he comments, 'surely nothing that lives is more vainglorious than man', and goes off to deceive Philoctetes with a sardonic effrontery, compared with which his villainy in Sophocles's play seemed 'gentle and candid'. Here he is the veteran *politique* valuing his reputation and advancement above both virtue and ease. But he is too intelligent to deceive himself about his motives or to be entirely self-satisfied. There is something almost Shakespearian, or at least post-machiavellian, in this self-consciousness.[28]

These last two plays provide further examples of how Euripides can distort a heroic quality into a contemptible fault. Ambition in the sense of desire for honour and glory—*philotimia*—is the main motive for heroic action in Homer and in much of later Greek literature. 'Ever to be best' was their ideal, and a hero who ignored it was quite exceptional. The same competition for excellence can be observed in Greek athletics and in the literary festivals. If Euripides himself had been entirely exempt from it he would not have competed for the prize at the Dionysia. Ambition can, of course, be a grave moral fault. But without it the whole heroic world would have collapsed in lethargy and torpor. Further, the Homeric Odysseus, as has been described, was much less under the influence of the desire to win glory than any other hero. With a few lapses, as in the Cyclops incident, he observed the Delphic maxim of 'Nothing in excess' almost as faithfully as Socrates. Lucian in his *Dialogues of the dead* (29) is more faithful to the Homeric spirit than Euripides in this matter. In Hades, Agamemnon asks Ajax why he had spurned Odysseus's friendly approaches (as described in chapter seven). Ajax reaffirms his implacable hatred. Agamemnon argues that, after all, Odysseus had only aimed at 'that most pleasant thing, renown' in the contest for Achilles's arms. His efforts to gain the prize were, he insists, just what one would have expected from any normal hero. The fact is that Odysseus's conduct in the earlier tradition gives no special grounds for charges of ambition and self-aggrandisement. Euripides is heaping on Odysseus the dislike he felt for the upstart Cleons of his own time.

It is seldom possible to prove that an author's attitude is identical with that of his characters, but most critics have agreed that Euripides is less detached from the opinions expressed by the sympathetic figures in his plays than Sophocles. His consistent tone of antipathy and disparagement towards Odysseus in the plays already mentioned —and a similar impression is made by the fragments of his plays on the Ulysses theme—in contrast with the two-sidedness of Sophocles's approach in *Ajax* and *Philoctetes*, seems to confirm the view that Euripides personally disliked the character of Odysseus as he saw it. What most repelled Euripides, apparently, was Odysseus's inhumanity in his treatment of the weak, no matter how much the doctrine of the greater good of the greater number seemed to justify it. Euripides had a unique sympathy for the individual in the grip of ruthless personal forces, and at times, unlike Sophocles, he seems to have allowed his feelings to overcome his dramatic technique. Euripides, again in contrast with Sophocles, had not been very successful himself in his own career. He had suffered much from the calumnies of witty and unscrupulous contemporaries. That is not to say that he was simply working off his personal spleen on Odysseus. But his own experience enabled him to understand the pathos of the losing side in life. Doubtless considerations of dramatic technique contributed to his villainization of Odysseus, but less, it would seem, than in Sophocles's more objective portraits.

Euripides's influence on the later Ulysses tradition was great, especially when reinforced by Seneca's adaptation of his *Hecuba* and *Troades*. As a result the standard role for Ulysses in European drama was that of the crafty man of policies, sometimes directing affairs with malign omniscience, sometimes merely executing the commands of others with inexorable precision. Obviously Euripides was not solely responsible for this.[28] Pindar, Aeschylus, Sophocles, and others to be mentioned in the following chapters, combined to bring Odysseus into contempt. But it was Euripides who most successfully enlisted the deeper feelings of his own contemporaries and of posterity against the grandson of Autolycus and favourite of Athene.

If one accepts Euripides's portrait of Odysseus as a cynical but unrepentant power-politician, a disillusioned but unrelenting careerist, the well-known scene at the end of Plato's *Republic* forms a fitting epilogue to his earthly life.[29] It comes at the end of the Vision of Er. The souls of Homeric heroes are assembling to choose bodies for their next reincarnation. Ajax, still angry at his defeat in the award of Achilles's arms, chooses to be a lion, symbol of unbounded strength and courage. Agamemnon takes the body of an eagle, unassailable lord of the sky. Thersites, ambitious for consummate buffoonery, would like to enter the body of an ape. Last of all comes the soul of Odysseus. He now knows the futility of all ambition. What he seeks is the life of some humble citizen unoccupied with public affairs. He searches for it among the lives that the previous heroes had tossed aside like unwanted bargains at a sale. It is not easy to find. When he comes to it, he seizes it gladly. Even if he had been given first choice, he says, he would have chosen this 'unofficial' life above all others.

Plato shows genuine sympathy here. If Odysseus had been all that fifth-century writers had said, ambitious, unscrupulous, unsuccessfully successful, disliked by the good, denounced by the honest, well might he have chosen the *fallentis semita vitae* for his next life. And from another point of view Plato's vision was uncannily prophetic. When after many vicissitudes in the literatures of Italy, France, Germany, England, and Spain, Ulysses came to choose his fullest and perhaps greatest metamorphosis since the *Odyssey*, he did take the body of a 'private, unofficial person'—the bourgeois 'hero' of Joyce's *Ulysses*.

CHAPTER IX

ULYSSES AMONG ALEXANDRIANS
AND STOICS

PLATO'S vision of Odysseus in the underworld is almost the last
product of true mythopoeic imagination in the classical Ulysses
tradition. Odysseus remained a favourite theme for poets, philosophers, and rhetoricians, until the end of the classical period. But
none of the creative writers of the post-Platonic period chose to
present an entirely new conception of Homer's hero. Certain
important features were added to the tradition, features which
would influence the medieval and modern tradition strongly, but
they were more arbitrary, more clearly the product of deliberate
policy, than in earlier phases. When Aeschylus, for example, had
wished to emphasize Odysseus's villainous treachery he was bold
enough to make a definite variation in the 'facts' of the myth by
alleging that Odysseus's father had been Sisyphus, not Laertes.
Similarly Euripides in his *Troades* seems to have invented the story
of how Hecuba took pity on Odysseus when he entered Troy as a
spy, simply to make a poignant contrast with Odysseus's ruthlessness
towards Hecuba after the capture of Troy. But the later Greek and
the Roman writers (except those who were deliberately anti-
Homeric, as will be discussed in the next chapter) tended to avoid
altering the myth itself. They preferred to get the effect they wanted
by offering new interpretations of the accepted episodes. The
difference can be put figuratively. The Odysseus of the period from
Homer to Plato changes his own colour like a chameleon or an
octopus—to use the analogies suggested by Eustathius and Theognis.
In the later periods he loses this personal adaptability: now the
changes in his appearance are due, as it were, to lights of different
colours thrown on him from outside, as on an actor in the modern
theatre—the green light of envy, the yellow light of jealousy, the
red light of anger, the rose light of romanticism, and (but rarely)
the white light of truth.

In other words Odysseus becomes more and more a puppet of
conflicting ideologies, less and less a figure charged with mythopoeic
power. His traditional qualities, especially the more ambiguous
ones, are now manipulated and re-orientated to suit prevailing

policies and doctrines. Literary, philosophical, political, and social cross-currents toss his reputation up and down like a cork on the tideway. If a Ptolemy or a Caesar happens to admire him, Odysseus is praised.[1] If state policy or court etiquette finds him reprehensible, he is duly reprehended by flattering bards and scribes. But he was too challenging a figure to be ignored, too adaptable to become stereotyped.

Meanwhile, too, by the end of the first century B.C. the whole literary tradition had become scattered and confused. European literature was no longer the perquisite of a few hundred square miles of Greek-speaking territory. After Alexander's Asiatic conquest new modes of thought and new attitudes to religion had confused and enriched the tradition. Now Alexandria, Antioch, Pergamum, Rome, Constantinople, and in time even Gaul, interpreted the Troy Tale in varying ways and in various languages. The comparatively simple Hellenic culture had passed into the complex Hellenistic congeries of cultures. A certain central Hellenism remained at the core of European literature to the end of the classical period, but the peripheral variations were immense.

No attempt will be made here to trace Odysseus's fortunes through all the by-ways of Alexandrian, Latin, and Byzantine literature. Most of the details have been collected elsewhere. As far as the main Ulysses tradition is concerned it will be sufficient to consider the effects of four new influences in the post-Platonic period. The three most important of these were Stoicism, Roman imperialism, and anti-Homeric propaganda. The fourth had no great effect on the classical tradition but became dominant for a while in seventeenth-century literature. This may be briefly discussed first.

The elaborate court etiquette, which became so marked a feature of later European monarchies, first entered the Hellenic world at Alexandria under the Ptolemies. With it came a certain niceness about the ruder manifestations of nature in the raw. This was an ambiguous attitude. Some might call it primness or prudery; others delicacy or refinement. At any rate, it is among Alexandrian scholars that one first finds a tendency to shy away from the cruder actions and expressions of the Heroic Age. Earlier critics had, as has been noticed, found fault with Homer's theology, philosophy, and ethics. But the Alexandrians were the first to be perturbed about his heroes' manners. Where feasible they introduced emendations to remove offending details or else recommended that the

passages containing them should be deleted. Where emendation
was impracticable, they recorded their censure in the margin. The
Odyssey shocked them more than the *Iliad*, because its situations were
less conventional. Consequently Odysseus incurred a good many
of their rebukes.[2] He had, for instance, an unfortunate habit of
appearing in a state of nakedness at times. Sometimes he could not
help it, as in his first encounter with Nausicaa (where he did his
best to clothe himself with a leafy branch). But need he have
'stripped off his rags' before his final attack on the Suitors? Should
we not save decorum (for this hero fighting his final deadly battle
against tremendous odds) by assuring ourselves that Homer intended
him to retain the minimum required for Alexandrian decency?
Then there were those references in the *Odyssey* which seem to
imply that young ladies bathed gentlemen in person. Would it not
be more proper to understand the verb used by Homer as having a
different force, so that the young princesses would simply 'cause to
be bathed', and all is *comme il faut*. Here the courtiers of Alexandria
bow in solemn collusion with a prime minister of Queen Victoria;
for Gladstone also pleaded for the more refined causative.[3] Alas,
stricter grammarians continued to prefer the unseemly transitive.
But some consolation might be found in the fact that according to
a late tradition Nestor's daughter (who personally bathed Telemachus) married him afterwards.

Objections were also lodged against Odysseus's healthy appetite[4]
—for the ethical gulf between a well-fed courtier and a shipwrecked
sailor is not easily bridged—and against his, and Homer's, racy
language. But no sustained indictment of Odysseus's manners has
survived from the classical period. One has to search through the
multifarious ancient commentaries on the Homeric poems to find
these scattered complaints. It was left to a seventeenth-century
French critic, René Rapin, to produce the most scornful and
vituperative attack on the manners of Ulysses and Homer in terms
of artificial decorum. His strictures, though Le Bossu and Fénelon
hastened to rebut them, had a lasting influence on Ulysses's reputation in France and England.[5] Even so ardent an admirer of Homer
as Alexander Pope was affected by them; and one still finds vestiges
of this appeal to decorum in contemporary Homeric criticism.

In view of the positive hostility to Homer that is found elsewhere
during the later classical period, one must remember that the
Alexandrians wished to justify Homer rather than to condemn him.
Even their most snobbish emendations and interpretations were, on

the whole, well meant. Homer's poems had been Alexander's bedside book during his campaigns, and they remained an object of veneration under the Ptolemies. But, though the motive of the Ptolemaic scholars was to improve Homer and to ennoble Ulysses, their criticisms eventually served to strengthen anti-Homeric and anti-Ulyssean feeling both in classical and in modern times. They had, however, much less influence on the development of the Ulysses tradition than the attitudes next to be considered.

Chronologically the Stoic influence is earlier, of course, than the Alexandrian. Zeno, the founder of the school, who flourished about 300 B.C., emphasized the moral value of the Homeric poems,[6] and wrote a commentary defending them from the strictures of 'Homer-scourgers' like Zoïlus. None of Zeno's specific references to Odysseus survives; but it was probably through him that the later Stoics came to admire Odysseus as the ideal *homo viator*. They paid more attention to Odysseus's Odyssean adventures than to his Iliadic career. Through their ingenious use of allegorical interpretation the *Odyssey* became a kind of Stoic *Pilgrim's Progress*. Special emphasis was laid on Odysseus's courage, resourcefulness, endurance, and piety, as displayed in his wanderings and his home-coming. Thus Epictetus[7] mentions him particularly as a type of the Stoic Citizen of the World, and as one who could be an outstanding figure even in rags (a reminder of the Stoics' debt to the Cynics). On the other hand, Epictetus admits that Odysseus is open to criticism for having been overtearful at times. Perhaps the philosopher was influenced by Roman austerity in this. Cicero had remarked (*Tusculan Disputations* 2, 21, 48 and 50) that Pacuvius in his version of the *Niptra* had done well to make Ulysses weep less after being wounded than he did in the play by Sophocles: 'for that most wise (or philosophical)[8] man of Greece should not make excessive lamentations'. Cicero specially commended Ulysses's moderation as portrayed by the Roman Pacuvius in the same play when in his dying words he exclaims

> To grieve at hostile fortune, not to bewail it,
> Is what becomes a man. Tears are for womanly minds.

'Thus', Cicero continues, 'the softer element in Ulysses's spirit obeyed the rational part, as a respectful soldier obeys a stern general. . . . In this lies the perfection of wisdom (or philosophy).'

Here the Stoic critics touch on a quality of the ancient heroes in general which has perturbed other readers. This is their proneness to abundant tears. These were not, indeed, tears of cowardice or weakness, but tears for the sorrows of their friends, tears for their own unhappiness or frustration, and even at times (as with Aeneas) *lacrimae rerum*, tears found in the nature of things. Achilles in indignation at Agamemnon's seizure of Briseis goes weeping to his mother on the seashore (*Il.* 1, 348 ff.). Odysseus never weeps in the *Iliad*. But in the *Odyssey* he often does, sometimes with extraordinary abandon.[9] Thus when Circe has told him (*Od.* 10, 496 ff.) that he must visit the Land of Shades before he returns to Ithaca, he rolls about in an agony of lamentation.

No one in the Homeric poems expresses surprise or scorn at these outbursts. But to later critics they seemed ridiculous as well as unstoical. Dryden expressed the British attitude, the tradition of the stiff upper lip, when he referred to Virgil's Aeneas as 'a kind of St. Swithen-Heroe, always Raining'.[10] Yet this sterner convention is only a convention, and one still honoured less in Mediterranean regions than in the colder North. And the convention has varied from era to era in the same country: Shakespeare's characters are nearer the Homeric pattern in this. It was chiefly in the seventeenth century that stoical imperturbability became the rule again for well-bred Europeans—to the detriment of literature and life. Decorum can demand too much of nature. To insist that a hero should not weep implies the fallacy that tears are necessarily a sign of weakness. They are seldom, if ever, this with Homer's heroes. For them tears bring welcome relief after dolorous deeds, or express their feelings when a desired consummation is prevented. Sympathy, mourning, anger, frustration, yearning, are the chief causes of their grief, not present pain or fear. If one of the Suitors, seeing Odysseus's tears when he met his dog Argos in Ithaca, had concluded that his spirit had been broken and his ferocity sapped by his wanderings, he would soon have learned his mistake. Here, once again, the Elizabethan poet-warrior, tearful in his sonnets, blood-thirsty in his boots, comes nearest to the Homeric Odysseus.

But, apart from his tears, Ulysses was generally an admired figure among Stoics, both Greek and Roman. His most famous eulogy was composed almost two centuries after Zeno and a century before Epictetus. It comes, rather unexpectedly, in the first book of Horace's *Epistles*. There, in the second letter of the collection, Horace tells his friend Lollius that he has been reading Homer again. Homer, it seems to him, is better than any professional Stoic or Academic at expounding what is beautiful, ugly, useful, and harmful in life. The *Iliad* displays the harm done by folly and passion. It shows how powerless wise men are at times to prevent the disastrous consequences of passion. Horace does not mention Ulysses yet. But his concluding remark on the Troy Tale will provide a contrast with Virgil's chauvinistic view. All the sufferings at Troy were due to uncontrolled passions:

> When leaders rage, the host must bear the blows.
> By plots, and wiles, and crimes, and lust, and wrath,
> Grave wrongs are done inside and outside Troy.

Here Horace transcends Euripidean or Virgilian partisanship, and sees, as every wise moralist, Christian and pagan alike, has seen, that the sources of war and violence lie not in racial differences but in the human heart.

Next Horace briefly considers the story of the *Odyssey*. Its message is different. It tells how much *virtus*—that great Romano-stoical concept—can achieve amid the harshest tribulations:

> And then, again, he sets before our eyes,
> Choice pattern of the manly and the wise,
> Ulysses; who when Troy he overthrew,
> With wise intent proceeded to review
> The cities and the ways of many men,
> And, o'er the wide sea, as he sought to gain
> Some means to compass the return to home
> Of him and of his comrades, did become
> Victim of many hardships, yet not doomed
> Beneath ill fortune's waves to be entombed.
>
> (Murison's translation)

What a contrast there is, Horace adds, between this stoical hero and such slack semi-Epicureans as himself, who spend their time in feasting and pleasure like Penelope's Suitors or the Phaeacians.[11] His final word of advice to Lollius is to master the enticements of pleasure, to control passion, and to avoid corruption.

Elsewhere Horace, with characteristic inconsistency, makes some conventionally disparaging remarks about Ulysses. But on the whole he seems to have admired him and to have sympathized with his sufferings.[12] The popularity of his Epistle to Lollius in medieval and neo-classical times ensured that Ulysses had one staunch defender in the Western tradition. The fact that the letter was not an incidental passage in some elaborate treatise, but a unity in itself, phrased with attractive informality, made it all the more effective among less erudite readers.

Other influential Romans were also on Ulysses's side. Cicero, also mainly for Stoic reasons, often refers to him appreciatively. His celebrated remarks (*De Finibus*, 5, 18, 49) on Ulysses's encounter with the Sirens have been mentioned in chapter five. His interpretation is essentially Greek in spirit. To a Roman (but Cicero does not say this) the Sirens would probably have offered power and glory, the kingdoms of the world. To a more sensual Greek than Ulysses the charm or novelty of their song's music might have been sufficient allurement. But, as Cicero points out, Homer saw that the greatest temptation to a man like Ulysses would be the offer of fresh knowledge, the promise that whoever stayed with them

> Post variis avido satiatus pectore Musis
> doctior ad patrias lapsus pervenerit oras.

In Cicero's rather laborious exposition, an interview with the Sirens begins to sound like an honours course in *Litterae humaniores* among the learned ladies of Tennyson's *Princess* or an audience with Molière's *Précieuses ridicules*. But his main point is sound, and his praise of Homer's skill and Ulysses's prudence is justified. Yet, curiously, it failed to convince Dante that Ulysses could resist the *discendi cupiditas*.[13]

Leaving for a moment the Stoic influence, one may note in passing what is perhaps a personal touch in Cicero's appraisal of Ulysses. In *De officiis* 1, 31, 113, he remarks on two special features of Odysseus's adventures in the *Odyssey*—his subjection to Circe and Calypso, and his unremitting affability towards all he met. The second quality had not been emphasized before. Why did Cicero remark on it specially? Was it because as a *novus homo* and an ambitious politician he had good reason to be aware of its social and political value? Among the Roman patricians Cicero must have felt sometimes what the grandson of Autolycus felt among the Aeacids and Atreidae at Troy. Among the plebeians he may sometimes have thought of the crude manners of the Cyclops and the Suitors. In the same passage he specifically notes how resolutely Ulysses bore the abuse of menservants and maidservants 'so that he might come to what he desired'. Possibly Cicero himself in the early stages of his career had endured the *contumelias servorum ancillarumque* in some aristocratic house, while he waited for an audience, like Samuel Johnson at Lord Chesterfield's. At all events there is no doubt about Cicero's final remark in this passage: Ajax would have preferred to suffer death a thousand times than to brook such indignities as Ulysses endured.

Other Latin writers followed Horace and Cicero in admiring Ulysses's patience, prudence, and fortitude. Seneca, when he was not writing plays in the Euripidean manner, praised him (with that other Cynic and Stoic hero, Hercules) as one 'unconquered by labours, scorning pleasures, victorious in all lands' (*De const. sap.* 2). The storms and sufferings of daily life are prefigured in the story of Ulysses (*Epistles* 88, 5); with Ulysses as an exemplar one can learn patriotism, love for one's wife and father (why not mother? one may ask), and how, even after shipwreck, one can reach the goal of an honourable life. If one is as prudent as Ulysses one can escape the Siren voices of pleasure, which in ordinary life allure us not from one rock alone but from every quarter of the world (*Epistles* 123, 12; 56, 14; 31, 1, 2). Seneca reproves (*Dialogues* 10, 13, 2; *Epistles* 12, 345) those who ignore the moral lessons of the *Odyssey* and pay attention only to academic speculations ('the Greek disease' as he calls it) as to how many rowers Ulysses had and whether his voyages were confined to the Mediterranean (as Aristarchus held) or extended also to the Atlantic (as Crates believed). Once, indeed, he seems to have felt rather tired of Stoic preoccupations with the *Odyssey*. He rebukes Lucilius (*Epistles* 88, § 7) for inquiring too zealously about the voyages of Ulysses and the chastity of Penelope when he should have been considering the perturbations of his own mind and the state of his own virtue. He is less edifying when he suggests, from his own experiences on board ship, that Ulysses was prone to sea-sickness. This is Seneca's most original contribution to the Ulysses legend.[14]

The influence of Stoic admiration for Ulysses can be traced continuously through the later tradition. It is found in Plutarch,[15] Apuleius, Marcus Aurelius,[16] several Fathers of the Church, and in the later ecclesiastical writers. Two features remain constant: first the tendency to dwell on Ulysses's Odyssean career rather than on his exploits in the *Iliad* and the Cycle. This evaded awkward questions about his conduct towards Palamedes, Philoctetes, and the captive Trojans; but from the literary point of view it did harm by dividing up the complex personality of the Homeric hero. The second feature, the elaborate use of allegorical interpretation, deserves further attention, for it greatly enriched the post-classical evolution of the Ulysses myth.[17]

As has been mentioned in chapter seven, allegory was used as

early as the sixth century B.C. by Theagenes of Rhegium as a
means of defending Homer from the strictures of Ionian philosophers. Little is known of this earlier school of allegorists. The
earliest surviving study of the allegorical aspects of the Homeric
poems is the *Homeric Allegories* of Heracleitos (first century A.D.),
already cited in chapter three.[18] It strongly influenced the later
allegorical tradition, and deserves special attention. The introduction makes it clear that its primary object is to defend Homer
from the strictures of fourth-century philosophers. Heracleitus
claims esoteric knowledge for himself and his school: 'Let us,
who have been purified in the sacred lustrations, trace back the
mystic truth, submitting ourselves to the discipline of the poems'.
As for the anti-Homeric philosophers—'Let Plato, the parasite, the
traducer of Homer, be thrown out. . . . Of Epicurus we take no
heed . . . ingrates both who, though they owe most of their knowledge to Homer, yet treat him with such impiety.' He goes on to
illustrate the allegorical method from Archilochus's poems on the
Ship of State and Anacreon's use of the metaphor of the skittish
filly to describe an arch woman. He notes that Ulysses himself used
the allegorical method when (in *Il.* 19, 222–4) he spoke of battle in
terms of harvesting.

   Heracleitus's main object is to exonerate Homer from the charge
of blaspheming against the gods. Their conduct in the *Iliad* can,
he claims, be explained quite satisfactorily by means of allegory.
His remarks on Athene (as cited already in chapter three) are typical
of his extraordinary ingenuity. When he turns from the 'energetic
and warlike' *Iliad* to the 'ethical' *Odyssey* (§ 60), he devotes less of
his attention to theology and more to utilitarian philosophy. If one
is willing to examine the *Odyssey* carefully, he asserts (§ 70) one
will find that the wanderings of Odysseus are, for the most part,
allegories. In fact, Homer took Odysseus as a kind of 'instrument
of all manly virtue' and expounded his philosophy through him,
because he hated the evils that batten on human life. The Lotus-
eaters represent the temptation of exotic food, the Cyclops the
menace of savage anger, Circe the allurement of strange vices,
Charybdis voracious extravagance, Scylla multifarious shamelessness, the Cattle of the Sun, the pangs of hunger. Odysseus's journey
to the Land of Shades is an allegory of the fact that intelligence is
prepared even to search out the secrets of the underworld. When
Odysseus listens to the Sirens he shows the desire to know 'the deep
lore of all the ages'. The *moly* plant which Hermes ('the rational

intelligence') gives him as a protection against Circe's magic is also an emblem of intelligence.

With such interpretations as these Heracleitus is convinced that he has entirely vindicated the poet. Homer, he enthusiastically asserts, is 'the great hierophant of Heaven and of the gods, who opened to men's souls the closed and untrodden paths to Heaven'. How misguided, then, of Plato to banish him from his Republic and Epicurus from his garden!

This energetic and arresting work was the foundation of a massive edifice of allegorical speculation in later times. Often these allegories were far removed from anything that Homer was likely to have dreamed of. Cleanthes, for example, argued that the *moly* was etymologically connected with the verb *molunein* 'to soften' and represented the reasoning faculty 'by which the impulses and passions are softened'.[19] Another commentator explained that the single eye of the Cyclops was (being unusually near the brain) a sign of special prudence, so that Ulysses's superior prudence was proved by his success in outwitting the monster.[20] Later, under neo-Platonic influence, the interpretations lost touch with the character of Ulysses, and strayed into trivial details, as in Porphyry's celebrated allegorization of the cave of the nymphs in *Odyssey* Thirteen. Here the imaginative element has become so strong that one can hardly describe the work as a commentary at all. Eventually, in fact, the allegorical method ceased to be a means of extracting Homer's esoteric meaning and became a source of creative literature in itself, as a later chapter will illustrate.

CHAPTER X

VIRGIL'S ULYSSES

AS the Roman people grew conscious of their political greatness, their writers began to create a national mythology to fill the blank spaces in the nation's pre-historic past. The first essential was to decide on an illustrious genealogy for the original dynasty of Latin rulers. All agreed that the Latins must have been named after a king Latinus and Rome after someone called Romulus or Roma. But, just as no respectable Irish chieftain was satisfied with a pedigree that fell short of Noah, the Romans and Latins felt that their origins should be traced back to the earliest recorded event in European history, the Trojan War. The problem was which side they should adopt as their progenitors. Enterprising Greek mythologists had made an early effort to enrol the Latins on the Greek side. The earliest evidence of this tendency is found in Hesiod's *Theogony* (vv. 1011–16): 'And Circe the daughter of Helios, Hyperion's son, in love with the enduring Odysseus, bore Agrios and Latinos, who was blameless and strong; and she also brought forth Telegonus by the will of golden Aphrodite. They then ruled among the renowned Tyrsenians (Etruscans) in a recess of the holy islands far away.' Unfortunately the authenticity of the passage is disputed; but even if interpolated it is probably earlier than all other references to the genealogy of Latinus.[1]

This (with some minor variations) was the pedigree that Greek genealogists offered the questing Roman writers. It provided a clear line of descent from Ulysses, and thence back to his great-grandfather Zeus. It had strong attractions. Long-established tradition had linked parts of the south-western coast of Italy with Odysseus and Circe. The *Telegoni iuga parricidae*, as Horace calls them, and the *Circaea terra* of *Aeneid* Seven, were familiar localities to Romans.[2] When Horace wrote of wine that matured in a Laestrygonian jar, his readers would accept the assumption that the Laestrygonians of *Odyssey* Ten were a primitive Italian tribe. The powerful *gens Mamilia* asserted that they were descended from Ulysses as well as from Tarquin the Proud. But the destiny of Rome lay with the *gens Iulia*.

There were stronger reasons why the Roman genealogists should

reject Ulysses as their heroic progenitor. Politically, although he
represented the winning side at Troy, he now, as a Greek, represented the losing side in the struggle for supremacy between the
Hellenistic and the Roman powers. Further, it would be remembered that Ulysses's dominions were insignificant compared with
Troy or the mainland kingdoms of Greece. Ethically, despite the
approval of the Stoics, his characteristic Greek resourcefulness and
subtlety conflicted with the deep-seated Roman admiration for
stability and directness. Livius Andronicus in his primitive version
of the *Odyssey* had translated Homer's ambiguous term *polytropos*
as *versutus*, 'the man of turns', aptly enough. But to a serious-
minded Roman senator of a century or so later, the man of *gravitas*
and *maiestas*, the term would suggest something of a mountebank
and a trickster, something, in fact, of an Autolycus, as to modern
cars 'the man of many turns' conveys a hint of the circus clown or
the music-hall actor.

There was, in fact, a fundamental difference of temperament
between the more characteristic Roman heroes, like Regulus, Cato,
or Pompey, and the more supple Greek type. Doubtless if Regulus
had exercised some ingenuity he might have twisted his way out of
his pledge to the Carthaginians by means of an Autolycan ambiguity.
But it meant far more for Roman morale that he preferred to give
a simple promise and honour it at the cost of his life. The younger
Cato, too, with his fidelity to the losing party, won Lucan's admiration, not the versatile ones who showed skill in shifting over to the
more comfortable side of the Ship of State.[3] One can see this
Roman scorn for mere resourcefulness and versatility in Juvenal's
famous diatribe on the hungry Greeklings who infested imperial
Rome.[4] *Non possum ferre, Quirites, Graecam urbem.*

Reasons like these, partly political, partly temperamental, made
Romans reluctant to accept the grandson of Autolycus as an
ancestor, even though on his father's side he was descended from
Zeus, and despite Homer's powerful patronage. In other circumstances the Roman mythologists might have chosen to emphasize
Ulysses's piety, endurance, courage, eloquence, and the special
favour of Athene, as the Stoics had done. But Virgil decided to
canonize Aeneas as the heroic ancestor of the Roman line—a por-
tentous decision for the development of the Ulysses tradition. He
could hardly have done otherwise if he wished to please Augustus
and the Roman people.

This second genealogical theory was at least as old as the fourth

century B.C., when the Sicilian historian Timaeus suggested that
the Latin kings were descended from Aeneas, prince of Troy, and
not from any Greek. It is uncertain whether this was his own
invention or based on an older tradition, and there is no evidence to
show why he advocated the Trojan pedigree. There was little
inducement for a Greek writer to favour the insignificant Romans
at that time. On the other hand, the motive of Lycophron, the first
poet to exploit this Trojano-Roman genealogy, seems clear. There
is every reason to believe that he wished to exalt the ascendant
Roman power. Writing at Alexandria some time after Timaeus
Lycophron accepted the view that Aeneas was the progenitor of the
Roman kings, and, what is more important for the present study,
decided that this demanded a corresponding vilification of the
Greeks in general and of Ulysses in particular. This was ungenerous
and unnecessary. A more magnanimous writer might have seen
that one could admit the good qualities of the conquerors of Troy
without detracting from the virtues of the defeated Trojans. But
Lycophron chose the more ignoble way. His Cassandra prefaces her
prophecy of the foundation of Rome by Aeneas's descendants with
a flood of embittered abuse against the Greeks, especially Ulysses.
Her denunciations rely for the most part on previously known
calumnies. Odysseus is 'the crooked Sisyphan fox', 'the dolphin-
ensigned stealer of the Phoenician goddess'.[5] The prophetess gloats
on the horrors of his Odyssean voyages (659 ff.). Accepting a
calumny completely alien to the Homeric poems, she emphasizes
the fact that Penelope played the harlot and wasted his wealth in his
absence. All the disasters of his last days, as imagined by the post-
Homeric writers, are then enumerated in a hodge-podge of confused
mythology. Cassandra triumphantly concludes: 'Then after he has
witnessed such a mass of woes he will go back again to Hades
(whence there is no return) without having seen a single calm
day in his life'.[6]

Had Lycophron been the only poet to combine belief in the
Aenean descent of the Roman kings with denigration of Ulysses,
Ulysses's reputation might have suffered little. The obscurity of the
Alexandra is notorious, and when one pierces the leaden curtain of
far-fetched allusion and sciolistic gloss there is little literary reward.
But when Virgil adopted the same double-edged policy in his
Aeneid the whole later tradition was drastically affected. Virgil's
political purpose was clear. He intended to write the great national

epic of the Romans, a poem to rival or surpass Homer's *Iliad* and *Odyssey*—*nescio quid maius nascitur Iliade*. But—and this is the question that concerns us here—what were his personal feelings about the Ulysses whom he for a political, indeed, it would hardly be unfair to say a chauvinistic, reason decided to vilify?

The cursory reader of the second book of the *Aeneid* can hardly be blamed if he gets a strong impression that Virgil detested Ulysses. He is described as harsh, dreadful, envious, plausible, cruel, and a 'deviser of crimes'. In other words the villainous power-politician of Euripides seems to come to life again under Virgil's hand. But, though the resulting portrait is similar, there is a fundamental difference between the motives of the two poets. When Greek Euripides deplored (or, at least, made his characters deplore) the ruthlessness and unscrupulousness of Greek Ulysses, he had to divest himself of natural bias towards the Greek cause. One can attribute this to disillusioned cynicism or to warm humanitarian feeling for a conquered people. But one can hardly attribute it to any desire for popularity or self-advancement on Euripides's part. He had little to gain except notoriety from exposing the faults of the Homeric Greeks. His plays won few prizes. It was quite a different matter for a Roman poet, writing for an imperial patron who claimed descent from Trojans, to denigrate the Greek leaders at Troy. Virgil had much to gain by presenting Ulysses, the ultimate vanquisher of Troy, as a scoundrel. Yet is it likely that so sensitive and reverent an artist as Virgil would stoop to such a policy of crude slander? After all, Ulysses was Homer's favourite hero, and though Virgil never explicitly states any veneration for the father of epic, his mind was obviously steeped in Homer's poetry. Plagiarism was not regarded as a crime in those days. But a poet who with one hand borrowed and adapted a predecessor's best lines and scenes and with the other blackened his most characteristic hero would be going, one feels, just too far. *Pietas* has its place in literature as well as in patriotism; and Virgil was the least likely of Roman poets to violate it.

It may be worth while then to re-examine the circumstances of Ulysses's denigration in *Aeneid* Two. At Dido's request Aeneas is recounting the capture and sack of Troy. 'Who among the Myrmidons or Dolopes, who even among the soldiery of harsh Ulysses, would restrain his tears in telling such sufferings?' It was not, Aeneas insists, a victory of valour over valour—what conquered general ever admitted that?—but a victory of Greek wile and treachery (*doli, error, insidiae*) over honest dealers. Later on Aeneas refers to Ulysses as dreadful (*dirus*). But he uses no more opprobrious epithet.

So far the attitude towards Ulysses and the Greeks is only what one would expect from a vanquished prince, especially in a Roman poem. Aeneas's epithets for Ulysses, 'harsh', 'dreadful', are not contemptuous. They belong to the normal language of the defeated refugee. It was only natural, too, that Aeneas should utter a curse when he sailed past Ithaca (3, 272–3). But a change comes over the tone of the narrative as soon as the despicable Sinon (who according to a late tradition was Ulysses's cousin) appears in it. Here Virgil separates himself, as it were, from the story by a further remove. For a while Aeneas no longer recounts events which he had experienced personally, but tells only what the false Sinon told. In other words we have neither Virgil's nor Aeneas's word for the subsequent denunciations of Ulysses, but only Sinon's.

Sinon clearly is not interested in truth. His sole object is to win the confidence of the Trojans. He knows that, since Achilles is now dead, the man they most fear is Ulysses. So he craftily curries favour with them by vilifying him. He introduces himself as a relative of Palamedes. After Palamedes had been killed 'through the envy of the plausible Ulysses', he, Sinon, had been compelled to lead a life of sorrow and obscurity. When he ventured to deplore Palamedes's death and to threaten vengeance, Ulysses had conducted a diabolical campaign of slander and popular agitation against him. This reached its climax when, at Apollo's demand for a human sacrifice from among the Greeks, Ulysses had coerced the prophet Calchas into proclaiming Sinon as the victim. Ulysses's violence towards the venerable prophet (whom medieval writers turned into a bishop) is emphasized: Ulysses 'drags' him out, 'demands' an answer, 'compels him with mighty shouts'.

Having described his subsequent escape, Sinon goes on to refer to the stealing of the Palladium by 'impious' Diomedes and Ulysses, the 'deviser of crimes' (*scelerum inventor*). The Wooden Horse, Sinon asserts, is nothing but a portent of Minerva's wrath at this sacrilege. If the Trojans will bring it into their city they will not merely survive the present war but will also be enabled in time to invade Greece.

The Trojans are very soon seduced by his crafty rhetoric.

The *ars Pelasga* triumphs over credulous virtue. Aeneas himself points the moral of the story:

> With such deceits he gained their easy hearts,
> Too prone to credit his perfidious arts.
> What Diomede, nor Thetis' greater son,
> A thousand ships, nor ten year's siege had done,
> False tears and fawning words the city won.
>
> (Dryden's version)

If one compares the references to Ulysses here (and the few others found scattered through the poem later) with those in Homer, Pindar, Horace, or Statius, one finds a marked distinction. Each of those poets gives his own view of Ulysses by means of epithets or comments in direct narrative. Virgil never does this. He leaves it to Aeneas and Sinon, and in later books, to Trojan Deiphobus, a companion of Ulysses's voyages, and a Rutulian prince, to make any comments that have to be made.[7] Why?

This is hardly an accident. Virgil often comments directly on other characters. Perhaps, then, this oblique method of depreciation was Virgil's device for avoiding a direct attack on Homer's favourite hero.[8] On the one hand Virgil was committed, by the fact that he was writing the national epic of the Romans, to exalting Trojan virtues and denouncing Greek wiles. On the other his literary *pietas* would make him disinclined to vilify the honourable figure of the *Odyssey*, the virtuous exemplar of the Stoics. This was why, if our conjecture is right, neither he nor his Aeneas stooped to slander Ulysses. He left that—perhaps with a touch of ironic satisfaction—to the admittedly false Sinon (whose task, incidentally, from a non-partisan point of view, demanded the greatest courage and address). Then, if (in that noble place of light which Dante set apart in Limbo for the five great poets of antiquity) Homer,

> quel signor dell'altissimo canto
> che sovra li altri com 'aquila vola,

had taxed Virgil with having plundered his poems and slandered his hero, Virgil could have answered the *poeta sovrano*: 'Homer, poetry as well as war has its *ineluctabile fatum*. You know this, you who praised the virtues of the Achaeans to please the Greek princes for whom you sang. Did you not represent the Trojans as having begun the war for the sake of an adulterous prince? Did you not say that the Trojans broke their solemn oath at the Truce? I had my prince and my people to please, as you had yours. But I did not

slander your Odysseus—and surely you, subtle master of the epic,
know it. You will find no comment of mine on him in any line of
my poem. Indignant Aeneas speaks of him in the manner of a
defeated soldier. Perfidious Sinon traduces him. But surely you see
that I transferred the chief burden of odium from your Odysseus
(whom your fellow-countryman Euripides did not spare) to Sinon,
who never appears in your poems. Sinon is my real villain, not
Ulysses'.

In a sense this would be a sophistry. But it would be the kind of
sophistry that artists must sometimes use to salve their consciences,
when they are caught in the grip of circumstance. Homer, one is
sure, would understand it, and accept the tortuous tribute without
rancour. *Habent sua fata libelli.*

But if Virgil never comments on Ulysses directly in the *Aeneid*
is there any clue to his own personal view, as distinct from his
On-His-Majesty's-Service attitude? There is no clear indication.
One can only, in Polonius's phrase, by indirections find directions
out. Perhaps it is significant that in Book Three (588 ff.), where
Virgil's debts to Homer are specially obvious, he contrives that his
readers should catch a glimpse of Ulysses's Odyssean virtues. There
it is related how Aeneas meets a lost companion of Ulysses[9] who
describes his experience with Ulysses, 'the unfortunate' (*infelix*, the
compassionate term is, significantly, used by Aeneas here), in the
cave of the Cyclops. This companion chiefly emphasizes the horror
of the incident. But unobtrusively Ulysses's better nature (*nec . . .
oblitusve sui . . . discrimine tanto*) is illustrated. Is it too far-fetched
to suggest that this was Virgil's way of acknowledging some of the
qualities which Homer and the Stoics had admired in Ulysses? It
is deftly done, for if some ultra-chauvinistic Roman had tried to
rebuke him for praising the arch-enemy of the Trojans, Virgil had
his answer. He had expressed no personal opinion. Surely, he could
argue, one Greek may be permitted to praise another even in a
pro-Trojan epic.

There is no proof that Virgil expressed his own personal opinion
of Ulysses through this Greek Robinson Crusoe rather than through
Sinon. It is only a possibility. Yet if Virgil wished to speak through
either, was he likely to prefer the lying deceiver? Quite possibly,
of course, he did not wish to speak through either. But the figure
of the lonely castaway—Philoctetes, Ariadne, Robinson Crusoe,
and, in a sense, Ulysses himself on Calypso's island—has often
appealed to imaginative poets. And Aeneas uses in his first descrip-

tion of the Greek exile a Virgilian key-word—*miserandus*. His was a genuinely pitiable condition. Sinon's *miseritudo* was feigned. This perhaps was Sinon's worst perfidy in Virgil's eyes, that he won the Trojans' trust by exploiting their pity—*capti dolis lacrimisque coactis.* That was the deepest pathos of Troy's fall, as Aeneas recounts it. The Trojans were not simply less clever and less perfidious than the Greeks; they were more pitiful, more humane, more endowed with that quality of tenderness which Homer had bestowed on both Odysseus and Hector. One can hardly blame Aeneas for calling the purposeful Odysseus of the Trojan campaign harsh: he did, too, call him *infelix* later. If one looks deeply into the *causas rerum* here, one finds that Homer and Virgil (as well as Homer's Odysseus and Virgil's Aeneas) are ultimately one in this golden quality of all humane letters—compassion.

This is a fundamental quality. There are also some more formal resemblances between Aeneas and Odysseus. Much of the first half of the *Aeneid* closely follows Odysseus's adventures in *Odyssey* 9–12.[10] The exordium of the *Aeneid* implied to the erudite reader an attempt to combine the two Homeric poems in one—the *arma* suggesting Iliadic battles, the *virum* the biographical nature of the *Odyssey*. At times Aeneas addresses his companions in close adaptations of Odysseus's phrases, as in

> O socii—neque enim ignari sumus ante malorum—
> O passi graviora. . . .

This has the authentic Odyssean ring. Further, Virgil often borrows from Homer suggestions for some of the most poignant scenes in Aeneas's journey. The parallel between the majestic silences of Homer's Ajax and Virgil's Dido in Hades has already been noticed. Similarly when Aeneas encounters the ghosts, first of his wife, then of his father, his frustrated embraces are derived directly from Ulysses's encounter with his mother's shade in *Odyssey* Eleven. There are many other parallels. Plainly Virgil was as conscious of Odyssean influence in his *Aeneid* as was James Joyce in his *Ulysses*. And, like Joyce, he must have recognized that a man who is portrayed within an Odyssean framework is bound to acquire some Ulyssean characteristics whether he likes it or not. Perhaps if Virgil had not been so closely committed to Roman imperialistic propaganda he might have portrayed an Aeneas who (like the Trojan Antenor in the older Troy Tale) could admire Ulysses and appreciate his innate integrity.

K

But Aeneas is, of course, far from being a mere Ulysses in Roman dress. Though the two heroes have much in common—piety, purposefulness, endurance, courage, eloquence, tenderness—they are fundamentally different. Aeneas is less impressive in personality, more impressive in destiny than Ulysses. As has been well said, 'The greatness of Aeneas is a kind of "imputed greatness"; he is important to the world as bearing the weight of the glory and destiny of the future Romans:

Attollens humero famamque et fata nepotum.

Odysseus is great in the personal qualities of courage, steadfastness of purpose and affection, loyalty to his companions, versatility, ready resource; but he bears with him only his own fortunes and those of the companions of his adventure; he ends his career as he begins it, the chief of a small island, which derives all its importance solely from its early associations with his fortunes.'[11] Or as another scholar has expressed it[12]: 'Vergil set before himself a Ulysses, perhaps even an Achilles. Nature set before him a St. Louis—a crusading knight and a *"holy* war". In the issue he hovers between the two conceptions—and fails. Yet there emerges from the failure something greater, at any rate in hope and suggestion, than any epical success: an ideal and mystical figure standing outside time and place, that seems to be now Aeneas, now Rome, now the soul of Man setting out on the pilgrimage of a dimly descried eternal glory.'

In this we see an essential difference in the typically Greek and Roman characters, the antithesis between the individualist and the imperialist. Ulysses's ultimate loyalty was to his own interests in the wide sense, his family, his kingdom, his companions, and, while reluctantly engaged in the Trojan campaign, to the Greek cause. His relations with the gods are primarily personal and individualistic: he is the victim of Poseidon, the favourite of Athene. The Virgilian *ineluctabile fatum* does not weigh so heavily on him as on Aeneas. Moreover, Ulysses's career moves in a circle described from Ithaca to Ithaca. Aeneas, on the contrary, moves in a widely curving, but never retrograde, arc from Troy to Carthage and Italy. He is the instrument of Destiny. Compared with its tremendous force, the intrigues of Juno and Venus seem secondary, almost puny. To some extent Aeneas's own personality is also dwarfed by the grandeur of his mission. As a person he is less attractive and interesting than Homer's Odysseus. As an impersonation of a tremendous historical force he transcends the merely personal. Odysseus argues with

Athene and even chides her once: he knows what he wants and expects his gods to give him his dues. Aeneas, often bewildered at the apparent injustices of heaven, often scolded by his divine patroness, is content to submit gravely to Heaven's will—*Sequimur te, sancte deorum, quisquis es, imperioque iterum paremus ovantes*. What made it impossible for Aeneas to be fundamentally like Ulysses was this Roman concept of *auctoritas*, this submission to a supreme *imperium* that would control religion and politics in Western Europe until the Renaissance revived the more individualistic Greek spirit.

In a sense, then, if one leaves out of account the beauty and power of Virgil's poetry, the greatness of Aeneas lies in political history, the greatness of Ulysses in the literary and philosophic tradition. Aeneas never lived as vividly again in the literary or artistic tradition of post-Virgilian Europe, as did Ulysses. Aeneas was constantly referred to; his words were constantly quoted; his pious devotion to his high mission was constantly cited as an example. But he always remained much as Virgil had made him. He had none of Ulysses's innate powers of adaptability. He was an Ajax who, by Heaven's grace, did not fail.

Yet though Virgil did not create in Aeneas so vivid and viable a figure as Ulysses, he did, whether he intended it or not, contrive to blacken Ulysses's character for some fifteen hundred years of the Western literary tradition. The later classical and medieval readers made no distinctions between what the poet said *in propria persona*, and what his characters Aeneas and Sinon had said, about the wily Greek. The general impression derived from *Aeneid* Two—always a primary source-book for the Troy Tale—was that Ulysses was a thorough scoundrel. Strengthened by the anti-Homeric denigrations of writers like Dictys of Crete (to be discussed later), this impression caused the writers of the medieval Troy romances, from the *Roman de Troie* to Lydgate's *Troy tale* and Caxton's *Recuyell of the historyes of Troye* to present Ulysses in a consistently unfavourable light. They, too, like Virgil, were writing to please monarchs who had ingeniously traced their lineage back to Trojan princes. It is mainly due to the combined influence of these medieval romancers and Virgil that one finds these entries in the *Oxford English Dictionary*:[13]

Trojan: a brave or plucky fellow; a person of great energy and endurance.

Greek: a cunning or wily person; a cheat, sharper, especially one who cheats at cards.

Ulyssean: characteristic of or resembling Ulysses in craft or deceit.[14]

CHAPTER XI

TRADITIONAL FEATURES IN OVID, SENECA, AND STATIUS

THE conflict between the Stoics and the Roman imperialists is the most notable feature of the Ulysses tradition in Latin literature. It was never finally resolved. Some writers, classical, medieval, and modern, followed Horace's presentation of Ulysses as a noble exemplar of virtuous living, others believed Virgil's Sinon that he was treacherous, cruel, and criminal. On the whole the more imaginative writers accepted the Virgilian portrait until the rediscovery of Homer's poems at the Renaissance re-established the original character of Ulysses.[1]

Many Latin poets, however, took neither side, preferring to follow the earlier classical tradition. Lyric and elegiac poets naturally tended to imitate the Greek lyrical attitude to Ulysses.[2] Tragedians for the most part emulated Euripides.[3] The comic dramatists, taking as their model Menander, who had nothing to say of Ulysses, generally ignored him.[4] Orators frequently praised his eloquence and wrote contemporary exemplifications of its style.[5] There is no need to survey all these multifarious conventional references here. But, when the Greek originals were inaccessible in Western Europe, writers drew much of their information about the Troy Tale from five Latin poets—Virgil, Horace, Ovid, Seneca, and Statius.[6] It now remains to consider how Ulysses was portrayed in the works of the last three of these.

Ovid was particularly well endowed by nature and art to appreciate Ulysses's personality. He was the most cosmopolitan and versatile of the Augustan poets, and a superb rhetorician. In his public life he suffered much from envy and malice. He found the company of women congenial and sympathetic. Later in life he came to understand the sorrows of exile. It is not surprising, then, that he seems to have found a kindred spirit in Ulysses. With two exceptions,[7] all his references to him are appreciatory.

Ovid's chief description of Ulysses is in some ways the least revealing. It is mainly a tribute from one skilful rhetorician to another. It emerges in a version of the celebrated, indeed, by that time hackneyed, contest for the arms of Achilles between Ulysses

and Ajax, in *Metamorphoses* 13, 1 ff. Ovid presents the opponents
in sharp contrast. First Ajax rises to speak, with a scowling look,
unable to control his anger. He is indignant that he must plead his
own cause beside the very ships which his valour had protected so
well, and against Ulysses, of all people. He is conscious that he
labours under a disadvantage; his forte is deeds not words. This
remark gives the essence of the whole passage. Ovid's intention is
to illustrate the recurrent conflict between men of action and men
of counsel, a literary commonplace as old as Homer and a favourite
topic in every period of classical and renaissance literature.[8] Ovid
does not disguise his own preference in the end. 'The event made
clear the power of eloquence: the skilful speaker won the brave
man's arms' (vv. 382–3).

Ajax, scorning any effort to conciliate his audience, launches into
an account of all Ulysses's faults and misdeeds: Ulysses is a coward;
he prefers to fight under cover of night; his lineage is ignoble (Ajax
assumes that he is Sisyphus's bastard); he feigned madness to escape
joining the Trojan campaign; he treated Philoctetes and Palamedes
disgracefully; when Nestor called for help, he ran on for safety;
when he was in terror of death, he, Ajax, had saved his life. Ajax
then contrasts his own valour. Where was the eloquent Ulysses
when the Trojans were trying to set fire to the ships? The best
feats Ulysses can boast of were the killing of Rhesus and the weak
Dolon, the capture of Helenus, and the taking of the Palladium—
all deeds done in the dark, and all done with the help of Diomedes.
Secrecy, stealth, fraud, and treachery, these are the martial virtues
of Ulysses. Is such a poltroon to win the arms of Achilles against
the mighty Ajax whose valiant arm and massive shield have so
often saved the Greeks from disaster? He ends by reiterating his
scorn for mere words. 'Let deeds be our proofs' (*spectemur agendo*),
he cries. Throw Achilles's arms into the midst of the Trojan ranks
and see which of the two competitors will bring them back.

Ovid has not spared Ulysses in this indictment. Ajax, despite his
expressions of contempt for verbal skill, makes as strong a case as
can be made against Ulysses. All the traditional calumnies are
included. They have been dealt with already in the present study;
but Ulysses's replies, as Ovid handles them, deserve consideration.
Before Ulysses begins, he fixes his eyes for a little while on the
ground (the pose which Antenor had described in the *Iliad*). Here,
however, his purpose seems to be less to give an impression of
modesty than to win an expectant silence. This achieved, he speaks

with an eloquence in which 'charm (*gratia*) is not absent'. His first
sentences contain a deft *captatio benevolentiae*. 'If your prayers and
mine had prevailed, Greeks, this contest would never have occurred:
Achilles would still be alive. But since fate forbade this'—and here
he seemed to dry some tears from his eyes—'who has a better right
to succeed to Achilles than the man through whose agency Achilles
joined the Greek host?' (By this he refers, as he explains later, to
his success in detecting Achilles among the maidens at Scyros and
in persuading him to come and fight at Troy.) He appeals to his
audience not to be prejudiced in favour of Ajax's slack-wittedness.
Whatever poor eloquence and wit he, Ulysses, possesses, has always
been at the service of the Greeks. Ajax boasts of his lineage—well,
one can hardly include one's ancestors among one's own personal
achievements: but even so, Laertes's grandfather was Zeus, and
Anticleia's grandfather was Hermes, which is as good ancestry as
Ajax can claim in the male and female lines. (Ulysses passes over
Ajax's reference to Sisyphus in silent contempt.)

'Ajax', Ulysses continues, 'claims that he has done more for the
Greeks than I. But, since it was I who brought Achilles to Troy,
all Achilles's deeds were ultimately due to me. Further, if I had not
persuaded Agamemnon to sacrifice Iphigeneia in the public interest
(*ad publica commoda*), and if I had not tricked Clytaemnestra into
sending her to Aulis, the Greek expedition would never have
reached Troy. It was I who was sent on the first dangerous embassy
to Priam. My counsel and my strength were always employed in
the service of the Greek host. By espionage, by advice, by consolation, by encouragement, by general serviceability, I sustained morale
for the whole nine years of the campaign. When in the tenth year
Agamemnon advised retreat and Thersites dared to assail authority,
it was I who averted the withdrawal. Is it not a fact that Diomedes
chose me alone from all the Achaean heroes to accompany him on
the dangerous night raid? Did I not extract the information we
needed about the enemy from Dolon before we killed him? From
that same raid did I not bring back the famous horses of Rhesus?'

Ulysses goes on to refute Ajax's charge of cowardice. He names
twelve Trojans slain by his hand, and claims many others not known
by name. Drawing aside his tunic, he displays his wounds. Ajax,
he asserts, has none to show. And to what avail were Ajax's boasted
deeds of valour? Hector survived his duel without a wound.
Besides, it was he, Ulysses, who rescued Achilles's body after his
death, and his armour with him. Who can doubt that he is strong

enough to carry that armour now? And, incidentally, it is armour of superb artistry. How could an ignoramus like Ajax appreciate its recondite beauties?

Ulysses returns to some of Ajax's allegations. 'Am I to be considered a coward for having tried to avoid conscription? Very well, you must then call Achilles a coward, too. He was held back by a loving mother; I by a loving wife. As for Palamedes, he was proved guilty of treason and executed by the common decree of the Greeks. It is by common consent, too, that Philoctetes has been marooned on Lemnos. He is needed back with the Greek host now. Let the eloquent and sagacious Ajax be sent to win him over! Absurd: as usual I shall be asked to undertake the task, and, as usual, I shall execute it with success—just as at great personal peril, I captured the Palladium on which the fortune of Troy depends. It is true that Diomedes, as Ajax says, was my companion on this and other exploits. Yes, I had one companion alone: Ajax prefers to have a crowd of followers and the protection of his impenetrable shield.' He goes on to taunt Ajax:

> Brawn without Brain is thine: My prudent Care
> Foresees, provides, administers the War:
> Thy Province is to Fight; but when shall be
> The time to fight, the King consults with me:
> No dram of Judgment with thy Force is join'd,
> Thy Body is of Profit, and my Mind.
> But how much more the Ship her Safety owes
> To him who steers, than him that only rows,
> By how much more the Captain merits Praise
> Than he who Fights, and Fighting but obeys. . . .
>
> (Dryden's version)

In his peroration Ulysses pleads that the Greeks should not forget all his services to them, implies that his wisdom will still be needed before Troy is captured, points to the Palladium, 'the fateful image of Minerva'—and wins the vote. Ajax kills himself on the spot. 'The event showed the power of eloquence.' And the composition shows the power of Ovid's rhetorical talent—but little more. Ovid's own personal feelings are not involved in the conflict. The reader's are hardly stirred. Neither contestant is a sympathetic figure. Ajax is too crude and arrogant, Ulysses too suave and self-confident. Besides, as even Ajax perceived, a debate between an Ajax and a Ulysses is not a contest on equal ground. Personalities fundamentally so different as these are incommensurable by any human scale of values.

On the whole, then, this is mainly an exhibition of Roman

rhetoric in a mythological setting. Ulysses has become, like Juvenal's Hannibal, a subject for declamations. But after Ovid had been exiled from Rome, he began to take a different view of Ulysses, finding a symbol of his own fate in Homer's descriptions of the wandering hero. He remembered how Ulysses, too, despite his prudence, had incurred divine anger (*Tristia* 1, 2, 9), and despite his self-control had tearfully yearned to see once more the smoke of his ancestral hearth (*Epistles* 1, 3, 33-4). It is true, Ovid admits, that Ulysses gives an example of 'a mind too patient' in his ten years' wanderings; but he had the consolations of Calypso's kindness, of hearing the Sirens sing, of having a chance to taste the lotus (*Ep.* 4, 10, 9 ff.). Ovid would gladly exchange his own miserable life among the barbarous Scythians for Ulysses's sufferings. Ulysses had a faithful band of companions with him; he had a strong and enduring physique, trained in military exercises; he had Pallas Athene to help him; he was on his way home, as a joyful victor. Ovid had none of these advantages (*Tristia* 1, 5, 57 ff.). 'Add the fact', he concludes, 'that most of *his* sufferings are fictitious, and you will see how much harder is my fate'. Adversity, indeed, is praiseworthy when nobly borne, and possibly, Ovid thinks, his own misfortune will add to his renown (*Tristia* 5, 5, 51; *Ep.* 3, 1, 53). But how much happier Penelope would have been if Ulysses had not won fame by leaving her. 'Believe me', he exclaims, 'if Ulysses were compared with me, his sufferings from Neptune's wrath would seem clearly less than mine from Jove's'.

At times Ovid seems to identify himself with Ulysses, at times he uses him as a stock mythological emblem. His attitude in some ways resembles that of the early Greek lyric poets as already described. But there is a difference. They found comfort and strength in Ulysses's courage and endurance. Ovid's tone is more querulous. Perhaps his fate was harsher than theirs. What is most noteworthy here for the general tradition is that Ovid provides the most striking example in Latin literature of a poet's self-identification with the exiled Ithacan. Modern examples of this experience will be given in a later chapter.

Ovid shows something of the same tendency to see himself in Ulysses when he dwells on Ulysses's relationships with women. He devotes the first of his *Heroides* to a letter from the lonely, loving Penelope to her wandering, and perhaps erring, husband. In *Tristia* 2, 375-6 he exaggerates the love element in the *Odyssey*— 'What is the *Odyssey*', he asks, 'but the story of a woman wooed by many suitors while her husband was away?' In a pleasant conceit he suggests (*Tristia* 5, 5, 2–3) that Ulysses even when exiled at the world's end perhaps celebrated Penelope's birthday, just as he, Ovid, now celebrates his own wife's. But the allusions are not confined to Ulysses's conjugal love. Ovid recalls how Ulysses had been helped in his distress by the sea-nymph Leucothea (*Ep.* 3, 6, 19–20). In earlier, more care-free days, too, Ovid had described (*Art of Love* 2, 123 ff.) how Ulysses, 'though he was not handsome', had racked sea-goddesses with love for him, and how Calypso especially had hung on his words. It is hardly rash to see something of Ovid's own fortunes reflected here. He is the first major poet in post-Homeric classical literature (as now extant) to dwell so much, and with such a personal note, on the affection and kindness of women towards Ulysses. His attitude is far from that of the modern writers who have magnified the erotic element in Ulysses's character into a dominant passion. But it does foreshadow the favourite renaissance and modern theme of Ulysses the Amorist.

In contrast with Ovid's personal sympathy with Ulysses, Statius offers a formal, stylized portrait in the first two books of his un-completed *Achilleis*. The poem has a special importance in the Ulysses tradition for an accidental reason. It happens to give the earliest extant account of Ulysses's cleverness in detecting Achilles among the maidens of Scyros. From it works like Metastasio's *Achille in Sciro* and Robert Bridge's *Achilles in Scyros* are ultimately derived. On the whole Statius tells his story without much bias. He, like Ovid, was a rhetorician and likely to be indulgent towards intelligence and cleverness. Ulysses is certainly portrayed as exhibiting craft and subtlety in his methods. But, if one concedes that the situation could only be successfully handled by subtle means, this is hardly reprehensible. Ulysses's actions are not undignified. He openly brings the gifts which eventually serve to reveal Achilles, and does not stoop to disguise himself as a huckstering merchant (as in later versions). His epithets vary: on the one hand he is described as 'watchful', 'smiling secretly', 'giving a sidelong glance', 'per-suasive', 'crafty'; on the other hand he is 'keen', 'sagacious', 'provi-dent'. Once, indeed, Statius plays the honest Roman and comments in person on Greek deceitfulness. When Lycomedes allows Ulysses to display his fateful gifts, the poet exclaims (2, 171–2):

> Alas, the simple one, too innocent!
> Those crafty gifts, Greek craftiness, and all
> Ulysses's variousness, he little knew.

But on the whole the balance of feeling towards Ulysses is not unfavourable. In a purely Greek story of this kind any strongly anti-Greek attitude would have been out of place.

Seneca is a Mr. Facing-both-ways, a Janus-like figure, in the Ulysses tradition. As a philosopher he admired Ulysses in the Stoic manner, as has already been mentioned. As a dramatist he followed Euripides in denigrating him. His *Troades*, a conflation of Euripides's *Hecuba* and *Troades*, had a great influence on the renaissance tradition, when Greek was still scarcely known to working playwrights. It preserves the Euripidean antipathy to Ulysses faithfully. Ulysses remains the same deceitful and unscrupulous *politique*— 'cautious', 'deceptive', 'an artist in crime', 'deviser of deceits'. We see him largely through Trojan eyes, as in Euripides. He threatens to torture Andromache if she will not reveal where Astyanax is hidden. 'Necessity has greater force than piety', he asserts. Andromache resists him with spirit, and almost convinces him that her son is dead. Ulysses is about to turn away when further doubts cross his mind. Then in a soliloquy he calls up his 'astuteness, deceits, and wiles—in fact all that is Ulysses'. He returns to subject Andromache to some subtler verbal tests. Eventually he discovers that Astyanax is alive. When he tries to justify the boy's execution on the grounds that the Greek interests must come first and that it was Calchas, not he, who demanded the killing, Andromache releases a flood of denunciation: Ulysses, and Ulysses alone, she asserts, is to blame for it all; even the Greeks have succumbed to his craft and malice; but no one ever succumbed to his warlike valour. The charge of cowardice Ulysses easily refutes:

> The Greeks well know the courage of Ulysses,
> The Trojans only too well. . . .

He says, perhaps sincerely, that he wishes he could indulge his pity for Andromache. He will at least grant what is within his power— time for her to take a long and tearful farewell of her son. But after a minute or two he breaks in impatiently and orders Astyanax to be taken away.

In its broader outlines this portrait is quite as unfavourable as that in Euripides's plays. But Seneca seems to show a grain or two more of sympathy for Ulysses in his thankless task.[9] As a Roman used to imperial discipline and to the harsher exigencies of power-politics he was better qualified than Euripides, the warm-hearted individualist, to understand Ulysses's inner feelings. Ulysses's first speech

excusing the sternness of his mission is more fully and more convincingly argued than its Euripidean prototype. He pleads that he
is merely the 'minister of a harsh decree': his demands are not his
own, but voice the will of all the Greek chieftains, who fear that if
a son of Hector survives, a war of revenge is bound to be declared
by the Trojans in the next generation. (Is there an echo of the
Carthaginian wars here?) Calchas has confirmed this fear with
prophecy. Only Astyanax's death can set their minds at rest. It is
an unpleasantly familiar argument—atrocity justified on the grounds
that it will prevent further atrocities. Later Ulysses gives it a more
personal application: if Astyanax does not die it will mean that
Telemachus may have to fight a second Trojan war. But afterwards, when Andromache appeals to him by his love for Penelope,
Laertes, and Telemachus, he hardens his heart. Perhaps it is significant that in the end Seneca spares him the abominable task of
having to hurl Astyanax with his own hand from the walls. The
child throws himself down; 'even Ulysses' is moved by his courageous spirit.

Much would depend on the acting of a part like this. It could be
presented as hideously villainous or as reluctantly stern. On the
whole the attitude of the neo-classical French writers in the Senecan
style, Garnier, for example, in his *La Troade* and Racine in his
Iphigénie, remain unfavourable to Ulysses. In such plays Ulysses's
degree of callousness varies, and his devotion to duty sometimes
carries more conviction. But wherever Seneca's influence[10] and the
Latin influence in general[11] prevailed, Ulysses never regained his full
prestige as a wise and magnanimous hero in the manner of the
Homeric poems or of Sophocles's *Ajax*. It was left to English
writers of the sixteenth and seventeenth centuries, under other
influence than that of Seneca, Virgil, and Euripides, to restore his
reputation for generous and sympathetic statesmanship.

CHAPTER XII

ULYSSES AND THE DISCREDITING OF HOMER

FOR the first eight hundred years of Ulysses's literary career Homer's powerful influence has supported him in most of his trials and vicissitudes, much as Athene had guided and protected him in the *Iliad* and the *Odyssey*. But now, towards the end of the first century of the Christian era, that support is destined to be undermined and removed. The time will soon come when it will be more to Ulysses's disadvantage than to his advantage to be known as Homer's favourite hero. It will be argued, and widely believed, that, since Homer himself was a liar and a cheat, his favourite hero must have been equally villainous. As a result, Ulysses's reputation reaches its lowest level at the end of the classical period and remains there for over a thousand years of the Western literary tradition. He enters, as it were, a Cyclops's cave of ignorant hostility, and he will only emerge safely from it when the uncouth ogre of the anti-Homeric tradition has been blinded by the torch of renaissance learning.

As has been described in a previous chapter, criticism of Homer had begun as early as the sixth century B.C. with strictures on his theological and scientific views. The fifth-century sophists had turned criticism more towards Homer's skill in the use of language and in the arts of rhetoric. In the fourth century Plato had attacked him on moral grounds. Soon afterwards, Zoïlus, the Scourge of Homer, probably prompted more by iconoclastic spite than by any moral fervour, had denounced him on many counts as a contemptible bungler and had written a eulogy of the Cyclops. By the middle of the third century the centre of Homeric criticism had moved to Alexandria. There, in a new environment and under kings descended from a captain of one of Homer's greatest admirers, Alexander the Great, Homer was treated for a while with more respect, though sometimes the courtier-scholars of the earlier Ptolemies felt it their duty to comment on a lack of decorum both in Homer's own style and in the conduct of his heroes.

All this had tended to undermine Homer's prestige in matters where Homer himself would have neither sought nor expected veneration. He had never set himself up as a theologian, or a scientist, or a rhetorician, or a moralist, or a historian, or as a writer on courtly etiquette. His aim had been to tell a semi-fictional story about a remote, fierce age, in a traditional oral style. It had been the fault of his later audiences that he had come to be regarded as a kind of universal oracle. But this fact did not prevent undiscerning minds from thinking that when his value as a recorder of facts and as a purveyor of moral lessons was decried his whole reputation as a poet was involved. There had, however, always been some influential voices on Homer's side. The Stoics, as has been described, took his part against the Academics. Aristotle in his *Poetics* had showed the ineptness of the typically sophistic kinds of captiousness, and had answered Plato's doctrines on the immorality of poetry. The greater Alexandrian scholars had followed Aristotle in regarding Homer as an admirable poet without claiming infallibility for either his technique or his facts. One finds the same tolerant, though not uncritical, admiration in the remarks of some Latin writers, Cicero and Horace among him.

Thus, of the period extending from Homer to Virgil one can say in general that despite severe criticism Homer's prestige both as a poet and as the earliest authority for European history, remained high. No matter what the subtler critics said or thought, the average man in Athens, Alexandria, Pergamum, and Rome, seems to have venerated him uniquely as The Poet. Yet this, as Theocritus, writing early in the third century B.C., rather bitterly remarks, made things hard for living poets.[1] 'Homer is good enough for us all' expressed the attitude of the average Alexandrian reader, it seems, when a new hexameter poem was offered to him.

In Theocritus's complaint—one is reminded of the young Bernard Shaw's attitude to Shakespeare, and Horace's towards Ennius and Naevius—it is possible to see the motive which drove less scrupulous authors to attempt to dethrone Homer from his traditional supremacy, as if he were an aged despot who would bear, like the Turk, no rival near his throne. This was not altogether a new attitude; but no definite attempt at assassination, so to speak, had been made by earlier victims of this alleged tyranny. Older poets had been content, on the whole, like Aeschylus, to live on the rich banquets of poetic material which Homer and the cyclic poets lavishly provided. Now, in the first century A.D., the standard of revolt is raised. Homer, it is alleged, is an impostor. His claim (which he had never in fact put forward) to be the supreme authority on the Troy Tale is entirely false. The true story has at last been discovered from unimpeachable sources. The time has come to burn your *Iliads* and *Odysseys* and to buy authentic stories of the Trojan War from Ptolemy Chennos,[2] or Philostratus, or Dictys of Crete, or Dares of Phrygia, as the case may be. It followed, of course, that Homer's praises of Odysseus and Achilles and the rest were entirely untrustworthy.

The motive of these forgers seems to have been primarily a selfish one—to win readers for their own works and to drive Homer's poems off the market. Some seem to have taken themselves less seriously than others. Dio Chrysostom, for example, in his *Trojan Discourse*, is hardly trying to do more than dazzle and astonish his audience in arguing that the Greeks lost the Trojan War, and that Homer's account was a tissue of partisan lies.[3] The oration is bland, persuasive, and superbly argued, but no intelligent person is likely to have believed it. Its aim is to gain admiration for skill in rhetorical technique and in sophistic arguments rather than to win lasting credence. Dio was clearly no fanatical or self-seeking opponent of Homer. On the contrary, in this discourse he affects to regard him with a patronizing tolerance, and he often praises him elsewhere.[4] Finally, unlike other anti-Homerists, Dio has nothing particularly offensive to say about Ulysses apart from pointing out that he was a liar like his author.

Despite the fact that Dio's work is primarily a *tour de force*, it reveals some of the profounder influences that were combining to undermine Homer's authority. The first was the tendency among Romans, mentioned in chapter ten, to regard the Greeks as fickle opportunists, ready to perjure themselves or to betray their brothers for a slight advantage. It suited Roman political propaganda in Greek lands from Sicily to Asia Minor that the Romano-Trojan stock should be venerated as the more majestic and more trustworthy breed, and that Greeks should be depreciated to the level of witty parasites and clever scribes. In other words, it would be well for Roman influence if Virgil supplanted Homer and Aeneas eclipsed Ulysses.

A second factor, though not emphasized, is discernible in Dio's *Trojan Discourse*. This is the growth of credulity. Dio's claim to have learned the truth about the Trojan War from an old Egyptian priest (who warned him that the Greeks were incorrigible boasters) is not a new literary device. Plato had used it long before. But in Dio's latter-day epoch of perfervid religiosity and ambitious thaumaturgy, when oriental cults were swarming through the

Mediterranean in competition with both Christianity and the Olympian gods, this kind of nonsense was more likely to be believed. Consequently some of the other chief writers in the anti-Homeric or anti-Greek tradition had no compunction in offering far-fetched explanations of their claim to have absolutely authentic information about the Trojan war and its heroes. Thus the unknown author of the impudently named *Journal of the Trojan War* (which he attributes to Dictys of Crete, an ally of the Idomeneus who fought for the Greeks at Troy) claims that this contemporary day-to-day record was preserved on linden bark in Dictys's tomb until an earthquake revealed it to some innocent and careful shepherds, whose master eventually had the precious discovery brought to Nero's notice. Philostratus goes further in his *Heroicus*. His informant, he states, was a vineyard-keeper in the Troad who had heard the true facts about the Trojan campaign from the ghost of Protesilaus. The third chief impostor, who masquerades under the name of Dares the Phrygian (ostensibly an ally of the Trojans), was less ingenious. He was satisfied to forge an introductory letter from the famous Cornelius Nepos recommending his fourth-rate chronicle as a trustworthy contemporary record. All three were eventually believed.

Another tendency helped in the dethronement of Homer. The creative vigour of classical mythology, and with it the ability of readers and audiences to enjoy the more imaginative flights of mythopoeic literature, had been dying out since the first century A.D. A few minor epics were still to be written in Greek and Latin, but the main creative impulse was gone among authors, and readers were becoming unable or unwilling to enjoy poems on the scale of the *Odyssey* and *Iliad*. The general public seems to have preferred to learn about mythology and the heroic age from epitomes and summaries,[5] just as many readers of the present day skim through literary digests of accepted masterpieces instead of reading the originals. In this condition of popular taste Dictys of Crete and Dares the Phrygian provided exactly what was wanted.

Further, Homer's influence was always weakened in Italy and the west of Europe by the fact that he wrote in Greek and in a Greek markedly different from literary Attic and the current *Koiné*. From the second century B.C. to the fall of the Western Empire most of the better educated Romans probably knew enough Greek to read the *Iliad* and the *Odyssey* fairly fluently and accurately in the original, if they wished. Many could, and would, visit Athens and learn to read Homer in the living Greek tradition. The more conservative

Roman schoolmasters and rhetoricians would continue to regard the Homeric poems as the foundation of a liberal eduction. But gradually, as Roman literature became more self-sufficient and as Roman rulers looked more to the West, the effort to learn Homeric Greek must have been harder to sustain. Already in the first century B.C. one finds evidence of a tendency to seek substitutes. A summary of the *Iliad* in a thousand and seventy Latin hexameters, about one-fourteenth, that is, of the original poem, appeared in the first century A.D. Combining simple language with a summary treatment, it was obviously designed to indulge a popular demand. Its title, *The Latin Iliad*, could be interpreted to mean that this was all the *Iliad* a loyal Latin need know.[6]

When one turns to consider how Ulysses fared in the writings of Philostratus, Dictys, and Dares, the three most influential detractors of Homer in the late classical period, one finds different methods but a similar result. Philostratus is much the most ingenious calumniator of the three. Early in the dialogue the vineyard-keeper who unfolds the truth about the Trojan heroes, as revealed by the ghost of Protesilaus, warns his Phoenician questioner that opinions of Ulysses have been unduly influenced by Homer. Homer, he explains, praised Ulysses above his merits because before composing his poems he had gone to Ithaca and consulted the ghost of Ulysses about the events at Troy. Ulysses's ghost had refused to tell Homer anything until he promised to eulogize his, Ulysses's, wisdom and courage in his poems. Homer agreed to this, whereupon the ghost told him the truth. When Homer had heard the whole story and was turning away, Ulysses's ghost called him back. Apparently the murder of Palamedes was still troubling his conscience, for he asked Homer not to mention Palamedes at all—'Do not bring him to Troy; do not use him as a warrior; do not say that he was wise. Other poets will say it, but it will be unconvincing if you have not mentioned it'. Homer consented to this *suppressio veri*. As a result, though he knew the truth about the Trojan campaign in his poems, he altered many of the facts to suit expediency.

One must admire Philostratus's ingenuity in both discrediting Homer and demonstrating the guilt of Odysseus at the same time. Homer's silence about Palamedes had always been a problem. Now the reason is made clear. It was simply, we are to believe, another example of Ulysses's astuteness. Philostratus implies what the average man's opinion of Ulysses's treatment of Palamedes was by telling of a farmer in the Troad who used to offer sacrifices to

Palamedes. This honest fellow in order to show his detestation for the man who killed his hero called his fawning and treacherous dog Odysseus and killed it contemptuously, all for Palamedes's sake. Later the same farmer told Palamedes's ghost, who came to visit him, that Ulysses was even more abominable than the dog, and expressed his regrets that Ulysses's tomb was not available for the desecration it deserved. Palamedes advised him not to trouble himself any more about Ulysses, for he had paid the penalty in Hades for his crime.

Here Philostratus obviously wants to build up feelings of scorn and dislike against Ulysses. Elsewhere he makes some definite attacks on Homer's narrative. He dismisses Ulysses's Odyssean wanderings as absurd and not even plausible in their motivation. Ulysses was, Protesilaus asserts, Homer's spoiled pet, and all the facts were distorted in his favour. Thus the real cause of the anger of Poseidon was not the blinding of Polyphemus but Ulysses's murder of the sea-god's grandson Palamedes. Various details of Ulysses's earlier career are also criticized. The story of his unwillingness to join the expedition is considered absurd: so ambitious a person would have welcomed the opportunity for greater fame. An elaborate account is given of how Ulysses became envious of Palamedes, that paragon of wisdom and learning, and of how he persuaded the Ithacans and Peloponnesians in the Greek host to stone him to death. The rest of the Greeks, especially Ajax, Achilles, and Protesilaus, deplored the cruel deed.

Philostratus devotes a long passage to a depreciatory description of Ulysses's appearance and talents. Granted that he had extraordinary eloquence and cleverness, these qualities were counterbalanced by his dissimulation, enviousness, and malice. You could tell the man's guilty thoughts by his downcast and concentrated expression. Far from being an expert in military affairs he was almost entirely ignorant of them. The Wooden Horse was his only remarkable achievement. His Odyssean wanderings were pure fables. It would be absurd to suppose, for example, that goddesses like Circe and Calypso would love a man past the age for amorous delights, undersized, with a snub nose, and with shifty, wandering eyes (because of his chronic anxieties and suspicions). That look of thoughtful concentration, which he habitually wore, was far from being conducive to love affairs.

Here Philostratus falls into sheer puerility in his attempt to vilify Ulysses. It would not be worthwhile to delay over the inherent

L

absurdities. But it is evident how low the reputation both of Homer and of his favourite hero had fallen when readers could be attracted by such gross travesties of the epic tradition.

Dictys[8] is less openly anti-Homeric and less ingeniously anti-Ulyssean than Philostratus. But the general tone of his narrative is sordid and unheroic. Though his personal bias is explicitly towards the Greek side, he tells a cynically realistic story of passion, treachery, and self-seeking, among Greeks and Trojans alike. The atmosphere of squalid intrigue and ruthless violence is very similar to that of Shakespeare's *Troilus and Cressida* (which may have been partly derived from Dictys's narrative) without any redeeming flashes of high eloquence or profound philosophy. The portrait of Ulysses (from whom Dictys has the impudence to say he got some of his information) is that of a clever, but ignoble, negotiator, an adept in defeating his rivals by treachery or intrigue, and a lover of contentious disputation. He is never actually called a liar or a villain, but his actions speak for themselves. Palamedes is presented as his superior in both character and practical wisdom. It is Palamedes who leads the first embassy to Troy and who always gives the Greeks the best advice in their deliberations, until Ulysses, envious of his virtue and eminence, conspires with Diomedes to assassinate him. 'Thus', remarks Dictys, 'a man whose counsel and valour were never ineffectual was outwitted and brought to an unworthy death by those whom it least befitted to slay him'. Similarly Ulysses is made to play an inferior rôle to Ajax. He carries home his plunder for him and only wins the contest for the Palladium (which Dictys substitutes for the Armour of Achilles) by gross favouritism on the part of the Atreidae. Ulysses's victory was so unpopular, we are told, that he had to be protected by a special bodyguard until he eventually left the Troad in fear of retribution. Here again Dictys does not disguise his prejudices. All the Greeks, he relates, 'scathingly denounced both of the kings and did not refrain from curses, being indignant that they should prefer their lust and desire for a woman to supreme military merit'. (Ulysses had saved Helen's life when Ajax wished to have her executed.) The possibility that Ulysses could have deserved to win the prize is not considered.

Other touches help to vilify Ulysses. After the first embassy to Troy he makes a speech 'more for the sake of argument than to achieve anything'. He is made entirely responsible for the deception that lured Iphigeneia to the sacrifice at Aulis. He is chased ignominiously by Telephus. He 'insinuates'. He curses the pitiable Priam who has come to beg for the corpse of Hector. He advises the killing of Polyxena. While his usefulness in negotiations is still well exhibited, no traces of his humaneness or sympathy remain from his Homeric prototype. He does, indeed, make the most powerful speech in the whole work, when he goes on the later embassy with Diomedes to Troy. But its tone is harsh, arrogant, and abrupt: it shows nothing of that initial modesty which had impressed Homer's Antenor so greatly. Significantly, Athene plays no part in his career as Dictys narrates it.

In the first five books of his *Journal* Dictys completes his account of the Trojan campaign. Then in his sixth and last book he sets out to describe how the chief Greek heroes went home and what their subsequent fortunes were. Here Ulysses receives much the greatest share of attention, and a remarkable narrative, differing radically from Homer's account, is evolved. Dictys tells how Ulysses was eventually carried in two hired Phoenician ships to Crete (all his own ships and companions having been destroyed by Ajax's father, Telamon, in revenge for the death of his son). There he told Idomeneus about his adventures after his departure from the Troad. First having plundered Ismarus, he had come to the Lotus-eaters (as in the *Odyssey*). Thence he reached Sicily, where he was ill-treated by two brothers named Cyclops and Laestrygon; lost most of his allies at the hands of their sons, Antiphates and Polyphemus. Later this humane Polyphemus had pity on them and treated them with kindness. This they repaid by attempting to carry off Arene, the king's daughter, who was 'dying for love' of one of Ulysses's companions named Alphenor. Their attempt was foiled, the girl was forcibly recaptured, and the Greeks were driven away. Passing through the islands of Aeolus, they came to Circe and Calypso, local queens. They stayed awhile with them, lured by 'certain enticements to their love'. Adventures with the Spirits of the Dead, the Sirens, Scylla and Charybdis followed. Eventually they fell in with Phoenicians and came to Crete (in contradiction to what was stated at the beginning of the chapter). Thence Ulysses was sent to Phaeacia, where Alcinous received him kindly. With Alcinous's personal help, apparently, in the slaughter of the Suitors, Ulysses regained his kingdom and married Nausicaa to Telemachus. When a son was born to them, Ulysses named him Ptoliporthus, Sacker of Cities, after himself.

Later on, Dictys proceeds, Ulysses begins to be alarmed by omens and dreams. A curious recurrent dream of his is described: a figure, half human, half divine, and of outstanding beauty, kept appearing to him from the same quarter. Every time it appeared, Ulysses would feel the utmost desire to embrace it. He would stretch out his hands towards it, only to be told by the figure, speaking with a human voice, that such a union would be wicked (since they were both of the same blood and origin) and that one of them would die by the other's deed. As (still in the same dream) Ulysses strove to find the reason for this doom, a 'sign' rose out of the sea and came between himself and the figure. Then at the figure's command it was hurled at Ulysses and they separated.

Interpreters agreed that this boded death and warned Ulysses against treachery from his son. As a precaution Ulysses banished Telemachus to Cephallenia, and withdrew himself to 'hidden and distant parts'. Soon Telegonus, his son by Circe, landed on Ithaca, and, after various misadventures, fatally wounded Ulysses with his lance (the point of which was made from the bone of a sting ray, causing the 'death off the sea' predicted by Teiresias). Father and son subsequently recognized each other in great sorrow. 'On the third day Ulysses died, an old man of advanced age, but not yet weak in natural force.'

Such is the strange farrago which for the best part of a thousand years was regarded in Western Europe as the true story of the wanderings, return, and death of Ulysses. It seems to have been concocted partly from puerile distortions of the *Odyssey*, and, in the latter portion, largely from the cyclic *Telegony*. As it adds nothing to the characterization of Ulysses and reveals no strong bias for or against him, it need not be dwelt on here. But the merits of the last portion of the narrative are considerable. The description of the dream is especially striking. It stimulated medieval writers on the Troy Tale to some remarkable elaborations.

Compared with these well written and plausibly argued narratives of Philostratus and Dictys, Dares's *History of the destruction of Troy* is a poor production. It attempts to cover the whole sequence of events from the voyage of the Argonauts (as a result of which the Greeks are alleged to have committed the first acts of aggression against the Trojans, thereby becoming ultimately responsible for the Trojan War) to the departure of the Greeks after their victory—all in about seven thousand words. One cannot expect any subtleties of characterization in so bald a summary as this. There was no room for exhibiting any special spleen against Ulysses, even if Dares in his pro-Trojan zeal had wished to do so. Ulysses appears only in his traditional rôle as leader of the Ithacans, as a regular envoy, and as a prominent counsellor. On the other hand, in order to increase the reputation of the Trojans, Dares represents Paris as having slain both Palamedes and Ajax by his arrows, thereby relieving Ulysses from all responsibility for their deaths. This paradoxical result of pro-Trojan bias naturally perplexed medieval chroniclers who found quite different accounts in Dictys.

As well as these casual references Dares gave one brief description of Ulysses which was destined to influence the whole medieval tradition. Ulysses, we are told, was 'strongly built, wily, with cheerful face, of medium stature, eloquent, wise'. The 'cheerful face' is the only unconventional feature. It caught the imagination of many writers on the Troy Romance from Benoit de Sainte Maure to Shakespeare. It may be simply intended as a sign of a good-humoured disposition. But this is hardly in character for either the much-enduring Homeric hero, or for the detested enemy of the Trojans. Even in Homer his smiles and laughs are generally sardonic or sinister. More likely Dares intended to suggest the sham *bonhomie* of W. B. Yeats's 'smiling public man', or the hypocritical friendliness of Pope's Atticus, skilled to 'assent with civil leer'. For, as Hamlet observes, a man 'may smile, and smile, and be a villain'. Yet Shakespeare in his *Rape of Lucrece* interpreted Dares's phrase (which he may have met in the original or else in some of the medieval English versions of the Troy Tale) rather more charitably, when he described how

> the mild glance that sly Ulysses lent
> Show'd deep regard and smiling government.

Apart from this touch of descriptive realism Dares's account of Ulysses is meagre indeed. Even when it was combined with Dictys's fuller account, the two provided poor material for mythopoeic amplification compared with the earlier classical tradition. In a way this very meagreness helped to enhance their authority in the eyes of western medieval writers and scholars. These plain narratives were, it was believed, the bedrock of history.[9] These were the authentic facts narrated by eye-witnesses in contrast with the poetic figments of Homer and Virgil. It was doubtless disturbing that Dares and Dictys disagreed on several points: one could not be sure for example, whether or not Ulysses had been to blame for the deaths of Palamedes and Ajax.[10] But these were small faults in comparison with the consistent disregard for truth that the poets had showed.

The imposture was astonishingly successful. All the writers on the Troy Romance and on the Troilus and Cressida theme from Benoit de Sainte Maure in the twelfth century to Caxton in the fifteenth believed that Dares and Dictys gave the authentic facts. The accepted view of Homer was, as Chaucer records, that he

> made lies
> Feyning in his poetries,
> And was to Greekes favourable.[11]

An effective effort to expose the fraud was not made until the sixteenth century, when Scaliger exerted his authority against it. Even then the truth was slow to gain general credence.[12]

In this way the victory of the anti-Homeric and anti-Ulyssean impostors was almost complete in the sphere of history and epic romance for many centuries. But they were unable to overthrow Homer's authority in the entire post-classical tradition. Even in the Latin-speaking West during the centuries when Greek was unknown to any but the rarest scholar, Homer's influence did maintain itself indirectly in some quarters, and Ulysses's Homeric renown was not entirely forgotten. From St. Paul's time onwards Christian apologists had recognized the value of the moral doctrines of the Stoics and had incorporated the Stoic method of allegorical interpretation into orthodox Christian apologetics. As a result, Ulysses continues to appear as a worthy example of natural virtue in the writings and sermons of Western as well as of Eastern clergy in every epoch of the Christian era. This has been discussed elsewhere.[13] A few typical examples will suffice to illustrate the general trend.

The early Fathers of the Church found it useful to refer at times to celebrated mythological figures as types of the Natural Man, partly as a contrast, and partly as a parallel to the supreme Christian Exemplar. Ulysses in his Odyssean adventures provided a convenient example of prudence, patience, and fortitude. So the Man of Many Turns, who had been the object of such obloquy from Pindar, Euripides, and Virgil, now had the surprising experience of being compared directly with Christ Himself. Both Origen and Hippolytus saw an analogy (though it is not to be pressed in details) between Our Lord on the Cross and Ulysses bound to the mast when his ship was passing the Sirens. Similarly Paulinus of Pella in one of his letters, having carefully explained that profitable lessons may be derived even from 'vain myths', exhorted Brother Jovius to emulate and excel Ulysses's self-control and prudence in face of Lotus-eaters and Sirens. The influential grammarian Fulgentius derived the name *Ulixes*, absurdly but appreciatively, as being from a Greek phrase meaning 'a stranger, or foreigner, in all things', 'because wisdom is alien to all worldly things': so Ulysses escapes from Scylla 'because wisdom scorns lust; whence also he is said to have as his wife the most chaste Penelope, because all chastity is joined to wisdom'. As the Church grew, Ulysses's good reputation spread beyond Mediterranean lands. When Abbot Immo in his life of Cadroe compared the Irishman's wanderings to those of Ulysses and Aeneas, 'whom the histories say endured many things', he can hardly have regarded Ulysses as a proverbial villain. The *Gesta Romanorum* provides a remarkable allegorization. After an account of the detection of Achilles in Scyros by Ulysses the reader is informed that in this incident Paris stands for the devil, Helen for the soul (or else all mankind), and Troy for Hell; Ulysses represents Christ, and Achilles the Holy Ghost. 'Ulysses represents Christ': what, one may wonder, were the thoughts of a medieval seeker after truth who read this interpretation in the light of Virgil's or Dictys's or Dante's portrait of Ulysses? It is true that allegory often produces astonishing results. But few characters in history or mythology can have been regarded in the same epoch as being both a type of villainous treachery and an analogue of the Incarnate Son of God.

Meanwhile, as Renaissance scholars were delighted to find, a living Greek literary tradition had survived in the Eastern Empire.[14] There, too, anti-Homeric and anti-Ulyssean propaganda had been strong. But, since there was no essential difference of language between Homer and educated Byzantine Greeks, Homer could always speak for himself against his detractors. If he was largely discredited as a historian, he was still venerated and studied as incomparably the greatest of epic poets. Orators still recommended their pupils to study his masterly speeches. Emperors still found models for wise government in his kings and princes. Poets still used his metre and phrases. And, what was most important of all for the revival of Greek studies in Western Europe, scribes continued to copy, and scholars continued to interpret, the works of both Homer and his admirers.

One author preserved by these late Greek scholars deserves special mention for his influence in restoring Homer and Ulysses to favour in Renaissance times. This was Plutarch,[15] the last great prose writer of the Greek classical tradition. No other figure of the Graeco-Roman world—he flourished about A.D. 90—did more to bring together all that was best in the Greek and Roman characters without chauvinistic prejudice or doctrinaire bias. He was devoted to Homer without being uncritical of his faults, and loyal to Stoicism without refusing to find good in other philosophies. He admired Ulysses both as a Homeric hero and as a prototype of the good Stoic. In the sixteenth century, when Western Europeans were wondering whether they should give their allegiance and veneration to the anti-Homeric writers or to Homer, Plutarch's impressive testimony did much to re-establish the older and nobler tradition and with it a more appreciative attitude to Ulysses.

CHAPTER XIII

THE MAN OF POLICIES

IT remains now to describe how the classical foundations of the
Ulysses myth have been used by vernacular writers. An exhaus-
tive study of this would require a volume to itself. Here it may
suffice to indicate the main lines of development.

The end of the Graeco-Roman period had left Ulysses's reputation
at a low ebb in Western Europe. The combined influence of the
pro-Roman and the anti-Homeric writers had established a generally
accepted conception of him as an unscrupulous, treacherous, contemptible intriguer. Some philosophers, it is true, had continued
to praise him as an example of prudent and virtuous living; and this
attitude had lived on in the writings and teachings of the Christian
Church. But after Benoit de Sainte Maure's *Roman de Troie* (written
about 1160) had become popular, the anti-Ulyssean faction domin-
ated the main literary tradition for the best part of three centuries.
Gradually, however, in the later part of that period, the revival of
interest in Greek studies removed the accumulated load of Latin
and Frankish odium from Ulysses. The beginning of this rehabilita-
tion may be dated near the 1360's, when Petrarch arranged to have
the *Odyssey* translated into Latin for Western readers.[1] Besides
Homer's growing influence, another eloquent champion soon began
to speak of Ulysses's good qualities. This was Plutarch, in whose
persuasive and inspiring works good Renaissance men could find
much scattered praise of Ulysses both as a Homeric hero and as an
archetypal Stoic. (The rediscovery of Sophocles and Euripides
helped Ulysses's reputation less, for on the whole his derogatory
portraits in *Hecuba* and *Philoctetes* outweighed his nobler appearance
in *Ajax*.) The whole atmosphere of the Renaissance with its
optimistic humanism, its richness, variety, and adventurousness, was
naturally congenial to a figure so versatile as Ulysses. The medieval
dichotomy between the warrior-knight and the learned clerk, both
in education and in life, had made it hard to comprehend his
double nature. But the men of the Renaissance, with their equal
interests in the martial and the liberal arts, could appreciate him
fully.

For a while the established Latin antipathy to Ulysses continued side by side with the renascent Homeric and Stoic admiration. But by the beginning of the sixteenth century the more favourable view prevailed among more progressive authors in England and France. In 1531 Sir Thomas Elyot in *The Governour* could recommend the wise, witty, courteous, resourceful, and nobly virtuous Ulysses to Henry VIII as an example of princely conduct. Elyot's eulogies of Ulysses, drawn mainly from Homer and Plutarch, are unstinted and unreserved. He quotes Ulysses's handling of the Thersites incident with approval to demonstrate 'That one soveraigne governor ought to be in a publike weale: and what damage hath happened where a multitude hath had equal authorite without any soveraygne'. This was a theme that Tudor monarchs would readily accept. Elyot finds equally good reason for praising Ulysses as he appears in the *Odyssey*.[2]

In France, too, for a while there were signs of a sympathetic attitude towards Ulysses. Joachim du Bellay's *Les Regrets* (1558) contained several appreciatory references to him besides the famous sonnet beginning *Heureux qui comme Ulysse*. Du Bellay also translated some portions of the *Iliad* and *Odyssey* into French. Ronsard seems to have had some liking for *Ulysse fin et caut*, as he called him, though he took Ajax's side against him in *Meslanges* 2. In 1604 Salomon Certon in the dedication of his translation of the *Odyssey* eulogistically compared the career of Henri IV with that of Ulysses (much in the manner of Chapman's prefaces to his English versions of Homer, in the same period).[3]

But Ulysses's reputation has never remained fixed for long. Before the end of the sixteenth century in France a fresh trend of literary taste began to revive antipathy against him. The crude old Trojano-Roman prejudice of the Troy Tale was replaced by a suaver and more sophisticated antagonism. Scaliger's attack on Greek literature and his championship of the Latin style (in his *Poetic* of 1561) marks the beginning of this counter-renaissance. Now Virgil and Seneca (instead of the naïve Dares and Dictys) become the arbiters of fashion in epic and dramatic poetry; and they were no friends of Ulysses. (Seneca's philosophic writings, in which, as has been described, Stoic admiration for Ulysses was often echoed, were less influential among French authors at this time.) The effect of this movement was soon seen in the plays of neo-classical dramatists like Garnier and Racine. It was strengthened by (and in turn helped to strengthen) the growing inclination of seventeenth-century French kings to present themselves in the style of Roman emperors—a marked change from the Greek interests of Henri IV and the English Tudor monarchs.[4]

The Augustan Age of French and English literature was not, however, entirely hostile to the Greekest of Greek heroes. After some acrimonious controversy about the morals and manners of Ulysses (very much in the idiom of the Alexandrian critics), which began with Rapin's ferocious attack in 1668,[5] he returned to favour under the patronage of Le Bossu and Fénelon. Similarly in contemporary England, after some less acrimonious criticism, Ulysses won equally influential support from Dryden and Pope (who acknowledged direct influence from Fénelon in his attitude to Homer's heroes). But the resulting Augustan portrait of Ulysses presented a rather too carefully groomed, too consciously monarchical, too gravely decorous, figure to stimulate much mythopoeic interest. It was not simply that he had become sad and reserved, losing the cheerful manner that even the Troy-romancers had conceded him. Meeting him now in Fénelon's *Télémaque* (1699) or in Pope's translations of Homer, one finds him just a little pretentious and rather a prig. Soon, it is clear, he may be simply a bore. It is all very well for Fénelon to hint at inscrutable secrets behind his majestic brow, or for Le Bossu to dwell on the governmental value of his wise and prudent dissimulation.[6] Where is the verve, the many-sidedness, the superb audacity, of Homer's hero? This decorous Augustan prince is as far removed from the affable ruler of Homer's Ithaca as Flaxman's smooth marbles from an archaic Greek bronze. One begins to wish for a few flaws in the dead-white façade. If this Fénelonesque view of the Homeric heroes was in Pococurante's mind when he confessed to Candide that he found *le plus mortel ennui* in Homer's poems, one can hardly blame him for his reaction. And Voltaire himself may have had the same reason for remarking, 'I do not know how it comes to pass, but every reader bears secretly an ill will to the wise Ulysses'.[7]

For these and other reasons (probably the growing regard for the scientific attitude, as will be illustrated from Vico in the next chapter, had some effect, too) no portrait of Ulysses fit to rank with those by Dante, Shakespeare, and Calderon, appeared during the eighteenth[8] or early nineteenth century. He remained a celebrated figure, especially in drama; but he had lost his imaginative qualities. One can see the typical eighteenth-century hero displayed in Metastasio's *Achille in Sciro* (first produced in 1736). Metastasio relies mainly on Statius's version of this incident. His Ulysses is honourable, generous, and magnanimous, as well as subtle, patient, and intelligent; and he uses no deceits to win over the reluctant Achilles from the arms of his loving Deïdameia. The total effect is spectacular and fine. Yet the prevailing Augustan tendency to strike an attitude and to conceal the deeper currents of human feeling makes this Ulysses seem wooden compared with his livelier portraits in earlier and later epochs.

With a few exceptions, this rather sterile kind of Ulysses is the typical product of the neo-classical and Augustan ages. It needed a literary revolution to break up this marmoreal image. The rise of romantic Hellenism in the nineteenth century provided this. Its effects will be seen later in Tennyson's *Ulysses*. There Augustan decorum is completely forgotten and a potent new symbol of restless modernism emerges. Since then the tradition has shown extraordinary variety. Once again the Ulysses-figure has become a receptacle for the conflicting moods and opinions of the time. Once again he plays the part of Everyman.

After this brief sketch of the general literary background it is not now intended to trace the development of the vernacular Ulysses myth in chronological order. Instead the intention is to consider the main modern variations on the classical portraits of Ulysses typologically. The word 'type' must be used in its broadest sense here, since the major presentations of Ulysses generally suggest a degree of moral and psychological complexity which transcends the narrower concept of type-character. Nuances of personality and of symbolism prevent him from being stereotyped as a conventional character. His inner qualities are too complex, his outward characteristics too adaptable, to conform to any ethical pattern for long.

But using the term 'type' in its broadest sense one may distinguish two Ulyssean types in the post-Homeric tradition, ancient and modern. One, broadly speaking, is that of the politician, the second (to be exemplified in a later chapter) that of the lonely wanderer. (Homer, it must be emphasized, had fully integrated the two; and attempts have been made to recreate this integrated personality in modern terms, as will be described later.) The first may be called the Iliadic hero. This Ulysses is the warrior, strategist, orator, counsellor, negotiator, and, if needs be, spy. In each of these rôles he is bold, purposeful, prudent, resourceful, firm-minded. Later, when authors began to value warlike qualities less highly than had the epic poets, the Homeric warrior-counsellor developed into the

statesman or (if unfavourably viewed) the party politician. The
Ulysses of Sophocles, Euripides, Virgil, and Seneca, is fundamentally
this kind of *politique*, essentially the public man, for good or evil.
This is his least sympathetic rôle, even when presented as favourably
as in Sophocles's *Ajax*. In this arena of public affairs Ulysses has
little chance of displaying either his gentler domestic virtues or his
adventurousness—his Odyssean qualities. Yet his reputation has
on the whole depended more on his conduct in this political rôle
than on anything else, and his popular notoriety chiefly results
from it.

The modern career of Ulysses the politician begins in the twelfth-
century *Roman de Troie* of Benoit de Sainte Maure. In it for the
first time in a major literary work Ulysses stands before us speaking
a vernacular language, wearing the armour of a medieval knight,
and—but this is still in a rudimentary stage—acquiring some of the
psychological traits of a Western European. Benoit and his numer-
ous imitators were in one respect nearer to Homer than most of
the later writers of the classical period, though this was the result
of historical environment and not of direct imitation (for they knew
little or nothing of Homer's poems): Benoit's heroes are primarily
warriors, not politicians, or philosophers, or symbolical figures.
Among these warring knights, 'Ulixès' is, as in the *Iliad*, the most
politically minded. He is 'wonderfully skilled in fine speech',
'prudent and courteous', but 'given to mockery and derision' (a
distortion of Dares's *ore hilari*), 'the greatest trickster in ten thousand
knights'. His conduct throughout Benoit's poem generally illustrates his more sinister and harsh qualities, in the manner of Dictys
and Virgil. Benoit is emphatically pro-Trojan and anti-Greek. Yet,
significantly for the later tradition, when he relates Ulysses's
Odyssean adventures (in direct imitation of Dictys) he seems to feel
some compassion for the storm-tossed hero. Here Benoit's Frankish
loyalties were less involved, leaving more room for personal,
humane feelings.

Benoit's presentation of Ulysses set the fashion for all subsequent
writers on the Troy romance in its ramifications from Russia to
Iceland during the following three centuries. In the more original
versions there are naturally some slight variations in attitude. Thus
Guido delle Colonne's influential Latin adaptation of Benoit's story
(in 1287) and Lydgate's *Troy Book* (1420) removed a few calumnies
from Ulysses's reputation. But on the whole he remained the
untrustworthy intriguer-knight. At the end of the medieval period

Caxton, in his *Recuyell of the historyes of Troye* (*c.* 1474), condemned him most harshly of all, making the Greek 'Thelamon' remark in the contest for the Palladium:

> Vlixes had in hym no prowesse ne vaillyance but onely subtylte and fayre spekyng for to deceyue men And by hym haue we goten to vs grete villonnye that where we myght haue vaynquysshid the troians by Armes Now we haue vaynquysshed hem by dysceyte and barate etc.

Ulysses repudiates the charge: but his reply is much less effective than in Lydgate's version of the incident.[9]

Early in the sixteenth century this medieval antipathy[10] to Ulysses the politician was counterbalanced by the reviving influence of Homer and the Greek philosophers. Yet it lingered on. As late as 1679 Dryden in his version of Shakespeare's *Troilus and Cressida* could still think it worth while to appeal to Trojano-British sentiment by ending his prologue with these stirring words:

> My faithfull Scene from true Records shall tell
> How Trojan valour did the Greek excell;
> Your great forefathers shall their fame regain
> And Homer's angry Ghost repine in vain.

One might be back again with Lydgate in the early fifteenth century as far as chauvinism and anti-Homeric prejudices are concerned. Dryden, who knew and admired Homer, can hardly have been entirely sincere about this[11]; yet clearly he was appealing to strong popular sentiment.

As has already been noticed, Sir Thomas Elyot's *Governour* (1531) marked the reaction towards a more favourable opinion of Ulysses in Tudor England; and it was the product of a general tendency throughout Western Europe. But Elyot's book was a prose treatise on the art of ruling, not a work of the creative imagination. Seventy years had to pass before the new view of Ulysses was expressed by an imaginative writer of the highest rank. Shakespeare's *Troilus and Cressida* (perhaps in 1602) presents the greatest portrait of Ulysses in the Renaissance style. Like so many other conceptions of Ulysses this complex figure has been a source of far-reaching controversies. What were Shakespeare's sources? Was he influenced more by medieval antipathy to Ulysses or by Renaissance admiration? Did he himself admire or dislike Ulysses? Had he personal reasons for portraying Ulysses as he did?[12]

A few excerpts will show how widely opinions vary on his

portrait of Ulysses.[13] 'The wily Ulysses, delighting in the caricature of his compeers, is the most ridiculous of the Greek heroes.' 'Ulysses is the real hero of the play, the chief, or at least the great, purpose of which is the utterance of the Ulyssean view of life; and in this play Shakespeare is Ulysses, or Ulysses Shakespeare.' 'Ulysses who is intended to represent the wise man of the play is as trivial of mind as the rest.' 'Shakespeare's Ulysses is a medieval knight of the legend of Troy who has been modernized into a *politique*—but who still retains a Greek touch of concern for "the still and mental parts".' 'And indeed Ulysses is wise, Shakespeare can make him utter searching truths about necessities of the social structure; but his wisdom is also shot through with grandiloquent emptiness and furthermore is guided by a mean calculating intelligence. . . . He is above all malicious.' '. . . wise, experienced, unscrupulous perhaps, the old fox who will use any means to attain his end. But he is not without nobility: the quality of his intellect—and he is all intellect save for certain moments when, in attendance upon Troilus, he charms us with his humanity—makes him a figure of worth. He has thought profoundly on political and social questions; he is familiar with the workings of the world; he can weigh, judge, and (usually) bring people to act as he wishes them to act.' 'The combination of psychological insight, cold malice, and artistic gusto with which Ulysses sets out to stir up trouble puts him in a totally different, and lower, camp from perpetrators of crimes of passion, reminding us, in retrospect, of Pandulph . . . and, in prospect, of Iago. . . . As a deranger of degree and fomenter of the very anarchy he pretends to hate, he turns out to be an advance agent of his own Universal Wolf.' 'Ulysses . . . is the much-experienced man of the world, possessed of its highest and broadest wisdom, which yet always remains worldly wisdom and never rises into the spiritual contemplation of a Prospero. He sees all the unworthiness of human life but will use it for high worldly ends . . . .' One of the most recent critics sees him as a person who 'towers right above the other Greeks in good sense and acute or sympathetic perception', but whose 'doctrine of honour is purely selfish and materialistic'; he (Ulysses) 'inhabits the world of convention and practises the maximum sympathy possible within that world'. James Joyce once paradoxically remarked: 'If you re-read *Troilus and Cressida* you will see that of all the heroes Thersites respects only Ulysses'. But in the play itself Thersites calls Ulysses 'that same dog-fox'.

To argue with each of these views separately would lead too far afield here. What follows is a short account of Ulysses's actions in the play and a personal opinion on his significance and Shakespeare's intentions.

Ulysses first appears in the Greek council of war in Act 1, Scene 3. 'After seven yeares siege, yet Troy walles stand.' What is the reason for the delay? When Agamemnon and Nestor have given their views, Ulysses with courtly compliments asks permission to speak, and begins his famous discourse on 'degree', the hierarchical system in society.[14] The theme goes back to Odysseus's words in *Iliad* Two, but it is weighted and embroidered with much medieval and Renaissance thought. The eloquence is superb. For the first time since his *orazion picciola* in Dante's *Inferno*, Ulysses speaks in the grand style.

Having exemplified Ulysses's magniloquence, Shakespeare goes on to exemplify his traditional knowledge of men. Asked what is the remedy for this sickness in the body corporate, Ulysses points to the main cause, the mocking pride of Achilles who is idling in his tent making fun of the more active Greek leaders. Then prompted by Nestor, Ulysses turns his attention to the second source of their frustration, Ajax with his stupid contempt for anything but brute force—a theme which Ovid had already exploited, as described in chapter eleven.

What is to be done? In a later scene with Nestor, Ulysses unfolds a plan. 'By device' the 'blockish Ajax' can be allowed to win the lottery for the privilege of fighting Hector. Then Achilles, when he sees how all the Greeks deliberately play up to Ajax as the worthier man, may be goaded into action. Here clearly is the Autolycan touch in this double deception of Ajax and Achilles. Some critics have considered it contemptible. But at least Ulysses had nothing personally to gain by it. It is entirely *pro bono publico* or at least *pro bono Graeco*. Nor will it do either Achilles or Ajax any great harm. Shakespeare in an age of machiavellian statesmanship can hardly have considered this a damnable deceit.

What is more, when Ulysses actually meets Achilles he rises far above mere trickery (3, 3). After a conventional ruse (like Hamlet's) with a book, and an equivocation about Ajax's forthcoming duel with Hector, Ulysses turns from deceit to high philosophical pleading. The result is another of the greatest speeches in the Ulysses tradition (and, by common consent, in Shakespeare's plays), his discourse on time and ingratitude. It leads back (though the parallel could not have been known to Shakespeare) to Ulysses's remarks in the prologue to Euripides's *Philoctetes*, and forward to Tennyson's Ulysses when he exclaims

> How dull it is to pause, to make an end
> To rust unburnish'd, not to shine in use.

This speech has been criticized on two counts. First Ulysses has been blamed for using purely selfish and materialistic arguments. But consider its hearer and its purpose. The Achilles of the later tradition was a fame-intoxicated, love-infatuated figure—irresponsible through his touchy pride and his secret passion for a Trojan princess, but indispensable to the Greeks for his consummate skill in arms. Ulysses's purpose is to persuade this bright bundle of needles to respond again to the magnet of glory (as, in different circumstances, in Metastasio's *Achille in Sciro*). This Achilles is no blockish Ajax to be easily fooled, but a man of a keen, though wayward, intelligence.

It is illuminating to observe how carefully Ulysses first lets Achilles display his own intelligence in explaining the enigmatic passage in the book; then emphasizes the rising fortune of Ajax; then manoeuvres Achilles into a self-pitying sense of man's ingratitude; and finally strikes with all the weight of his philosophical eloquence. It is true that the appeal is mainly to self-interest. But this was no occasion for sermonizing or moralizing. The argument, though phrased in splendid abstractions, is an *ad hominem* appeal to Achilles's special virtue, the doing of glorious deeds.[15] In other words Ulysses is performing the first duty of a diplomat or a politician, to accommodate his speech to his audience's mind and mood. This first effort fails. After some rather ominous words on statecraft,[16] Ulysses tries one more argument—what will Achilles's son think of his father if it is Ajax who vanquishes Hector? Then Ulysses leaves without waiting for a reply, hoping no doubt that this last dart will sink deep. Later events show that it, too, has failed.

This failure to persuade Achilles provides grounds for a second criticism of Ulysses in this scene, the argument being that, if one embarks on deceit, failure is an added disgrace. But there were two technical reasons why Ulysses had to fail. First, an unsuccessful attempt by Ulysses to restore Achilles to the fighting line had been an established part of the tradition since Homer's account of the Embassy in *Iliad* Nine. Unless Shakespeare could find a very good dramaturgical reason for reversing the tradition, it would have to remain so. Secondly, Ulysses's failure here did in fact suit

M

Shakespeare's purpose very well, if critics are right in seeing *Troilus and Cressida* (in its political as distinct from its romantic aspects) as illustrating the ultimate powerlessness of prudence and reason against passion and pride. Ulysses, the personification of practical wisdom, can persuade Agamemnon, Nestor, and Menelaus; for they are still in a reasonable frame of mind. With Achilles, it is shown, he can go a certain distance: then the bronze doors of pride and passion clang to, and reason is powerless to enter. To Ulysses's credit he takes his defeat without rancour or self-exoneration. It is hard to see how the scene could have been intended to vilify him.

This is the end of Ulysses's main political part in the play. Shakespeare now lets the element of passion take command among the Greeks and Trojans alike. But Ulysses does not sink into obscurity like a defeated party politician or an incompetent diplomat. On the contrary he is given some striking opportunities to demonstrate his intuitive wisdom, self-control, and (in the most significant scene) his gentleness—the very qualities, it will be remembered, Homer's Athene had liked best in him. In Act 4, Scene 5, he first sums up Diomedes's character with a shrewd deduction from 'the manner of his gate'. Then, when Cressida enters and receives a cordial welcome from the other Greeks, he (in Dowden's phrases) reads her at a glance, seeing to the bottom of her sensual, shallow nature, and, in contrast with his subsequent courtesy towards the 'most gentle and most valiant Hector', flouts her in her own pert idiom. Thoughts of Penelope and Ithaca are clearly irrelevant here: the incident grows directly out of the characters of Ulysses and Cressida as Shakespeare conceived them. Yet this rejection of Cressida's kiss does accord perfectly with Homer's conception of a Ulysses entirely faithful to Penelope at Troy.

In these short but notable exchanges Ulysses shows two of his more personal qualities, intuitive shrewdness towards Diomedes and Cressida, marked courtesy towards Hector. The second might be dismissed as merely conventional in this play of passion-shattered chivalry, if it were not for a further series of episodes, which may give the final clue to Shakespeare's opinion of Ulysses.

Soon after Ulysses's meeting with Cressida and Hector, he has an opportunity of giving his opinion of Troilus. Here his worst critic cannot find any base reason for him to be generous and magnanimous. Yet he is both (4, 5, 96 ff.). He particularly admires Troilus's firmness of speech, level-headedness, perseverance, and generosity. The first three qualities are unusual in a prince 'not yet mature', as Ulysses describes him. In making Ulysses emphasize them Shakespeare's intention may have been to imply that the much-experienced Greek and the not yet disillusioned Trojan had much in common.

Finally, in Act 5, Scene 2, Ulysses stands beside Troilus while he witnesses, broken-hearted, the perfidy of his Cressida with Diomedes. At first Ulysses spares the young lover no revelation. Troilus must know the full extent of Cressida's mutability. But when he sees that Troilus is near the breaking-point, he tries to lead him away. Troilus insists on remaining. Ulysses appeals to him for patience and self-control. In the end, to Troilus's copious words of disillusionment, he, the eloquent Greek, confines himself to the briefest replies. He attempts no explanation or consolation. He simply stands by the distraught and ranting Trojan, listens to his heart-broken words, and replies less by phrases than by his tone and his subdued presence. His last words, after a speech that might have provoked an Ajax to voluble sympathy, are simply 'I'll bring you to the gates'. The final comment is left to Thersites, who can see nothing but wars and lechery in it all.

Ulysses enters the play only for a brief speech later, calling on the Greeks to show courage at the crisis of the battle. His last words are in praise of Ajax for redeeming his faults by sheer valour. The play itself breaks into fragments of fighting, treachery, and cursing.

It is in his scenes with Troilus that Ulysses has the best opportunity of revealing his more intimate qualities. But once again the perennial ambiguity of his actions confronts us. Some critics have seen flattery, sadistic enjoyment, and sardonic pessimism, in his handling of Troilus. Endless argument is possible here. What now follows is only the personal opinion of a reader who has arrived at the problems of Shakespeare's Ulysses not, as is more usual, from a previous study of medieval and modern literature, but from a pursuit of the Ulysses tradition from Homer downwards.

Seen in the full perspective of the Ulysses myth these scenes between Ulysses and Troilus most resemble those between Odysseus and Telemachus in the *Odyssey*, and, later in the tradition, the last scene between Leopold Bloom and Stephen Dedalus in Joyce's *Ulysses*. In all of these scenes the patient, much-enduring hero converses with an idealistic, inexperienced young man, partly in the spirit of *maxima debetur puero reverentia*, and partly in awareness that they have much in common despite discrepancies in age and policy. In the *Odyssey* there was a physical bond as between father and son. In *Troilus and Cressida*, as in Joyce's *Ulysses*, the bond is that of compassionate humanism, which Shakespeare is more likely to have learned from his own heart than from any study of the Ulysses tradition. Then what Shakespeare may have ultimately perceived was, perhaps, this: the medieval accounts of the bitter feud between Greeks and Trojans failed to recognize that both parties consisted of human beings, passionate, proud, deluded, sometimes well-meaning, sometimes ill-intentioned, sometimes crafty, sometimes foolish, but, still, human beings. The pure-souled Trojans and evil-hearted Greeks of the conventional accounts were false abstractions. Take the two apparently most unlike figures of the old Troy tale, the romantic Troilus and the hard-bitten Ulysses. Bring them together in a moment of deep emotion. What will happen? They will forget their traditional antipathies and realize their common humanity, their common victimization, so to speak, in the scheme of things. The worldly-wise Ulysses and the freshly disillusioned Troilus are brothers under their skins—and so, too, in a less emphasized way, are Thersites and Pandarus, Nestor and Priam, Menelaus and Paris.[17] Once again it is Horace's view: *Iliacos muros intra peccatur et extra.* In other words, Shakespeare wrote here, as far as his conception of Ulysses is concerned, not as a medievalist or as a neo-classicist, but as a humanist in the tradition of both Homer and the Renaissance.[18]

'Others abide our question. Thou art free.' Matthew Arnold's sonnet warns against attempting to see Shakespeare's personal motives behind his plays. Yet, with emphasis on its purely speculative nature, a brief suggestion may be allowed here. First, a curious coincidence: if, as is generally agreed, *Troilus and Cressida* was written about 1602, Shakespeare was then about thirty-eight.[19] This was the age of Leopold Bloom on the fateful day described in *Ulysses* and also the age of his author, James Joyce, when he was putting the finishing touches to his novel in 1920. Is this pure accident? Perhaps not, for if we take Shakespeare's Seven Ages of Man as a norm, a man in the later thirties has passed through his lovelorn ballad-writing years and is coming to the end of his career as a reputation-seeking soldier. His Troilus and Achilles days are over; a few years, and he will be the sententious, round-bellied justice, 'full of wise saws and modern instances'. Romanticism is past; ambition is sated or disillusioned; he begins to wonder what can be saved from the ruins left by amorous passion and self-seeking conflict—and this in a world peopled with creatures like Ajax, Pandarus, and Thersites, a world of stupid men of honour, clever men of shame, and scurrilous mockers. Further, if a man at this time of life has any public spirit or humane feelings left after his disillusionment, he will consider how his experience can best be used to help the people he lives with, or at least to help those of them who are not, like Ajax and Pandarus, beyond all human help. So Bloom as he goes about his ordinary business through the streets of Dublin meditates on many ingenious devices for reforming society. So, too, at the same age James Joyce abandoned the self-centred autobiographical attitudes of his earlier works for the more social and political outlook of *Ulysses*.

Perhaps it was for the same reason that Shakespeare turned from the warriors of his historical plays and the young lovers of his romantic plays to a deeper study of traditional society. In *Troilus and Cressida*, within the framework, that is, of the Troy tale, he surveyed the devastation caused in the social order by lust, pride, violence, insubordination, and treachery. In that legend there was only one character who presented some hope for the maintenance of hierarchical order and decency: a man disillusioned but not embittered, self-controlled but not hardened, disciplined but not ruthless, public-spirited but not inhumane, wily but not fundamentally dishonest, firm but not ungentle—Ulysses.[20] Why then Shakespeare should have let anarchy and ruin prevail at the end of the play is another question.

The breadth of Shakespeare's comprehensive humanism can be illustrated by the contrast between his Ulysses and that of the neoclassical French tragedians. There both the Senecan style and the Senecan attitude to Ulysses prevented any indulgent portrait.[21] Robert Garnier's *La Troade* (1579), as its title implies, closely followed Seneca and Euripides. Opinions vary about the degree of Ulysses's odiousness as Garnier presents him, but in general he is the inflexible emissary of a harsh decree. He retains his eloquence, self-possession, firmness of purpose; but one will look in vain for humane compassion. The plot, the style, and the accepted attitude, prevent it. Racine's *Iphigénie* (1674) presents much the same unsympathetic figure.[22] His Ulysses is perhaps a trifle less repellent than the Gauleiter of Garnier's *La Troade* and a little more independent than the shifty go-between of Euripides's *Iphigeneia at Aulis*; but his appeals to honour, patriotism, and glory, in the scene with Agamemnon ring very false. His manner is, as Racine's idiom

demanded, dignified and fine. But he is far from that *beau caractère*,
that *esprit délicat et fort*, that man whose reputed wiliness must be
taken *en bonne part, pour adresse, prudence*, whom Racine had found
in the *Odyssey* twelve years previously.[23] The Latin anti-Ulyssean
genius had prevailed once more.

Meanwhile the Netherlands had produced a political Ulysses in
whom one does not have to discern ethical nuances, for he is a
thorough-going villain. Joost van den Vondel's *Palamedes, or
Murdered Innocence*, appeared in 1625.[24] Its theme is the most
discreditable incident in Ulysses's career, the slaying of Palamedes.
Here Ulysses is mainly a mask for political pamphleteering in the
conflict between Remonstrants and Counter-remonstrants. The
'martyred' Palamedes represents the leader of the oligarchical
Republican party. The guilt for his death is laid on Ulysses (who
stands for a leading Counter-remonstrant), assisted by Diomedes.
Ulysses leads the conspiracy against his innocent rival, and, inspired
by a vision from Hell of his father Sisyphus, presses the false charge
home. In other words, a wicked Calvinistic Ulysses (supported by
a Calchas who is a caricature of ultra-predestinarian dogmatists)
triumphs despicably over an innocent martyr to goodness and truth
—or so one is expected to believe.

Little could be gained by delaying over Ulysses's characterization
in a mainly propagandist play of this kind. Ulysses is merely a pawn
in a religious and political conflict. But even as a pawn in seventeenth-century affairs, he made some curious moves. Vondel saw
him as an intriguing Calvinist. Within the next thirty years writers
like Calderon and Jacopo Ugone would present him as a worthy
personification of post-Tridentine Catholic truth, as will be described in the next chapter. Others would piously compare him
with Biblical figures. But in these allegorical and propagandist
portraits of Ulysses the personality of the hero himself counted for
little.

Conventional representations of Ulysses continued throughout
the eighteenth[25] and early nineteenth centuries. In general they
followed the Augustan and Latin style, as has been exemplified in
Metastasio's play. Ulysses remains a figure more fit for Versailles,
or for Alexandria under the Ptolemies, than for Troy, Ithaca, and
Fairyland. As the nineteenth century advanced, the movement now
called Romantic Hellenism transferred literary interest to the
Odyssean wanderer-hero. But not, however, entirely: occasional
portraits of the *politique* recurred. Thus one minor poet produced

an adaptation of Sophocles's *Philoctetes* which contained one of the bitterest denunciations of Ulysses ever written[26]:

> His tongue drops honey: his lip
> Smiles gently, smoothly, innocently mild:
> His heart is as the very lees of hell.
> Ay, he will reel you off the name of the gods,
> And weep the earth's impiety and sigh
> The innocent old days back, searching the while
> Where he may surest stab and end you out.

But blackening a traditional villain is an easy task.

The period between the first and second world wars of the present century produced one outstanding presentation of the Iliadic hero. Here Ulysses's problem is not to win a war (as in the *Iliad* and in Shakespeare's *Troilus and Cressida*) but to prevent one—an urgent problem in 1935 when Jean Giraudoux wrote *La guerre de Troie n'aura pas lieu*. The theme of this brilliant play is the Greek embassy to Troy to demand back Helen before the outbreak of war (as mentioned in the *Iliad* and described in detail in the *Cypria* and in the medieval Troy tale). Ulysses is the only traditional Greek figure to appear—and this only in two scenes. But the impact of his portrait is fresh and strong. He appears first as an ambassador among a group of leading Trojans. His manner is forthright, brusque, but not disagreeable, more reminiscent of the scenes with Cressida and Hector in Shakespeare's play than of anything in Euripides, Seneca, or Racine. A salty Homeric humour and an unusual candour of phrase make it clear that this is neither the discreet negotiator nor the callous power-politician.

In the next scene Ulysses remains alone with Hector. Each with an intuitive confidence in the other speaks frankly of himself and his motives. Hector describes himself as a figure of young manhood, devoted to his young wife and to the child that is to be born. His is *la joie de vivre, la confiance de vivre, l'élan vers ce qui est juste et naturel*. Ulysses in reply characterizes himself as *l'homme adulte*, devoted to a thirty-year-old wife and a growing son, valuing *la volupté de vivre et la méfiance de la vie*. They continue in a kind of confessional litany: Hector stands for *la chasse, le courage, la fidélité, l'amour*; Ulysses for *la circonspection devant les dieux*—a notable, though possibly ironical, reference to his long-forgotten Homeric piety—*les hommes et les choses*. Hector compares himself to a Phrygian oak and a falcon who stares into the sun; Ulysses chooses the symbolism of the olive tree and the owl. In the end Hector admits that he feels unequal to Ulysses.

They turn from this symbolical, almost poetic, self-appraisal to the problem of the war. Here Hector speaks in conventional, rather naïve, terms. In contrast Ulysses shows himself as a realist who has thought deeply on the paradoxical causes of human conflict. His rationalistic irrationalism perplexes, even shocks, Hector, who tends to harp on a traditional belief in a fundamental enmity between Greeks and Trojans. Ulysses refuses to accept these generalizations. War and peace, his experience and thought have shown him, depend on common human qualities. *Iliacos muros intra peccatur et extra.* When Ulysses makes his final proposal about Helen, Hector becomes suspicious for a moment—*Est-ce là la ruse d'Ulysse ou sa grandeur?* Ulysses replies that if there is any ruse it is only against *le destin*, and avers his sincerity. Hector trusts him, apparently with reason. They separate as friends, Hector assured now that it is *noblesse* which has led Ulysses to his decision. Ulysses in his last words says, No, not *noblesse*, but because the fluttering of Andromache's eyelashes reminded him of Penelope's. The phrase, characteristic of his almost frivolous refusal to accept pretentious generalizations in this play, suggests both ironical self-depreciation and also reminds us for an instant of the gentler aspect of the Odyssean hero. In the last scene the peaceable settlement is wrecked by the boorishness and treachery of a Trojan Thersites. The Trojan War will take place after all.

Giraudoux's Ulysses is a brilliant sketch, combining a Racinian lucidity of phrase and thought with a Homeric and Shakesperian sympathy for Ulysses's essential Greekness. Like all the greater conceptions of Ulysses, this figure succeeds in personifying apparently hostile qualities. He is both fatalistic and energetic, realistic and compassionate, logical and imaginative, flippant and serious. Hardly a trace remains of the Troy Tale's sinister intriguer or of the Euripidean power-politician. Instead one recognizes, despite Giraudoux's twentieth-century ethics and idiom, the innate honesty and tolerance of the Homeric hero. There is much here, too, of Shakespeare's *Troilus and Cressida* in both Ulysses and Hector, as well as in the ultimate triumph of chaos over order, passion over reason, brutality over civilization. But here it is the folly of the populace, not the folly of princes, that causes the disaster. As in the *Iliad* and in *Troilus and Cressida* the Ulysses of *La guerre de Troie n'aura pas lieu* stands for the civilized mind in a world of undisciplined passion. This is his highest function as a *politique*.

CHAPTER XIV

THE WANDERER

SUCH were some of the post-classical vagaries of the Iliadic Ulysses. What, now, of the Odyssean hero? In Homer's *Odyssey* Ulysses remained the alert, prudent and resourceful person that he was in the *Iliad*. But his environment had changed. He was no longer a compeer of great heroes whose conduct was regulated by recognized customs and conventions; and he no longer moved in the arena of public life under the critical gaze of rival chieftains. Instead, in the unconventional conditions of the *Odyssey*—for even when Ulysses has reached home he must play the part of a beggar —he is compelled to be mainly the individualist and the opportunist. He does, indeed, have some occasions for using his skill as a *politique*. But the Iliadic world of formal debates and embassies is now left behind, and a paradoxical world of magic and disorder has taken its place. In other words Ulysses has been moved from a classical to a romantic environment. As a result, it was his Odyssean aspects that appealed most to the romantic writers of the later tradition.

One can distinguish three main phases in Ulysses's career in the *Odyssey*. Homer introduces him first (as described in chapter four) as a mournful exile, yearning for Ithaca after seven years of indolence on Calypso's island. Next he appears as the adventurous traveller in unexplored lands. Finally, in the last twelve books, he becomes the King-who-comes-into-his-own-again, the Avenger-in-disguise, the Husband-who-returns-at-last. There Homer's narrative ends. But later writers (as described in chapter six) imposed further journeys on the weary wanderer. Modern versions of these four phases will be now considered in turn.

First, Ulysses as the exile yearning for home: in the post-Homeric tradition Ovid, the Stoics, and some of the early Christian Fathers, had made notable use of Ulysses as an emblem for nostalgia or for spiritual aspiration. Ovid, when exiled from Rome, found personal comfort in it. The philosophers and the churchmen took it as an allegory of man's yearning for the Heavenly City. These two attitudes, the personal and the moralistic, continued throughout the vernacular tradition. The allegorical interpretation is a common-place and need not be illustrated. The personal attitude is hardly less hackneyed, but one famous example of it deserves special consideration. It comes at the beginning of Joachim du Bellay's celebrated sonnet:

> Heureux qui comme Ulysse, a fait un beau voyage,
> Ou comme cestuy là qui conquit la toison,
> Et puis est retourné, plein d'usage et raison,
> Vivre entre ses parents le reste de son aage !
> Quand revoiray-je, hélas, de mon petit village
> Fumer la cheminée, et en quelle saison
> Revoiray-je le clos de ma pauvre maison
> Qui m'est une province, et beaucoup d'avantage.

Despite its brevity and conventionality, this use of the emblem has a poignancy unrivalled in the whole Ulysses tradition. It is more than a mere simile: it is a deeply felt self-identification. Circumstances had made the Ulysses image particularly apt for du Bellay's own feelings. When Ovid used the same figure he was, it is true, an exile, but an exile *from* Rome, eager to return to its splendours and excitements. Du Bellay was an exile *in* Rome, eager to leave it for the quiet peace of Lyré and *la doulceur angevine*, just as in the *Odyssey* Ulysses had yearned to escape from the richness and beauty of a demi-goddess's island to rugged Ithaca. Like du Bellay, Ulysses must have been conscious that this might seem a foolish choice. But, as he saw it, affection is better than luxury, charm brings more happiness than beauty. Ulysses had learnt that in time a man tires of heroic effort and spectacular surroundings, and will want to return—not, indeed, as a nonentity or as a failure, but as a man satisfied and completed by experience and knowledge—to his own little kingdom. This, unlike Ovid's querulous cravings to renew a metropolitan career, is the authentic spirit of the Odyssean hero.

Many other modern writers have used Ulysses as an emblem of their exilic emotions.[1] But few recaptured the Odyssean note as effectively as du Bellay. Others tended to tarnish the silver clarity of the emblem with feelings of self-pity, indignation, or rancour. Du Bellay neither whines nor rages: he merely affirms in superbly concrete images, partly Homeric,[2] partly Renaissance, that having seen the greatest glories of the world he prefers his own undistinguished homeland. For a moment he and Ulysses become identified by a sudden flash of imaginative sympathy, and a faultless symbolism results. References elsewhere in his poems suggest that this sense of spiritual kinship with Ulysses was not a passing fancy.

A recent poem, deliberately written as a modern variation on du Bellay's theme, deserves to stand beside his sonnet as an expression of the exilic mood in Odyssean terms. This is 'On a foreign line' by the Greek poet George Seferis, written in London in 1931.[3] Beginning with a Greek adaptation of du Bellay's first line, Seferis describes how an exile's love of home surges in his veins 'with an indestructible rhythm'. He tells how again and again he seems to see the ghost of Odysseus: the hero's eyes are red from the sea brine and from his 'desire to see again the smoke that rises from the warmth of his home and his dog that has grown old waiting at the door'; he is tall and bearded; his hands are calloused from the rope and the helm, his skin tanned by the wind and the heat and the snow. He appears to be trying to prevent the intrusive figures of the 'superman' Cyclops, the Sirens, Scylla and Charybdis—'so many complicated monsters'—from obscuring the fact that he (like the poet) was a man 'who wrestled with the world, the soul, and the body'. The poet imagines that Odysseus has come like this to advise him how he, too, can make a wooden horse for himself and with it win his Troy. Odysseus speaks humbly and serenely 'as if he knew me like a father, or like those old sailors who would lean on their nets when the winter came and the wind went mad, and tell me, in the days of my childhood, the romance of Erotocritus, their eyes full of tears'. Odysseus tells of the pain that comes when 'you feel the sails of your ship inflated with memories and your soul straining like a steering wheel'. He has known what it is 'to be all alone and darkling in the night, out of control like a straw on the threshing-floor: the bitterness of seeing your comrades overwhelmed by the elements, submerged, one by one'. He recalls (from his experience in the Land of Shades in *Odyssey* Eleven) how, strangely, you can find a manly strength in speaking with the dead, when the living left with you are no longer able to help you. The poem ends: 'He speaks ... and I can still see those hands of his ... presenting me with the unruffled blue sea in the heart of winter'.

Seferis's poem reaches out much further than du Bellay's into the bitter bereavements of life. Du Bellay thought only of exile: the Greek poet goes on beyond the initial emotion of yearning for home to see the whole of life as an odyssey among dangers and desolations. In other words, he is nearer in the end to the Stoic conception of Ulysses than to Homer's and Ovid's. And though Ulysses and he are in close sympathy they remain separate beings throughout the poem: in du Bellay's sonnet for a moment the poet and the hero were one. But as a lyrical expression of modern emotions in the traditional Odyssean symbols Seferis's poem deserves to be remembered.

As Homer recounts the exploits of Ulysses in the *Odyssey* this exilic phase is presented first. But in actual time it was preceded by the fabulous wanderings. In these Homer provided a never-failing storehouse of material for imaginative writers in every epoch of European literature. Even in the darkest ages of Western Europe, when the *Odyssey* itself was unknown and even Dictys's distorted and desiccated summary was neglected, the more famous episodes lived on in popular tradition and in scholastic allusion, wherever classical learning had penetrated. The Cyclops and the Sirens, at least, were never entirely forgotten. But in the times when the Homeric canon was unknown curious variations were bound to occur, as one would expect in the free treatment of such fanciful material. No attempt will be made here to record all the various amplifications of the Dictys version of Ulysses's wanderings, which are to be found in Benoit de Sainte Maure and subsequent writers on the Troy romance.[4] They are not without some peculiar conceits and misunderstandings. But once Homer was rediscovered they were rapidly neglected and no major creative work derived from them.

The first great vernacular portrait of Ulysses the wanderer appears in the twenty-sixth canto of Dante's *Inferno*. This is a paradoxical, Janus-like figure: one face looks sombrely back to the conventional Latin conception of Ulysses as the treacherous conqueror of the Trojans; the other gazes, with astonishing radiance, on towards the spirit of the Renaissance and of nineteenth-century romanticism. Next to Homer's conception of Ulysses, Dante's, despite its brevity, is the most influential in the whole evolution of the wandering hero.

Dante comes with Virgil, his guide, to the part of the Malebolge reserved for fraudulent counsellors. The flames that devour these deceivers shine as thick as fire-flies in the dark gulf. One flame, curiously cloven at the top, arouses Dante's curiosity. He asks who is in it. Virgil answers:

> 'Tormented there,' said he, 'Ulysses goes
> With Diomede, for as they ran one course,
> Sharing their wrath, they share the avenging throes.
> In fire they mourn the trickery of the horse,
> That opened up the gates through which the high
> Seed of the Romans issued forth perforce;

There mourn the cheat by which betrayed to die
Deïdamia wails Achilles still;
And the Palladium is avenged thereby'.

(Dorothy Sayers's version)

Apart from the dignity of Dante's poetry, this passage might be a mere transcription from any of his predecessors in the Greek and Latin anti-Ulyssean tradition—Euripides, Virgil, Seneca, Philostratus, Dictys of Crete—or from any of the contemporary anti-Ulyssean writers on the Troy tale. This Ulysses is the familiar figure of Latin execration, the perfidious arch-Greek, the crafty trickster. Significantly it is Virgil who speaks his indictment here, not Dante himself; for in the *Aeneid* (though with the reservations mentioned in chapter ten) Ulysses had been described as a 'deviser of crimes', a 'forger of speeches', 'harsh' and 'plausible'. Now, under a Christian poet, he is condemned to eternal punishment for his successful stratagems against the Trojan ancestors of the Roman seed.

Yet, if one stands aside for a moment from the anti-Ulyssean tradition, Dante's inexorable verdict provokes some protest. Is it not a fact that Ulysses simply did his duty as a Greek leader when he conquered the Trojan ancestors of the Romans by stratagem and deceit? Did the ancient conventions of warfare (and has Christianity changed them so greatly?) forbid or even deprecate deceitful tactics against the enemy? If the evidence cited in chapter two is typical, they did not. No doubt it was natural for the outwitted Trojans to complain that they had been conquered by cunning and not in the open field. But the stealing of the Palladium and the ruse of the Wooden Horse were not outrageous crimes against any recognized code of international law, as the Latin writers imply. It would seem that their motive for denouncing Ulysses was based less on righteous indignation than on angry chauvinism. In fact, this first part of Dante's judgment on Ulysses is propagandist, not moralistic or judicial. It differs very little from the kind of judgment delivered in post-war trials when the victors try and condemn the leaders of the vanquished in the name of absolute justice—for it must be remembered that when Dante wrote the *Divine Comedy* the Latin tradition was victorious throughout Western Europe.

Dante's interview with Ulysses would probably have ended here if Dante had seen nothing more in him than the execrable *politique* who had secured the defeat of the Trojans. But Dante was apparently not satisfied with this conventional verdict. Perhaps another aspect of the tradition had some effect here—the pro-Ulyssean arguments which Dante might have known from Cicero, Horace, and some of the Fathers of the Church, who had insisted that the Odyssean Ulysses provided a noble example of wisdom and fortitude. But Dante's own genius for understanding the inner springs of human conduct and his imaginative sympathy even for the objects of his severest condemnation are more likely to have led him to these further questionings about Ulysses. Or perhaps it was due to instinctive obedience to that great maxim of Roman justice, 'Hear the other side'. The result, in any case, was an entirely new mutation in the tradition of Ulysses the wanderer.

Dante relates that a sudden desire seized him to hear Ulysses speak for himself. At his earnest request, Virgil consents to ask Ulysses, with a marked courtesy and a curious indirectness, 'where, being lost, he went to die'. Then the taller peak of the ancient flame begins to shudder and murmur. A voice—Ulysses is not named—plunges without greeting or preface, for it is the voice of a man in unending agony, into a stark narrative. Ulysses tells a tale never heard before[5] of his last voyage: how after leaving Circe

> Nor fondness for my son, nor reverence
> Of my old father, nor return of love,
> That should have crown'd Penelope with joy,
> Could overcome in me the zeal I had
> T' explore the world, and search the ways of life,
> Man's evil and his virtue. Forth I sail'd
> Into the deep illimitable main,
> With but one bark, and the small faithful band
> That yet cleav'd to me.
>
> (Cary's translation: as below)

In terse, metallic phrases he describes how he sailed on relentlessly. At length he and his companions, now old and slow (one must not press the chronology), reached the pillars of Hercules, prescribed by classical writers as the limit to legitimate exploration. There he took his fatal decision. In one of the most famous examples of Ulysses's proverbial eloquence he roused his enfeebled companions to a last effort:

> O brothers! I began, who to the west
> Through perils without number now have reach'd,
> To this the short remaining watch, that yet
> Our senses have to wake, refuse not proof
> Of the unpeopled world, following the track
> Of Phoebus. Call to mind from whence we sprang:
> Ye were not form'd to live the life of brutes,
> But virtue to pursue and knowledge high.

They sailed on southwards. A dim mysterious mountain appeared
in the distance. They were filled with gladness. Suddenly a whirl-
wind struck the ship:

> Thrice it whirled her round
> With all the waves, the fourth time lifted up
> The poop, and sank the prow: so fate decreed:
> And over us the booming billow clos'd.

When Ulysses has finished speaking his flame becomes 'erect and
still'. Without groan, boast, or curse, he moves firmly away. His
austere and majestic self-restraint, worthy of a Regulus or a Cato,
contrasts with the abject lamentations of the fraudulent counsellor
who comes next to Dante's view.

·Both in its mythology and in its moral implications this is a
revolutionary version of the final voyage of Ulysses. Mythologically
its revolutionary feature is that Ulysses never goes home from his
Odyssean wanderings at all. Instead, he goes straight from Circe to
pursue his inordinate desire for knowledge and experience of the
unknown world. Moralistically Ulysses now becomes a symbol of
sinful desire for forbidden knowledge. This gives Dante his ultimate
reason for condemning him as a false counsellor, because by persuading his comrades to follow him in the quest for knowledge he
led them to destruction. It was a far weightier charge against
Ulysses than any chauvinism could provide.

Many objections could be made to Dante's conception of the
Odyssean hero in the light of the earlier tradition. Homer's Ulysses
was an eminently god-fearing, self-controlled man; it was his
companions who were sacrilegious and reckless. He was outstanding
both in the *Iliad* and in the *Odyssey* for his sense of social duty, his
love of home, his appreciation of peaceful rule and reverent piety.
Now under Dante's guidance we see him as a scorner of religious
and social ties, a man overpowered by one great passion, the
characteristically Greek desire to know.[6] Homer had, indeed,
suggested that Ulysses was more eager than the other heroes for
knowledge, and had portrayed him as more of an individualist than
any of his associates. But the controlling motive of the *Odyssey*, as
du Bellay recognized, was essentially social, leading homewards
towards his little kingdom in Ithaca. In place of this centripetal,
homeward-bound figure Dante substituted a personification of
centrifugal force. By doing so he made Ulysses symbolize the
anarchic element in those conflicts between orthodoxy and heresy,

conservatism and progressivism, classicism and romanticism, which vexed his own time and were to vex later epochs more tragically. When he condemned this Ulysses he condemned what he thought to be a destructive force in society. Perhaps, too, as has been suggested elsewhere,[7] he was also condemning a tendency to over-adventurous speculation and research in his own mind. If so, it would explain the paradoxical feeling of admiration which is evident in Dante's portrait of the doomed hero; for even if one accepts the justice of his doom, he remains a figure of majestic nobility, like Milton's Satan or Melville's Captain Ahab. The contrast with the sneaking Ulysses of the Trojan propagandists could hardly be greater. If Dante had once himself experienced the zest of the intellectual explorer, the lonely joy of a mind voyaging through strange seas of thought alone, he could hardly have failed to let some admiration for the Greek spirit remain even when by sending Ulysses to destruction he remorselessly killed the thing he loved. Here is a new ambiguity in the Ulysses tradition. The older moralists had been perturbed by the ambivalence of his practical intelligence with its power for good or evil. Dante points to the subtler ambivalence of the pursuit of knowledge for its own sake.[8] In contemporary terms: are those who lead us into new realms of scientific knowledge false counsellors, luring us on to atomic destruction, or are they prudent and trustworthy guides conducting us to higher levels of civilization? The modern verdict on the Dantesque Ulysses depends on the answer to this question.

Doubtless Dante intended his Ulysses to convey a terrible warning to the medieval world in general. But within a few years the first stirrings of the Renaissance began to alter his underlying assumption that experiment and exploration were better avoided. Yet the Augustinian antipathy to intellectual curiosity continued to exert its influence against Ulysses for some time afterwards. Thus in 1390 the English poet Gower in his *Confessio Amantis* painstakingly related how Ulysses became the supreme polymath of the heroic age:

> He was a worthi knyht and king
> And clerk knowende of every thing;
> He was a gret rethorien,
> He was a gret magicien;
> Of Tullius the rethorique,
> Of king Zorastes the magique,
> Of Tholome thastronomie,
> Of Plato the Philosophie,

Of Daniel the slepi dremes,
Of Neptune ek the water stremes,
Of Salomon and the proverbes,
Of Macer al the strengthe of herbes,
And the Phisique of Ypocras,
And lich unto Pictagoras
Of Surgerie he knew the cures.

But, alas, this erudition led him on to seek forbidden knowledge. He turned to sorcery: and

Thurgh Sorcerie his lust he wan,
Thurgh Sorcerie his wo began,
Thurgh Sorcerie his love he ches,
Thurgh Sorcerie his lif he les.

The moral is the same as Dante's. The difference lies in the range of reference. Gower's mind, limited to the conventional explanations of his own age, could only understand Ulysses's inordinate curiosity in terms of the Black Art. Dante's imagination, ranging far beyond the superstitions of his own age, created a symbol relevant to every age of advancing science. As it happened, Western Europe found a more congenial symbol of uncontrolled desire for knowledge in Faust, and Dante's Ulysses had no immediate effect on the main tradition. It was only when an English poet came to reject gothic romanticism in favour of a new romanticized Hellenism that Ulysses's 'false counsel' began paradoxically to sound like a gospel of salvation to modern writers.

Classical writers had not, on the whole, emphasized the vein of intellectual curiosity in Ulysses, though they did not entirely neglect it. They preferred to dwell on Ulysses's reactions to the various sensual temptations which beset him on his homeward voyage—the song of the Sirens to tempt his ears, the Lotus to tempt his palate, the perfumes and amorous enticements of Circe and Calypso, and so on. Renaissance writers generally followed antiquity in this, and agreed that Ulysses had, on the whole, come through his ordeals with credit. Two excerpts from Roger Ascham's *The Scholemaster* (1570) are, apart from one special feature, typical of the renaissance attitude:

Yet, if a ientleman will nedes travell into *Italie*, he shall do well, to looke on the ife, of the wisest traueler, that euer traueled thether, set out by the wisest writer, that euer spake with tong, Gods doctrine onelie excepted: and that is *Vlysses* in *Homere*. Vlysses, and his trauell, I wishe our trauelers to looke vpon, not so much to feare them, with the great daungers, that he many tymes suffered, as to instruct

N

them, with his excellent wisedome, which he alwayes and euerywhere vsed. Yea euen those, that be learned and wittie trauelers, when they be disposed to prayse traueling, as a great commendacion, and the best Scripture they haue for it, they gladlie recite the third verse of *Homere*, in his first booke of *Odyssea*, conteinyng a great prayse of *Vlysses*, for the witte he gathered, and wisedome he vsed in his traueling.

For, he shall not alwayes in his absence out of England, light vpon a ientle *Alcynous*, and walke in his faire gardens full of all harmlesse pleasures: but he shall sometymes, fall, either into the handes of some cruell *Cyclops*, or into the lappe of some wanton and dalying Dame *Calypso*: and so suffer the danger of many a deadlie Denne, not so full of perils, to destroy the body, as, full of vayne pleasures, to poyson the mynde. Some Siren shall sing him a song, sweete in tune, but sownding in the ende, to his vtter destruction. If *Scylla* drowne him not, *Carybdis* may fortune swalow hym. Some *Circes* shall make him, of a plaine English man, a right Italian. And at length to hell, or to some hellish place, is he likelie to go: from whence is hard returning, although one *Vlysses*, and that by *Pallas* ayde, and good cousell of *Tiresias* once escaped that horrible Den of deadly darkenes.

This is mainly the doctrine of the Stoics and Horace (whom he cites). What Ascham adds is a touch of patriotism, of pride in the 'plaine English man', and a flavour of puritan piety.[9]

In the next generation Chapman maintained this reverence for the Odyssean Ulysses. In the preface to his *Odysses* (1616), addressed to the Earl of Somerset and his 'Ulyssean patience', he affirms that the *Odyssey* is a demonstration of 'overruling wisdom', of 'the Minds inward, constant and unconquered Empire; unbroken, unaltered, with any most insolent tyrannous infliction'. In his translation and commentary, too, Chapman loses no opportunity of praising Ulysses as 'the much-sustaining, patient, heavenly man', 'the wise and God-observing man', 'whose genius . . . turns through many and various ways towards the truth' (which is Chapman's explanation of *polytropos*, Homer's initial epithet for him in the *Odyssey*). Chapman does, indeed, show some touches of English chauvinism in his eulogies of Homer, deriding the follies of 'quiddi-tical Italianists'. But this is incidental. His sustained tone of fervent admiration for Homer and his heroes, coloured at times with a tinge of mystical ardour, became one of the most potent influences in reviving English enthusiasm for the Greek tradition in the nineteenth century, as Keats's famous sonnet testifies. But Chapman's fervour made few converts in his own century.[10]

The preceding chapter has mentioned how the literary inclination of the seventeenth and eighteenth centuries turned away from the more imaginative aspects of Ulysses. Some, like Rapin, denounced him as a despicable scoundrel. Others, like Fénelon, tried to groom him for admission to the Court of Louis XIV. In these centuries attention was chiefly focused on the political career of Ulysses, not on the fairy-tales of the *Odyssey*. The romantic and allegorical elements in the tradition were ignored or minimized in these epochs of *étatisme* and scientific thought. The vogue was for wit, not for fancy. *Gulliver's travels*, with their underlying political satire and their remarkable 'scientific' precision in detail[11]—and without any trace of mysticism or active supernaturalism—suited the taste of *le siècle sans étonnement* better than Ulysses's adventures in wonderland.

This being the case, it is not surprising that an effort was made in the eighteenth century to reduce Homer's work to political and scientific terms by the familiar method of allegorical interpretation. Giambattista Vico in his *Scienza nuova* (1725) took the view that the incidents described in the Homeric poems were symbolical representations of historical forces and movements. He regarded Ulysses as a type of heroic jurisprudence, which 'looked to what Roman jurisconsults called civil equity and we call reason of state'. In one way remarks like these are commonplaces of the tradition. One is reminded, for example, of Shakespeare's Ulysses in *Troilus and Cressida*. But there is a fundamental difference. Shakespeare, being a Renaissance humanist, was concerned with exploring the effects of such 'heroic jurisprudence' on the lives of human beings in a particular situation. Vico was not interested in Ulysses as a human being, but only in so far as his archaic heroism illustrated an abstract theory of political science. In the earlier tradition Ulysses had, indeed, often been a mere mask for various kinds of propaganda. But never before was he so much depersonalized, so much reduced to scientific terms, as in Vico's exposition. In Vico's theory the hero who traditionally excelled in exploiting political devices became a mere symbol of abstract political processes, a puppet in a mechanistic theory of civilization.

Some further remarks by Vico will exemplify his methods of interpretation[12]:

The suitors of Penelope invade the palace of Ulysses (that is the kingdom of the heroes), arrogate to themselves the title of kings, devour the royal substance (having taken over the ownership of the fields), and seek to marry Penelope (claiming the right to *connubium*). In some versions Penelope remains chaste and Ulysses strings up the suitors like thrushes on a net. . . . (That is, Ulysses binds them to cultivate the fields like the laborers of Achilles, just as Coriolanus sought to reduce the plebeians who were not satisfied with the agrarian law of Servius Tullius to the condition of the laborers of Romulus. . . .) Again, Ulysses fights

Irus, a poor man, and kills him (which must refer to an agrarian contest in which
the plebeians were devouring the substance of Ulysses). In other versions Penelope
prostitutes herself to the suitors (signifying the extension of connubium to. the
plebs) and gives birth to Pan, a monster of two discordant natures, human and
bestial. This is precisely the creature *secum ipse discors* of Livy, for the Roman
patricians told the plebeians that, if they were to share with them the *connubium*
of the nobles, the resulting offspring would be like Pan, a monster of two discordant natures brought forth by Penelope who had prostituted herself to the
plebeians.

Similarly he explains that the legends of Circe and the Sirens 'portray
the politics of the heroic cities', since 'the sailors, travelers and
wanderers of these fables are the plebeians who, contending with
the heroes for a share in the auspices, are vanquished in the attempt
and cruelly punished'.

The absurdities and inaccuracies of these explanations are obvious.
Vico makes no distinction between the fabulous nature of Ulysses's
wanderings and the quasi-historical quality of his Iliadic exploits.
He fails to see that the primary function of the Homeric poems is to
tell a story about human beings. He ignores the fact that an outstanding feature of Homer's Ulysses is his ability to rise above class
distinctions and social conventions. His attitude is not anti-Homeric
or anti-Ulyssean. It is more radically destructive: it is anti-human-
istic. Historically Vico is, of course, famous as a prophet of the
Marxist theory of political evolution and a herald of the proletarian
revolution, so that to judge him simply in terms of his few remarks
on Ulysses would be absurd. But his rigorous use of political science
as a means of interpreting Homer serves as an extreme example of
the prevailing thought of his epoch. Clearly it was an uncongenial
climate for mythopoeic imagination.

This chilling scientific attitude, combined with the equally chilling
Augustan insistence on decorum, prevailed until well into the
nineteenth century. An unpretentious little book provides evidence
of the turning tide. This was Charles Lamb's *Adventures of Ulysses*
(1808). Based largely on 'one obsolete version' of the *Odyssey*—a
significantly phrased allusion to Chapman's translation, which
Pope's disapproval had helped to drive out of use—Lamb's charm-
ingly childlike narrative revived the older sense of mystical allegory
in the *Odyssey*. 'The agents in this tale', Lamb observed in his
preface, 'besides men and women, are giants, enchanters, sirens:
things which denote external force or internal temptations, the
twofold danger which a wise fortitude must expect to encounter in
its course through this world'. This was clearly a reaction from the

scientific attitude. Against his publisher's objection to breaches of decorum in Homer's narrative, Lamb stoutly replied, 'If you want a book, which is not occasionally to shock, you should not have thought of a tale so full of anthropophagi and wonders. I cannot alter these things without enervating the book, and I will not alter them, if the penalty should be that you and all the London book-sellers should refuse it.'[13] Lamb's determination was justified by the results. Soon his book became a favourite among children, and also among adults, as he had hoped. Reaching the minds of school-children in their most impressionable years, its influence in restoring the imaginative, non-scientific approach to the Odyssean Ulysses was great. From it, for example, James Joyce first became interested in Ulysses: 'I was twelve years old when I studied the Trojan War', he remarks, 'but the story of Ulysses alone remained in my recollec-tion. It was the mysticism that pleased me. . . .'[14] Lamb's *Adventures of Ulysses* had kindled in him an awareness, however vague, of that long tradition of allegorical mysticism which reaches back through Chapman and Ascham, to Neo-Platonists, Stoics, and the earliest epochs of Homeric interpretation. As far as Homer's own artistic intentions are concerned, this mode of interpretation may be as gratuitous as Vico's. But at least Ulysses remains a human being in it and does not become a mere personification of historical movements.

Minor variations in allegorical interpretations of Ulysses's fabu-lous adventures need not be pursued here. But an outstanding use of allegory for dramatic purposes deserves special notice, partly for its own merit and partly because it is one of Spain's richest contribu-tions to the Ulysses tradition. This is Calderon's interpretation of Ulysses's encounter with Circe in *Love the greatest enchantment* (*El mayor encanto amor*: 1635) and its Christianized revision, *The soceries of sin* (*Los encantos de la culpa*).[15] In the first of these plays Ulysses enters the most exotic and luxurious environment in his whole literary career. It is as if he has stepped out of Western literature into *The Arabian Nights*. He himself, however, remains the 'pilgrim of the sea', 'the eloquent Greek', one (in terms better suited to the era of Cervantes and Calderon than to Homer's or Virgil's):

> in whom the sword and pen
> Woke in turn the same responses.

In Calderon's Circe, as Calderon portrays her, Ulysses meets the most formidable combination of erudition and voluptuous beauty

that ever came his way. The catalogue of her intellectual accomplishments rivals Gower's testimonial to Ulysses's own learning.
In her intoxicating environment of sensual and intellectual delights
he is tempted and for a while succumbs to her double charms.
Eventually his companions (as in the *Odyssey*), assisted by the ghost
of Achilles, manage to rescue him from amorous sloth. Shocked
into recollection of his heroic destiny, Ulysses, like another Aeneas,
steals away in Circe's absence. She, returning to see his ship far out
at sea, pleads with him, curses him, and at last sinks in death beside
the ruins of her magic palace. Calderon shows no Virgilian tenderness for his Dido. Ulysses is the hero; she, merely the beautiful and
accomplished villainess. The last lines proclaim a festival in honour
of Ulysses's triumph.

This was Calderon's first version. Apart from the opalescent
richness of its style, its development is conventional enough. But it
poses a problem which Calderon faced in his revised version, after
he had abandoned secular life to become a priest. The problem is
an old one in the Ulysses tradition. How could a man who yielded
to the amorous enticements of Circe (and Calypso) be regarded as
a noble example of prudence and virtue? This has been considered
in terms of its Homeric setting in an earlier chapter. The later
classical and earlier Renaissance traditions never quite solved it.
Advocates of Ulysses's goodness generally tended to ignore his
weaker moments (as when Ascham spoke only of his resistance to
Circe's magic cup and not of his yielding to her amorous proposals).
Depreciators emphasized them. Calderon in his first play implied
that if a man can eventually escape from a Circe when duty calls
(and the freshness of her company is dulled), that is all that matters.
But a priest in Holy Orders could not be so nonchalant; and in his
'sacramental allegorical Auto', *The sorceries of sin*, Calderon presented
what was virtually a recantation of his former play.

The scenes mostly correspond with those of the first play. But
now the note of allegory is dominant. Ulysses has become 'the
Man', a cosmic figure. He sails in a 'mystic boat' piloted by
Understanding and the Five Senses. The temptations of Circe and
her palace are expressed in terms of a struggle between the Senses
and the Understanding. The Hearing enticed by Flattery is turned
into a chameleon; Smell, by Calumny, into a lion; Taste, by
Gluttony, into a pig; Touch into a bear, by Lasciviousness; Sight
into a tiger, by Envy. Even Understanding is hard put to it to resist
the assaults of Pride with her poisoned Cup. Ulysses is at first

inclined to follow the Senses. But, hearing of their bestial trans-
formations, he prays to Heaven for forgiveness, confesses his sins,
and repents. Penance appears in person, sent by 'the mighty Jove'
to rescue 'Christian-born Ulysses' from the 'proud bewitchments'
of Sin. When Penance goes she lets fall, as a protective charm (like
the *Moly* of Hermes) a bunch of flowers

> all dappled
> O'er with virtues from the life-blood
> Of a Lamb, whose crimson altar
> Was a tree's unmeasured hardness

But further temptations follow. Voluptuousness enters with a
silver goblet, and others with similar emblems. Then Sin herself
(who is Circe) exerts all her powers of rhetorical and sensuous
persuasion, on Ulysses, whose name, we are told, means

> in Grecian parlance
> An astute-soul'd man (astuteness
> Being, as 'twere, a twin with talent).

Ulysses resists and compels her to restore the Senses to their original
form.

But Sin is subtle. Ulysses suddenly decides that he would like to
examine this remarkable woman alone, dispensing with the duenna-
like attentions of Understanding. He is especially attracted (being
always the inquisitive Greek) by her offer to show him her 'deep
researches . . . all the secrets of her science'. (Here the Dantesque
Ulysses is to be seen for a moment.) These include sorcery, necro-
mancy, and divination by birds and flowers. (Here Gower's theory
of Ulysses's inclination to the Black Art is confirmed.) When his
mind has been delighted by these marvels, his body is subtly led on
to seek other pleasures:

> In a word, delicious joys,
> Raptures, ravishments, entrancements,
> Pleasures, blisses, fondest favours—
> Sports and plays, and songs and dances.

As Sin lures him on, the flowers of Penance fall from Ulysses's hand
one by one. A magnificent palace springs up before them. Ulysses
and Sin enter, hand in hand.

Subsequently Understanding and Penance succeed, after a sharp
theological disputation with Sin (who desperately quotes Scripture
for her purpose), in persuading Ulysses to depart. He sails away,
once more the fully Christian Ulysses, in 'the saving vessel of the

sovereign Church', voicing a final curse on 'cruel Circe'. Circe's counter-curses fail. Her palace disappears. She is left alone in the desert. Ulysses sails off to cries of 'Happy voyage!' from his angelic supporters.

Dramatically and stylistically this is a dazzling play. Despite its strongly propagandist intention it keeps remarkably close to the framework of the Circe incident in the *Odyssey*. Though boldly adapted to seventeenth-century Spanish customs and thought, Calderon's Ulysses retains most of his archetypal qualities, his intellectual alertness, his love of learning new things, and his self-control (though this last is here externalized into Divine Grace). Like Homer, Calderon emphasizes that the Circe episode was only a passing incident in Ulysses's life. But since Circe is now equated with Sin, and Ulysses not so much with prudence as with piety (Penance is much stronger than the Understanding here), the last scene is harsher and more melodramatic than in Homer's briefer version. The final impression that Calderon's contribution to the tradition leaves in the mind is not so much of triumphant piety (for Ulysses rather makes the best of both worlds before he departs) as of unrivalled sensuous richness in setting, style, and symbolism. As to the old problem of how Ulysses could both enjoy Circe's favours and also be a virtuous example, Calderon solves it by the *deus ex machina* of Penance. Nothing could make a greater contrast in attitude or in style with Dante's Ulysses-figure. Dante's story is as sparely functional as a Doric temple, Calderon's as opulent as a baroque cathedral. Dante's Ulysses is hurled down to Hell: Calderon's sails blandly on to salvation.

For almost two hundred years after Calderon's masterpieces no great new portrait of Ulysses the wanderer appeared in European literature. But Germany nearly produced one. In 1770 Goethe began to study Homer in the Greek. He fell deeply under the influence of Ulysses's personality.[16] For a while his reading, thinking, and even his way of living, became centred on Ulysses and Homer. Climbing in the Alps, he would encourage himself on the steeper slopes with recollections of Ulysses's endurance. Could he find a cowherd to listen in the high valleys, he would tell him tales from the *Odyssey*. Ulysses became the pattern of what Goethe himself wished to become. He admired Ulysses's freedom of action, his fixity of purpose, his iron endurance, his all-pervading alertness and intelligence. Goethe found it convenient, too, in his infidelities to Christiane to recall how Ulysses, though faithful in mind to

Penelope, had not been impervious to the divine charms of Circe and Calypso and had felt no sense of guilt for his liaisons.

In 1786 Goethe announced that he had begun working on a tragedy to be called *Ulysses auf Phäa*. It was to supplement and interpret Homer's account of Nausicaa's meetings with Odysseus in the *Odyssey*. Homer's restrained, realistic episode would be thoroughly romanticized. Nausicaa would fall deeply in love with the handsome stranger. He would withhold his name and the fact that he was married until her passion was unquenchable. She would only discover his identity when she had publicly announced her love for him, and then would kill herself for shame and frustration. Ulysses and Nausicaa were to represent the *Urmenschen*, the unspoilt, uninhibited, primal humanity that Goethe thought he had found in the pure state in the Homeric epics. But 'the world order would be revealed as inhumane: inhumane the daemonic power of attraction in Ulysses's character; inhumane the love that drives the girl to destruction'.[17]

Full of this project, Goethe set out six months later on a journey to Sicily, which was by common consent one of the lands visited by Ulysses on his voyages. (A hundred years later Samuel Butler succumbed so far to its Homeric atmosphere as to identify the site of Nausicaa's home with Trapani and to make her the authoress of the *Odyssey*.) As he sailed across from Naples to Palermo, Goethe felt himself to be a Ulysses indeed. The Mediterranean scenery delighted his philhellenic eyes. 'The *Odyssey* ... ceased to be a poem: it seemed to be nature itself.' As the people of the *Odyssey* were the true *Urmenschen*, so its scenic descriptions, now actualized in what Goethe saw for himself in Sicily, were the true *Urlandschaft*. In the luxuriant vegetation of the public gardens in Palermo he felt himself back with Ulysses among the *Urpflanzen* in the fabulous gardens of Nausicaa's father, King Alcinous. It was all just as he had dreamed. Yet soon, somehow, his interest turned from the *Urmenschen* to the *Urpflanzen*: 'the theory of the primary plant ousted the sufferings of *Nausicaa* from his mind'.[18]

The play receded but was not entirely abandoned. In 1798 he wrote to Schiller about it. Nausicaa was to display the '*Rührung eines weiblichen Gemüts durch die Ankunft eines Fremden*', Ulysses '*die Gestalt des sprachgewaltigen, überredenden, überklugen Abenteurers*'. The title was changed to *Nausikaa*. Goethe was perhaps losing interest or finding some impediment in his self-identification with Ulysses. But the arrangement of the play was settled: Act 1,

Nausicaa meets Ulysses; Act 2, Ulysses meets her family; Act 3, Nausicaa falls in love with Ulysses; Act 4, Ulysses reveals his identity and departs, promising (with quite un-Ulyssean obtuseness) to arrange for Nausicaa to marry Telemachus; Act 5, Nausicaa kills herself. Something under two hundred lines of jottings and draft speeches survive. There is an energetic and vividly-phrased speech by Ulysses after his awakening on the Phaeacian shore, in which he describes himself Homerically as

> Der Städtebändiger, der Sinnbezwinger

and '*der Vielgeplagte*', and then, rather more Don Juanically than Homerically, as

> Der Bettgenoss' unsterblich schöner Frauen.

Later Nausicaa tells how she considers him different from the many smooth-spoken, boastful strangers she has already met, and apostrophizes him:

> Du bist ein Mann, ein zuverlässiger Mann,
> Sinn und Zusammenhang hat deine Rede. Schön,
> Wie eines Dichters Lied tönt sie dem Ohr
> Und füllt das Herz und reisst es mit sich fort.

But inspiration failed, and no more was written.[19] Similarly his projected *Achilleis*, in which Ulysses's treachery was to have been made responsible for Achilles's death, petered out. One catches a glimpse of Ulysses again in *Werther* and in the Classical Walpurgisnacht of *Faust*. Goethe had obviously found Faust with his sorceries and medievalism a more congenial symbol for his Everyman.

Why had Goethe lost interest in Ulysses? Was it for temperamental reasons? Despite his Hellenic mind, Goethe's heart was essentially Teutonic and Gothic. Homer's Ulysses is the supreme *homo mediterraneus*, a product of the sun-scorched sea coasts of Greece. Goethe was essentially, like Pindar, a landsman, an inlander with a continental mind, naturally antipathetic to the Navigator Hero. Besides, his youthful conceptions of Ulysses as a half-daemonic, half-Rousseauesque figure, as a noble but sinister Primal Man, were, as he would find on closer acquaintance with the Homeric world, a chimera. Further, the situation between the veteran Ulysses and the girlish Nausicaa was hardly adequate for the kind of tragedy Goethe planned, unless he was prepared to make radical changes in Homer's assumptions. As Homer presents it, the tone of the Phaeacian incident is relaxed, easy-going, self-indulgent, the mood of Shaw's *Caesar and Cleopatra* rather than of Shakespeare's *Antony and Cleopatra*. To turn Ulysses into a sardonic Don Juan and Nausicaa into a youthful Dido would be false to the whole spirit of the *Odyssey*.[20]

In the nineteenth century the growth of romantic Hellenism[21] stimulated many minor adaptations of Ulysses' fabulous wanderings. Each passing phase dressed Ulysses, Circe, Calypso, and Nausicaa, more or less in its own costume—Zolaesque or Pre-Raphaelite or Swinburnian. The general tendency was to minimize Ulysses's power of self-control and to emphasize the erotic element in his travels,[22] though a few moralists still pointed to firmer qualities. The effect of these conflicting influences will become apparent in subsequent pages.

The third phase of Ulysses's career, his return to Ithaca, as described in the *Odyssey*, provided little scope for controversy in the post-Homeric tradition. The circumstances were straightforward, and Ulysses's part in them was hardly open to much disparagement. He returns as a King to claim his rightful kingdom and as a husband to rescue his wife from insolent suitors. Poetic justice prevails. The good are rewarded: the bad are punished. Ulysses is clearly the leader of the good party. Though some might cavil at the nature of his subterfuges and disguises—how, for instance, could a true prince have demeaned himself by playing the part of a beggar so thoroughly?—everyone who valued legitimate sovereignty and orderly family relationships had to approve of his final success. Romantic writers, having less interest in the social order, would, indeed, find this part of the *Odyssey* rather dull, and would prefer to avoid or to discredit it. But less anarchic spirits[23] cherished its story of legal rights recovered and of domestic felicities regained.

Plainly the triumph of loyalty and prudence (in the persons of Ulysses, Penelope and Telemachus) over dissolute self-seekers (the Suitors) provided comfortable material for moralists and allegorists. On the whole their interpretations followed obvious lines. One of the more ingenious deserves to be mentioned. In 1655 Jacopo Ugone asserted that the *Iliad*, *Odyssey*, and *Aeneid*, were allegorical revelations of post-Tridentine Catholic truth.[24] In the second half of the *Odyssey*, he argued, Ulysses represents St. Peter, while Penelope is Mother Church threatened by wicked Reformers in the guise of the Suitors. (That Homer prophetically intended this last

allegorism is indicated, Ugone points out, by the obvious identification of Melanthios with Melanchthon, and of Antinous, emended
to *Artinous*, anagrammatically with *Martinus* Luther.) Telemachus,
then, prefiguring the Pope, protects Mother Church until St. Peter
returns and triumphs over the heretics. Thus it happened that
within a century, Ascham saw Ulysses as an example for English
Protestants, Vondel as prototype of Dutch Calvinists, Calderon as
an emblem for Spanish Catholics, and Ugone as a prefiguration of
St. Peter.

For contrast one can turn to the fustian hero who appears in
Ulysses, a tragedy by Nicholas Rowe (1706). Rowe presents the
Return of Ulysses in the Restoration style with its characteristic
combination of formal elegance and moral sordidness. Rowe, in
order to suit the prevailing fashion, invents a series of amorous
intrigues for the Suitors and the ladies of Ithaca. In one scene
Ulysses acts as the procurer of his own wife. It would be a waste of
time to unravel the intricacies of the far-fetched plot. A description
of Ulysses (spoken by Ulysses himself in disguise) will exemplify
how flat the style and characterization are:

> He was my Friend,
> I think I knew him; And to do him right,
> He was a Man indeed—Not as these are,
> A Rioter, or Doer of foul Wrongs;
> But boldly just, and more like what Man shou'd be.

The play as a whole reveals less about the Ithacan than about
Nicholas Rowe, who tries in alternate scenes to titillate the fancies
of Wycherley's former patrons and to persuade the neo-puritans
that he is on the side of moral reform. One cannot expect much
contribution to heroic mythology from such a source. Samuel
Johnson's criticism of its theme has been mentioned in chapter one.

In a play like that Ulysses is merely a lay-figure to be dressed in
the current fashion by authors who value external manners more
than inner qualities. A similar process of superficial adaptation can
be seen crudely in operation a century later in the Netherlands. By
this time the cult of Ossian had swept over Western Europe. So the
Dutch poet Bilderdyk conceived the notion of producing an
Ossianic Return of Ulysses (1808). The plot remains basically that
of Homer. But Ulysses is now called Kormak, Penelope Moine,
Telemachus Makdulf, and all behave as Ossianic characters should
behave.[25] Adaptations of this kind have little significance, except as
further proof of Ulysses's traditional adaptability.

These examples represent the superficial kind of originality which was generally applied to the Return of Ulysses in the neo-classical period. The romantic atmosphere of the nineteenth century tended to neglect this theme in favour of Ulysses's more exotic adventures. But it was still occasionally handled with some distinction, as in *The return of Ulysses* by Robert Bridges (1890), a close dramatization of the climax of the *Odyssey*, and in *Ulysses* by Stephen Phillips (1902).[26] But these are mainly derivative plays and add no permanent element to the myth.

In 1914, however, the story of Ulysses's return to Ithaca became the subject of one of the most unusual plays in the whole tradition— *The bow of Odysseus* by the German poet, Gerhart Hauptmann.[27] Its Ulysses is a baffling creature. In his outlines he is recognizably Homeric, but his mind and motives are more obscure than in any earlier phase of the ancient or modern tradition. For the framework of his play Hauptmann chose a part of the *Odyssey* which had not been exploited before in the vernacular tradition—the succession of incidents at the steading of the swineherd Eumaeus as described in *Odyssey* 13–17. Hauptmann kept to the main Homeric pattern in his earlier scenes, but transferred the Trial of the Bow and the Slaying of the Suitors to the Swineherd's hut. By this drastic alteration he achieved a complete unity of place and effectively concentrated the dramatic action. His chief innovation in the *dramatis personæ* is the invention of a grand-daughter of Eumaeus named Leukone. This good-living and high-principled girl is set in contrast with Melanto, the disloyal and evil-living servant who is in favour with the Suitors. Penelope's part is completely eliminated, and her influence on Odysseus is minimized.

Hauptmann opens his play with a scene between Leukone and Melanto. From what they say it is clear that things in Ithaca are in a bad way through the arrogance of the Suitors and the demoralization of Odysseus's retainers. Soon Odysseus approaches, looking like an abject pauper. He addresses the women in obsequious beggar's cant. He is obviously almost overwhelmed by fatigue and privation. Indeed, through most of the play his spirit seems near to breaking point as a result of his suffering and privation. When told that he is in Ithaca he is slow to believe it, fearing that the Spirits (*Daemones*) may be deceiving him. When convinced at last, he breaks into a characteristic exclamation of his traditional patriotism:

> Sieh, hier dieser Staub
> Ist köstlicher als Purpur, köstlicher

Als alle Frachten der Phönizier!
Ist wundervoller als Kalypsos Bett!
Süsser als Kirkes Leib, der Zauberin,
Und schmeichlerischer anzufühlen! Biete
Mir Helena—ich bin ein Bettler, habe nichts
Ausser diesen Lumpen!—biete mir
Die heilige Troja, wie sie ging und stand:
Ein Korn von diesem Staube wiegt sie auf!

Immediately afterwards he has to exert his proverbial resource-fulness. Asked 'Who are you?' he, still dazed with weariness, unguardedly answers 'Odysseus', but swiftly covers the lapse by adding '. . . was my friend'. Leukone warns him not to mention even Odysseus's name to Eumaeus, for he has been cheated too often by beggars with fraudulent stories of his beloved lord. This is an ingenious innovation. Like other touches to follow, it creates a bitterly ironic situation for the disguised hero. It frustrates his skill in devising apt tales about himself (which is so copiously illustrated in Homer's account of the Return), and makes his hope of success-fully establishing his identity all the more remote.

In the second Act, after Odysseus has grimly endured the mockery of Melanto, Telemachus arrives back from Sparta. He has become convinced that his father will never return now and that he must take his place as ruler of Ithaca. Odysseus bides his time to reveal himself. The strain on his self-control becomes almost unbearable. He conceals it by acting a grotesque idiotic part with clownish gestures, mixing truth and nonsense in what he says. Once, for example, he leaps up exclaiming

Here I am! Baa! Bury me: I am Odysseus.

The hearers regard this as mere lunacy. But the words also express Odysseus's sense of frustration and hopelessness. Here he is, restored to his son and to his most loyal servant; yet, as things are, he cannot claim their affection and loyalty. He is Odysseus, but he might as well be dead and buried. Later he raves in disgust at his present condition, and then denounces himself as he was when king. Rebuked, he beats himself savagely. He calls himself Noman (as in the Cyclops's cave). His vacillations between truth and idiocy border at times on sheer lunacy. In the mingled feelings of pity and horror that he evokes there is something suggestive of the mad Lear. But all the time a sense of lurking daemonic force remains and gradually gains strength. The dramatic suspense hinges now, as in the *Odyssey*, on the question whether Odysseus will reveal himself prematurely or not, and whether, when he does reveal himself, he will be accepted as the true Odysseus. But Hauptmann adds a psychological complication: will this almost maniacal Odysseus ever recover his characteristic equanimity again, or has extreme suffering paralysed his heroic fortitude into a permanent state of sub-human degradation?

Another deliberately grotesque incident follows to strain Odysseus's powers of endurance still further. When Odysseus has left the scene for a while, his father enters in such a miserable condition of neglect that at first he is mistaken for the mysterious beggar. When Odysseus returns to the scene he and Laertes converse, or rather grope for each other's meaning, in half-understood phrases. Eventually Odysseus tells Laertes that he is his lost son. Laertes in senile humour takes this as a pawky joke and, entering clumsily into the spirit of it, dances with Odysseus in a croaking mockery of the joy he would really have felt if his son had truly returned. The bitter irony of the situation stabs Odysseus to the heart. Once again Hauptmann has completely changed a Homeric episode to suit his mordant style, with undeniable dramatic success.

After further taunts by some bystanders and interchanges with the insolent Suitors (who have now arrived) it would seem that Odysseus's cup of frustration and woe must be filled to the brim. But Hauptmann adds another minim. Odysseus, left alone with Telemachus, tries obliquely to reveal his true identity. Fearful of failure, he very gradually infuses into his assumed idiocy some hints and indications of the truth. Telemachus becomes conscious of momentous and mysterious implications in what is being said to him, but fails to divine the full meaning. Odysseus sinks into despondency again and resumes his imbecilic manner.

This exaggerated idiocy, combined at times with an almost maniacal violence, is the most unusual element in Hauptmann's characterization of Odysseus. Some passages in the *Odyssey* remotely suggest something of the kind, but Hauptmann has developed it into the main feature of his play. The word *närrische*[28] recurs like a refrain. Such a portrait of idiocy combined with cunning and latent strength could be a re-creation of the pre-Homeric Odysseus, the Wily Lad or Cunning Clown of prehistoric folklore. Or else Hauptmann may have decided that in the circumstances this is how Odysseus would most naturally have behaved. What makes interpretation difficult is that it is often not clear when Odysseus's mixture of madness and stark sanity, of raving and prophesying, is intended as a pose and when it is a genuine state of mind. In fact, something of a Hamlet problem, as well as a Lear motif, arises here.

This uncertainty is reflected in a conversation between Telemachus and Leukone in the next scene. Both agree that the mysterious stranger is no ordinary crazy beggar. He is *stark wie ein Dämon*. Is he man, god or daemon? They begin to wonder can he possibly be Odysseus in disguise after all. Telemachus recalls a story Helen had told him in Sparta about the time when Odysseus had successfully played a beggar's part as a spy in Troy. They consult Eumaeus, but he refuses to admit any hope that the beggar can be the King.

The play now moves towards its climax. When Odysseus enters again, his mysterious power seems to have increased. A stage direction describes him as a stooping figure, strong and silent like a gigantic Satyr (*ein gigantischer Waldmensch*). Telemachus calls him 'the Daemon' without qualification now. When Odysseus speaks, his words are awesome. Now the Suitors—Hauptmann wisely reduces them to four—come on the scene again. They mock Odysseus, much as in the *Odyssey*. His replies are strange and ominous, but his pose as an idiot prevents any suspicion. At the end of this act (the fourth) Telemachus, who has been watching Odysseus closely in these last trials, begins instinctively to obey him. At length he cries 'My father!' and the act ends.

The rest of the play is straightforward and based mostly on the Homeric dénouement. Odysseus is accepted as the returned king by Eumaeus. Telemachus and Odysseus converse as son and father at last. Odysseus's main desire now is for blood and revenge. The Suitors fail in the Trial of the Bow. Odysseus succeeds, and (with cleverly contrived dramatic variations) slays them all. His last words to Telemachus are:

> Patience, patience, there's plenty still to do.
> But what will your Mother say, Telemachus,
> Now that I've smashed her prettiest plaything?

Presumably the last phrase refers to the Suitors, or possibly, in view of a remark by Melanto in the opening scene, to Eurymachos in particular. But in any case it is a curiously quizzical reference to the absent Queen who counts for so little in the rest of the play. It hardly augurs well for her reunion with her much-travelled lord.

One hesitates to attempt any precise definition of this often obscure, and at times almost inarticulate, characterization of Ulysses, the strangest in the whole tradition. It calls for a histrionic rather than a critical interpretation of its complex moods and elemental passions. The influence of Goethe and of the German ethos may be discerned in the daemonic quality already discussed and in the suggestion at times of the *Urmensch*. Hauptmann's description of Odysseus as resembling a gigantic creature of the woods is significant. Homer has little to say of chthonic creatures of this kind, and they play no prominent part in extant Greek literature until the drama of Aeschylus. Indeed, if it is worth while to describe Hauptmann's Odysseus in terms of ancient literature at all he is an Aeschylean rather than a Homeric figure.

Two of the most recent major adaptations of the Ulysses theme have also emphasized the psychological implications of Ulysses's long-delayed return to Ithaca. Jean Giono in his *Naissance de l'Odyssée* (1938) has the distinction of presenting the most mendacious Ulysses in the modern tradition. The true Ulysses, we learn, was a loose-living, rather cowardly sailor who had been slouching round various Greek ports with various Greek women since the fall of Troy some ten years ago. Now he would like to return to Ithaca and Penelope. But he dreads her attitude to his long and inexcusable absence, and is terrified to hear that she has a muscular lover living with her. One evening, as Ulysses drifts apprehensively homewards across the Peloponnese (here and elsewhere Giono's superb talent for describing Mediterranean scenery helps to redeem his novel from gross ugliness), an attentive audience inspires him to invent some sensational stories about himself. A listening bard hearing these wonderful tales of divine women and demonic monsters turns them into a saga. It becomes popular, and soon brings the (wholly fictitious) fame of Ulysses to Penelope in Ithaca. She, greatly impressed, drives out her lover, Antinous. Ulysses, by a further series of accidents, becomes established as a great hero in his own country, instead of being despised as the sordid old hypocrite that he really is. But towards the end of the book the shadow of a suspicious and resentful Telemachus falls over his path, menacing his precarious prosperity.

In terms of the classical tradition this book lies half-way between the anti-Homeric inventions of authors like Philostratus and the gross, sometimes obscene, humour of the comic and burlesque writers on the Ulysses theme. Homer's narrative is assumed to be entirely false; Ulysses himself is presented as a self-indulgent

o

impostor. In terms of the modern tradition Giono and his Ulysses illustrate the non-moral, indeed, one might say the anti-moral, attitude. The Ulyssean prudence and self-restraint emphasized by Renaissance and neo-classical writers has been replaced by a sordid and slovenly opportunism, in which the last traces of classical balance and moderation have disappeared. Even Autolycus, one may surmise, must have been a less disreputable figure than this scallywag. Yet Giono's rogue-hero has two redeeming features—a magnificent imagination and a profound mystical consciousness of the gods immanent in nature.

More recently the Swedish novelist Eyvind Johnson has produced a more elaborate version of Ulysses's return in *Strändernas Svall* (1946). The actual time of this novel[29] is that between Ulysses's departure from Calypso and his slaying of the Suitors. But by copious use of the 'flashback' technique this author manages to include most of the incidents in the *Odyssey*. The book keeps faithfully enough to the structural outline of the *Odyssey*, though it rationalizes some of Ulysses's adventures in Fairyland. The characters also are mainly Homeric in name and in their superficial qualities. But there the traditional element stops. Ulysses is no longer the energetic forward-looking hero of the main tradition, but a battered, worn-out ex-soldier, hating almost everything he does and submitting to the successive compulsions of destiny with apathy or disgust. Only the will to survive, together with an occasional flicker of erotic desire, seems to keep him from complete inertia, except when the gods intervene to drive him homewards. When finally, drawing on the dregs of his heroic valour, he triumphs over the Suitors, Penelope hears of the carnage regretfully. She sees it as the end of her freedom. She yearns that some young strong man should come and remove this triumphant old man and say to him: 'Go away, you old thing, you war-battered wreck, you all too long absent and all too long waiting one, go away, disappear, for if she opens the door and shows you out then Happiness can sneak in and stay with her. Give her freedom to choose, it is hers not yours. . . .' For Penelope has, it seems, kept young, supple, and eager for pleasure, while Ulysses has shrivelled, physically and spiritually, into the mere husk of a hero—an implausible situation which Homer as mentioned in chapter four, avoided.

Johnson supplies a wealth of descriptive detail about his characters as he pictures them in body and mind. One learns about the exact state of Ulysses's teeth, the condition of all five fingers on his left hand and of one on his right, the peculiarities of his eyes, nose, lips, neck, arms. Penelope's contours are precisely surveyed and the number of grey hairs in her head is recorded. If one wants information about Ithacan politics and economics (with statistics) or about the conduct of cats and house-flies in Ithaca, it is to be found here. Conversations or motifs, which Homer sketched quite sufficiently in a few lines, are expanded to several pages.

The total impression is one of much fertile inventiveness and little genuine creativeness. A group of commonplace contemporary characters—shrewder, perhaps, and more sex-ridden, than the average, but nevertheless commonplace in thought and motive—have been dressed in Homeric costume and made to act within the pattern of a Homeric plot. One reader, at least, would prefer the dynamic squalour of Giono's Ulysses to this lust-shattered ruin of a warrior hero, haunted by guilty memories and exulting with a 'wry, evilly grinning face' as he kills the Suitors at last. Even this final massacre, as Johnson presents it, is clearly only another chain-reaction in a saga of disillusion and futility—without loyalty, without constancy; without wisdom, affection, generosity, or compassion: a world of ethical automatism, where heroism and villainy can scarcely exist, where even a Ulysses becomes only a rather more complicated automaton than the mechanisms that surround him. This curious dehumanization of the tradition (despite Johnson's elaborate efforts to give physiological reality to his figures) is, one feels, less a fault of this author's technique than (like Vico's interpretations) a product of contemporary ideology. Deny the power of prudence and self-control in human conduct and you deprive Ulysses of his reason for existing in European mythology at all. Of all character-images he is the least amenable to a behaviouristic interpretation of life. Whether hero, villain, or Everyman, his quintessential characteristic is the ability to overcome the obstacles that destiny and nature place in his homeward path. Once he becomes acquiescent, apathetic, merely instrumental, he ceases to be himself. This is where Johnson's hero fails, and, as will be argued later, Joyce's Ulysses, despite many superficial resemblances to Johnson's, triumphs.

The fourth phase in the career of the wandering Ulysses is not directly derived from Homer. Homer implied that Ulysses would die quietly in Ithaca amid the prosperity of his people. But the prophecy of Teiresias was open to misunderstanding and was later interpreted as predicting a tragic death for Ulysses. The *Telegony* described further wanderings by Ulysses, though making him return to Ithaca in the end. Subsequent writers made the radical change of placing Ulysses's death in a foreign land.[30] But no ancient author seems to have portrayed Ulysses as a victim of mere wanderlust: his reasons for leaving Ithaca again were political, religious, or economic, rather than psychological—that is, as far as one can judge from the scanty references that survive. It was Dante who revolutionized the interpretation of Ulysses's final fate by presenting him as a man possessed by an irresistible desire for knowledge and experience of the unknown world. This conception of an outward-bound, home-deserting hero inspired some remarkable modern presentations of Ulysses, now to be considered.

The earliest was Tennyson's lyrical monologue, written in 1833 when the poet was still grief-stricken from the death of his friend Arthur Hallam. The poem, as Tennyson himself remarked, gave expression to his own feelings 'about the need of going forward and braving the struggle of life perhaps more simply than anything in *In Memoriam*'.[31] But a recent poet-critic finds a very different spirit in it. 'What is *Ulysses*', he asks, 'but a covert . . . refusal to be a responsible and useful person, a glorification of the heroic dandy?'[32] Once more the characteristic ambiguity of the greater portraits of Ulysses challenges interpretation.

Within its seventy lines *Ulysses* is a poem of remarkably varied moods. Tennyson's Ulysses speaks with five different voices, each of which can be recognized by direct quotations and allusions. These voices are those of Homer's Odysseus, Dante's Ulisse, Shakespeare's Ulysses, Byron's Childe Harold, and Tennyson's own Grenville. Yet the total effect is unified and what emerges in the end is a recognizably heroic, though bewildered, figure, a permanent and influential contribution to the Ulysses myth.

Homer's voice is the least significant here. The *Odyssey* provides some phrases and the scenery (but Ithaca has now become repulsive, not lovable, to Ulysses) and the *dramatis personæ*. From his opening words, however, this Ulysses is clearly not the social-minded, home-loving prince of the Homeric poems. He is Byronic in his mood of peevish discontent with normal life, Byronic in his romanticized description of himself as 'always roaming with a hungry heart', and Byronic in his determination 'to drink life to the lees'.[33]

But Byron's spirit does not prevail for long. Before the end of the poem's first movement Tennyson-Ulysses (for no one is likely to

deny the poet's empathy here[34]) begins to see himself in another
rôle. In place of the irresponsible heroic dandy he becomes

> this gray spirit yearning in desire
> To follow knowledge like a sinking star
> Beyond the utmost bound of human thought.

This is the voice of Dante's doomed hero, and it, despite some
wavering, remains dominant to the end of the poem.[35] By its
power, and that of another traditional influence to be mentioned
later, the Byronic demon of boredom and disgust is exorcized and
yields to a spirit of high heroic endeavour. In the end Ulysses's
romantic solipsism—the earlier part of the poem is insistently
egoistic—is dissolved in a desire for new experience[36] and in a
classical sense of comradeship, 'one equal temper of heroic hearts'
(as Byron, at the end of his life also, to do him justice eventually
overcame his egoism in dying for the sake of Greek independence).

Later in the poem a fourth Ulysses speaks. Though only a
momentary influence, yet it shows the living continuity of the
tradition; and psychologically its undertones may have done much
to help Tennyson to overcome his mood of lethargic despondency.
Suddenly Ulysses exclaims

> How dull it is to pause, to make an end,
> To rest unburnish'd, not to shine in use.

This is a paraphrase of Ulysses's words in *Troilus and Cressida*:

> perseverance, dear my lord,
> Keeps honour bright: to have done is to hang
> Quite out of fashion, like a rusty mail,
> In monumental mockery.

The imagery is the same, but the context is significantly different.
Shakespeare's Ulysses, an eminently extrovert figure, had addressed
these words to Achilles in his sulky sloth. Now—a portent of the
subjectivism that will dominate the Ulysses tradition during the
next century—Tennyson's Ulysses has to address the exhortation
to himself.[37]

In the second movement of the poem the Byronic mood returns
again for a moment. This time it expresses itself in ironical contempt
for the home-loving Telemachus, 'centred in the sphere of common
duties', decent, pious, blameless—in fact (Ulysses implies) intoler-
ably complacent and priggish.[38] Then at the beginning of the third
movement the decisive influence begins to make itself felt. What

takes control now is a boldness derived from the exploits of Elizabethan sea-dogs and strengthened for Tennyson's generation by
Nelson's recent triumphs. This, from the point of view of the
Ulysses tradition, is the poem's most original feature, a characteristically English contribution to the myth. Under its influence
Ulysses turns his attention from himself and from the causes of
his personal discontent to the dark, broad seas and his veteran
'mariners'. His words to his comrades do, indeed, recall the last
words of Dante's Ulysses. But there is a new quality in them, a note
which will sound louder in Tennyson's later poems, a resonant,
firm note. Grenville in *The Revenge* will voice it more tersely:

> For he said Fight on! fight on!

Dante, like Goethe and Pindar, was fundamentally a landlubber
poet: Tennyson's poetry, like Homer's, glistens with sea salt.

   Though some touches of despondency return before the poem is
ended, what finally triumphs is a mixture of a Dantesque desire for
knowledge and the reckless courage of the English sea legends.
Dante had seen only danger and destruction as the final fate of
Ulysses the explorer. Tennyson, living in a post-Columban age,
familiar with the deeds of English explorer-adventurers from Cabot
to Cook, impressed by the expanding power of England's empire
and navies, could adopt the Navigator Hero as an emblem of
justifiable scientific enterprise and of a commendable pioneering
spirit. Though the modern strain of discontent and uncertainty
never quite leaves the poem—these heroes are 'made weak by time
and fate'—yet, for a while at least, the English poet is roused and
energized by Ulysses's traditional call to heroic action. Finally as a
result of these many moods and influences a modern Ulysses is born,
a pagan patron saint for a new age of scientific optimism and
colonial expansion. In the end, by a curiously circuitous route
Tennyson has arrived back at something like the Ulysses of Homer's
Odyssey, but with one fundamental difference: this Ulysses follows
Dante's pointing finger, outwards, away from home, into the
unknown, not towards Homer's Ithaca or du Bellay's Lyré.[39]

   Tennyson's poem leaves many questions unanswered. In what
direction will Ulysses sail? Will the gulfs wash him down, or will
he touch the Happy Isles and see the great Achilles again? If he
does reach the Happy Isles, is there not a risk that their delights,
stronger than the temptations of Lotus Eaters and Sirens, may
quench his burning desire for knowledge and frustrate his heroic

ardour once again? What then will Ulysses's final fate be—further disillusionment or beatific achievement; Hell or Heaven? Sixty years later an Italian poet answered these questions strangely, in terms of his own personal philosophy. Pascoli's intention in his *Ultimo viaggio* (published in *Poemi conviviali*, 1904) is clear. He states in a note that his poem was an attempt to reconcile Dante's[40] and Tennyson's conceptions of Ulysses with Teiresias's prophecy that Ulysses would die 'a mild death off the sea'. This was a difficult, one might almost have thought an impossible, task. It meant combining the positive and negative symbols, as it were, for Ulysses's death. In mathematics the two would cancel out. Actually, in a paradoxical way, this is what Pascoli's solution finally amounts to —nothingness, but not nothing.

Pascoli's hero (now called Odysseus again for the first time in a major contribution to the vernacular myth) retains the centrifugal desires implanted in him by Dante and Tennyson. But plainly he has lost almost all his heroic confidence and energy. Having performed the inland pilgrimage prescribed by Teiresias, he returns home and sits drowsing at his fireside, waiting for the prophesied *morte soave, molto soave*. But death delays; and the hero's sense of loneliness and futility increases as the seasons pass and re-pass. No longer are there crowded banquets in his halls, with rich meats, music, and epic songs. He feels as desolate as the oar he planted at Teiresias's command in the deserted valley far from the sea.

For nine years he hears the cranes pass oceanwards in the autumn crying 'Plough' to the farmer and 'Rest' to the helmsman. Gradually discontent gnaws deeper into his heart. As he sits brooding at the fire the ageing Penelope, the skilful housewife, sits opposite, silently observing him. At last she, *la veneranda moglie*, sensing danger in his reveries, breaks in to remind him of how they had sat together just like that at the hearth (but he still disguised then, and unrecognized) immediately before their joyful reunion nine years ago, when he had come home tired of war and of the sea. Ulysses does not respond. His mind is absorbed now in half-dreaming, half-remembering, his voyages.

In the tenth Spring he hears the song of the swallow announcing the season for voyaging again. He makes his decision. Taking the helm from where it hangs above the hearth, he goes down to the sea. On the shore, after many symbolical incidents, he finds his old companions awaiting him. He addresses them with a gentle nostalgic eloquence, far removed from the spare vigour of his speeches in

Homer and Dante, saying much of his own feelings. He tells them that he is like the sea ('our sea'), vari-coloured and changeful:

> Compagni, come il nostro mare io sono
> ch'e bianco all'orlo, ma cilestro in fondo.

He tells of his yearning to see once more the violet-covered fields of Calypso's island, the wonders of Phaeacia and Aeaea:

> And lo! his speech colours the heart of all
> with the azure colour of far distant lands. . . .

Soon he and his companions embark and sail away from Ithaca for ever, singing as they go a child's Swallow Song to the sound of Phemius's lyre. After a storm they come to Circe's island. Expectantly Odysseus goes to seek her well-remembered palace and her enchanted beasts. He finds nothing left. He hears only the rustling of the leaves in the forest and far, far away the everlasting music of the sea:

> cantare
> lontan lontano eternamente il mare.

There his beloved rhapsodist, Phemius dies; but his lyre hung on an oak-branch still plays delusive love-songs in the wind. Sadness now begins to invade the heart of Odysseus and his companions. A leaden feeling of frustration grows. They come to the land of Cyclops. There, too, they fail to find anything to re-create their former deeds of heroism. They pass the Sirens, the Lotus-eaters, the Laestrygones, the Land of the Dead, the Cattle of the Sun, the Wandering Rocks, Scylla and Charybdis, without danger and without adventure, as if these wonders, once so vivid, were now no more than the insubstantial fantasies of an opium-dream.

Eventually their wanderings bring them back in a wide circle to the flower-strewn meadow of the Sirens. Odysseus calls to them over the waveless sea. He beseeches them to tell him the truth about mankind and about himself:

> Solo mi resta un attimo. Vi prego!
> Ditemi almeno chi son io! chi ero!

The Sirens make no reply. The hero's gaze falls on a great heap of men's bones and shrivelled skins that lie near them on the shore; and he sadly understands the symbolism. He has hardly finished speaking when the ship shatters itself on the reef.

Odysseus is alone now. The azure sea carries him to Calypso in her *isola lontana*. Gladly he sees again the verdant vine, the cave, the alders and odoriferous cypresses, the wild birds, the meadows of violet and wild parsley, that he had known so well for seven years before he returned to Ithaca. The wave carries him ashore 'to the solitary Concealer' (for *Kalupso* suggests 'She who hides' in the Greek) in her desert island:

> alla Nasconditrice solitaria,
> all'isola deserta che frondeggia
> nell'ombelico dell'eterno mare.

But Odysseus is dead now. Calypso hides his body in the cloud of her flowing hair. A mysterious cry goes mournfully over the deserted tides, announcing that the best fate for man is annihilation, non-existence:

> Ed ella avvolse l'uomo nella nube
> dei suoi capelli; ed ululò sul flutto
> sterile, dove non l'udia nessuno.
> —Non esser mai! non esser mai! più nulla,
> ma meno morte, che non esser più!—

So the poem ends. No paraphrase could do justice to the gentle, subtle melancholy of its imagery and melody. Its interpretation of the last would-be heroic adventure of Ulysses contrasts profoundly with its immediate prototypes in Dante and Tennyson. The root of this contrast lies in each author's conception of God and man. Dante, believing in the absolute sovereignty of God and the absolute dependence of man on God's will, had condemned the typical Greek hero, with his avid desire for knowledge, to eternal damnation: but he had also revealed him as a man of truly heroic energy and wilfulness. Tennyson, keeping the expression of his religious faith after Hallam's death for the pages of *In Memoriam*, left all theological and social considerations out of his conception of Ulysses, making him a personification of the dauntless sea-rover who could rise above the disillusionments and frustrations of daily life. Pascoli, in *The last voyage* at least, has no confidence either in the over-ruling justice of God or in the indomitable spirit of man. Against Dante, he believes with Tennyson's Ulysses that 'death closes all', so that Heaven and Hell are irrelevant to his portrait of a hero. But Tennyson's optimistic humanism is equally ineffective for this *fin de siècle* figure. Tennyson's Ulysses had exclaimed

> something ere the end,
> Some work of noble note, may yet be done.

Pascoli's Odysseus, having wistfully attempted to do some work of noble note, meets only illusion and disillusionment. Instead of a new heroic adventure outwards, onwards, to new experiences and new glories, his last voyages turn out to be essentially retrograde, a *recherche du temps perdu*. Like all such efforts to recapture the past, it fails. Pascoli sees only too clearly that the crowded hour of glorious life is irretrievable. One cannot be a hero in the same way twice. One can never relive the past. There is always an inner change and an outer change. A heart once engulfed in the depths of discontent and disillusionment can never regain its young heroic rapture. The best ending for a veteran hero, who cannot rest in contentment at home, is, Pascoli suggests, annihilation, absorption into the infinite. Perhaps Pascoli's use of Calypso as a symbol for Nirvana is meant to imply a touch of compassion at the end, as if his Infinite were not the scientific Void of Lucretius and the Atomists, but an element endowed with feminine tenderness. But this hardly disguises the ultimate pessimism of his poem. Whatever faults Ulysses had shown in his earlier portraits, his energy—whether for the benefit or harm of his companions, whether for his own salvation or damnation—had never been denied. Now this fundamental heroic quality, energy either to endure or to overthrow, has been taken from him. In Pascoli's poem a late nineteenth-century agnosticism has destroyed both his Homeric piety and his Dantesque defiance, and a contemporary mood of sensitive, quivering aestheticism has refined away his Tennysonian boldness and bravado. If one asks what, apart from these historical influences, was the metaphysical reason behind this mystical fable of heroic evaporation, Pascoli enigmatically replies, 'The All has a sorrowful son: his name is Nothingness'. In such an environment Ulysses is No-man, indeed.[41]

If the evolution of the Ulysses myth were an organic, single-stemmed process Pascoli's *Last voyage* would be its absolute end, its atomic, Lucretian, dissolution. But true to his reputation as the man of many turns, Ulysses recovered rapidly from this misadventure, even in Italy. It was one of Pascoli's immediate successors, Gabriele d'Annunzio, who reacted most violently from Pascoli's mood. In Dante's Ulysses d'Annunzio found a dynamic emblem of something far removed from Pascoli's evanescent nihilism. Instead, the Navigator Hero became for him an avatar of the Nietzschean super-man, self-centred, self-assertive, self-willed. Dante had obviously disapproved of Ulysses's readiness to repudiate his love of his family and his social responsibility for the sake of his 'mad voyage'. D'Annunzio glories in that repudiation. Better by far, he blasphemously asserts,[42] the figure of Ulysses burning in the Inferno than that of Christ in Galilee:

> 'Nè dolcezza di figlio . . .' O Galileo
> men vali tu che nel dantesco fuoco
> il piloto re d'Itaca Odisseo.

Dante had conceived Ulysses's attitude in his last fatal decision as being one of austere self-dedication to a scientific purpose. D'Annunzio changes this to a grandiose solipsism aiming at vague self-exaltation[43]:

> Sii solo della tua specie,
> e nel tuo cammino sii solo,
> sii solo nell' ultima altura.

If d'Annunzio could explain what the *Ultima altura* is and where it is to be found, we might accept the validity of his interpretation. Granted

> ché necessario è navigare,

in what direction must we steer, what do we seek, what is our compass? D'Annunzio, like Tennyson, offers no answer: we must simply fight our way, he says, to some unspecified ultimate height and hold our place there till someone else pushes us off, if he can. Neither Christianity nor humanity must ever stand in the way of our self-aggrandisement. Elsewhere, too, d'Annunzio sounds the same note of bombastic self-assertiveness, with the same vagueness about the ultimate purpose of Ulysses's new efforts. Thus, for example[44]:

> Contra i nembi, contra i fati,
> contra gli iddii sempiterni,
> contra tutte le Forze
> che hanno e non hanno pupilla,
> che hanno e non hanno parola,
> combattere giovami sempre. . . .
> Sol una è la palma ch'io voglio
> da te, o vergine Nike:
> l'Universo! Non altra.
> Sol quella ricever potrebbe
> da te Odisseo
> che a sé prega la morte nell' atto.

The magnificent diction here, as elsewhere, does not entirely conceal the flatulence of the substance. What d'Annunzio actually says differs little from the cruder slogans of the contemporary business tycoon—'The sky's the limit'. There is nothing here of Ulysses's steel-edged determination to discover new realms of knowledge, nor, at the other extreme, of Pascoli's gentle nihilism. D'Annunzio sounds the loudest and brassiest note in the whole tradition in solemn conviction that this is the true essence of heroism.

If this had been merely a literary solecism, one could pass it by without further regret. But it became something far more harmful. Dante's vision of total destruction for this Ulysses and his companions was all too clearly justified by the sequel to this kind of heroics in modern Italy. As is well known, d'Annunzio's gospel of aggressive heroism both predicted and helped to create the Fascist régime, with its screaming rodomontade, its colossal railway-stations, and the glorious conquest of Abyssinia. The Italian disasters of 1944 confirmed Dante's judgment that the end of this road is destruction. Yet, as the next chapter will show, there were answers to Dante's interpretation.

Tennyson, Pascoli, and d'Annunzio are the three most significant Western writers on the fortunes of Ulysses after his return to Ithaca. Other modern poets and novelists handled the same theme, but with less distinction. A French writer, for instance, emphasized Ulysses's sensuality in his final wanderings;[45] an English novelist in collaboration with the classical scholar Andrew Lang, contrived that Ulysses should have various pseudo-mystical experiences in Egypt;[46] an Italian poet, in close imitation of Dante, conceived him as an early Christopher Columbus.[47]   In turn sentimentalists, cynics, and hedonists[48] invented what they considered appropriate endings for the hero's wanderings. In these minor versions Ulysses is hardly more than a lay figure to be dressed and posed as each author desires. The emphasis is laid on novel experiences rather than on character or symbolism. But in his greater portraits, as described earlier in this chapter, it almost seems at times that it is the mythical hero who is in control, not the author; as if, when intensely imagined as by Dante, or Tennyson, or d'Annunzio, he could prophesy future dangers or unravel present perplexities like the ghosts in the Odyssean land of shades, who had to drink blood before they could speak. So, too, it seems, with Ulysses: if he drinks the heart's blood of an imaginative writer he speaks truths about the nature and destiny of man which only a timeless spirit can know.

CHAPTER XV

THE RE-INTEGRATED HERO

WITH one exception every portrait of Ulysses described in the previous chapters has been incomplete. Homer alone presented the whole man—the wise king, the loving husband and father, the brave warrior, the eloquent and resourceful *politique*, the courageous wanderer, the goddess-beloved hero, the yearning exile, the deviser of many ruses and disguises, the triumphant avenger, the grandson of Autolycus and the favourite of Athene. Subsequent writers in the tradition usually selected one, or a related group, of these roles to suit their personal inclinations or artistic purposes. A few, though specializing in a single facet of Ulysses's character and career, did, indeed, also suggest some of the deeper perspectives of his personality. Dante, though his main concern is to show the sinfulness of Ulysses, does not entirely ignore Ulysses's love of home and his heroic nobility. Shakespeare's Ulysses is primarily the man of policies; but his gentleness towards Troilus helps to reveal a tenderer side to his nature, reminiscent of his affection for Telemachus in the *Odyssey*. Giraudoux by means of symbolism and allusion implies much more in his portrait of Ulysses as an ambassador than do Racine and Seneca in theirs. But no author in ancient or modern times has attempted to rival the comprehensiveness of Homer's account until the present century, when an Irish novelist and a Greek poet have produced two contemporary interpretations of the much-enduring hero: James Joyce in his *Ulysses* (1922) and Nikos Kazantzakis in his *Odyssey* (1938).

What strikes one first about these two works is their sheer bulk. In this they far surpass all previous contributions to the Ulysses tradition. Even the combined *Iliad* and *Odyssey* are considerably shorter.[1] Some might see this merely as a product of twentieth-century diffuseness. But in fact both Joyce's novel and Kazantzakis's poem fully justify their bulk by their developments of the theme's content and symbolism. It says much for the vitality of the myth that its greatest extensions should emerge almost three thousand years after its first appearance in literature.

Another quality distinguishes these works from other post-classical versions of the myth. We are familiar with Ulysses in vernacular plays, lyrics, novels, and moral discourses. But Joyce's prose narrative and Kazantzakis's poem are nearer to heroic epic than to any of these genres. This epic quality[2] enables these authors to treat Ulysses with a greater objectivity than in lyric, a greater narrative freedom than in drama, and a greater weight of heroic symbolism than in a novel. Here, in fact, we return after a long interval to the heroic-romantic atmosphere of the *Odyssey*, an atmosphere less strictly epical than that of the *Iliad*, but closer to it than to any other genre of classical literature, and an atmosphere specially congenial to the versatile and often unorthodox heroism of Ulysses.

In contrast with these Homeric qualities of spaciousness and epic objectivity, one could list many unhomeric features in these two highly modernistic writers. But most of these are the result of assimilation to modern fashions and techniques and need not be dwelt on here. The main question for the present study lies before us: are Joyce's and Kazantzakis's conceptions of Ulysses as well integrated and as satisfying as Homer's?

Joyce's *Ulysses* consists in the thoughts and actions of two Edwardian Dubliners, Stephen Dedalus, a young university graduate, and Leopold Bloom, a thirty-eight years old, married, advertising agent. These are the Telemachus and Ulysses of the story in its Odyssean aspect. Their actions and experiences are commonplace enough—breakfast, business, casual encounters, a funeral, lunch; visits to a public house, a hospital, and a brothel; a late supper at Bloom's house, and his last thoughts before sleep. What gives the work its bulk, complexity, and significance, is, first, the abundance of naturalistic detail, and, second, the fact that it is deliberately multi-dimensional. This second feature calls for some discussion before the characterization of Ulysses-Bloom can be satisfactorily considered.

Both in form and content *Ulysses* is intended to be understood as something much more than a naturalistic (and at times expressionistic) novel of modern city life. Joyce, as is well known, constructed it to the pattern of Homer's *Odyssey*.[3] As Dedalus and Bloom make their ultimately converging ways through the streets of Dublin, they re-enact the experiences of Telemachus and Odysseus among modern equivalents of Odyssean places and characters. Lotusland now centres on a turkish bath, Hades on a suburban cemetery; Nestor has become a tedious schoolmaster, Circe a brothel-keeper. Sometimes the Odyssean order is dislocated or telescoped, and sometimes the analogies are rather far-fetched. But Joyce kept the parallelism constantly in mind, both as a structural model and as a symbolical undertone.

Besides having this formal ambivalence, the narrative of *Ulysses* is polysemous in the fourfold Dantesque manner.[4] Literally it is a description of events on a certain day in the city of Dublin. But it can also be understood allegorically, moralistically, and (in a sense) anagogically. Allegorically it belongs to the school of those philosophers and churchmen who regarded the *Odyssey* as a kind of *Pilgrim's Progress*—a school best exemplified in the modern tradition by Ascham, Chapman, Calderon, and Charles Lamb (whose *Adventures of Ulysses* first attracted Joyce to the Ulysses legend by its 'mysticism'). As Calderon presented his Ulysses as 'the Man', a baroque Everyman influenced by fleshly weaknesses but ultimately saved by faith and penitence, so Joyce presents Bloom as a twentieth-century, megalopolitan Everyman, justified in the end not by any religious piety but by his own bourgeois virtues. With due allowances, Dante's description of his *Divine comedy* in a letter to Can Grande fits Joyce's human comedy closely: 'If the work be taken allegorically, its subject is Man, in so far as by merit or demerit in the exercise of free will he is exposed to the rewards or punishments of Justice'. Bloom's rewards and punishments are mainly personal and subjective—exaltations or miseries in his own heart. But they are none the less real. For him hell, purgatory, and paradise, are in Dublin.

The fourth aspect of a polysemous work as defined by Dante, the anagogical, is not represented by any spiritual dimension in *Ulysses*. The one salient characteristic of Homer's Ulysses which is lacking in Leopold Bloom is piety. He is no longer the god-fearing, god-resembling, god-beloved man. Originally a Jew, then vaguely Protestant and Catholic in turn, Bloom is now an agnostic humanist. If he were militantly atheistical, or a deliberate defier of God's will like Dante's explorer-Ulysses or Gower's sorcerer-Ulysses, the anagogical sense might still be operative. But Bloom is simply not interested in God, and, so far as Joyce's indications go, God shows no interest in him. (Dedalus, on the other hand, is intensely conscious of religious doctrines and duties, but is moving towards their repudiation.) In place of this spiritual dimension Joyce substitutes the heroic dimension. Bloom's pattern and archetype is Ulysses, not Christ. His lost Eden is the heroic world (and, in another sense, the Promised Land of his Jewish ancestors), not Adam's Paradise.

Clearly, then, Joyce's Leopold Bloom is not simply a Ulysses in modern dress, nor is *Ulysses* a sordid naturalistic version of the tradition in the style of Giono or Johnson. It is a complex four-dimensional work, capable of literal, allegorical, moralistic and (in a humanistic sense) anagogical, interpretations; and its total meaning lies in the perspective of all these four dimensions. Unlike Giono's novel (and its predecessors, the seventeenth-century burlesques, the Roman *Priapea*, and the Greek comedies on the Ulysses theme), it is not mock-heroic or anti-heroic. Though it contains many sordid details,[5] it is essentially a study in compassionate humanism, by means of pity and salaciousness effecting its catharsis of suchlike tendencies. In the end Ulysses emerges, as he does from the *Odyssey*, as a man who by prudence and endurance, can overcome the dangers and disasters of life. One can see that the differences between Bloom and Homer's Odysseus in manners and ideology are not fundamental, if one allows for the principle of historical assimilation so prominent throughout the tradition. The basic humanistic elements in conduct, motive, and environment, are identical for the Prince of Ithaca and for this humble citizen of Dublin (and, further, the underlying symbolisms are the same).

One other complication needs unravelling before Bloom's Ulyssean qualities are discussed. This is the relationship between the three figures, Bloom-Ulysses, Dedalus-Telemachus, and Joyce himself. As has been illustrated in earlier chapters, many writers on the Ulysses theme identified themselves explicitly or implicitly with Ulysses. Did Joyce? To some extent, apparently, yes, but with a difference. We must consider the matter on two time-levels. In so far as *Ulysses* is a record of an actual day in 1904, when Joyce was twenty-two, it is Dedalus who represents the author at that time, and some of Dedalus's thoughts and actions are doubtless auto-biographical. But as the title implies, and the narrative establishes, Bloom is the central and pivotal figure. To what extent, then, is he a character-image of Joyce himself? On the second time-level, that is, in the period between 1914 and 1922, when *Ulysses* was being laboriously composed (with painstaking study of the earlier tradition[6]), Joyce had much in common with Bloom—agnosticism, cosmopolitanism, polymathic curiosity, uxoriousness, exilic yearnings, a respect for Jews, and a love of music, for example. Bloom's ultimate philosophy of life may well have represented Joyce's at the time when he had grown out of his Dedalus *imago*. But this self-projection is not emphasized by Joyce. On the contrary, he adopts a strictly detached attitude to his 'favourite hero',[7] and on the whole Bloom remains an objective, self-sufficient character in the true epic tradition.

But Stephen Dedalus is never merely a subsidiary figure. By deepening the psychological interest of this Telemachus and by creating a stronger bond of sympathy between him and his Ulysses, Joyce enriched the tradition significantly. In Homer's *Odyssey* the relationship between father and son was never more than conventional, and Telemachus never became an arresting figure in himself. Fénelon was the first to place him in the centre of the stage (as a model for the Dauphin's son), but his new adventures in *Télémaque* failed to make him anything more than a lay figure for moralization. Tennyson, though much nearer in age to Telemachus than to Ulysses when he wrote his *Ulysses*, showed little sympathy for the young prince's 'slow prudence'. With better judgment Joyce preferred Telemachus as a symbol for youthful discontents, rather than the middle-aged Ulysses. What is more, he used Dedalus-Telemachus as a means of solving a radical antimony in the tradition—the conflict between the conceptions of Ulysses as a home-deserter and as a home-seeker, or, as Joyce himself phrased it, between the centrifugal and the centripetal hero. In general Dedalus-Telemachus represents the centrifugal, rebellious, destructive, home-abandoning element in the *homo ulixeanus*: soon he will spread his wings like the Cretan Dedalus and escape from the labyrinth of Edwardian Dublin. Like Dante's Ulysses, he will be deterred by no love of family or home from travelling into the unknown world to find new knowledge and experience. Bloom, on the other hand, like the Ulysses of Homer, Shakespeare, and Giraudoux, represents the centripetal, conservative, and constructive element in society. Dedalus rejects and struggles to overthrow; Bloom accepts and tries to improve. Dedalus denies; Bloom affirms. Dedalus stands for *Athanasius contra mundum*, Bloom for a 'general improvement all round'. In this way Dedalus marks the negative pole of the Ulyssean character, Bloom, the positive. Between them they encompass the whole cosmos of the tradition.

One must allow for another complexity in this relationship. It results from what Joyce himself called the 'consubstantiality of the Father and the Son'.[8] Though Bloom has mastered the centrifugal impulses of his Ulyssean nature so that they cannot disrupt the normal course of his existence, they still have power to affect his inner, imaginative life, as will be illustrated later. This deepens his

P

sympathy for Dedalus in their few hours of symbolical fatherhood
and sonship. But Bloom, true to his Homeric prototype, ultimately
returns to Penelope and to his Ithaca, while Dedalus resolves, like
Tennyson's Ulysses, to abandon his home and kindred for ever. He
will become an exile physically as well as mentally. Bloom, in
contrast, manages to harmonize his inner sense of exile—from Zion,
from the heroic world, from all but the humblest kinds of pleasure
and prosperity—with patient acceptance of his commonplace
diurnal destiny.

In presenting the Homeric aspects of his hero Joyce concentrates
attention mainly on Bloom's Odyssean adventures and characteristics. But some Iliadic qualities are also noticed. Bloom, though
thwarted by his social condition from any prominence in politics,
is not without secret ambitions to excel as a *politique*. In his delirium
in Nighttown, he sees himself as 'alderman sir Leo Bloom', later to
be the popular lord mayor of Dublin. In the final catechism before
his return to his wife it is revealed that his political hopes are not as
selfish as those of the Euripidean Ulysses. If he were given a chance
he would try to be a genuine political and social reformer—'because
at the turningpoint of human existence he desired to amend many
social conditions, the product of inequality and avarice and international animosity'. He had thought deeply on justice and on what
Shakespeare's Ulysses calls 'degree'. He had loved rectitude from
his earliest youth. Schemes for increasing Ireland's wealth and
prosperity abound in his fertile brain. But in his more realistic
moments he knows he will never be a national leader. The best use
he can, and does, make of his sagacity and tact is to pacify and
moderate the passions and follies of his bourgeois associates. Yet
mutatis mutandis, is this much different in the end from what Ulysses
tried to do with the passions and follies of Agamemnon, Achilles,
Ajax, and Thersites, both in the *Iliad* and in *Troilus and Cressida*?

Similarly, though an ordinary citizen of Dublin had little opportunity to show the martial valour of an Iliadic hero, yet Joyce
indicates that, given an opportunity, Bloom could be as brave in
conflict and as loyal to a companion as ever Homer's Odysseus had
been. In the incident at Barney Kiernan's public house (a modern
Cyclops's cave where uncouth nationalism represents Polyphemus[9]
Bloom defends the Jews with firm courage, standing alone in a
circle of wrathful enemies as staunchly as Odysseus in *Iliad* Eleven.
Later, protecting Dedalus as he lies helpless on the street, Bloom
shows himself to be a worthy successor to the hero who fought

so stubborn a rearguard action over the body of Achilles in the *Aethiopis*.

Other qualities of Homer's Odysseus are to be found in Bloom —prudence ('Gob, he's a prudent member and no mistake'), caution ('Mr. Cautious Calmer'), wiliness, resourcefulness, tactfulness, self-control, skill in negotiation, intellectual and manual versatility, endurance, emotional resilience. These need not be illustrated in detail. But three other traits, present but not stressed in Homer's *Odyssey*, deserve special attention. They are the salient traits in modern portraits of Ulysses as the wanderer, and Joyce's treatment of each is significant. These are: the desire for knowledge; the yearning (exilic or escapist) for far-away lands; and the erotic impulse.

The erotic aspects of Ulysses's career had already been emphasized sporadically in the earlier tradition. But they had not become a dominant theme until the second half of the nineteenth century. Joyce makes as much of this erotic element as any writer before or after him. Indeed, the worst piece of literary blasphemy in the whole of *Ulysses* is a result of this—the Nausicaa incident, which he deliberately reduces to a nauseating mixture of noveletish sentimentality[10] and furtive eroticism. His treatment of Calypso is only a little less sordid. But his adaptation of the Circe episode reaches a degree of phantasmagorical horror and bestiality unrivalled in the tradition. Finally, Homer's faithful Penelope becomes the faithless adulteress of the post-Homeric legend. If Swift had handled these themes he could hardly have presented them more unheroically. Yet, though Joyce is Swiftian in his readiness to expose the least decent aspects of his hero and heroines, he shows none of Swift's fierce moral indignation. More like Homer, he avoids revealing any personal attitude except (and this only by implication) one of humane compassion. And like Homer's Odysseus, Bloom feels no remorse for his erotic experiences. His amorous infidelities are controlled only by prudence—the quintessential Ulyssean quality— not by any sense of sin or shame. The fact that his wife is as unfaithful as himself—and much less secretively so—balances the marital accounts in this unmoral (and unmoralized) relationship.

If one seeks for a reason to explain the sordid eroticism of *Ulysses* —yet a sordidness ultimately relieved by the author's prevailing compassion—it can best, perhaps, be found in the principle of historical assimilation. Ulysses-Bloom's eroticism is mainly that of the Edwardian era, both in life and in literature. Joyce's worst sacrilege in the eyes of a reader familiar with the Homeric archetypes is his rendering of the Nausicaa interlude. But it is a sacrilege prompted by an intense conviction of artistic propriety. With sardonic insistence it exposes the modern world's cheap substitutes, in literature and in love, for the golden aura of the heroic age. This is the same devaluation of mythological coinage as has already been observed in the plays of Sophocles and Euripides and in the propaganda of the later anti-Ulyssean writers. But Joyce's intention is not anti-Ulyssean: it is partly an indictment of his own epoch and partly an expression of his own pity for the predicament of twentieth-century man.

Joyce goes further. With his customary skill in solving classical problems in a modern idiom, he achieves Bloom's greatest triumph within the context of this eroticism. Here the parallelism with Odysseus's conduct in the *Odyssey* is paradoxical and yet satisfying. As Homer tells the tale, in terms of the archaic admiration for victory by slaughter (an admiration not shared by Homer himself), the supreme climax of the *Odyssey* comes in Book Twenty-two, when Odysseus, throwing off his disguise, slays the Suitors remorselessly. After the carnage, it will be remembered, Odysseus prevented Eurycleia from gloating over the slain—not because he felt any remorse, but because he knew that he was essentially the instrument of the gods in exacting divine retribution for injustice. Here Homer had distinguished Odysseus from the normal hero, both in self-control and in philosophic piety.

But despite Homer's modification of the brutality inherent (being doubtless derived from a pre-Homeric source) in the Slaughter of the Suitors, Joyce found this whole episode 'unUlyssean', mainly, no doubt, because Joyce himself had a contempt for war and violence.[11] His problem, then, was how to contrive that Ulysses should triumph over the paramour of his Penelope without using crude force. Joyce never showed greater ingenuity in adapting his traditional materials than here. Prompted, perhaps, by Odysseus's restrained speech after the slaughter of the Suitors in *Odyssey* Twenty-three, he substituted a psychological victory for a physical one. Bloom finally triumphs over the suspicions, fears, jealousies, and frustrations, in his own heart (which, we are to understand, are the modern equivalent of the unruly Suitors), by—to use Joyce's own terms—'abnegation' and 'equanimity', by recognizing 'the futility of triumph or protest or vindication: the inanity of extolled virtue: the lethargy of nescient matter: the apathy of the stars'. In this way Bloom regains his Ithaca, achieves peace of mind and even a vestigial happiness, as he deferentially salutes his faithless Penelope and falls asleep. Some may think this unheroic, pusillanimous, lacking in moral indignation. Joyce, for his part, disregards all questions of praise or blame. He is satisfied to complete his modern *Odyssey* by showing how a modern Everyman, without religious faith, without high philosophic principles or a highly cultivated humanism, without true friends or even a loyal family, can, by self-knowledge, prudence, humility, and resignation, regain his kingdom in Ithaca.

Joyce did not neglect the traditional quality of intellectual curiosity in his portrait of Ulysses. Though Bloom is not as well educated or as well read as the young university graduate Dedalus, he is, in his limited way, something of a polymath. His meagre library includes two books on astronomy[12] and one on geometry (the primary Greek sciences), besides odd volumes on theology, philosophy, history, and travel. Bloom's many other intellectual interests have been listed elsewhere.[13] They extend from aspects of ventriloquism to problems concerning foot-and-mouth disease. Through all his fleeting speculations some essentially Greek qualities prevail—a childlike sense of wonder, an omnivorous curiosity, a gift for seizing on the essential point, a freedom from dogmatism, a readiness to admit ignorance and to ask questions. His lack of training prevents him from systematic thought, but it also preserves him from the besotting influences of academic jargon, though some abstruse terms, like metempsychosis and parallax, affect him with an almost religious awe. It is also noteworthy as an intellectual trait that, despite his carnality, Bloom sometimes approaches that sensuous admiration of pure form which so often raises Greek art above the merely mundane; and he loves music, the most spiritual of the arts and the basis of Greek education. In this (as Buck Mulligan put it, with a different reference) 'he is Greeker than the Greeks'. And his Semitic ancestry enhances his mental quickness: 'Jewgreek is greekjew'.

This supreme Ulyssean cleverness has always exacted a bitter penalty throughout the tradition. From Homer to Joyce, Ulysses is lonely and often unpopular, especially in masculine society. Bloom suffers the same fate. In the Cyclops Scene the anonymous narrator (like Thersites in *Troilus and Cressida*, on whom he is directly modelled) ironically calls him 'the distinguished scientist Herr Professor Luitpold Blumenduft'. The assembled Goths detest his 'jawbreakers about phenomenon and science and this phenomenon and the other phenomenon'. 'Mister Knowall', they call him in loutish mockery. Once, earlier, a note of approbation is heard, in Lenehan's remark to M'Coy: 'He's a cultured allroundman, Bloom is. . . . He's not one of your common or garden . . . you know. . . . There's a touch of the artist about old Bloom.' But this is quite exceptional and evokes no response. At home, too, he has tried to awaken some intellectual interest in his Penelope, and has failed. She prefers less cerebral means of approach to the Tree of Knowledge. Similarly Bloom's effort to establish a lasting intellectual companionship with Dedalus fails. When, towards the end of the book, Dedalus finally leaves him, Bloom feels a 'lonechill' like 'the cold of interstellar space, thousands of degrees below freezing point, or the absolute zero of Fahrenheit, Centigrade or Réaumur'. So Joyce, half, perhaps, in parody, expresses the *de profundis* of Everyman in the Scientific Age.

What now of Joyce's interpretation of Ulysses as the wanderer? As has been noted, Joyce had transferred much of the centrifugal force of the Dantesque Ulysses from Bloom to Dedalus, his Telemachus. But a Ulysses without some adventures in far-away lands would be less than half himself. So, though Bloom has no opportunity for physical wanderings, his imagination ranges far beyond the boundaries of Dublin and Ireland. As soon as he leaves his house after breakfast he begins to think of 'somewhere in the east . . . turbaned faces going by. Dark caves of carpet shops. . . . Wander along all day. . . .' The motif often recurs; when, for example, he looks into the window of a tea-merchant's shop and on the sea shore. In the Hospital Scene he is twice named 'the traveller Leopold', and we are reminded of his 'many marches environing in divers lands and sometime venery'. His few books at home include *Three Trips to Madagascar*, *Voyages in China*, and *In the Track of the Sun*. When Bloom and Stephen converse with the garrulous old sailor in the cabman's shelter, his nautical stories rekindle Bloom's desire to see strange cities and peoples. Here Joyce deftly works in allusions to other famous wanderers, the Ancient Mariner, the Flying Dutchman, the Wandering Jew.

The classical Ulysses was never a voluntary wanderer. Prolonged absence from home was exile, not escape, for him. Joyce strengthened the exilic tradition by introducing a new heredity for his Ulysses. Bloom's father was a Hungarian Jew,[14] and Bloom himself retains an ancestral yearning for Zion. Here a distinction must be noticed. Bloom himself is never conscious that he is a metempsychosis of Ulysses: only Joyce knows that. But, in contrast, Bloom is intensely aware of his Hebraic qualities. He is shaped from inside, as it were, by his Jewish heredity; from outside by the Homeric parallelism. For Joyce, and for the instructed reader, the houses and streets of Dublin represent the islands and straits of Homer's wonderland: but for Bloom their ancient analogue is the waters and willow trees of Babylon. As a result of this new symbolism the traditional exilic yearning of Ulysses is deepened by an inheritance of wandering and exile which goes back far beyond Homer's Odysseus, to Abraham and even to Adam. This is a far more complicated emotion than the simple, personal nostalgia of Ovid and du Bellay. Heine with his Jewish blood comes nearest to Bloom in this respect, but his Ulysses poem is too short to convey the wider associations of Zionism.

Just before Bloom finally returns to Penelope the wanderlust (kindled by his conversations with the outward-bound Dedalus) seizes him again. He imagines himself visiting the most famous scenes in Europe, travelling on to 'Thibet' and the Eskimos, steering by the stars over the sea. Thence, as his imagination soars on its last free flight, he conceives a vast interstellar odyssey and a spectacularly heroic return:

Ever he would wander, selfcompelled, to the extreme limit of his cometary orbit, beyond the fixed stars and variable suns and telescopic planets, astronomical waifs and strays, to the extreme boundary of space, passing from land to land, among peoples, amid events. Somewhere imperceptibly he would hear and somehow reluctantly, suncompelled, obey the summons of recall. Whence, disappearing from the constellation of the Northern Crown he would somehow reappear reborn above delta in the constellation of Cassiopeia and after incalculable eons of peregrination return an estranged avenger, a wreaker of justice on malefactors, a dark crusader, a sleeper awakened, with financial resources (by supposition) surpassing those of Rothschild or of the silver king.

This is the supreme adventure of Bloom's adventurous mind. It is a conception beyond anything in the previous Ulysses tradition, carrying with it much of that potent scientific romanticism which modern astrophysicists have inherited from ancient astrologers, and much, too, of the spirit of Dante's doomed hero. The last phrase incorporates a characteristically Joycian touch of irony.

But Joyce's hero is always the prudent realist in the end. With characteristic self-knowledge Bloom soon reminds himself of his limitations and goes quietly to bed. As he falls asleep, the wanderer motif returns for a moment. His last moments of consciousness dwindle away in an evanescent repetition of the Sinbad-the-Sailor theme.[15]

Here once more there is pathos in Bloom's destiny. Cosmic wanderer as he is in imagination, it is clear that in actual fact the greatest voyage he will achieve can, at best, be no more than his 'longcherished plan . . . of travelling to London via long sea', though 'he was at heart a born adventurer though by a trick of fate he had consistently remained a land-lubber'.

To this modest orbit of travel has the twentieth-century reincarnation of Homer's and Dante's wanderer come, 'by a trick of fate', by a revolution in literature and in life. Yet can one say, leaving aside all prejudices about heroism, classicism, and romanticism, that this Ulysses is more contemptible or that he has learned less about human vices and virtues than his predecessors in the tradition? Though he has no Athene to guide him through the maze of life and has had no aristocratic education to keep him in the path to excellence, he remains the humane, much-enduring, serviceable, widely experienced, resourceful hero of the Homeric pattern, undaunted by the long littleness of life, the tricks of fate, and the apathy of the stars.[16]

The *Odyssey* of Kazantzakis and the *Ulysses* of Joyce have been brought together in this chapter primarily because they present the most elaborate portraits of Ulysses in the whole post-Homeric tradition. A full comparison between the style and substance of each work is not feasible here; but some salient similarities and differences may be mentioned. The two works differ considerably in hypothesis, scope, and pattern. The working hypothesis of *Ulysses* is the same as that of Homer's *Odyssey*: it assumes that Ulysses's controlling motive is to reach home safely, and that he does not seek adventure for its own sake. This, the classical conception, is to be found as clearly in du Bellay and Heine as in Ovid and Homer. Similarly, in so far as the political hero of the *Iliad* is portrayed in *Ulysses*, Joyce remains faithful to the classical conception. Bloom has no desire to be a revolutionary force in his country or in the world at large. The height of his ambition—apart from making a few minor improvements in the settled order—is to make the best of things as they are, and to check disruptive passions. In this Bloom sides with the Ulysses of Sophocles and Elyot, of Shakespeare and Giraudoux.

In contrast Kazantzakis adopts the non-Homeric hypothesis that Ulysses was an incurable wanderer at heart and after his return from Troy set out from home again to seek further adventures.

The Greek origins of this hypothesis have already been described in chapter six. Dante made it a dominant element in the vernacular tradition, to be followed by Tennyson, Pascoli, d'Annunzio, and others, as we have seen. This is the essentially romantic conception of the Odyssean hero, owing something to Byron and Nietzsche as well as to Faust and Columbus. When applied (as it sometimes was) to Ulysses as a politician it tended to produce either an over-bearing *Duce* or an insatiable anarchist. Kazantzakis when he turns his attention from the wandering to the political Ulysses succeeds in avoiding these extremes; but his hero is never the cautious statesman of the classical tradition.

This difference in their hypotheses—the one hero centripetal and conservative, the other centrifugal and experimental—has led Joyce and Kazantzakis into differences in the scope and pattern of their works. To adapt a comparison suggested by Joyce himself, *Ulysses* resembles one of those elaborately illuminated manuscripts of the early Irish Church in which the well-known words of the Gospels provided the basis for inwrought linear patterns of the highest possible complexity. Joyce spoke of the most famous example of this style, the Book of Kells, in the following terms: 'It is the most purely Irish thing we have, and some of the big initial letters which swing right across a page have the essential quality of a chapter of "Ulysses". Indeed you can compare much of my work to the intricate illuminations.'[17] Just as those Irish illuminators did not interfere with the canon of the Gospels, so Joyce kept faithfully to outlines of the Ulysses myth as described in the *Odyssey*. But, like the Irish monks, on this accepted, familiar foundation he wove an astonishing structure of erudition, imagination, and symbolism. One can find the same labyrinthine art-form in the structure of Bloom's inner monologue, that unspoken stream of his thoughts which forms so much of *Ulysses*. From chapter to chapter the various thoughts, actions, and sensations of Bloom's minute-by-minute experiences are interwoven, loop by loop, spiral by spiral (and each theme as in the Celtic manuscripts is coloured with its own imaginative colouring) into a complex, variegated unity of design. This analogy with the closely confined patterns of Celtic art is strengthened by the fact that spatially Bloom's movements and actions are kept within a narrow area. His whole odyssey is woven within the space of about one square mile (while, in contrast, Kazantzakis's hero ranges on an uncurving path from Ithaca through Crete, Egypt, Africa, to the Antarctic regions). As a result Bloom's adventures must arise mainly from the agility of his imagination and the subtlety of his senses: an ordinary tea-merchant's shop, for example, sends his mind off on a vivid flight of fancy to the Far East. Here, too, we see the characteristic style of the Book of Kells, where a single word of the text may flower into almost as much detail as the façade of a Gothic cathedral.

In contrast with this closely-woven texture the design of Kazantzakis's *Odyssey* is spacious and uncomplicated. As the hero moves steadily forward on his trans-continental wanderings, each new scene provides ample imaginative and symbolical stimulus by its own immediate impact. Further, being free from the restrictions of the Homeric canon, Kazantzakis was not compelled to linger reverently over familiar scenes. Instead he could compose a vast apocryphal, gnostic gospel on the Ulysses theme, retaining the central figure but allowing himself every licence that invention could provide. Curiously enough, this freedom from the Homeric canon enabled him to re-create an Odysseus more Homeric in many ways than Joyce's hero: for Bloom, constricted by the limitations and conventions of Edwardian Dublin, bears all the marks of the post-Descartian age: the proof of his heroic identity lies in his thoughts rather than in his physical actions. *Cogito sicut Ulixes: ergo sum Ulixes.* Kazantzakis's Odysseus is no less intelligent, imaginative, and thoughtful, than Bloom, but being set in a freer environment he comes much closer to the Homeric extrovert figure, exhibiting his heroic powers once more in a series of spectacular heroic deeds and decisions, not in aspirations or yearnings.

These are some of the differences between the modern Greek and Irish versions of the myth. Some general resemblances also deserve mention. First there is the fact that both Joyce and Kazantzakis admire and like Ulysses, and to some extent feel themselves to be kindred spirits with him. To them he is not simply a manageable pawn in some propagandist campaign, or a useful exemplification of moral (or immoral) qualities, or a convenient type-figure for a conventional plot, but a means of exploring the predicament both of modern man and of the authors themselves.[18] Other writers had already, of course, used the character-image of Ulysses in this way— but none so comprehensively. Giraudoux, Shakespeare, Calderon, Dante, Euripides, Sophocles, and the other social-minded contributors to the tradition, had shown the purposeful intelligence of Ulysses at work in various limited spheres of human life. Joyce and Kazantzakis try to show him in almost every typical activity of life—from a visit to the privy to the leadership of a revolution. Further, unlike most of their predecessors in the tradition, these two authors see Ulysses not as a regional, or a national emblem, but as a cosmopolitan, supra-national figure. He bears, in a sense, the hopes and fears, the wisdom and folly, both of contemporary European society and of the whole European literary tradition. Further, he bears this accumulated load of eagerness and anxiety at a time when Europeans are uncommonly apprehensive for the welfare of European civilization, and acutely conscious of the need for a new supra-national organization of society. Under the weight of this ideological burden the Ulysses of Joyce and the Odysseus of Kazantzakis begin to resemble Virgil's Aeneas. For Aeneas in contrast with Homer's Odysseus was endowed (as described in chapter ten) with a kind of 'imputed greatness', bearing on his shoulders not only *famamque et fata nepotum*, but also the destiny of the Roman Empire. In the same way the Ulysses of these two modern writers seems to carry with him much of the fate of twentieth-century man. . . . But here we perhaps do an injustice to some of the earlier contributors to the tradition. Perhaps in their time their conceptions of Ulysses seemed fully as fateful to contemporary thinkers, Shakespeare's Ulysses to Elizabethans, Sophocles's to fifth-century Athenians, and so on. One can never entirely enter into the thoughts and feelings of ages long past. It may be that our understanding of those earlier portraits of the enduring wanderer is deficient. But at least the mid-twentieth-century critic can record with confidence that the Ulysses-figures of Joyce and Kazantzakis do present unusually comprehensive symbols of contemporary aspirations and perplexities.

One further similarity: both Joyce and Kazantzakis are rebels, or perhaps exiles would be a better term, from the traditional beliefs of their ancestors, Joyce from those of Latin Western Europe, Kazantzakis from those of the Greek and Slavonic East. In politics they have repudiated narrow nationalism, in religion coercive orthodoxy. This personal exile is reflected in their portraits of Ulysses. But they have used their exile, not in tearful yearnings like those of Ulysses in Calypso's island, but as a means of seeing the problems of contemporary life in a clearer perspective. Finally, it is singularly apt for the theme of this chapter, the re-integrated Ulysses, that between them—Joyce with his profound understanding of the Western Catholic, and Kazantzakis of the Eastern Orthodox, way of life—they fully embrace the two hemispheres of European civilization. It is as if Virgil and Apollonius Rhodius had both written epics on Ulysses in the same generation.

To turn now to the content[19] of Kazantzakis's *Odyssey* (published 1938). In the opening scenes Odysseus has killed the Suitors, controlled the Ithacan mob, and related his Odyssean adventures. Now (in something like the mood of Tennyson's Ulysses) he begins to feel stifled in his island kingdom. He chooses new companions, gets drunk with them, and sacks his own palace. A ship arrives bringing Nausicaa to Ithaca. Odysseus marries her to Telemachus. After the marriage celebrations Telemachus plots with some other princelings to overpower Odysseus and seize the throne. Odysseus, surmising their intention, challenges Telemachus who replies that he is unwilling to live under the shadow of Odysseus's overbearing personality. His father joyfully welcomes this proof of his son's high spirit, and Telemachus in turn experiences the supreme joy of feeling Odysseus's full paternity within himself. Odysseus promises to set sail for ever from Ithaca next morning. Next day he keeps his promise. As he sails away his companions gaze longingly back towards their homeland. 'Look no longer at Ithaca', he says. 'We shall never see it again. Regard it no more than a sprig of some sweet-scented herb hung for a while above our ear: let it fall away unregarded.'

Odysseus and his companions sail on, letting the voyage ripen itself like a fruit. Then the scene changes for a while—to Helen who is walking and sighing among the oleander trees of Sparta, tired of her soft, shallow life with Menelaus, now fat and complacent. (He, it should be remembered, had reached home soon after the fall of Troy, nine years or so before Odysseus's return.) In the night she opens her arms and yearns for another Paris to take her away from her tedious life at Sparta. Meanwhile Odysseus with sleepy eyes lies outstretched at the prow of his speeding ship. As he drowses, he sees a dream-shape, like a white bird at first, perched motionless on the bows. Soon he knows it to be Helen, 'her lily-like face, dewy, gleaming, as if shaped from ivory'. Waking with a shudder, Odysseus turns the ship towards Sparta.

At Sparta he encounters the beginnings of a peasant revolt against Menelaus. By an adroit ruse—he terrifies them all with a cry that barbarian hordes are advancing on the city—he restores harmony and enters the palace, already sensing the presence of Helen close at hand. Inside Helen awaits him. They speak, and 'Troy is rekindled in their eyes'.

Menelaus emerges and embraces his old friend. He, unlike Helen, is flabby and contented. At a banquet Odysseus tries to revive some heroic spirit in his heart with threats of an imaginary barbarian invasion (which does actually arrive later) and of a terrifying new chthonic god. Menelaus does not respond: instead he complacently takes Odysseus to admire his treasures. Odysseus is filled with contempt for this easy-going self-satisfaction. He makes one more effort to rekindle the heroic flame in him. Menelaus drowses off even while he is speaking. In disgust Odysseus determines to take Helen away from this sluggard prince. He goes to the tower where Helen has been expecting him. They sail away together to Crete.

At this point it would seem as if the narrative were about to follow a familiar pattern. Odysseus has passed through what might be called his Tennysonian phase: he has put an end to his discontent with Ithaca by leaving it for ever. But Tennyson, though strongly influenced by Byron, had not hinted at any erotic impulse in his hero. Here it seems that Kazantzakis has set the stage for amorous adventures in the manner of Calderon and Johnson. But it is not so. The relationship between Helen and Odysseus does not develop in this way. Kazantzakis has explained it[20]:

Odysseus had no erotic motive when he carried Helen away from Sparta. Helen could not endure Sparta any more. She wanted to go away; and Odysseus wanted to take her with him as a new 'Wooden Horse', in order to bring about the fall of the already shaky civilization of Crete.

On another level of meaning, Helen is the Beauty of the Achaeans which creates the Greek civilization by mingling with the Dorian barbarian. As soon as Odysseus sees that this purpose is fulfilled—i.e. when he saw Helen in the barbarian's embrace—he goes away, leaving Helen to accomplish her mission: to breed, to transubstantiate within her womb the barbarian seed, and to bear a son—Hellen. Naturally, however, Odysseus does not part from her without pain. He goes away with the unhealing bitterness which every man is bound to feel when he sees a beautiful woman in someone else's arms, even if he has not had personal designs on her. Helen was a warm body, not a fleshless idea, so that Odysseus could not part with her for ever without pain. Yet he had to go, and he did go away. What could he do with Helen? It was not his unique purpose to contribute to the creation of a Greek civilization by uniting the Achaeans with the barbarian Dorians. Helen was only one of the stages of his journey.

In this Kazantzakis has returned to the spirit of the early Greek epic tradition, though in a modern idiom. Homer made it clear both in the *Iliad* and the *Odyssey* that there had been mutual admiration and understanding between Helen [21] and Odysseus, but nothing more. An early post-Homeric writer described how Odysseus had been one of the Suitors of Helen but had prudently retired in favour of Menelaus. Probably the ancient writers with their sound common sense appreciated that a marriage between the most intelligent and the most beautiful of the Greeks would be unlikely to succeed. No later classical writer went against this precedent. Andrew Lang and Rider Haggard in their novel *The world's desire* were the first to make a search for Helen (now mysticized into a vague emblem of spiritual beauty) the motive for Ulysses's last wanderings (which they placed in Egypt, anticipating a later scene by Kazantzakis). There was also a note of mystic love in Pascoli's *Ultimo viaggio*, but there the magnet is Calypso and she is a vague symbol of Nirvana.

Kazantzakis's Helen is no vague symbol, but a full-blooded woman, something in the manner of Calderon's Circe. Odysseus may be in love with her, as a beautiful woman and a free soul. But if so it is a 'Platonic' love: he has no carnal relations with her. He recognizes that her beauty is intended for a purpose distinct from his. She must remain in the decaying heroic Greek world to bear, by a barbarian mate, the ancestor of the new Greek world. He must continue on his centrifugal course. Knowing this, he characteristically uses her to effect a political purpose, the overthrow of a decadent tyranny in Crete, before they part.

To resume the narrative. Odysseus and Helen arrive, after a storm, at Crete. There, like characters in a Hemingway novel, they witness a bull-spectacle (such as one sees depicted in Minoan art: the importance of its symbolism for Kazantzakis's thought will be discussed later). After it he uses Helen as a bait to delude Minos, King of Crete. When emissaries from the barbarians (the migrating Dorians) arrive, Odysseus helps them (as at Sparta) to unite with the local proletariate and establish a new dynasty. This done, he sails away to Egypt.

He is now in the thick of politics again, no longer, for a while, the far-ranging wanderer. In Egypt he finds a third example of decaying civilization. (Kazantzakis emphasizes this theme in the earlier part of his work: possibly some Marxian influence may be deduced here.) Once more Odysseus joins the revolutionaries. He is imprisoned (like Joseph, as well as the hero of *The world's desire*) in Egypt. In order to escape he carves an image of a god, which first takes his own form and then develops into a horrifying visage. With it he terrifies Pharaoh into releasing him. Now, like another Moses, he leads a band of freedom-loving souls across the desert. He conceives the notion of finding the sources of the Nile (always an aim of exploration and speculation in antiquity). His new companions follow him wearily, like the toiling crew of Dante's questing hero. But Kazantzakis adds another traditional motif—it is not to be assumed, of course, that these are all conscious revivals—by making Odysseus become a Magian, adept in esoteric knowledge: this recalls Gower's Ulysses with his fatal addiction to Sorcerie. It is significant, though, that neither his desire to explore unknown lands nor his practice of magical arts brings this Odysseus to the destruction he met in Dante's and Gower's versions of the myth. The antithesis between the Greek belief in the rightness of pursuing all forms of knowledge to the end and the medieval distrust of 'inordinate desire' for knowledge is plain.

Ulysses presses on southwards. The Egyptians follow wearily. Eventually they come to an immense shining lake. They have found the unknown source of the Nile. What now? This is the recurrent problem for the hero when he has reached his goal. Pascoli could see only a life of subsequent disillusion and frustration, Johnson of disgust and fatigue, d'Annunzio of strutting bombast and self-assertion. But Kazantzakis's hero holds to the creed of Ulysses in *Troilus and Cressida*:

> Perseverance, dear my lord,
> Keeps honour bright: to have done, is to hang
> Quite out of fashion, like a rusty mail
> In monumental mockery. Take the instant way;
> For honour travels in a strait so narrow
> Where but one goes abreast: keep, then, the path.

Another traditional feature of the hero becomes more apparent in his subsequent wanderings. Odysseus has grown conscious of increasing loneliness as each adventure ends. (A scene with one of his comrades, whom he leaves behind with exhortations to heroic endeavour, seeing him poignantly as an emblem of his own lost youth, has just emphasized his aloneness.) Now he leaves his followers and climbs a mountain alone.[22] At the summit he adopts the posture of a mystic; plunges himself into austere contemplation; ascends the scale of mystical enlightenment, rising above all mundane concepts, the Ego, Race, Mankind, the Earth itself; and achieves a dazzling vision of the universe. He is seeking to receive by divine revelation (like Moses on Sinai) a new Decalogue for the Ideal City which he intends to build. The divine revelation comes. First God appears in the form of three earlier hero-strivers: Tantalus (the would-be lover of Hera, Queen of Heaven: a symbol, presumably, of Don Juanism and its tantalizing nemesis of never being

satisfied); Hercules (the laborious benefactor of mankind, who had
already been used by the Stoics as a parallel emblem, with Ulysses,
of indefatigable virtue), who urges Odysseus to sail on beyond his
Pillars (in direct challenge to Dante's philosophy of restraint); and
Prometheus (the titan who brought fire down from heaven to
mortals, defying Zeus, for which he was tortured on the Caucasus).
Finally God appears in the form of an old vagabond, bent down,
chewing a morsel of bread, exhausted and out of breath, stumbling
over the stones as he climbs. Odysseus connects this vision with a
voice he has heard just before: God struggles eternally to extricate
Himself from the flesh and from earth; He has become afraid that
He will perish with the human race; and now He is tired, lonely,
and frightened. Odysseus accepts the paradox, and decides to found
his city in the desert as God's last citadel on earth. Man is to become
God's companion-at-arms in the battle for freedom.

Two traditional features are apparent here: the piety and the
political constructiveness of Ulysses. But both are much altered by
non-classical influences. The element of piety in Ulysses's character
was strongly emphasized by Homer and by most of the Greek
writers who admired Ulysses. It was almost totally absent from the
medieval and early renaissance tradition. Shakespeare and the
French neo-classical dramatists ignored it. Calderon revived it to
suit his propagandist purposes, but presented it very much as an
external and, one might even say, mechanical force. The Augustan
writers for the most part had been content with the 'divine machinery' of the Homeric poems. (Fénelon, as befitted an Archbishop,
had, however, emphasized the significance of Athene's favour a
little more than most writers of his epoch.) In nearly all the nine-
teenth- and twentieth-century contributions to the theme one finds
a secular-minded, more or less godless, hero, from Tennyson's
Ulysses to Joyce's Leopold Bloom. Kazantzakis's conception of
God's part in the life of Ulysses (and of all mankind) is obviously
far removed from the previous tradition, both pagan and Christian,
though perhaps parallels could be found in some of the more bizarre
visions of the Desert Fathers of the early Church. (Kazantzakis
himself had formerly spent some time in the practice of mystical
asceticism among the Orthodox communities at Mount Athos.)
Some elements in the vision on the mountain seem to be attributable
to Buddhistic influences, others, perhaps, to the modern existentialist
tendency to find paradoxes, even apparently ludicrous paradoxes,
at the sources of human thought and belief. At all events, whatever

the influences at work, here for the first time in many centuries we have a Ulysses who seeks God.

Odysseus's decision to found a city is also a development of a traditional motif. Illustrations of Ulysses's constructive statesmanship have been cited from many phases of the myth. But hitherto he has tended to be a conservative: his policy has been to maintain the *status quo* as wisely and as fruitfully as possible. Here in the desert, for the fourth time in this new *Odyssey*, he shows himself to be an innovator. But while in Sparta, Crete, and Egypt he had to overthrow in order to recast, here he tries to create an entirely new city in the wilderness. And, as we shall see, his efforts show a political idealism which he never approached in the earlier tradition, except in Leopold Bloom's daydreams. The new city as he conceives it is to be better than all other cities on earth. It will combine something of Plato's Republic, something of St. Augustine's City of God, and something of the Marxian Utopia. But it fails.

After his paradoxical vision of God Odysseus formulates his own Decalogue. It emphasizes God's dependence on man and man's duty to love not merely the rest of mankind, but animals, and plants, and the whole of creation. One recalls that another famous mythical wanderer already associated with Ulysses, the Ancient Mariner, came to a similar creed at the end of his journey:

> He prayeth best, who loveth best
> All things both great and small.

Having formulated his creed and decalogue Odysseus descends from the mountain. With his companions—the scum of the earth— he prepares to build the City. They will share everything, the land, government, even the family. He lays the foundation-stone with mystic rites. Emblems are engraved on it: flames, a bloodstained path spiralling upwards, trees, wild animals, waves, a sharp-prowed ship, and a small bird, Liberty, with blood-bespattered breast. . . .

In other hands the epic might have ended at this point. The wanderer has, it seems, found a place to build a new and better Ithaca; he has laid the foundations of a Brave New World. But Kazantzakis knows, with St. Augustine, that the City of God cannot be built by human hands alone. The narrative soon proves this. When Odysseus's City is completed, there is a ceremony of inauguration; Odysseus dresses up as God; a few moments later a volcano erupts with devastating force; the City is entirely destroyed. The few inhabitants who escape are led away by the last of

Q

Odysseus's companions to rebuild the City somewhere else. Odysseus is left entirely alone, his hair snow-white from the shock of seeing his City destroyed and of losing all his companions.

Now the tenor of the story changes. Hitherto Odysseus has been a hero in the classical sense, a man of heroic action, a leader of men. After the catastrophe he abandons the cult of doing for the cultivation of being. To put it in other terms, the Homeric hero seems to give way to a figure more like an Indian Yogi.[23] His aim is no longer to change the order of things and to seek change in travel and adventures. Though his wanderings do in fact continue, he no longer uses physical and political means to express himself and to improve his environment. He now seeks self-knowledge and self-improvement in asceticism and in the exploration of personal relationships with people who are also seekers after the inner secrets of being and non-being. For a while he roams the jungle, free at last, physically free from possessions and companions, emotionally free from hope and fear, from desire and pride. He lives in spontaneous, joyous communion with plants and beasts and all nature. He smiles. He dances. In time many suffering people come to visit him, desiring to have his blessing. His pity for the human race is unbounded.

After this Kazantzakis introduces a lyrical interlude (rather in the manner of a Sanscrit play). Odysseus plays his flute and lulls five persons to sleep: a dancing-girl, an old king, a fierce wanderer, a young singer, and a sturdy slave. A kind of play ensues in which each of the five dream that their desires are fulfilled, five different dreams involving—here one thinks of Pirandello rather than of Kalidasa—each of these same five characters. The interlude ends. Now a tempter appears: why does Odysseus not commit suicide and thus liberate himself? Odysseus rejects the temptation calmly: 'I am the liberator, and there is no liberation from the world'. Next comes a young embittered prince, who sees death and decay in everything. He, like Odysseus, is empty of hope: but he cannot bear it and he fears death, whereas Odysseus regards death as the salt of life. Later he seems to become partly converted to Odysseus's view. He follows Odysseus who (ironically?) rides on his white elephant.

Odysseus meets a beautiful and famous courtesan, Margaro. She begs the holy man—which he has now become—to fill her empty soul. He does so by telling her that there are seven hidden ways of salvation: the play of the mind, fruitful and diligent goodness of the

heart, proud and lofty silence, fecund action, manly despair, war,
and love (the most hidden path of all). He asks Margaro what are
the fruits of her own experience. 'Two', she replies. 'Only you and
I exist in the world; and you and I are one.' To this Odysseus adds
a third discovery, the supreme secret: this One is as insubstantial as
the wind. The young prince, who has been listening, decides to
cast away all his earthly possessions. He has chosen the *via negativa*.
But Margaro and Odysseus choose the way of acceptance: they will
endeavour to fill the vacuum of life with joy. In this episode the
Odysseus of Kazantzakis rejects the ultimate nihilism of Pascoli's
Ulysses, just as he has earlier rejected the hollow heroics of d'Annunzio's Navigator Hero.

Odysseus now begins to travel towards the sea, towards death.
He was born near the sea and near the sea he purposes to die. He is
bidding farewell to the world. The ascetic cycle is complete. The
flesh has become spirit and the spirit flesh. But other encounters
still await him. He meets another holy man and talks with him.
This man had been a king who saw life bitterly, without a smile.
So he became an austere anchorite; but now, near death, he wishes
he had enjoyed life. Next Odysseus meets a singer. This man sings
a song about an imaginary king who became a singer by sending
each of his seven sons (one for each string in his lyre) to death.
Thus he became free: the singer, too, is free. Odysseus meets
another free figure called Lord One, a lonely pathetic warrior,
reminiscent of Don Quixote. Then he comes to the lord of a tower
in the middle of marshlands. He is a gross hedonist and a universal
mocker. Though he, too, knows the Secret, he disgusts Odysseus.
Next Odysseus witnesses a savage ritual in which a father is torn to
pieces and eaten by his sons. All these figures, it seems, are types of
freedom.

At last the hero reaches the sea. He sees an effigy of Buddha and
greets him as a kindred spirit. In a tavern he hears the tale of
Odysseus. Unlike Giono's rascally hero in similar circumstances, he
is pained at the divine qualities attributed to him. As he wanders
through the streets of the port, an old prostitute pities him and offers
him some pomegranates. (Later it is she, as a kind of Calypso-
figure, who bids farewell to him when he embarks for his final
voyage.) Odysseus builds his last boat, small and coffin-like. Some
fishermen arrive. Among them is a young Christ-like man, who
talks to him of love, universal salvation, the fatherhood of God, and
suchlike topics. Odysseus tells him the Secret as he sees it: 'All is as

insubstantial as wind'. The youth retorts: 'All except the One'. Arguing, Odysseus strikes him. The youth turns the other cheek meekly. He practises what he preaches.

Odysseus embarks and sails ever southwards, like Dante's hero. (Tennyson's post-Columban mariner sailed west.) He reaches the last limit of mankind, the terrible twin rocks, Yes and No. He goes between them: they prove to be ordinary cliffs inhabited by sea-birds. Now the sun weakens, yet remains in the sky to watch over the last days of his old comrade. The intense cold begins. Odysseus thinks death is imminent. But he comes to a village of people like Eskimos who live on the ice. Their lives, he finds, are governed by hunger and fear. The ice melts. They all perish. Odysseus escapes by climbing on to an iceberg. On it he sees Death sitting opposite him. His figure looks like a mirror-image of Odysseus himself, now old and weak. They converse in friendly terms.

The time has come for the hero to prepare for death. He says good-bye to his ancestors, his homeland, women, animals, his senses, the elements, and his mind. Then with a supreme effort he summons all the spirits of those who held the Faith—*Adeste fideles*. In turn his companions appear, and Helen, and all the free men and women whom he met on his travels. Something like an Apotheosis of Odysseus ensues. Two monks and two ancient Greeks (indicating, presumably, the most fundamental influences on a modern Greek) join the company of the Faithful. The ancient Greeks ask Odysseus for his 'deepest word'. What he offers them is not hope, or despair, or beauty, or sweet play, or truth, but a significant smile. (So far has Ulysses's smile evolved in the myth: first the grim smile of triumph when he was about to deceive Dolon to his death in *Iliad* Ten; then in the *Odyssey* his sardonic smile when insulted by a Suitor, his merciful smile to Medon, and his fatherly smile to Telemachus; then his politic, public smile in Dares Phrygius and the urbane statesman's smile in Shakespeare; now the enigmatic, all-accepting and all-rejecting smile of a Buddha.)

The hero's last moment has come. He calls upon his dearest temptation: the making and unmaking of the world. The temptation appears—another paradox at the heart of things—in the form of a little negro boy (an emblem, presumably, of the African element in Kazantzakis's spiritual ancestry and of the African admixture in Crete). They talk playfully for a while. The boy falls asleep at Odysseus's feet. The hero dies peacefully on the huge iceberg. . . .

Even from the preceding bald synopsis, a few pages for some two

hundred thousand words, one can appreciate something of Kazantzakis's remarkable additions to the Ulysses legend. We need not
dwell on what may be called the episodic and spatial enrichments of
the myth. It is clear from the synopsis that these are on a scale,
both physical and imaginative, far beyond any contribution since
Homer's. What concerns us here is the character of the hero. Has
Kazantzakis made any fundamental change in the mind and motives
of Ulysses? The answer seems to be that, without adding an
entirely new dimension to Ulysses's personality, Kazantzakis has
given in his portrait of Ulysses a profound and comprehensive
exposition of what is perhaps the most characteristically twentieth-
century feature of the Ulyssean mind.

In trying to define the essence of this neo-Greek Ulysses we may
leave the classical Greek and Roman traditions aside. Kazantzakis
has, indeed, derived many of his hero's qualities and adventures
from the early Greek epic. But in essence his Ulysses is an avatar of
Dante's centrifugal hero,[24] and derives from the tradition which
leads from Dante through Tennyson and Pascoli to the present day.
Tennyson's Ulysses is nearest to Kazantzakis's in essence; for, though
Tennyson makes his hero's expressed motive the same as that of his
prototype in Dante, namely, the desire

> To follow knowledge like a sinking star,
> Beyond the utmost bound of human thought,

yet his immediate motive is to free himself from his domestic
environment in Ithaca. Pascoli's hero shares this desire for freedom;
but it is muffled in nostalgic yearnings for scenes of his bygone
heroism. Kazantzakis has singled out the wish to be free as the
dominant passion of his hero. In fact, psychologically his epic is an
exploration of the meaning of freedom.

Freedom, *eleutheria*, has long been the political and spiritual ideal
of the Greek mind—at times a deluding will-o'-the-wisp, at times
a spur to greatness. The Athenians at Marathon, the Greeks of the
War of Independence (with Byron as a heroic emblem among
them), the Greeks of the campaign against the invaders in the
second World War; Socrates, the Desert Fathers of the early
Church, the ascetic monks at Athos: these, and many more, at
different times and in different ways, spent their lives in seeking
freedom. But the Greeks were never vague sentimentalists. Being
very much a Greek, Kazantzakis in the course of his epic finds out

the true nature and the full price of this freedom, and then makes
his hero pay it, a terrible price, boldly and cheerfully.

The quest for freedom is already clear in the earlier parts of the
work when Odysseus is still the man of heroic deeds. In the later
part—the epic of being and becoming, rather than of doing—it
dominates .every stage of Odysseus's pilgrimage: now his chief
concern is to search his own mind and the mind of other freedom-
loving persons for the essence of liberty. To signify this difference
Odysseus is generally described in the earlier stages as the Killer
and the Man of Many Devices: that is, he is still imposing his will
and wisdom on the world. In the later stages his commonest title
is the Athlete (presumably in an ascetic sense, as in St. Paul's meta-
phorical description of the Christian as an athlete striving for a
heavenly prize): for now his chief task is to discipline himself in the
way of true liberty. But, significantly, from beginning to end he is
the Lonely One.

The Lonely One: here is the nemesis of absolute freedom.
Kazantzakis does not flinch from its terrors (though perhaps he
lessens them a little for his hero at the last by introducing the negro
boy in the death scene). Absolute freedom means absolute separation from one's fellow-men; and each degree of freedom must be
achieved by giving up some element in social life. The hermitage,
the ivory tower, the mountain top, are familiar emblems of the
effort to find freedom by rejecting society. Kazantzakis sends his
hero, when he has freed himself in turn from the Ego, the Race,
and the World, to a much more desolate place—to the wastes of
polar ice. One is reminded of the 'lonechill' that Leopold Bloom
felt after Stephen's departure. But that was only a momentary
feeling: soon Bloom was asleep in the warm double bed. Bloom
has accepted ordinary life with all its restrictions and humiliations:
he is the centripetal hero. The Odysseus of Kazantzakis has pursued
personal liberty to the zero-point of the earth. The hero is not
simply liberated by death. He had rejected that path in an earlier
temptation. Death for him is not the cause, but the consequence of
his quest for liberty. His decision to seek the desolation of the
Antarctic was his own.

Yet there is no note of black pessimism in the hero's last moments.
Instead, as he grows more conscious of the price of liberty he becomes more cheerful, even humorous and playful. This cheerfulness
changes from wild merriment soon after the destruction of the city
into a quieter and more innocent humour as his asceticism proceeds.

It culminates in the Smile which he finally offers as an answer to the riddle of life. It remains to the end in his playful talk with the negro boy on the iceberg. There is something essentially Greek in this indomitable cheerfulness. From the earliest times the Greek word for good-bye has been *Chaire, Be cheerful*: in contrast with the Semitic wish for peace (*salaams*), the Roman for health and strength (*salve, vale*), and the Christian for divine protection (*Good-bye, Adieu*). Even when death came, the final word of the Greeks was still *Be cheerful*. There was no trace of frivolity, or levity, or inanity, in this. Everyone who faces the problems of life philosophically must choose to become a follower of the laughing philosopher Democritus or of the weeping philosopher Heracleitus. Odysseus and the majority of the Greeks generally chose the rule of cheerfulness.

Obviously Kazantzakis's conception of the hero may be disliked or decried. His *Odyssey* offers as much scope for ethical, theological, and artistic controversy as Joyce's *Ulysses*. Some have seen it as a Jeremiad of decaying Western civilization, or as an apotheosis of nihilistic egoism. Others as a serene and satisfying epic of human destiny. At least it is a substantial proof of Ulysses's ability to symbolize contemporary modes of thought.

In surveying the evolution of the Ulysses myth it usually is not possible to give each writer's own interpretation of the hero. But Kazantzakis has provided his.[25] Himself a Cretan by birth, he has explained his Odysseus in terms of what he calls 'the Cretan vision of the world'. (Crete, it will be remembered, was the cradle of Mediterranean civilization in the Minoan age, and has always been a stepping-stone between Greece and Africa.) He sees his hero as the product of over three thousand years of Greek history. In those three millennia many different racial strains have enriched the Greek stock. Some Greeks of the present day would like to prune away all post-classical accretions and recover the pure antique tradition as they imagine it. This policy Kazantzakis rejects. Far better, he thinks, to create a synthesis of all those varied racial elements and to find a way of expressing their variegated richness. His *Odyssey* embodies his conception of this synthesis, and is an expression of this 'hyperhellenic' tradition. 'Ulysses', he says, 'expresses not only, in general, the modern man who aspires to a new and higher form of life, but also, in particular, the Greek who must resolve the basic dilemma of his destiny. Ulysses chooses to live according to the solution that seems most appropriate; he does not seek to prune his life; he renounces nothing; he seeks the synthesis.'

This use of the term 'synthesis'—presumably in a Hegelian sense— would not help much to clarify our understanding of Kazantzakis's hero, if he did not explain it further. He does so in terms of Western and Eastern attitudes to life. The chief characteristic of the Greek ethos, he asserts, is 'to strengthen, at the price of abundant efforts, the I, the inner stronghold which subjects the forces of instability, the primitive demons, to the illumination of the human will. The supreme ideal of Greece is to save the I from anarchy and chaos. The supreme ideal of the Orient is to unite the I with the infinite until it is lost in it. Passive contemplation, the bliss of renunciation, an utterly trustful self-abandonment to mysterious and impersonal forces: such is the essence of the Orient.' The oriental ethos is quite opposed to the hero of his *Odyssey*, Kazantzakis insists. It is true that Odysseus does not follow the Greek tendency to cast a veil over the chaos of human life: even at the moment of his death he raises himself erect to face this chaos with a clear eye. A typical Greek, Kazantzakis claims, would not have met his death with such a clear-eyed acceptance of 'chaos'. So his Odysseus is not just a typical Greek. What, then? Here Kazantzakis looks back to his own native Crete, where Minoans, Greeks, Arabs, and Venetians, have had their turn to reign. In his own Cretan heredity he finds neither a Greek nor an Oriental essence, neither anarchic chaos nor will-less resignation, but a synthesis. He sees this as 'The I gazing on the abyss, without perturbation but rather enabled to concentrate better on itself, to become more filled with pride and courage, as a result of this fixed gazing on life and death—which I call Cretan'. (Elsewhere he writes[26]: 'What is our duty? To hold ourselves in front of the abyss with dignity. No tears, no laughter, to hide our fear. No closing of the eyes. To learn calmly and silently to gaze upon the abyss, without hope and without fear.')

In explaining what he means by the Cretan view of life, Kazant-zakis makes much of the cult of the Bull in the Minoan epoch. Unlike the modern Spaniards the Minoans did not kill the bull in the arena. They played over it and round it with graceful acrobatic feats. If, as the ancients held, we are to understand the bull as a symbol of the earthquake and its terrible abysses, then these bull-games symbolically denote that the Cretans did not fear the abyss or the terror of death, but could transform the moment of terror (the 'moment of truth' as the Spanish bull-fighters call it) into a superb game. According to Kazantzakis the present generation is the Epoch of the Bull, an epoch of ferocity, in which 'courtesy, harmony, balance, the pleasure of life, happiness, are virtues and joys which we must not hope to see again'. Frail spirits cannot gaze resolutely on the face of this monstrous epoch. They turn away. Even the artists and writers of our time have not dared to face the depths of the abyss which threatens to engulf our civilization. Only the Cretan spirit, which is the spirit of Kazantzakis's hero, can endure the sight: so Kazantzakis believes.

At first sight this seems an entirely new interpretation of the Ulysses theme. Certainly its symbols and modes of thought are new. But, when one looks further into it, is it not essentially the attitude of the Stoics, who also, as we have seen, employed Ulysses as a favourite emblem of the virtuous life? The good Stoic had to be fully as able as Kazantzakis's Cretan to face the Coming of the Bull, when the final conflagration came to consume the world— *dies irae, dies illa*. And, further back than Stoicism in the tradition, did not Homer's Odysseus gaze into the abyss of Charybdis and into the Cyclops's burning eye without flinching?

Kazantzakis has found many new ways of understanding Ulysses in terms of modern thought. He has devised many new and significant adventures for him. He has presented a fully integrated portrait of the hero—as wanderer and politician, as destroyer and preserver, as sensualist and ascetic, as soldier and philosopher, as pragmatist and mystic, as legislator and humorist. He has combined many scattered elements in the ancient and modern tradition. But the earnestness with which he urges his Cretan view of life must not make us accept his Odysseus as an entirely new conception of the hero. On the contrary this neo-Greek hero is something much more like a 'synthesis' of the whole post-Homeric myth. And the prevailing mood is fundamentally that of the Stoics. As one studies Kazantzakis's philosophic writings in general one constantly recalls the *Meditations* of Marcus Aurelius.

This chapter, and the whole survey of the tradition, may fitly end with another quotation[27] from the critical writings of this Cretan inventor of a 'Cretan' Ulysses. Here he speaks more calmly —not as a prophet of the *Dies Irae*, but as an heir of the European literary tradition:

As far as I am concerned, no age is more epical than ours. It is in such ages— when one Myth fades away and another struggles to come into being—that epics are created. As I see it, the 'Odyssea' is a new epical and dramatical attempt of modern man to find deliverance, by passing through all the stages of contemporary anxiety and by seeking the most desperate hopes. What deliverance? He does not know it at the start: he keeps creating it with his joys and his deceptions, with his successes and his failures—struggling. This, I am sure, is the struggle, whether conscious or unconscious, of the true modern man who lives profoundly his own age.

In such periods of interregnum, a spiritual endeavour can either look back to justify and judge the old civilization that is falling apart, or look ahead and attempt to prophesy and express the new civilization. Odysseus in his struggle looks ahead. This may be—though none but our great-grandchildren will know for certain— because we are not very far away from the new Myth. In any case, Odysseus goes on, ceaselessly, his neck stretched forward, like the leader of birds migrating.

CHAPTER XVI

EPILOGUE

SUCH were the main vagaries in Ulysses's fortunes during the twenty-seven centuries from archaic Greece to the present time. As suggested in the first chapter, their explanation lies partly in external influences common to the evolution of all traditional figures and partly in the remarkable adaptability of Homer's archetypal Ulysses. One can see the external influences at work in every major phase of the tradition. Historical assimilation[1] accounts for many changes in manners, idiom, and thought. Linguistic anomalies alter the quality of Ulysses's eloquence and, at times, his thought and character. The exigencies of the chosen genre sometimes reduce Ulysses's elastic personality to a conventional type—villain, machiavel, amorist, glutton, or the like. This last tendency has been exemplified even within the works of single authors: as when, for instance, Sophocles converted the generous-hearted hero of *Ajax* into the diabolical sophist of the *Philoctetes*, and when Racine, despite his earlier expressions of admiration for the Homeric Ulysses, presented him as a Senecan *politique* in his *Iphigénie*. Similarly the varying motives of propagandists and the varying standards of moralistic writers have had clearly discernible effects on the tradition.

These historical, linguistic, technical, and ethical variables do not, of course, work in isolation. On the contrary, as the Ulysses tradition amply illustrates, they generally combine to produce complex results. In fact, the greater the writer's genius, the more complex the resulting presentation of Ulysses is likely to be. For example, in Calderon's second play, *The sorceries of sin*, the Ulysses theme is used for three distinct purposes: as a subject for a spectacular *pièce de théâtre*, as an allegory on human life, and as a means of strengthening faith in the Church. So, too, Dante's portrait of the hero combines a symbolization of the desire for knowledge with traditional anti-Ulyssean prejudices and current theological doctrines. Joyce's conception of Ulysses incorporates idioms and attitudes of mind as diverse as those of St. Thomas Aquinas and *Peg's Paper*, of *Hamlet* and public-house talk.

One other external influence, external, that is, to the pre-existing tradition, has been often mentioned in the preceding chapters. It deserves some further attention now, for it can cause some of the most unexpected changes in the tradition; and it is also one of the most disputable factors in literary composition. This is the personal factor, consisting of each author's personal reaction to the *persona* of any traditional figure. The subtler subjective aspects of this relationship had best be left to expert psychologists. What concerns us here is its observable effects on the characterization of Ulysses.

First it should be emphasized that this personal factor may not perceptibly influence an author at all. Among writers on the Ulysses theme, Sophocles, Seneca, Racine, and Landor, for example, seem to have been entirely objective in their treatment of the hero. Whether others like Giraudoux, Shakespeare, Dante, Euripides, and Homer, were equally detached is less certain. The possibility of some self-expression in their portraits of Ulysses has been suggested earlier, but it can only be conjectural, and many may prefer to regard their portraits of Ulysses as entirely objective. There is, however, clear evidence of self-interest on the part of other authors. One can see it in varying degrees of intensity and complication. It occurs in its simplest form in the examples quoted from Ovid and du Bellay. There Ulysses is little more than a simile, providing a well-known analogy for the author's feelings during his exile from home. Yet Ovid's and du Bellay's attitude to Ulysses in their similes is not entirely objective. Some transfusion of feeling occurs, so that when we read du Bellay's sonnet, *Heureux qui comme Ulysse*, we understand more about Ulysses's (as well as about du Bellay's) emotions as he yearned for home. Most of the innumerable references to Ulysses in classical and medieval similes are little more than mere mythological embellishments. But in Ovid and du Bellay there is a note of sympathy combined with self-pity.

Another form of this personal reaction is to be found in the use of Ulysses as an example not so much of general morality as of personal behaviour. Long before the Cynics and Stoics adopted Ulysses as an exemplar of prudence and endurance, Archilochus had found a source of strength for himself in phrases and incidents from the *Odyssey*. The fascination of Ulysses's personality for Goethe illustrates a stronger degree of this power of finding self-realization and self-encouragement under the direction of a traditional hero. One might call it a kind of hero-possession. Its effects on Goethe soon passed off, apparently, and his projected portrait of Ulysses eventually failed to appear. But the psychological experience provides a remarkable example of Ulysses's power to grip the imagination.

Curiously enough, classical antiquity provided an analogy to this. Philostratus, as described in chapter twelve, affirmed that Homer had written the Homeric poems at the dictation of Ulysses's ghost. Though this fiction was apparently prompted by Philostratus's desire to vilify both the poet and the hero, it contained allegorical truth, in that some authors (and possibly Homer among them) seem to have had an almost clairvoyant power of seeing and hearing traditional heroes as if they were living spirits.

Tennyson's *Ulysses* is one of the surest products of this personal interaction between author and traditional figure. We have the poet's own statement that this portrait of the hero as an old man expressed some of his own feelings after the death of Hallam. The resulting poem as we have it shows how both the poet and the traditional Ulysses were changed. Ulysses absorbed much of Tennyson's sense of tedium and doubt (as well as being affected by certain literary and historical influences in Tennyson's mind at the time), and thereby entered into his first genuinely nineteenth-century personification. Tennyson, we know, gained new courage and strength for 'going forward and braving the struggle of life'.

Pascoli, too, seems to have experienced a similar self-realization in his version of Ulysses's last voyage. But here the final discovery, for the hero as well as for the poet, brought no renewal of strength or heroic perseverance. Its symbolism was of disillusionment, frustration, and ultimate annihilation, for hero and poet alike. In reaction from both Pascoli and Dante, d'Annunzio found a very different message in the Ulysses myth—a message of self-assertive conquest, of ruthless solipsism, and of indefatigable energy. Plainly here, too, the poet projected something of himself into Ulysses. One finds the same interplay of feeling between the traditional hero and a modern writer in the works of Kazantzakis.

Other examples of this self-identification or self-discovery[2] in Ulysses have been mentioned in previous chapters. Sometimes the hero seems to impose his personality on the author. Sometimes the author shapes the traditional outlines of the hero to resemble himself: sometimes there is a full interaction between the two personalities.[3] There are versions of the myth in which the autobiographical or egotistic elements form merely a part of an author's final portrait of the hero—in Joyce's *Ulysses*, for example. In a few instances this egotistic element can be proved from external evidence. In others it can, perhaps, be reasonably conjectured.[4] But one must be careful to avoid the fallacy[5] that there is always and necessarily some discernible link between the personality of an author and the personalities of his heroes as they finally appear in his work.

These personal, historical, linguistic, ethical, and technical considerations were the main external factors in the evolution of the Ulysses theme from the time of Homer onwards. But every traditional hero is open to these influences. Why then was Ulysses's evolution so unusually varied? Why have the figures of Achilles and Hector, Nestor and Diomedes not gone through as many vicissitudes? And why among post-classical character-images do only Faust and Don Juan approach Ulysses in adaptability. Relative antiquity cannot provide an answer here. Agamemnon and Menelaus, though as old in the European tradition as Ulysses, remain more or less fixed types in every epoch, while it is Don Juan, comparatively a newcomer, who comes nearest to him in the variety of his reincarnations.

One explanation of this difference has been given in the earlier chapters on Homer's characterization of Ulysses. Homer presented Ulysses—whether one simply reckons the amount of poetry devoted to him, or considers the quality of the interest shown in him—much more fully than any other hero. Ulysses has a considerable and subtly impressive part to play in the *Iliad*: he is the central figure of the *Odyssey*. The personalities and talents of the other heroes are displayed in one single setting, and that a narrow one—the environment of an invading army. Ulysses is also displayed as an adventurer in unexplored and magical lands, as a disguised avenger in his own land, and as husband, father, conspirator, and king. Naturally this ampler canvas gave later writers scope for wider developments and adaptations, especially when Homer in the richness of his imagination had left so many incidents sketched in mere outline.

One might rest content, then, with saying that Ulysses's adaptability was the result of the unparalleled richness of his qualities and exploits as displayed by Homer. But Homer's poems themselves were not created out of nothing. They were the product of long literary development. Belief in a pre-Homeric literature makes it unsatisfactory to say that Ulysses became the most versatile figure in European mythology because Homer made him so. Why did Homer make him so?

Once more the folklore figure of the Cunning Lad, the Wily One, the Grandson of Autolycus, suggests an answer. To watch, with awareness of his cleverness, a clever person at work is one of

the most entertaining and instructive spectacles in life and art. Some
may watch with admiration, some with dislike; some with a desire
to imitate, some[6] with an instinct to shout to the victims of his
cleverness, 'Look out, he's tricking you!' As life and literature
evolve from folk-society to higher forms of civilization, men's
reactions to cleverness, intelligence, prudence, wisdom—whatever
it may come to be called—will change. But the fascination of
watching 'brains', *nous*, at work, for good or evil, will remain. And
what audiences enjoy, professional writers will naturally produce.

But if this view of cleverness provides the best rationale both of
Ulysses's adaptability (for cleverness and versatility go together)
and of his popularity or unpopularity (for cleverness always interests, whether we like it or not), why are Faust and Don Juan[7] his
chief rivals for popularity in mythological revivals? Faust is the
simpler figure of the two. He is mainly a specialized, and gothicized,
form of a single quality in the more comprehensive figure of
Ulysses. Faust represents the intellectual passion to know more, and
thereby to become more powerful, than other men. In the Middle
Ages Dante and Gower had seen something of this quality in
Ulysses. But since Ulysses's traditional nature included prudence as
well as intellectual curiosity, the imprudent Faust provided a better
emblem for showing how this inordinate desire for knowledge
could lead to destruction.

What, then, of Don Juan? He, like Faust, is unclassical in the
sense that he ignores the maxim of 'Nothing in excess'. He, too, is
a man driven by passion; but his is sensual passion in contrast with
Faust's intellectualism. In the recent European tradition Juan has
proved to be a stronger character-image than Faust. Don Juanized
Fausts are commoner than Fausticized Don Juans. The reason is,
perhaps, that Juan represents the whole force of an elemental passion
while Faust's passion to know is only a part of intelligence in its
fullest form. But when the Juan element has conflicted in the
Ulysses tradition with the full force of intelligence as personified in
Ulysses, it has generally lost the battle—this battle royal between
the two ruling forces in human life, 'passion to urge and reason to
control'.

Homer implied this. His Circe and Calypso to some extent, at
least, personified non-domestic passion and affection, while Penelope
embodied passion and affection within the home. Penelope prevailed. Similarly in Joyce's *Ulysses* the hero turns to Penelope at the
end. So, too, Calderon's Circe is finally rejected. From the time

of the Cyclic poets, it is true, there have always been some writers to argue that a centrifugal, Juanesque, impulse would drive Ulysses away from Penelope in search of old or new loves. But in the tradition as a whole the authors who believe in the ultimate triumph of reason over passion in Ulysses's heart command the weightier authority.

There is some risk here of being driven back to an allegorical interpretation of the Ulysses theme. Charles Lamb, it will be remembered, saw the 'agents' of the *Odyssey* as 'things which denote external force or internal temptations, the twofold danger which a wise fortitude must expect to encounter in its course through this world'. In this he spoke for two thousand years of Homeric allegory. But one need not become an allegorist to value the Ulysses theme. In the past, authors and readers in every stage of the tradition have been satisfied to see him simply as a person, as a supremely intelligent, many-sided person grappling with multifarious difficulties; a personality as actual, in a sense, as Themistocles, or Cicero, or Cecil, or Richelieu.

One aspect of the whole story needs final emphasis. Contrary to casual opinion, a heroic figure like Ulysses—but especially Ulysses—is something more than a name attached to certain fixed characteristics and exploits, chiefly useful 'to point a moral or adorn a tale'. In some way these traditional heroes retain a dynamism and a momentum of their own. When Goethe and Tennyson and others established so close a relationship with the *persona* of Ulysses it was not a matter of simple imitation or veneration. A mutually energizing power was exchanged between the author and the hero. Precisely how, is for others to determine.[8] But, whatever its psychological implications, this *rapport* between living persons and a dead (or mythical) hero follows a long established custom. For the ancient Greeks, when they needed guidance in doubt or perplexity, did not always consult the oracles of the gods at Delphi or Cumae. They occasionally preferred to commune with less awful powers. Then they would go and inquire at the traditional shrines of the heroes; and at times they, somehow, received an enheartening response.

NOTES TO CHAPTER I

[1] Samuel Johnson, *Lives of the English poets, Nicholas Rowe*, ed. G. B. Hill (Oxford, 1935), ii, 68.

[2] John Keats as quoted by Leigh Hunt in *The Indicator* of December 8, 1819: 'Talking with a friend about Dante he observed that whenever so great a poet told us anything in addition or continuation of an ancient story, he had a right to be regarded as a classical authority. For instance, said he, when he tells us of that characteristic death of Ulysses in one of the books of his Inferno, we ought to receive the information as authentic, and be glad that we have more news of Ulysses than we looked for'. See further in Douglas Bush, *Mythology and the romantic tradition* (Cambridge, Mass., 1939), p. 118, to whom I owe the quotation.

[3] See E. M. Butler, *The fortunes of Faust* (Cambridge, 1952), and John Austen, *The story of Don Juan* (London, 1939).

[4] See index for other references to these controversial terms.

NOTES TO CHAPTER II

The fullest collection of references to Ulysses in all epochs of the classical period will be found in Wüst and Schmidt: see also Cesareo. The titles of works cited by the authors' names will be found in the list of books given at the end of this book. Where no author is named the article is by the present writer.

[1] Decipherments of the Minoan and Mycenean records have suggested no reference to Ulysses yet. Dubious Egyptian parallels (especially in the Wen Amun story) are discussed by Vikentiev, Hittite by Lesky, Semitic by Bérard, Indian by Carnoy and Fries, Babylonian by H. Muchau (*Bursian's Jahresbericht*, clxxxii (1920), 251–4 and 256–64), and also by A. Ungnad, *Gilgamesch-Epos und Odyssee* (Breslau, 1923). (But on the last possibility, G. R. Levy, pp. 143–4, has remarked: 'The character of Odysseus is that the very antithesis of that of Gilgamesh, whose Homeric counterpart is Achilles . . .', though both are presented in the first lines of their epics as heroes of unusual mental powers.) Patroni's elaborate theory of 'Mediterranean' sources for Ulysses's characteristics is based on the slenderest foundations, cf. *Journal of Hellenic Studies*, lxxii (1952), 129. For comparisons between Ulysses and Old Testament figures (a favourite study in the seventeenth and eighteenth centuries) see Fabricius, *Bibliotheca Graeca*, i (4th edn., Hamburg, 1790), 533.

[2] For a list of Odysseus's epithets in the Homeric poems see R. J. Cunliffe, *Homeric proper and place names* (London, 1931), p. 29. Those which are confined to Odysseus alone and not shared with any other hero refer to his ability in planning and giving counsel, his wide experience, his wiliness, resourcefulness, and endurance. A remarkable feature is his virtual monopoly of epithets in πολυ- among male Homeric figures (see note in *Classical Philology*, xlv (1950), 108–10) by which Homer indicates the unique richness and complexity of his personality. Sheppard has discussed some significant arrangements of his epithets; see also Osterwald and Kretschmar. R. von Scheliha has criticized the view that some of Odysseus's epithets in the *Iliad* prove an earlier legend (as, e.g., argued by Robert, p. 55), but admits that there must have been some pre-Homeric Odysseus tradition.

[3] For discussions (to 1937) of variation in the Greek spelling of Ulysses's name see Wüst, and since then especially Kretschmer in *Glotta*, xxviii (1940), 253–4, and in *Anzeiger Akad. Wissen. Wien, phil-Hist. Kl.*, lxxxii (1945), 90–3 For Etruscan variations (also unparalleled) see E. Fiesel, *Namen des griech. Mythos im Etruskischen* (Göttingen, 1928), p. 28; and also s.v. *Utuse* in Roscher. Illyrian or Anatolian origins have been suggested for the *Oulixes* form. The variation between -*d*- and -*l*-, if accepted as a normal linguistic mutation, must belong to a pre-Homeric stage of Greek. The suggestion that Οὖτις, Ulysses's pseudonym in the Cyclops incident, is connected with 'Οδυσσεύς, or with the Etruscan *Utuse*, is dubious.

[4] For a tentative suggestion that *Ulixes* and *Odysseus* were originally quite different names see van Leeuwen on *Od.* 19, 407–9. It would be convenient to identify the knavish elements in Ulysses's character with a proto-Ulixes and the heroic elements with a proto-Odysseus, but there is no evidence at all for such a dichotomy. Homer may have adopted the -*d*- form to suit an etymology: see n. 11 below.

[5] For 221 versions of the Cyclops legend see Frazer's *Apollodorus*, Appendix xiii, with references to fuller discussions; also A. B. Cook, *Zeus*, ii, 988 ff. Some additions will be

found in the Warburg *Bibliography of the survival of the classics*, 1 (London, 1934), 14 and 18. Folklore parallels to other Odyssean episodes are mentioned by Tolstoi (citing many earlier studies), Crooke, Lang, and Stith-Thompson, *Motif-index of folk-literature* (Bloomington, Indiana, 1932–5). These parallels are generally much closer than those cited by the authors mentioned in n. 1. For the many explicit references to Ulysses in recent fairy-tales see M. H. Eastman, *Index to fairy-tales, myths, and legends* (Boston, 1926 and 1937).

⁶ For Ulysses as a historical figure see Croiset, and contrast M. P. Nilsson, *The Mycenaean origin of Greek mythology* (Cambridge, 1932), pp. 95–100. W. Aly, *Homer* (Frankfurt, 1937), p. 59, thinks that he was originally a Cretan sailor. For U. as a pre-historic sea-god, see Mayer; as a sun-god, or year-daimon, Menrad (criticized by J. A. Scott in *Classical Philology*, xii (1917), 244–52), Seeck, Murray, and Thomson. L. R. Farnell, in *Greek hero cults* (Oxford, 1921), p. 326, mentions cults of Odysseus in Laconia, Aetolia, and Libya, but warns against taking these as evidence for any aboriginal godhead. Carnoy suggests that Ulysses was originally a fire god like Mātariçvan of the Vedic hymns, comparing the Germanic Loki and the Celtic Lugh, and finding the root of the Latin *lux* 'light' in the name 'Ολύξης. For the view that Odysseus was originally a chthonic deity combining elements from prototypes of Hermes and Poseidon see Mario Untersteiner, *Odissea Libro XI* (Florence, 1948), pp. 37–42.

⁷ Ulysses as a kind of Wolf Dietrich is discussed in Radermacher and Thomson; as a hibernating bear, in Carpenter and Thomson. His connection with horse-cults is discussed with strong reservations by Thomson. There is little or no evidence for any of these speculations.

⁸ For problems of fact and fiction in Homer see especially Carpenter.

⁹ The Autolycan, or Shifty Lad, element in Odysseus's character was emphasized by Andrew Lang in *Anthropology and the classics* (Oxford, 1908), p. 60, cf. Thomson, pp. 14–17, and Philippson (who explains it as a 'chthonic' characteristic derived from Hermes). W. Crooke, in *Folklore*, ix (1898), 100, and 114 had noted that Sisyphus (Odysseus's father according to a non-Homeric tradition) belonged to 'the Master Thief cycle'.

¹⁰ 'Maui-of-a-thousand-tricks: his Oceanic and European biographies', by K. Luomala, *Berenice P. Bishop Museum Bulletin*, 198 (Honolulu, 1949). Some of the resemblances with Ulysses are remarkable.

¹¹ Problems in Homer's etymology of Odysseus's name are discussed in *Classical Philology*, xlvii (1952), 209–13, with references to earlier studies. Homer connects it with forms of *ὀδύομαι denoting anger, displeasure, dislike. This may have been his own fancy, or else an earlier folk etymology. On the other hand some modern philologists concede that it could be the genuine explanation of the name. Others prefer to connect *Odysseus* with *duk*—'a leader'. Wüst mentions a suggested connection of the form *Ulixes* with the Celtic *Lixovius* (hence *Lisieux*), and Thomson (pp. 17–18) derives it from *luk*- 'a wolf'.

¹² According to the post-Homeric tradition Hermes was Autolycus's father, but Homer does not imply it. See *Il.* 5, 390 and 24, 24 for references to his thievish talents. Philippson discusses the Hermes element in Odysseus's character, and expounds its polarity with the Athene element as will be discussed in chapter three. She emphasizes Hermes's direct interventions in Odysseus's adventures in that part of the *Odyssey* where Athene is absent (*Od.* 5, 43 ff.; 10, 275 ff.); but is he anything more than the messenger of the gods there (though he has no expressed instructions from them in the second case)? For an older view see Osterwald who identifies Odysseus with Hermes (p. 147). Hermes is described as πολύτροπος (Odysseus's special epithet in Homer) in *Hymn to Hermes* 13.

¹³ Wüst. See Wüst and Roscher on *Autolykos*, and Philippson, for folk-lore traits in early references to him. The fact that Homer describes Autolycus's sons as using magical incantations to heal Odysseus's wound in the boar hunt (*Od.* 19, 457–8) also suggests folk sources. M. Miller in *Journal of Hellenic Studies*, lxxiii (1953), 46–52, finds several other Autolycuses in Odysseus's ancestry: but I can find no good authority for any of them.

¹⁴ Arkeisios's mother was a bear according to a later tradition first attested in Aristotle's *Constitution of the Ithacans*—presumably an etymological fancy: but Carpenter, pp. 128 ff., takes it as genuine folk tradition. As Croiset notes, the name might just as plausibly be derived from ἀρκεῖν 'to defend'.

¹⁵ Sophocles, Frag. incert. 880 (Nauck): ὀρθῶς δ' 'Οδυσσεύς εἰμ' ἐπώνυμος κακοῖς πολλοὶ γὰρ ὠδύσαντο δυσσεβεῖς ἐμοί.

¹⁶ Geddes bases his theory of the authorship of the Homeric poems on a distinction between a 'Ulyssean' writer (author of the *Odyssey* and *Il.* 2–7, 9, 10, 23, 24) and the author of the 'Achilleid' (as Grote determined it). His theory has been refuted by Shewan and others, but I owe many useful observations on the character of Odysseus to his study.

[17] For the neutrality of the word δόλος in Homer see, for example, the scholia on *Il.* 2, 114; 3, 202; Eustathius on *Il.* 3, 358 and 10, 383. Cf. the Latin conception of *dolum malum* as distinct from *dolum bonum*.

[18] Alexander Pope, generally a shrewd critic of Homer's characters, explains (in the note to this line in his translation of the *Iliad*) it as meaning no more than 'that behaviour which is commonly remarkable in a modest and sensible man who speaks in public'. If so, no other hero is presented by Homer as modest and sensible when he speaks in public. But Homer's strong terms—αἰδρεῖ φωτὶ ἐοικώς and φαίης κε ζάκοτόν τέ τιν' ἔμμεναι ἄφρονά τ'αὔτως—seem to imply more than a mere modesty of bearing or a preliminary pretence of diffidence in the manner of Cicero. The ancient commentator referred to in the next sentence in my text is the scholiast A on *Il.* 3, 217.

[19] E. N. Gardner in *Journal of Hellenic Studies*, xxv (1905), 24–5, argues rather dubiously that the match must have been a draw, because Odysseus was 'surely' the last man to surrender his right to a prize.

[20] In Dictys of Crete (3, 18) Odysseus does compete, as one would have expected, in the archery contest. For Odysseus's pride in his skill as an archer see *Od.* 8, 215–22, and see later in chapter five.

[21] *Il.* 4, 339, καὶ σὺ κακοῖσι δόλοισι κεκασμένε, κερδαλεόφρον. The last term had already been applied to Agamemnon himself by Achilles in *Il.* 1, 149, but preceded by a phrase which implies arrogance, not deceitfulness. κέρδος is another of Homer's ethically ambiguous terms. It varies in meaning from 'good counsels, plans' to 'artful, self-seeking devices', hence 'gains, profits'. See further on Odysseus's acquisitiveness in chapter five.

[22] Eustathius on *Il.* 9, 309, takes it that the remark is intended as a preface to Achilles's own candour (as if he were naturally a reticent man). But the scholia B & T understand it as a taunt directed against Odysseus's oratorical devices: cf. the noteworthy scholium on *Od.* 1, 1, which suggests that early critics took Achilles as the type of the *homo simplex* and Odysseus of the *homo duplex* on the basis of Achilles's remark here. Odysseus himself uses Achilles's phrase in *Od.* 14, 156–7, 'Hateful to me as the gates of Hell is the man who, yielding to poverty, utters deceptive words': but it is a carefully restricted adaptation.

[23] Achilles's form of address to Odysseus in the Land of Ghosts (*Od.* 11, 473–4) is much more friendly; but perhaps there is a slightly patronizing tone in his 'Pertinacious one (σχέτλιε) what even greater deed have you contrived now?'—in other words, 'You're always bent on some bigger feat, aren't you, Odysseus?' Compare Athene's tone in *Od.* 13, 330, as discussed in the next chapter.

[24] Telemachus says just this about Odysseus in *Od.* 17, 347 (quoted by Socrates in *Charmides* 161A).

[25] For an ampler analysis of Odysseus's lies see *Hermathena*, lxxv (1950), 35–48. Sir Maurice Bowra in *Sophoclean tragedy*, pp. 270 ff., argues that the Greeks in general considered lying an evil practice and cites support from some of the more austere Greek moralists, but it may be questioned (in view of remarks like those in Xenophon, *Memorabilia* 4, 2, 13–15, Aeschylus frags. 301, 302, and the instances cited in Herodotus 4, 201, and Thucydides 3, 34, 3, for example) whether the average attitude was so firm; cf. Mahaffy, *Social life in Greece* (3rd edn., London, 1877), pp. 27–9. At all events, this severer view is not to be found in Homer. Hesiod is sterner towards falsehood and fiction, but as Jaeger observes (p. 153), the concept of truth as 'a new universal category to which every personal preference must yield' derives from sixth-century Ionian philosophy. Gladstone (*Juventus mundi*, p. 385) sadly concedes Homer's 'tenderness . . . for fraud under certain conditions', finding Achilles alone exempt from its influence. Cf. Snell, p. 166. For Odysseus's lies in *Od.* 13–19 see C. R. Trahman in *The Phoenix* vi (1952), 31–43, and R. B. Woolsey, 'Repeated narratives in the *Odyssey*', *Classical Philology* xxxvi (1941), 167–81.

[26] Socrates in Plato, *Republic* 382 c; Polyaenus, *Strategemata*, Introduction, 4 ff. with special reference to Odysseus and Autolycus; Leo, *Strategemata* passim. For the technique of deception by fallacious oaths, in which Autolycus excelled, see Eustathius on *Od.* 19, 395 ff., 'as when one swears to a truce for so many *days* and then attacks by *night*'.

[27] Davaux, to whose study I owe several points in this and the following chapter, notes that Odysseus avoids telling a flat lie whenever he can, preferring to use misleading ambiguities, even when dealing with an enemy like Dolon. Davaux finds some signs of grace in this. But I doubt that it necessarily implies any respect for truth: a clever deceiver scorns the simplicity of a simple untruth. Chaignet, p. 192, remarks, however: *il ne faudrait pas être injuste envers Ulysse . . . Ulysse n'est pas faux, n'est pas perfide; il ne ment pas pour mentir; il ne trompe pas pour tromper.*

[28] Frank Budgen, *James Joyce and the making of 'Ulysses'* (London, 1934), p. 16.

[29] Cf. Geddes, p. 322: 'We must carefully distinguish . . . between a natural and unconscious ethical purpose and a didactic and conscious one. The latter has no place in either poem.' He cites from Goethe's *Autobiography* (1, 469): 'A good work of art can, and will indeed, have moral consequences, but to require moral ends of the artist is to destroy his profession'.

[30] *Od.* 5, 173–9, 356–9; 13, 256–88.

ADDITIONAL NOTE. Odysseus's reputation in the *Iliad* for wiliness could, of course, be explained, without direct reference to Autolycus, as the result of such incidents in his career before the landing at Troy as his feigned madness or his ruses in the detection of Achilles (if these were current in Homer's time: see chapter six). But these examples of clever dealing, too, were presumably consequences of his Autolycan heredity.

NOTES TO CHAPTER III

[1] Besides the three main interventions by Athene in Odysseus's career in the *Iliad*, which are to be described in detail in this chapter, she also prevents him from pursuing Sarpedon in *Il.* 5, 676, thereby saving him from Zeus's anger, and in *Il.* 11, 437–8, she prevents the spear of Sokos from inflicting a mortal wound. Neither of these interventions is emphasized.

[2] For an analysis of personal interventions of deities in the affairs of individuals in the *Iliad* see L. A. MacKay, *The wrath of Homer* (Toronto, 1948), pp. 68–71. Athene makes more use of Achilles and Diomedes than of Ulysses to check the Trojans, but Homer makes it clear that she favours Achilles mainly as an instrument for slaughter and Diomedes less for his own sake than because he is the son of her former protégé Tydeus (see *Il.* 5, 124 ff., 406 ff., 800 ff.), though there is a touch of personal affection in her phrase 'thou who hast found favour in my heart' in *Il.* 8, 826. In general Athene uses Achilles and Diomedes when physical valour is needed and Odysseus in matters demanding prudence and tact. Athene's special regard for Odysseus is emphasized by Nestor in *Od.* 3, 218–24. Diomedes (as Davaux notes, p. 5) actually intervenes more often in the council of elders than Odysseus, but this may indicate boldness rather than wisdom. See further in n. 2 to chapter five.

[3] Odysseus's consciousness of Athene's constant surveillance, as expressed here, struck Epictetus (*Discourses* 1, 12, 3) as a notable example of religious faith.

[4] Apuleius, *De deo Socratis*, 18, remarks that in the Doloneia Odysseus is the intelligence (*consilium, mens, animus*), Diomedes the physical force (*auxilium, manus, gladius*) in this episode.

[5] The scholia A on *Il.* 10, 249, note Odysseus's modesty here, and explain the contrasting boastfulness of his self-description in Phaeacia (*Od.* 9, 19–20) as being necessary to win enough respect to be granted an escort home. His self-praise in *Od.* 8, 166 ff., is forced by Laodamas's direct insult. For his remarks to Sokos see later in this chapter.

[6] For the more formal aspect of Odysseus's piety see especially Zeus's testimony in *Od.* 1, 66–7. 'More than other mortals has he offered sacrifices to the immortal gods'. Odysseus's actions throughout the *Odyssey* illustrate his personal piety. Even in his worst sufferings he never blames the gods (except Poseidon whose wrath is admittedly justified) or accuses them of 'envy' as others do (e.g. in *Od.* 4, 181; 5, 118; 23, 211). His single moment of petulance against Athene in *Od.* 13, 316 ff. is discussed later in this chapter. Contrast Achilles's threats against Apollo (*Il.* 22, 20 ff.) and his defiance of the river-god Scamander (*Il.* 21, 130 ff.).

[7] The Locrian Ajax, who was the swiftest of the Achaeans (*Il.* 14, 521–2).

[8] The scholiast on *Od.* 13, 89, uses a similar comparison: 'like a mother putting a dear child to sleep Athene speaks a word of praise to Odysseus'.

[9] I have used Rieu's translation in the last two paragraphs both for its liveliness and to avoid any risk of subjective interpretation to suit my own views.

[10] Hart, pp. 263 ff. Apropos of this scene he discusses Odysseus's freedom from the dominance of passion and his carefulness in considering possible courses of action, citing *Il.* 11, 401 ff.; *Od.* 5, 465 f.; 6, 141 ff.; 10, 151 ff.; 18, 90 ff. I cannot agree with his view that Odysseus is characteristically sceptical towards the gods here and in *Od.* 5, 173, 356, but prefer the explanation offered in chapter two.

[11] This interpretation connects ἐπητής and ἐπητύς with ἔπω 'to tend, attend to'. Others derive it from ἔπος and render it as 'talkative, eloquent'; but this meaning is weak in *Od.* 13, 332, and incongruous at *Od.* 18, 128, and 21, 306. Cf. Chaignet, p. 197.

[12] It is assumed in this paragraph that ἀγανοφροσύνη and ἠπιότης are similar to ἐπητύς in denoting aspects of gentleness and kindness. The quality denoted by the post-Homeric πρᾶος and πραότης (as in the Beatitude 'Blessed are the meek', St. Matthew v. 5), which seems to

have been like that implied by ἐπητύς is attributed to Odysseus by Eustathius on *Il.* 2, 337, and the B scholia on *Il.* 3, 196.

[13] *Od.* 2, 47 = 2, 234 = 5, 12. Other tributes to Odysseus's gentleness are to be found in *Od.* 4, 689–91; 14, 62–7; 138–9; 16, 443–4.

[14] Cf. *Gorgias* 516 C, where Socrates attributes to Homer (perhaps on the basis of *Od.* 4, 120, or 9, 175) the belief that the δίκαιοι are ἥμεροι.

[15] For the special affection shown towards dogs in the *Odyssey* and the 'Ulyssean' books of the *Iliad* see Geddes, chapters sixteen and seventeen. (But his argument that this is evidence for difference between the authorship of the *Odyssey* and the 'Achilleid' fails if one remembers that dogs are naturally repugnant on battlefields where they devour the dead and naturally cherished in hunting and in domestic life.)

[16] For Odysseus's tearfulness see chapter nine.

[17] Cf. G. M. A. Grube, 'The Gods of Homer' in *Studies in Honour of Gilbert Norwood* (Toronto, 1952), p. 9: 'Certainly, Odysseus cannot claim any outstanding moral rectitude; in fact, the slaying of the suitors and, in particular, of Amphinomus and Leodes, with the revolting massacre of the maidservants, is the most deliberately savage episode in the two poems'. While I agree in general with Grube's view that Homer's gods and heroes are mainly amoral, I question the view that Odysseus's slaughter of the usurping suitors and disloyal maidservants would have been regarded as particularly savage by Homer or his audience: cf. Agamemnon's view in *Il.* 6, 55 ff., and Achilles's in *Il.* 22, 346–8. O. did try to warn off Amphinomus, the only gentle suitor.

[18] The special implication of 'fidelity' in Achilles's use of ἐχέφρων is paralleled in its post-Homeric application to faithful dogs: see Liddell and Scott.

[19] *Juventus Mundi*, p. 392. See also Gladstone's discussion of Odysseus's patience and endurance as an active quality based on moral courage (p. 389). At times this active self-control merges into dogged endurance (cf. the comparison with a dog in *Od.* 20, 13 ff.: Odysseus's self-control there is specially admired by Socrates in *Republic* 441B and *Phaedo* 94D). Odysseus is the only hero who is called τλήμων in the *Iliad* (5, 670, cf. 10, 231–2, where the quality is specially emphasized, and 498): see Geddes's study of this and similar terms, pp. 88–9 and 226.

[20] *Od.* 22, 411 ff. Some commentators (going back to a scholiast ad loc.) take εὐχετάασθαι as meaning 'to pray, offer supplication'; but this hardly suits the context as well here as it does in *Il.* 6, 267–8.

[21] Odysseus broke his own precept in exulting over the slain Sokos in *Il.* 11, 449 ff. But, as the scholia note, the circumstances were extenuating: Sokos had just wounded him after a taunt (with a definite incitement to boast). This is an answer to Geddes's view that *Il.* 11, 449, is a proof that the Ulysses of the Achilleid appears to be 'entirely ignorant of the ethical injunction of the Ulysses of the *Odyssey*'. Similarly the usually merciful and compassionate Menelaus in *Il.* 17, 19, prescribes something like the same rule—'Surely it is ignoble (οὐ καλόν) to boast with excessive violence'—but breaks it without great provocation in *Il.* 13, 620 ff.

[22] *Od.* 18, 130 ff. A similar melancholy pessimism is found in Glaucus's words to Diomedes in *Il.* 6, 144–9, and more markedly in Achilles's to Priam in *Il.* 24, 525–33; but the first makes no reference to the gods and the second accuses them of caring nothing for men's sufferings, while Odysseus accepts the divine will without criticism. Cf. n. 6 above.

[23] In giving this mere opinion I must apologize for not entering more deeply into the perplexing problems of Homer's theology. For a convenient discussion of recent views see Grube, loc. cit. in n. 17 above. Taking the view that Homer certainly does not intend the conduct of his gods to be a moral example, Grube does concede 'the very first glimmerings' of a moralistic attitude to divinity in his poems.

[24] Cf. E. R. Dodds, *The Greeks and the irrational* (Berkeley, 1951), p. 54, with a reference to Nilsson's *Minoan-Mycenaean Religion*, 2nd edn., pp. 491 ff. See also C. Ghislau, *Beschouwingen over de Athene figur bij Homerus* (Leiden, 1929), pp. 41–3.

[25] Cf. C. Seltman, *The twelve Olympians* (London, 1952), pp. 50–51, for Athene as Palace Goddess. On pp. 59–60 he admits some symbolism in the myth of Athene's birth from the head of Zeus but begs a large question in calling it the 'mind' and 'brain' of Zeus. He concludes: 'So Athene, sprung from the brain of Zeus, is the symbol and the patroness of *sophia*, which means "skill-plus-wisdom", and therefore is the protectress of every man and woman who is definitely keen on and good at his or her job'. This fits her attitude to Odysseus well, but Seltman is referring here to the fully developed post-Homeric concept of Athene. Chaignet, p. 192, discusses Athene's two aspects, as Πρόμαχος and as Μηχανῖτις, in connection with Odysseus.

²⁶ Paula Philippson: cf. n. 13 to chapter two.

²⁷ Also, to some extent, Patroclus, to whom the epithet ἐνηής in *Il*. 17, 204; 21, 96; 23, 252; and μειλίχιος in *Il*. 17, 691; 19, 300. He by his death as a consequence of Achilles's anger offers a parallel to the death of the gentle Hector as a consequence of Paris's offence.

²⁸ For a different conclusion, but on similar lines, cf. Levy, p. 144: 'the shift of focus [between the *Iliad* and the *Odyssey*] from spiritual conflict to equilibrium seems rather to belong to the old age of the real or symbolic author of the Greek epics. At the conclusion of the dark era, it may be conjectured, the non-epic qualities came to be admired. The *Odyssey* represents an involuntary revolt against the bitter and joyful (?) heroism of the *Iliad*, on the part of an old man or a dying epoch'. And p. 145: 'The self-control of Odysseus makes him a hero no longer dependent upon *menos* or *mana*. He is without passion (?), like Rama and Aeneas, and so belongs to a new civilization. This is an epic of transition'.

NOTES TO CHAPTER IV

¹ Menelaus speaks of Odysseus with affection in *Od*. 4, 169 ff., but that was nine years after the fall of Troy. He shows no signs of special friendliness to him in the *Iliad*. Ajax's words in *Il*. 9, 642, do not imply any special intimacy. There is a statement in *Od*. 19, 247, that Odysseus honoured his herald Eurybates above all his companions because he 'saw eye to eye' (Rieu) with him. Eurybates is signalized there with a remarkable description, and one feels he had a significant part in some version of the legend; but Homer says nothing more of him. Eustathius *ad loc.* tells some extraordinary tales about him: cf. Pauly at *Eurybates*.

² Odysseus's loneliness is not specially emphasized in the classical tradition. It becomes a dominant feature in his characterization by Fénelon, Tennyson, Pascoli, and Joyce.

³ *Il*. 2, 260; 4, 354.

⁴ *Il*. 2, 292 ff. The Venetus B scholiast regards this passage as a prelude to the affection of Odysseus and Penelope as portrayed in the *Odyssey*, i.e. as a piece of 'poetic economy'.

⁵ Eustathius in his introduction to the *Od*. 6 distinguishes the erotic love of Circe and Calypso from the affection of Athene which is based on the pleasure of dealing with an intelligence and wisdom like her own. The earliest insinuation that Athene was amorous of Odysseus is, so far as I know, made by Poseidon in Stephen Phillips's *Ulysses*: see chapter fourteen. For Odysseus's relationships with women in the Homeric poems see Hart, Müller, and Woodhouse.

⁶ The tragic potentialities of this licence are exemplified in the case of Phoenix (*Il*. 9, 449). Teucer also was an illegitimate son (*Il*. 8, 286).

⁷ That is so far as Homer's narrative goes; the *argumentum ex silentio* is supported by Odysseus's known conduct. The Venetus A scholiast on *Il*. 1, 182, and the B and Townleian scholiasts on *Il*. 1, 138, say that Laodice, the daughter of Cycnus, was allotted to Odysseus. Athenaeus (13, 556D), discussing illegitimate children, cites Aristotle (fr. 162 Rose) for the statement that only Menelaus was without a concubine at Troy; but Aristotle seems to have explained the problems involved by suggesting that most of the women slaves awarded to the various heroes (including Nestor) were 'as an honour' (εἰς γέρας) not 'for use' (εἰς χρῆσιν).

⁸ This view is presented in Plutarch's *Bruta animalia ratione uti* (*Gryllus*): the transformed men give reasons for preferring to remain animals. This Cynic paradox became influential in the vernacular tradition after Gelli's version of the Circe legend in 1548: see E. M. W. Tillyard, *The Elizabethan world picture* (London, 1943), p. 26.

⁹ *Od*. 10, 472: the Companions begin δαιμόνι᾽ ἤδη νῦν μιμνήσκεο, which can be colloquially rendered 'You're a surprising man. Isn't it about time that you remembered . . .?' Calderon in his *Love the greatest enchantment* emphasizes the difficulty of freeing Odysseus from Circe's fascinations: see chapter fourteen.

¹⁰ It was not always so, as Homer's discreet remark in *Od*. 5, 153, implies: 'since the nymph *no longer* delighted him'.

¹¹ The symbol of the smoke from Odysseus's hearth fire became a favourite motif in the later tradition: cf. Ovid, *Epistles* 1, 3, 33–4; du Bellay's sonnet *Heureux qui comme Ulysses*, and the 'azure pillars of the hearth' in Tennyson's *Princess*. Clement of Alexandria (*Exhortation to the Gentiles* 25) remarks that Odysseus should have yearned for the celestial radiance of the Heavenly City rather than for a mere wisp of mundane smoke.

¹² Cf. L. A. Post, *From Homer to Menander* (Berkeley, 1951), p. 14: 'a united family is the goal'.

[13] Cf. Lucian, *Vera historia* 2, 29, where Odysseus secretly sends a letter from Ithaca to Calypso; cf. Philostratus, *Life of Apollonius* 7, 10.

[14] I owe this interpretation to Müller's imaginative study in the symbolism of the Odyssean voyages.

[15] Homer repeats that Odysseus's liaison with Calypso was 'perforce' in *Od.* 4, 557; 5, 14; and he uses the verb 'held back' (κατέρυκε) in 1, 55; 23, 334. Is it accident or a stroke of subtle policy that Odysseus does not refer to any such compulsion on Calypso's part, in his speeches to the Phaeacians (7, 244 ff.; 12, 448 ff.)?

[16] See E. F. D'Arms and K. H. Hully, 'The Oresteia story in the *Odyssey*', *Transactions of the American Philological Society* lxxvii (1946), 207–13. They note parallels and contrasts between Odysseus and Agamemnon, Penelope and Clytaemnestra, Telemachus and Orestes, the Suitors and Aegisthus. Their view that Homer intended these implicit comparisons to ennoble the 'provincial' royalty of Ithaca is questionable.

[17] J. W. Mackail in *Love's looking-glass* (London, 1891).

[18] Woodhouse (to whose analysis I am much indebted in what follows).

[19] Plutarch (*Quomodo adulescens*, 27) admits that Nausicaa's wish that 'such a man as this should dwell here and be my husband' (*Od.* 6, 244–5) would be bold and licentious, if uttered without a knowledge of Odysseus's good character (which, he assumes, she has already got by observation and intuition).

[20] *Od.* 8, 457 ff.

[21] Cf. Woodhouse, p. 64: 'Who does not feel that there is something hard and unsatisfying in this ending of her first passion? We feel perhaps just a little sorry that, after all, there is a Penelopeia patiently waiting in the background. In the original old story . . . here so sadly mutilated and dislocated, everything went as the heart would have it'. Cf. L. A. Post, op. cit. in n. 10 above, p. 22. The theory that Nausicaa was originally a typical fairyland princess whose role in the pre-Homeric tradition was to be wooed and won by a mysterious stranger was first developed, as far as I know, by van Leeuwen's article in *Mnemosyne* xxxix (1911), reprinted with additions in his *Commentationes Homericae* (Leyden, 1911). W. R. Paton added further possibilities in *The Classical Review* xxvi (1912), 215–16. Some of the arguments offered in its favour are unconvincing, as when Paton says that Odysseus's hot bath in *Od.* 8, 449 ff., is 'obviously the wedding bath'—but what is more natural than that a man should bathe before a public banquet, after a day at an athletic contest and among a people whose love of hot baths was unusually great?

[22] Goethe in the fragments of his unfinished play, *Nausikaa*: see chapter fourteen.

[23] Mackail loc. cit. in n. 17 above.

[24] For references to the fact that Penelope yearned for Odysseus and hated her life without him see *Od.* 16, 37–9; 17, 272–4; 19, 136.

[25] This interpretation was already known in antiquity: see Seneca, *Ep.* 88, 8. For arguments in its favour see P. W. Harsh, 'Penelope and Odysseus in *Odyssey* xix', *American Journal of Philology* lxxi (1950), 1 ff.; cf. Post, op. cit. in n. 10 above, pp. 24 and 275. But R. Merkelbach, *Untersuchungen zur Odyssee* (Munich, 1951), p. 237, argues that if Homer had intended this subtlety he would have said so explicitly, e.g. 'But she knew in her heart that it was Odysseus'.

[26] *Od.* 19, 103 ff.: especially vv. 115 ff., 166, 209 ff.

[27] *Od.* 23, 85 ff. In what follows I discuss especially 113 ff., 156 ff., 174 ff., 209 ff.

[28] Cf. Post, op. cit. p. 23: 'It is not merely Odysseus' knowledge of the secret that assures Penelope of his identity; his righteous indignation discloses a passion that she recognizes'.

[29] The element of paradox: Eustathius on *Od.* 19, 488.

[30] Eustathius on *Od.* 23, 110 ff. At times his urbane humanism resembles that of another famous prelate who interpreted the Ulysses story, Fénelon, Archbishop of Cambrai.

[31] πεπνυμένος.

[32] Notably Fénelon in his *Télémaque* and James Joyce in *Ulysses*. Tennyson in his *Ulysses* makes Odysseus rather contemptuous of his 'most blameless' son: see chapter fourteen.

[33] *Od.* 24, 244 ff.

[34] *Od.* 24, 240: πρῶτον κερτομίοισ'ἔπεσιν διαπειρηθῆναι.

[35] The scholiast on *Od.* 11, 177, suggests that Odysseus, aware that mothers-in-law usually dislike their daughters-in-law, tactfully left his inquiry about Penelope to the end; and that Anticleia, wishing to please her son, answered that question first. But Aristarchus took the reversal in the order simply as an example of Homeric hysteron proteron, which may be right. Cf. *Oxyrhynchus Papyri* viii, 1086, 16 ff.

[36] Tributes from Eumaeus in *Od.* 14, 62 ff., 137 ff. (v. 147 implies a special degree of friendly veneration), 167 ff.: for others see n. 13 to chapter three.
[37] *Od.* 7, 237–9.

NOTES TO CHAPTER V

[1] For studies of Odysseus's general characteristics in Homer see especially Shewan, chapter twenty (containing a survey of older views), Geddes (subject to Shewan's corrections), and Lang (*H. and the E.*, chapter eight), besides the less discursive surveys in Pauly and Roscher. Shewan, p. 150, quoting Wolf and Mure, argues effectively against Wilamowitz's early view that it is foolish to talk of a single Homeric Odysseus. Mure remarks elsewhere (*Critical history*, etc., 1, 412) 'like the fabulous Lycian sphinx, which combined the nature of the lion and serpent with its own proper body of Chimaera, Ulysses, whether the king, the beggar, the warrior, or the traveller, is still in word and deed Ulysses': cf. Hole, pp. 143–4: 'the more minutely it (Ulysses's character) is examined, the more evidently we find that the design, however bold, is exceeded by the happiness of the execution'. Since this was written I have seen two other notable discussions of Homer's conception of Odysseus: Hubert Schrade, *Götter und Menschen Homers* (Stuttgart, 1952), pp. 225–59, in which Odysseus is characterized as the first *uomo universale*, a prototype in some respects of the Sophists, but differing from them in his all-pervading piety; and E. Beaujon, *Acte et passion du héros* (Geneva, 1948), in which some new symbolical interpretations of Odysseus are examined.

[2] Odysseus admits inferiority in martial valour to Achilles (*Il.* 19, 217 ff.) while claiming superiority in intelligence, which he tactfully attributes to his greater age. (See additional note below.) The common soldiers rated Ajax, Diomedes and Agamemnon as fighters next to Achilles (*Il.* 7, 179–80). Hyginus, 114, gives statistics of the 'kills' recorded by the Greek champions: Achilles leads with 72, followed by Teucer (30) and Ajax (28). Odysseus is second last with 12 to Menelaus's 8. Lang (*A. and C.*, pp. 60–61; cf. *W. of H.*, p. 250) holds that it 'would not be hard to show that Odysseus is really the hero of the *Iliad*, as well as of the *Odyssey*, the man whom the poet admires most ...' (one may admit the second view without agreeing with the first: a poet's hero is not necessarily the same as his poem's hero). Against this see also Jaeger, p. 7, where Achilles is viewed as the golden mean between the rigid Ajax and the slippery Odysseus, and M. H. van der Valk on 'Ajax and Diomede in the *Iliad*', *Mnemosyne* v (1952), 269–86. But taking the two poems together Homer certainly merits the title φιλοδυσσεύς, which Eustathius (on *Od.* 19, 583) gives him.

[3] Athene's other great favourite, Tydeus, was also a low-sized man (*Il.* 5, 801). Other details of Odysseus's appearance in Homer: he had the normal fair or auburn (ξάνθος) hair of an Achaean hero, but possibly with a dark beard (see Eustathius on *Od.* 6, 230, and 16, 176, and my note on *Od.* 16, 175–6), darting, lively eyes (*Od.* 4, 150), expressive eyebrows (*Od.* 9, 468; 12, 194; 21, 431), large, fine thighs, broad shoulders and chest, powerful arms (*Od.* 18, 67–9). See additional note below. Roscher, col. 639, gives details of post-Homeric descriptions. Many of them present a despicable conception of a hero, e.g. suggestions by Tzetzes and Isaac Porphyrogennetos that he was pot-bellied and Philostratus's that he was snub-nosed: but we can probably attribute caricatures like this to general anti-Ulyssean prejudice. Lycophron's description of him as 'the dwarf' (*Alexandra*, 1242 ff.) is a good example of propagandist distortion of a Homeric description.

[4] As in Patroni's elaborate but insubstantial theories on Odysseus before Homer. Patroni believes that there is even some surreptitious anti-Achaean propaganda in the Homeric poems, Homer, too, being of Mediterranean race.

[5] Contrast Homer's indication of the positive ugliness of Thersites (*Il.* 2, 216–19) and Dolon (*Il.* 10, 316).

[6] For references to Odysseus's appetite in Attic comedy see Schmidt in *Jahrb. Cl. Phil.* For philosophical criticism see n. 7 below. Alexandrian depreciations will be discussed in chapter nine. Among late writers Athenaeus accuses him bluntly of gluttony and greed (*Deipnosophists* 412 b-d and 513 a-d), alleging that even Sardanapalus would not have made Odysseus's remark in *Od.* 7, 219 ff., 'But my belly ever bids me eat and drink and makes me forget what I have suffered and bids me fill it up'. Athenaeus ignores the fact that Odysseus is speaking of the effect of extreme hunger, not of any Sardanapalan cravings. Lucian (*Tragodopodagra* v, 261–2) alleges that Odysseus died of gout as the result of over indulgence. Cf. Eustathius on *Od.* 18, 55, and the scholia on *Od.* 7, 216.

⁷ *Republic* 390ʙ. Probably what most provoked philosophers in Odysseus's praise of banquets was his use of the word τέλος which later came to mean something like the *summum bonum*. Even Heracleitus Ponticus, that staunch champion of Homer against Platonic carpings, felt that Odysseus's remark could only be justified on the grounds that he was not himself but only 'the remnant (λείψανον) of Poseidon's wrath' when he said it (*Homeric Allegories*, 79). With Plato's view cf. Lucian, *De parasit.* 10, where he takes Odysseus's remarks as praise of the parasite's life. According to Athenaeus 513a, Odysseus's remarks were explained by Megacleides, the fourth-century Homeric critic, as a venial piece of opportunistic flattery based on Alcinous's earlier remark on the Phaeacians' love of music and feasting (*Od.* 8, 248) —which is the most sensible explanation, cf. 8, 382–4, where Odysseus praises the Phaeacians' skill in dancing.

⁸ There is a choice modern example of this out-of-context criticism in a recent (1948) study of the Homeric poems: Odysseus's voracity in *Od.* 6 and 7 is explained as a 'propitiatory rite'. Is it unreasonable to insist, in the light of both common experience and Odysseus's own reiterated statements, on a simpler explanation—that extreme hunger compels men to eat grossly?

⁹ This is the view of Monro, *Odyssey*, p. 305, and others. Shewan (pp. 168–9) questions it, citing Teucer, Philoctetes, Meriones, and Apollo, as reputable bowmen and concluding, 'That the bow was in common use as an auxiliary weapon is certain . . . and that it was held in contempt is not proved'. Wilamowitz suggested that *Telemachus* (Far-fighter) was named from Odysseus's skill in archery. For the use of the bow by Homeric heroes see H. L. Lorimer, *Homer and the monuments* (London, 1950), pp. 299 ff.

¹⁰ Odysseus's poisoned arrows are referred to in *Od.* 1, 260–1; 2, 329. Eustathius and a scholiast on *Od.* 1, 259 ff. suggest that they were necessary for the ultimate slaying of the Suitors, to make every wound fatal (as Heracles killed Nessus with an arrow dipped in the blood of the Hydra). Or they may have been intended for hunting. Murray, p. 130, claims to find traces of the use of poisoned arrows in war in some phrases of the *Iliad*.

¹¹ Cf. Eustathius on *Il.* 2, 157 and 337.

¹² See on *Il.* 3, 216 ff., in chapter two, and Leaf and Bayfield for the 'level tone'. 'Habitual' is implied by Homer's use of the frequentative or iterative forms στάσκεν, ἴδεσκε, ἔχεσκεν. Odysseus's power of holding an audience is emphasized in *Od.* 17, 518–21; 11, 334; 13, 2. Tributes to Odysseus's oratorical powers by later rhetoricians are very frequent, see Roscher, col. 640. The BT scholia on *Il.* 3, 216, note that Odysseus's oratory was 'firm' or 'robust' (πυκνός), the ideal kind, resembling that of Demosthenes, while the styles of Menelaus and Nestor are compared to those of Lysias and Isocrates respectively.

¹³ Shewan, pp. 165–7, has refuted the allegations of Geddes and others that Odysseus is deliberately vilified here and in *Il.* 11, 414 ff., by the poet of 'the Achilleid'; cf. Houben, pp. 3 ff. Note also Odysseus's firm and effective opposition to Agamemnon's proposal to retreat in *Il.* 14, 64 ff. For post-Homeric tributes to his courage see Roscher, col. 639.

¹⁴ See the article cited in n. 2 to chapter two. The A scholia on Odysseus's epithet πολυμήχανος in *Il.* 8, 93, give a long list of his various accomplishments, as ploughman, shipwright, carpenter, hunter, steersman, and so on. Homer clearly admires this kind of versatility.

¹⁵ Jaeger, p. 98, describes Odysseus as 'not so much a knightly warrior as the embodiment of the adventurous spirit, the explorer's energy, and the clever practical wisdom of the Ionian', and cf. p. 20, 'the cunning storm-tossed adventurer Odysseus is the creation of the age when Ionian sailors wandered the seas far and wide'.

¹⁶ Barker, p. 6.

¹⁷ A friend has asked me to reconsider this view, claiming that Odysseus's motive for visiting the island of the Cyclops was simply a desire to get information on his whereabouts (as in *Od.* 10, 190 ff.). But the phrasing of *Od.* 9, 174–6 still seems to me to imply a special kind of curiosity.

¹⁸ See the Homeric lexicons at δῶρον. Aelian, *Var. Hist.* 4, 20, observes that both Menelaus and Odysseus resembled Phoenician merchants in the way they acquired wealth on their travels: cf. the young Phaeacian's taunt against Odysseus in *Od.* 8, 161–4. Comments on Odysseus's love of gifts will be found in the scholia on *Od.* 7, 225; 13, 103; and in Eustathius on *Od.* 10, 571. Plutarch, in *How to study poetry*, 27, explains why Odysseus need not necessarily be convicted of avariciousness in checking his Phaeacian gifts so carefully on his arrival in Ithaca (*Od.* 13, 215 ff.): he may simply have wished to see if the Phaeacians were honest and truthful men; or for rejoicing at Penelope's receiving of gifts (*Od.* 18, 281–2): he may merely have been glad at the Suitors' over-confidence. But both excuses are rather

weak. It is better to admit that Odysseus, like the other heroes of his time, delighted in acquiring wealth: see Chaignet, pp. 271–4, and Snell, 156–7, and cf. n. 21 to chapter two.

[19] The scholiast ad loc. admits that this was 'over quarrelsome' (φιλονεικότερον) but adds that it would give some consolation to the injured feelings of the Greeks.

[20] A far-reaching problem opens up here; and a greater emphasis on Homer's debt to his predecessors would demand a quite different view of the characterization of Odysseus in *Od.* 9–12. But I must leave it to others to explore this line of interpretation. See D. L. Page, 'Odysseus and Polyphemus', *Latin Teaching*, 1949, 8–26, and, more generally, D. Muelder in *Hermes* xxxviii (1903), for possible signs of imperfectly digested material in the Cyclops incident, and cf. n. 3 to chapter two above. C. C. van Essen in *Mnemosyne* lviii (1930), 302–8, suggests an Etruscan origin for the Cyclops and Odysseus.

[21] For the Sirens as a kind of 'poetical gazette' see Allen, p. 142, n. 1, who quotes Sextus Empiricus, *Adv. math.* 1, 11.

[22] Cicero, *De finibus* 5, 18: see further in chapter nine. For the view that the Sirens appealed especially to those ambitious for ἀρετή see Xenophon, *Memorabilia*, 2, 6, 11.

[23] Cf. H. Fraenkel, *Dichtung und Philosophie des frühen Griechentums* (New York, 1951), pp. 123–4. Chaignet, p. 193, sums up his impression of Odysseus in the Homeric poems thus: *au fond Ulysse est un idéal de la vie morale en même temps qu'un représentant de toutes les qualités de sa race. C'est le type non pas le plus sympathique, le plus noble, mais le plus complet du héros grec.*

ADDITIONAL NOTE: The evidence for Odysseus's age in the Homeric poems is inconclusive. Antilochus, in *Il.* 23, 790–91, describes him as being 'of an earlier generation and of earlier men' and also as ὠμογέρων. The last term is ambiguous: it could denote a person in the early stages of old age, or an active old man, or one who is prematurely aged. Considering that Odysseus's only son was then barely ten years old and that Laertes was still active ten years later, he can hardly have been far advanced in years. Antilochus was a very young man and to such even the moderately middle-aged often seem old. If Odysseus was in his late thirties and Antilochus was eighteen or nineteen, he might loosely be described as 'belonging to an earlier generation'. This would place him in the late twenties when he left Ithaca and in the late forties on his return home, which seems to fit the general implications of the poems best. On the other hand, the flagrant inconsistency in the implied ages of Neoptolemus (see commentators on *Il.* 19, 326 ff.) warns against assuming chronological consistency in matters of this kind. If ὠμογέρων meant having a prematurely aged look, as some ancient commentators held, it would be in character for a man like Odysseus: and Idomeneus (whose brother Odysseus pretends to be in *Od.* 19, 181) is described as 'half-grey' in *Il.* 13, 361. But the description of Odysseus in *Od.* 13, 430–34, seems to preclude any premature ageing in his appearance.

NOTES TO CHAPTER VI

For the very controversial background to this chapter (brief because there is so little evidence for the motivation of Odysseus's actions in the Cycle) see especially Bethe, Robert, Severyns, Schmidt. There is a convenient translation of the cyclic epitomes and fragments in *Hesiod, the Homeric hymns and Homerica*, by H. G. Evelyn-White (London, 1914).

[1] T. W. Allen in *The Classical Review*, ii (1908), 64–74 and 81–8, concludes on the evidence for the length of the poems and their contents that they were 'bare catalogues of events', especially the *Little Iliad* and the *Sack of Troy*. In the same articles he reviews earlier discussions and warns against far-fetched theories: 'Upon scanty quotations and a jejune epitome a tedious literature has been built'.

[2] The following incidents in Odysseus's career as described in the cyclic poems are not mentioned by Homer: his attempt to evade conscription; his skilful handling of the Telephus affair (but cf. *Od.* 11, 519); the sacrifice of Iphigeneia at Aulis (but the remains of the Cypria do not specifically mention Odysseus); the abortive landing at the Troad; the visit to King Anios and the Oinotropidai at Delos (but perhaps this was when Odysseus saw the famous palm-tree mentioned in *Od.* 6, 161–5; cf. schol. on v. 164 and Severyns, p. 311); Odysseus's purification of Achilles after the killing of Thersites; the murder of Palamedes; the capture of the Palladium; the slaughter of the Trojans; and the various post-Ithacan adventures described later in this chapter. The following incidents, briefly mentioned or implied by Homer, were amplified in the cyclic epics: the mustering at Aulis; the embassy to Priam; the fate of Philoctetes; the rescue of the corpse of Achilles; the contest with Ajax for the arms of Achilles; the Wooden Horse. The following events, which fall within the period

of the Trojan campaign, are referred to by Homer but not found in the cyclic remains; the enlisting of Achilles (*Il.* 11, 765 ff.; cf. 7, 127; 9, 252 ff.; 667–8); the wrestling with Philomeleides in Lesbos (*Od.* 4, 342 ff., and 17, 133 ff.); the quarrel between Odysseus and Achilles on the relative merits of valour and intelligence (*Od.* 8, 75 ff.). (The last two may well be Homer's own fictions to enhance Odysseus's prestige; similarly M. H. van der Valk has suggested that the description of how Odysseus got his bow from Eurytos in *Od.* 21 is another fiction by Homer to emphasize the bow's importance.) The story of how Odysseus tricked Protesilaus into landing first on Trojan soil (thereby incurring death, as predicted by an oracle) is first attested by Ausonius in the fourth century A.D.

Professor J. A. Davison has suggested (in *Göttingische Gelehrte Anzeigen* ccviii (1954), 44) that the unexplained quarrel between Odysseus and Achilles referred to in *Od.* 8, 75 ff. (cf. n. 8 to chapter eleven), was in fact concerned with the fate of Palamedes—an interesting possibility but not provable. For other attempts to explain it see the note *ad loc.* in my edition of the *Odyssey*.

³ The remains of the *Cypria* do not actually mention Odysseus's part in the wooing of Helen, but it is implied in the story of his enlistment for the Trojan War. It is first found in a fragment of the Hesiodic *Catalogue of Women* (Rzach 94), which may go back to the eighth century B.C. There we learn that Odysseus 'knew in his heart that blond Menelaus would win, for Menelaus was pre-eminent in possessions'—a characteristic example of Ulyssean prudence, as was his oath binding the losing suitors to punish anyone who interfered with Helen's marriage (for which see Severyns, pp. 274–5; he thinks the oath was first described by Stesichorus).

⁴ It is not known how the cyclic tradition motivated Odysseus's marriage with Penelope: according to one later account he competed successfully in a race for her; according to another, Icarius (doubtless having observed Odysseus's prudence in his suit for Helen) offered Penelope to him. Pausanias, 3, 20, records a curious development of the second version: Icarius desired Odysseus to live on with him and Penelope in Sparta. Odysseus refused and drove away with Penelope in his chariot. Icarius pursued them and made a final appeal to Penelope to stay with him. Odysseus sternly told her to choose once and for all between husband and father. She veiled her face in a gesture of modest submission to her husband—thereby escaping a permanent father-fixation according to F. L. Lucas, *Literature and psychology* (London, 1951), p. 63. Icarius solaced himself by setting up a statue to Modesty at the place where he had been defeated. Sir James Frazer, in *The Golden Bough* (*The Magic Art*, ii, 300), infers from Icarius's action that Odysseus would have inherited his kingdom through Penelope.

⁵ *Achilles in Scyros*, cf. Ovid, *Metamorphoses* 13, 301, as quoted in chapter eleven.

⁶ See *Od.* 24, 118–19. But Eustathius *ad. loc.* considers that the story of Odysseus's pretended madness and of Palamedes's ruse is silly prattle: he notes that Homer says Odysseus was persuaded, not compelled, to go. Cicero (*De officiis* 3, 26, 97) says that there is no hint of this affair in Homer and observes that it would have been *utile* but not *honestum* for Odysseus 'to reign on and live at ease with his parents, wife and son'.

⁷ Frank Budgen, *James Joyce and the making of 'Ulysses'* (London, 1934), p. 16.

⁸ The whole career of Palamedes presents many perplexities: see further in Pauly, Roscher, Lang, *W. of H.* 188–96, and Robert, pp. 1128 ff. He is a kind of superfluous Prometheus in his inventiveness and a superfluous Odysseus in his prudent counsels. Andrew Lang argued that he was a post-Homeric culture hero foisted into the Troy tale by anti-Achaean influences in the epic cycle. The fact that the Argive Diomedes was associated with Odysseus in his murder may indicate some border hostility between Argos and Nauplia where Palamedes lived: hence it has been suggested that Diomedes was the prime mover in his death. But, on the other hand, Diomedes's association with Odysseus may be explained by the fact that his father, Tydeus, was a West Greek (Aetolian). A later tradition makes Odysseus suffer for his part in the murder: Nauplius, Palamedes's father, sent news to Ithaca that Odysseus was dead, and in despair his mother hanged herself. But this contradicts the account of Anticleia's death in *Od.* 11, 197 ff. (see Eustathius on v. 202).

⁹ This in a sense was a preparation for his similar disguise after his return to Ithaca. Milton aptly compared Odysseus's exploits in disguise with King Alfred's adventures in humble dress after his defeat by the Danes (*Outlines for tragedies*, Columbia ed., xviii, 243).

¹⁰ Horace, *Odes* 4, 6, 13 ff. Neither Homer nor the cyclic writers explicitly state that Odysseus devised the stratagem of the Horse. Homer only says that Epeios ('Horse-man') constructed it (*Od.* 11, 523). But the later tradition assumes that it was Odysseus's invention and any other inventor among the remaining Greeks seems inconceivable. Odysseus was

supreme commander inside the Horse (*Od.* 11, 524–5; 4, 271 ff.), and a very drastic one, to judge by his handling of Anticlos (*Od.* 4, 286 ff.; cf. Pascoli's poignant poem, *Anticlo*).

[11] For the killing of Astyanax see especially Robert, pp. 1259 ff. The *Little Iliad* ascribed it to Neoptolemus, the *Sack of Troy* to Odysseus. It is probable that on this occasion Odysseus spoke the grim line, 'Fool is he who slays the father and leaves the child': cf. his remarks in Seneca, *Troades* 589–93. The scholiast on Euripides, *Hecuba* 41, says that the *Cypria* attributed the killing of Polyxena to Odysseus and Diomedes, while Euripides followed Ibycus in ascribing it to Neoptolemus. This is a good example of the flexibility of the Cyclic as distinct from the Homeric tradition.

[12] Lang, (*W. of H.*, 188 ff.) argues strongly for anti-Ulyssean bias in the *Cypria*; but his view that it was due to Ionian prejudice against the 'Achaean' tradition is hardly tenable now. For other attempts to distinguish differences of attitude towards various heroes in the cyclic epics see especially Bethe 2, 251–2, Severyns, and Jebb in *Ajax* xvi, followed by Davaux, 49–53. Besides the Palamedes affair the only other noteworthy possibility of shameful conduct on the part of Odysseus has been deduced from later versions of the theft of the Palladium in which Odysseus is represented as having tried to murder Diomedes in order to get the whole credit for himself: see O. Jahn, 'Der Raub des Palladion', in *Philologus* i (1846), 47, who sees Odysseus in the *Little Iliad* as a sly and cunning coward, cf. Frazer on Pausanias 1, 22, 6. But there is no certain evidence that the *L.I.* gave any such account of Odysseus's part in the Palladium episode: Hesychius's alternative ascription of the proverb 'Diomedean compulsion' may not refer to the villainous conduct described in Suidas (an anti-Ulyssean writer) at all, but might point to the tradition first found in Sophocles's *Lakainai* that the heroes had to escape from Troy through a narrow and filthy sewer. Bethe (*Homer* 2, 251–2) seems to have better reason for rejecting the story entirely from the *L.I.*, in which, he holds, Odysseus is the most favoured hero. Besides, it is unlikely that a cyclic writer should oppose Homer's authority on a matter of this kind: the Doloneia is an eloquent tribute to the mutual trust and confidence between Odysseus and Diomedes, as well as to Odysseus's indifference to getting the credit for their joint exploit, as described in chapter two.

[13] *Od.* 15, 343–5; cf. *Od.* 10, 464; 21, 284. But Homer himself was not completely unaware of the feeling of wanderlust: see the remarkable simile in *Il.* 15, 80–83.

[14] Here I agree, I find, with M. H. van der Valk's view as expressed in criticism of Merkelbach's opinion (in *Untersuchungen zur Odyssee*, Munich, 1951) that the *Odyssey* contains material from the *Telegony*: see *Bibliotheca Orientalis* ix, 3–4 (1952), 148 For a survey of the widely varying interpretations of Odysseus's inland journey after his return to Ithaca see van der Valk, *Beiträge zur Nekyia* (Kampen, 1935), pp. 13–32. He holds that the story is Homer's own invention, and does not go back to a pre-Homeric myth: but I feel dubious about this. Severyns (pp. 409 ff.) concludes that the *Telegony* is *un genre nouveau, celui du roman en prose.*

[15] For the various post-Homeric accounts of Odysseus's last days see especially Hartmann, Severyns, Pauly, Roscher, Svoronos, Frazer on *Apollodorus* Epitome 7, 34–40; and (for Latin versions) Martorana, pp. 27–40. Dictys's bizarre version will be discussed in chapter twelve. For the legend of Odysseus's final death in Etruria see W. R. Halliday, *The Greek Questions of Plutarch*, p. 80, Robert, p. 1448, and Phillips. For his connections with Rome see chapter ten. For Odysseus's eighteen children and six consorts, as alleged in the post-Homeric tradition, see Roscher, col. 632. Eustathius on *Od.* 16, 118, dismisses such genealogies as superfluous and depraved. The killing of Odysseus by his son is an example of a well-known folk motif. Psychologists who believe that myths are symbols of suppressed desires and passions (see Highet, pp. 523–4) have found special significance in the fact that according to one version Telegonus then married Penelope—a case of Œdipus complex, it is suggested; but Telegonus had never seen either Odysseus or Penelope before. The converse motif is found in the legend of Euryalus, Odysseus's son by Euippe, who through Penelope's jealousy was killed in ignorance by Odysseus. It was, perhaps, but dubiously, the subject of Sophocles' play, *Euryalus*: if it was not, the story is not attested until Parthenius (*Erotica* 3). Sextus Empiricus, *Adv. gramm.* 1, 12, gives other curious anecdotes.

[16] The perplexed geography of Ulysses's wanderings as recorded in the Homeric poems and in post-Homeric writings has been recently surveyed by Phillips, citing the main earlier authorities. See also Alfred Klotz, 'Die Irrfahrten des Odysseus und ihre Deutung im Altertum', *Gymnasium* lix (1952), 289–302. As Wüst notes, various late classical authors claimed that Ulysses reached Lisbon, Scotland, and Germany; and modern scholars have sent him even further afield. For ancient depreciation of the ethical value of such studies see Seneca, *Epistles* 88, 7, and Aulus Gellius, *Attic nights*, 14, 6, 3.

ADDITIONAL NOTE: No attempt has been made here to discuss the various cults of Odysseus in Greece and Italy as recorded in Pausanias and other authors (see Wüst) as, apart from a few exceptions which I cite (e.g. in n. 3 above), they do not seem to illuminate the literary tradition.

NOTES TO CHAPTER VII

For previous studies of this phase of the tradition see especially Wüst, Cesareo, and Roscher.

[1] The loss of Stesichorus's works is specially regrettable, as he seems to have had highly original views on the heroic tradition. According to him the emblem on Odysseus's shield was a dolphin (Plutarch, *De sollert. anim.* 36), an apt symbol of his vigorous seamanship. Among the later choral lyrists, the fragments of Bacchylides's account (fr. 15, Snell) of the visit of Menelaus and Odysseus to Troy to demand Helen back before the war (cf. *Il.* 3, 205 ff.) contain no significant addition to the myth.

[2] Alcman, fr. 80 (Diehl).

[3] It is perhaps not accidental that among the titles of Cratinus's lost comedies are Ἀρχίλοχοι and Ὀδυσσεῖς.

[4] Archilochus, frs. 11, 60, 65, 67a (Diehl) and cf. Bergk, *Poetae Lyrici Graeci* ii, 698, 700. For other Odyssean echoes see Snell, pp. 47 ff.

[5] *Elegies* 1123–8.

[6] *Elegies* 213–18. Hudson Williams in his edition suggests that a direct allusion to *Od.* 5, 432 ff., is intended in this comparison with the polypus, but it may be taken directly from nature. Similar references to the advantages of imitating the polypus's protective changes of colour are quoted by Athenaeus (513 C–D) in connection with the second passage: Pindar, fr. 235 (Bowra), and Sophocles, fr. 286 (Nauck: from the *Iphigeneia*). They were perhaps spoken by Odysseus in their full contexts. See also Ion, fr. 36, and Bergk on Theognis 213.

[7] The ambiguous word for crafty or complex here is πολύπλοκος, perhaps a paronomasia on πολύτροπος.

[8] Mahaffy in his pioneer article on the decline of Odysseus's reputation (see bibliography) suggests that Epicharmus was the first to denigrate Odysseus (in his *Cyclops*, *Philoctetes*, *Sirens*, *Odysseus shipwrecked*, and *Odysseus the deserter*). Epicharmus, he argues, being debarred by the Sicilian despots from criticizing politicians, applied his comic and satirical talents to mythological figures. Pindar, then, would have derived his anti-Ulyssean bias from contacts with Epicharmus's work in Sicily. There is no firm evidence for this; and a distinction must be made between comical treatment of Odysseus's conduct (which even Homer provides, in the Irus and Thersites episodes, for example) and moralistic denunciations in the manner of Pindar or Euripides. Besides, nothing is really known about Odysseus's part in the plays cited, except from the papyrus fragment of *Odysseus the deserter*. This has been generally assumed to have presented Odysseus as a poltroon, but I have offered arguments against this view in *Classical Philology* xlv (1950), 167–9. Andrew Lang (*W. of H.*, pp. 160 and 189) rejects Mahaffy's theory in favour of his own view that the denigration of Odysseus began with the anti-Ionian and anti-Homeric poets of the epic cycle, whence he claims Pindar derived it. But there is no evidence for this. The fact remains that the first definite denunciation of Odysseus as a liar in extant post-Homeric literature is Pindar's.

[9] For a similar sympathy with the loser compare the closing scenes of the Cyclops incident in *Od.* 9, 446 ff.: from the time when the blinded monster converses affectionately with his pet ram (under which Odysseus hangs in an agony of suspense) Homer seems to want to make us feel some sympathy for him, and Polyphemus by no means has the worst of the final exchanges with Odysseus.

[10] *Od.* 11, 547. According to the scholia on Aristophanes, *Knights* 1056, the *Little Iliad* contrived that the verdict was given on the basis of some remarks overheard from Trojan girls. In Sophocles, *Ajax* 1135, Teucer blames Menelaus for falsifying the votes in the contest for the arms of Achilles, thereby exonerating Odysseus from Pindar's calumnies in *Nemeans* 8, 26–7. See Severyns, pp. 328 ff.

[11] For Pindar's views on Odysseus cf. Farnell's edition 1, 215–16. Pindar also hints at Odysseus's obliquity in *Isthmians* 4, 36–40, and apparently deprecated his conduct in the Palamedes affair as well, to judge from fr. 275 (Bowra). N. O. Brown in 'Pindar, Sophocles, and the Thirty Years' Peace', *Transactions of the American Philological Association* lxxxii (1951), 1–28, argues that in *Nem.* 8 Aeacus represents the perfect union of virtue, wisdom, and power; Ajax virtue without prudence; and Odysseus 'a crooked kind of wisdom without virtue',

which is equated by Pindar, he thinks with the new bourgeois order in contemporary society and especially the revolutionary imperialism of Athens. He thinks that Sophocles in *Ajax* was deliberately rebutting Pindar's opinion. For criticism of Brown's theory see V. Ehrenberg, *Sophocles and Pericles* (Oxford, 1954): grave uncertainties in chronology are involved.

[12] Since the portrait of a 'blockish' Ajax (as Shakespeare calls him in *Troilus and Cressida*, probably following Ovid in *Metamorphoses* Thirteen) is canonical in medieval and renaissance English literature, it may be well to emphasize that Homer never, with one exception, implies any unusual stupidity or obstinacy on his part (cf. Jebb's edition of Sophocles's *Ajax*, pp. x–xii). The exception is when Hector calls him βουγάιε, 'lumbering ox' or 'loutish boaster' in *Il.* 13, 824, but an enemy's insult of this kind is likely to be grossly exaggerated.

[13] For Aeolo-Doric influence on Pindar see Schmid-Stählin, 1, 1, 77 n. 1. Schmidt in *B.S.* notes as possible other causes of Pindar's antipathy to Odysseus: influence of cyclic poems (which I doubt), a landsman's dislike for a seafarer, a preference for *breviloquentia* against *eloquentia*, and aristocratic dislike of Odysseus's readiness to undertake humiliating tasks.

[14] For Pindar's attitude to Homer in general see S. Fitch, 'Pindar and Homer', *Classical Philology* xix (1924), 57–65. He holds that the opposition between Ajax and Ulysses is traceable to the cyclic poems, but not to Homer.

[15] Early criticisms of Homer are discussed by Schmid-Stählin 1, 1, 129, and J. E. Sandys, *History of Classical Scholarship* (3rd edn., Cambridge, 1921), chapter two. See also chapter twelve below.

[16] ψεύδεα πολλά . . . ἐτύμοισιν ὁμοῖα (Hesiod, *Theogony* 27 = *Od.* 19, 203). It is possible but not, I think, probable that no allusion to Homer's poetry is intended.

[17] For the authenticity of the sophistic discourses quoted in the following paragraphs see Pauly at *Gorgias, Alkidamas, Antisthenes*, and n. 23 below.

[18] The terms used by Gorgias are φθόνῳ, κακοτεχνίᾳ, κακουργίᾳ. Nothing noteworthy is said about Odysseus elsewhere in this excessively stylized speech. In Plato, *Phaedrus* 261B, Gorgias's oratory is jestingly compared with Nestor's and Odysseus's with that of the sophists Thrasymachus and Theodorus.

[19] Plato, *Apology* 41B.

[20] For sympathetic feeling towards Palamedes see, e.g., Plato, *Ep.* 2, 311B, and n. 25 to chapter eight below.

[21] Aristotle, *Rhetoric* 3, 3, 1406b, 12–13.

[22] The only originalities, from the point of view of the Ulysses tradition, in Alcidamas's discourse are some alleged details of Palamedes's delinquencies.

[23] Ragnar Höistad, *Cynic hero and Cynic king* (Uppsala, 1948), pp. 94–102. This author gives a list of studies on Antisthenes and discusses the authenticity of his discourses, agreeing with Blass and others that they are genuine. His discussion of Heracles and Cyrus as patterns for the ideal Cynic king reveals some illuminating parallels with Odysseus. Antisthenes's favourable attitude to Odysseus influenced Dio Chrysostom, as will appear later. (Antisthenes wrote books on Homer, the *Odyssey*, and Odysseus, according to Diogenes Laertius 6, 15.) In view of the remarks on Archilochus earlier in the present chapter it may be noted that Antisthenes also was something of a half-breed, his mother having been a Thracian. For a controversy on whether Antisthenes treated Odysseus allegorically or not, see Höistad and J. Tate in *Eranos* xlix (1951), 16 ff. and li (1953), 14–22. Tate establishes that in the strict sense of the word Antisthenes was not an allegorist.

[24] For Odysseus's voluntary self-mutilation see *Od.* 4, 244, and Severyns, pp. 348–9. His sufferings in beggar's disguise among the Suitors were, of course, many and varied in *Od.* 17 ff. until he achieved his purpose of slaying them in Book 22. It was a curious anticipation of Cynic terminology when Odysseus in his famous soliloquy on endurance in *Od.* 17, 283, used the word κύντερον.

[25] Höistad (pp. 99–100) notes some similarities between Plato's portrait of Socrates and Antisthenes's description of Odysseus. Cf. *Symposium* 220c.

[26] For signs of a reaction against Odysseus among later Cynics see n. 11 to chapter nine.

[27] Scholium on *Od.* 1, 1. The text is much confused. No interpretation is certain. I have chosen the one which seems most consistent with Antisthenes's views on Odysseus elsewhere. Other appreciations of Odysseus by Antisthenes are to be found in the scholl. on *Od.* 5, 211 (Odysseus wisely prefers Penelope's moral qualities to Calypso's beauty, and knows that lovers' promises are untrustworthy, cf. schol. on *Od.* 8, 257) and on *Od.* 9, 525 (Odysseus knows that it is Apollo, not Poseidon, who is the healer god).

[28] For a discussion of the arguments for the two most likely meanings of πολύτροπος ('much-travelled' or 'versatile') see T. Kakridis in *Glotta* xi (1921), 288–91. He refutes Lehrs's support

for the second view and establishes the former as the most likely for Homer's time. In this he is supported by P. Linde, 'Homerische Selbsterläuterungen', *Glotta* xiii (1924), 223–4. For the many ancient views see the scholiasts and Eustathius on *Od.* 1, 1. They on the whole incline to an ethical interpretation, contrasting Odysseus, the versatile hero, with the ἁπλοῦς type like Achilles and Agamemnon. Eustathius takes πολύτροπος as indicating one who is ποικιλόφρων or who has πολυειδῆ ἐνέργειαν though he notes that τρόπος does not mean ἦθος in Homer. He compares the adaptability of the chameleon (which is the first use of this analogy in connection with the Ulysses tradition). The curious variant reading πολύκροτον, 'much-knocked-about', in *Od.* 1, 1, is best explained as an early parody.

²⁹ Höistad (p. 101) notes a foreshadowing of Puritanism here; just as there is obviously an anticipation of Christian asceticism in Antisthenes's attitude to Odysseus's voluntary sufferings.

³⁰ For more favourable views of Odysseus see Xenophon, *Memorabilia* 1, 3, 7 (Odysseus's self-control), 4, 6, 15 (Odysseus's oratorical ability), Plato, *Phaedo* 94D (self-control in *Od.* 20, 17–18), *Laches* 201B, *Laws* 706D, *Phaedrus* 259B. Simmias's remark about the raft in *Phaedo* 85D is typical of many incidental allusions to Odysseus's adventures: it also points on to the Stoic idealization of the *Odyssey* as a kind of *Pilgrim's Progress*, as discussed in chapter nine below. The praise of Odysseus by Socrates in the *Lesser Hippias* is not, of course, to be taken seriously.

³¹ Plutarch, *Alcibiades* 2 and 24, calls Alcibiades πολύτροπος doubtless with deliberate Ulyssean implications. The populace is similarly styled *polytropos* in Pseudo-Phocylides 95; cf. Pericles's remark according to Thucydides 2, 44, that the Athenian populace had been reared ἐν πολυτρόποις ξυμφοραῖς, and see Gomme's note on Thucydides 1, 70, 8. But as warning against always assuming a Ulyssean implication in the term it may be observed that God is described as having spoken πολυτρόπως to the Patriarchs in the Epistle to the Hebrews 1, 1.

³² Historical causes of the decline in Odysseus's prestige are discussed at greater length in *Hermathena* lxxiii (1949), 33–51, and lxxiv (1949), 41–56, with references to earlier studies. Since then Delebecque has made a wider survey with special reference to Euripides's attitude.

³³ Note Gylippus's remark during the Athenian campaign in Sicily (Thucydides 7, 66): 'When men have been checked in the sphere where they claim superiority, even with what is lost of their self-esteem they are weaker than if they had never conceived it: unexpectedly tripped up in their elation they give ground more than their actual strength warrants'. Versatility and intelligence had been the sphere in which the Athenians had claimed superiority earlier in the Peloponnesian war.

NOTES TO CHAPTER VIII

For special studies of this phase in the tradition see especially Garassino, Marcowitz, and Schmidt; also *Hermathena* lxxiii (1949), 33 ff., lxxiv (1949), 41 ff.

¹ *Agamemnon* 841–2: 'Odysseus alone, the man who sailed against his will, once he was yoked (to the Greek cause) readily shared the burden with me'. If, as Fraenkel argues, Agamemnon is viewed in a favourable light, as a tolerably wise and well-meaning ruler, such praise from him would be to Odysseus's credit. But if, as I argue elsewhere (in a forthcoming article in the *Classical Review*), Aeschylus intends us to see Agamemnon as a man lacking in the ability to discern true friend from flatterer (hence Clytemnestra's ease in deceiving him) the praise would be worthless, as Odysseus might have courted his favour successfully without having felt any disinterested or sincere fidelity (cf. Garassino 221). Against what I argued in *Hermathena* lxxiii (1949), 37, I now think the second view is right and that there is no evidence in Aeschylus for an appreciatory view of Odysseus.

² *Bone-gatherers, Circe, Ghost-raisers, Judgement of the armour, Palamedes, Penelope, Philoctetes.* Possibly Odysseus was also prominent in such plays on the Troy tale as *Iphigeneia, Mysians, Telephus.*

³ Dio of Prusa, *Orations* 52, 4–10.

⁴ Schmidt (*B.S.*, p. 449) thinks this Sisyphus parentage was foisted on Odysseus by one of the early genealogists. Wilamowitz (*Heimkehr*) attributes it to pro-Dorian and anti-Corinthian influences. W. R. Halliday (*The Greek questions of Plutarch*, p. 182) explains it as an example of mythological syncretism.

⁵ In studying the characterization of Odysseus in Sophocles I have been chiefly helped by Sir Maurice Bowra's *Sophoclean tragedy* (Oxford, 1944), H. D. F. Kitto's *Greek tragedy* (London, 1939), T. B. L. Webster's *Introduction to Sophocles* (Oxford, 1936), W. K. C.

Guthrie's article, 'Odysseus in the Ajax', *Greece and Rome* xlviii (1947), 115–19, and Davaux's unpublished thesis, besides Jebb's editions and the authorities cited in n. 1 above. I had not the opportunity of considering the illuminating remarks of F. J. H. Letters in *The Life and work of Sophocles* (London, 1953), pp. 127, 144, and 263 ff., which on the whole support my views. But he takes a more favourable view of Athene in *Ajax*. See also Cedric H. Whitman, *Sophocles* (Cambridge, Mass., 1951), pp. 46 and 65 ff. A. von Blumenthal, *Sophokles*, pp. 132 ff., believes that Odysseus speaks for Sophocles himself in *Ajax*; cf. J. C. Opstelten, *Sophocles and Greek pessimism*, translated by J. C. Ross (Amsterdam, 1952), pp. 14, 100, 114, 154. See also N. O. Brown, loc. cit. in n. 11 to chapter seven.

⁶ Guthrie, p. 117. The subsequent quotation is from Bowra, p. 37. For Athene's unsympathetic role in the play see further in Guthrie.

⁷ In v. 24 Odysseus emphasizes that he has undertaken the task of spying on Ajax 'as a volunteer'. I am not sure whether this is a reference to his general character as the 'serviceable man' in Homer (for this term cf. H. T. Wade-Gery, *The poet of the Iliad*, Cambridge, 1952, p. 45) or a slightly depreciatory suggestion of a prying busybody.

⁸ v. 103, τοὐπίτριπτον κίναδος. But Garassino (p. 320) holds that the epithet means 'subtle, astute' (*fina*) not 'accursed' (*maladetta*) here. In any case the phrase is obviously vituperative. This is the first time in European literature that Odysseus receives his often recurring title of the fox, unless the pseudonym Αἴθων which he assumes in *Od*. 19, 183, refers to a fox's proverbially torchlike tail (cf. his description in Lycophron 344: τῆς Σισυφείας δ'ἀγκύλης λαμπουρίδος). The fox was, of course, notoriously resourceful: e.g. Alcman (Diehl, Supplement 22, 7) ποικιλόφρων ἀλώπα and the proverb 'The fox knows many things: but the hedge-hog knows one big thing' (which implies a preference for the ἁπλοῦς character, like Ajax's, over the complex Ulyssean type: cf. Aeschylus's *Judgement of the armour*, ἁπλᾶ γάρ ἐστι τῆς ἀλαθείας ἔπη).

⁹ Davaux explains Odysseus's egoistic argument in his scene with Agamemnon as a concession to Odysseus's bad reputation among Athenians at that time: he emphasizes the low reputation he also had with Ajax, Teucer, and the Chorus, in the play. This is clearly possible, but I prefer to retain the view that Odysseus assumes a self-centred philosophy here in order to win over the self-opinionated Agamemnon.

¹⁰ This is mainly Davaux's view (pp. 101–7). For the importance of Athenian prejudice in favour of Ajax see Jebb, pp. xxx–xxxii, Bowra, p. 16, and F. Allègre, *Sophocle* (Lyons, 1905).

¹¹ The views cited in this paragraph are those of H. Weinstock in *Sophokles* (Leipzig, 1931) and Mario Untersteiner in *Ajax* (Milan, 1933) as discussed in Davaux, pp. 90–5.

¹² Here are some further views of Odysseus in the *Ajax*: 'neither the brave, resourceful hero of epic nor the cold and remorseless plotter which he becomes in the Philoctetes. We have a very human figure, reluctantly consenting to an ally, who is divine only in the sense of being more powerful' (Guthrie); 'a pattern of virtue . . . a fair-minded observer . . . the modest man who humbles himself before the gods and keeps to the Mean . . . (Sophocles's) serious, modest, compassionate Odysseus bears little resemblance to the gay (?), enterprising, reckless (?) hero of Homer and still less to the cold-blooded Odysseus of Euripides . . . the embodiment of sanity and decency' (Bowra); his 'magnanimity . . . springs from high intelligence as much as from chivalrous sentiment . . . the wise moderation which the gods love . . . his habitual reasonableness and prudence' (Jebb); 'une grande figure dont la noblesse donne une impression de réconfort et corrige ce qu 'avait de pénible, par moments, la seconde action de la tragédie' (G. Dalmeyda in *Revue des études grecques* xlvi, 1933, 9); he 'attains moral grandeur' (Kitto).

¹³ Odysseus's role in *Philoctetes* is fully discussed by Bowra. But, with A. J. A. Waldock in *Sophocles the dramatist* (Cambridge, 1951), 200 ff., I cannot accept the view that the key to the play is that Odysseus misinterpreted or misapplied the oracle of Helenos. On Odysseus's fetish of success and his contempt for honour in this play Bowra remarks (p. 286) that he 'resembles other men produced and corrupted by war'. Davaux (pp. 143–52) offers a spirited defence of Odysseus against Grégoire's description of him as *un être abominable*. He pleads that Odysseus was acting under divine compulsion (vv. 610–18, 989–90) and *pro bono publico*, and emphasizes that Dio found Sophocles's Odysseus 'gentler and more straightforward' than in Euripides's *Philoctetes*. Similarly E. Howald (*Die Griechische Tragödie*, Munich, 1930, pp. 123–4) finds some mitigating features.

¹⁴ Even in his Homeric career Odysseus had once instructed a young man to tell lies. In *Od*. 16, 281 ff., he tells Telemachus to give the Suitors an untrue reason for removing the arms from the dining-hall. But the Suitors were avowed enemies, while Philoctetes was a comrade-in-arms.

[15] Davaux argues convincingly that Neoptolemus's statement (vv. 359 ff.) that Odysseus refused to give him the arms of Achilles is simply one of the many lies in his story to Philoctetes and not (as some have argued) a factual variation of the narrative in the *Little Iliad*, in which Odysseus gave the arms to Neoptolemus on his arrival in Troy. The point is important, for it relieves Odysseus of an additional burden of cynicism (as imputed, e.g. in Masqueray's introduction to *Philoctetes*, 2nd edn., Paris, 1942, p. 97) and Neoptolemus from a dishonourable complaisance.

[16] The meaning of σωφροσύνη ranges from 'healthy-mindedness' or 'whole-mindedness', the *mens sana* which is not maimed or inflamed by passion and folly, to the narrower and more negative concept of 'self-control, temperance'. It is doubtful whether the second meaning was as prevalent in fifth-century literature as is sometimes—mainly as a result of Plato's and Aristotle's influence—assumed.

[17] It is significant that Odysseus addresses his impious prayers for help in his deceits (vv. 133–4) to Hermes, god of trickery, and Nike, deification of success, as well as to his Homeric patron Athene.

[18] Cf. the scholium on *Philoctetes* 99, 'The poet is accusing the party politicians (ῥήτορας) of his own era'.

[19] Odysseus figured prominently in many of Sophocles's lost plays, but few of the fragments are sufficient to establish any definite attitude: see Pearson's edition and some comments in Svoronos. In the *Syndeipnoi* Odysseus was called a busybody in whom the ancestry of Sisyphus and Autolycus was very clear, but whether the speaker's opinion was intended to be accepted by the hearers or not is uncertain (the frag. is quoted by the scholiast on *Ajax* 190, where Ajax refers to Odysseus as being τᾶς ἀσώτου Σισυφιδᾶν γενεᾶς). Two quotations of unknown provenance refer to Odysseus (Pearson 913, 965). In the first someone describes him as a πάνσοφον κρότημα—a scarcely translatable phrase combining a notion of toughness (as of welded metal) and knowingness. (Cf. αἱμυλώτατον κρότημα applied to Odysseus in *Rhesus* 498–9 and his description as a κρόταλον δριμύ in *Cyclops* 104). These terms have a rather slangy tone, like others applied to Odysseus elsewhere: see Liddell and Scott at ἄλημα, κόπις, πανοῦργος, τρίβων. See also n. 15 to chapter two.

[20] On the whole Odysseus's part in *Cyclops* is courageous and reputable (cf. Schmidt in *C.R.*) at least for a satyr play. His Homeric presence of mind and loyalty to his companions is clearly displayed (cf. *Orestes* 1403–5). His sceptical remark about the existence of Zeus (354–5, cf. 606) is, of course, quite unhomeric and thoroughly Euripidean. But Schmidt (in Roscher) goes rather too far, I think, in describing Odysseus in this play as 'zweifelsuchtige und von des Gedankens Blässe angekrankelt' on the basis of these touches of contemporary thought. Masqueray, pp. 196 ff. (and similarly in *Euripide et ses idées*, p. 233) after a comparison of Odysseus's speech to Polyphemus and the Cyclops's reply finds the second more attractive and believes that Euripides preferred the monster's *logique épaisse* to the fine but ineffective phrases of cautious and sophistical Odysseus (so, too, Grégoire loc. cit. in n. 21 below). Masqueray comments: *Ce Gargantua stupide, vigoureux et sans bedaine l'a séduit comme une des force intactes de la nature.* But what evidence is there that Euripides could admire such gross and selfish hedonism? I prefer the view of Schmid-Stählin 1, 3, 535, that the Cyclops is a caricature of current atheistic materialism—if the play is anything more than a boisterous frolic.

[21] *Rhesus* is definitely depreciatory of Odysseus. His penchant for trickery (vv. 498–9, 625, 709) and the humiliating nature of his disguise when he went as a spy to Troy (vv. 710 ff.) are emphasized. Diomedes takes the lead and patronizes Odysseus in a manner quite different from that of the Doloneia in *Il.* 10. The barbarian Rhesus denounces stealth in war (v. 510 ff.). But Odysseus's courage is admitted by both Hector (v. 499) and the Trojan chorus (v. 707) and his actions are both brave and adroit. Without deviating greatly from the Homeric narrative the author has managed to give the impression that despite his courage Odysseus was a person of inferior ethical calibre. For similarities with the characterization of Odysseus in *Hecuba* see H. Grégoire in *L'Antiquité Classique* ii (1933), 125–6 and 130, and cf. R. Goossens, ibid., 1 (1932), 101. Grégoire argues for a Rhesus-Hecuba-Epeios-Cyclops tetralogy, all hostile to Odysseus.

[22] This remark prompts Masqueray to a superbly-phrased paragraph on Odysseus's pragmatic attitude to words: once they have served their purpose, they leave as little trace in his mind as a bird's flight does in the air.

[23] Scholium on *Hecuba* 241. Cf. Masqueray, pp. 199–200.

[24] For the odiousness of Odysseus's part in *Hecuba* see especially Masqueray, H. J. G. Patin, *Etudes sur les tragiques grecs* (5th edn., Paris, 1877–9), *Euripide* i, 377, ends a finely

S

balanced opinion of Odysseus's conduct here and in Sophocles and Racine thus: '*personnage qui ne peut assurément compter sur notre sympathie, mais qui obtient de nous cet intérêt qu'excite toujours le spectacle d'un caractère énergique, d'une forte intelligence aux prises avec une situation hasardeuse et difficile*'. Louise E. Matthaei, *Studies in Greek tragedy* (Cambridge, 1918), pp. 130 ff. and 146 ff. says all that can be said in excuse for Odysseus's conduct in *Hecuba*, emphasizing his duty to the Greek cause. For criticism of Miss Matthaei's plea see E. L. Abrahamson, 'Euripides's Tragedy of Hecuba', *Trans. Americ. Philol. Assocn.* lxxxiii (1952), 120–9: Odysseus's speech in vv. 306–12 is not a true justification of Nomos but 'a masterpiece of pseudo-idealistic rhetoric'. It was probably only for technical reasons that Euripides ascribed the actual killing of Polyxena to Neoptolemus (cf. n. 2 to chapter six) and not in order to relieve Odysseus of any odium.

25 When this chapter was being written I had not seen E. M. Blaiklock's analysis of Ulysses's part in *Hecuba*, in *The male characters of Euripides* (Wellington, New Zealand, 1952), pp. 103–7. He sums up: 'Here was the old conflict between the claims of humanity and the claims of the community', and compares Ibsen, *An enemy of the people*, Act 4: 'The majority *never* has right upon its side, etc.'. Odysseus is 'perfectly reasonable, eminently convincing, and all the more repulsive for the fact'.

26 For the Palamedes trilogy see Gilbert Murray in *Greek Studies* (Oxford, 1946), chapter six. A poignant note of sympathy for Palamedes's death—he was presumably murdered treacherously by Odysseus in the version adopted by Euripides—is expressed in the fragment (Nauck 588): 'You have slain, you have slain, O Greeks, the all-wise one (πάνσοφον doubtless in contrast with Odysseus the πανοῦργον), the Muse's nightingale who never caused pain to any man.' The cynical remark on money-making in fr. 580 may have been spoken by Odysseus, and 583–5 against him. Schmid-Stählin 1, 3, 477, queries Welcker's view (*Griech. Trag.* 503–4) that Odysseus represented the warmongers (especially Alcibiades) and Palamedes the pacificists (especially Nicias) in this play.

27 Ancient commentators on Homer argued that there was little basis, in Homer at least, for this portrait of Odysseus as a seeker of popular favour (δημοχαριστής), especially in view of his rough handling of Thersites, the proto-demagogue: see, e.g., Eustathius on *Il.* 2, 200. But Euripides could have pointed to the fact that Odysseus did in fact act so as to win the favour of most of the common soldiers in that scene: cf. *Il.* 2, 270 ff., and Eustathius on *Il.* 2, 337. Blaiklock, op. cit., p. 104, notes that Euripides's notion of the mob is anachronistic in a Homeric context.

28 See Nauck for fragments and testimonia of Euripides's *Philoctetes*. Dio's *Discourses* 52 and 59 give a fair idea of its tone. The depth of Odysseus's infamy in this play lay, perhaps, in the fact that he did not hesitate to tell Philoctetes a string of flat lies (contrast his Homeric practice as mentioned in n. 26 to chapter three), and to include a denunciatory reference to the betrayal of Palamedes, pretending that he was one of Palamedes's persecuted friends (like the perfidious Sinon in *Aeneid* 2). Doubtless the imputation of competitive avarice among the gods (fr. 794) was spoken by Odysseus, and perhaps the sceptical fr. 795. Nothing significant is known about Odysseus's part in the notorious *Telephus*: he is mentioned (fr. 715) as not being the only rogue alive 'for necessity makes even the slow-witted clever'.

The references to Odysseus in the fragments of the minor Greek tragedians are few and insignificant (see Nauck, pp. 747, 785, 797, 801, 840). Some character in Theodectes's *Ajax* (Aristotle, *Rhetoric* 2, 23, 1399 b 29) was impudent enough to argue, in face of Diomedes's praise for Odysseus in *Il.* 10 that Diomedes had chosen Odysseus as his colleague in the Night Raid not because he honoured him but because he wanted a companion inferior to himself: in other words, Odysseus could now be viewed as a kind of Sancho Panza and Diomedes as a man bent on monopolizing all its glory for himself in this incident—which shows how low the conception of a hero had fallen in Theodectes's time.

29 Cf. Margaret E. Hirst, 'The choice of Odysseus', *Classical Philology* xxxv (1940), 67–8.

ADDITIONAL NOTE: The few references to Odysseus in the fragments of Greek comedy are discussed by Schmidt in *Jahrb. Cl. Phil.* They add nothing noteworthy to the tradition: cf. n. 8 to chapter seven and n. 6 to chapter five.

NOTES TO CHAPTER IX

Wüst, Roscher, Cesareo, and Martorana have collected and discussed aspects of the Ulysses theme in the Graeco-Roman period.

1 Ptolemy Euergetes admired Odysseus (see F. W. Walbank in *Classica et Mediaevalia* ix (1948), 171–2); so, too, Marcus Aurelius (as cited in n. 16 below) and Julian (*Orations* 3, 114;

Letters 7, 33; 58, 13). Caligula, to judge from his description of his great-grandmother Livia Augusta as 'a Ulysses in petticoats' (*Ulixem stolatum*, Suetonius *Vit. Calig.* 23), did not. The effect of Caracalla's preference for Achilles is noted in chapter ten. Perhaps it was significant that Nero took only Ulysses's statue from the group of Greek heroic statues mentioned at Olympia by Pausanias (5, 25, 8). The response of the Pythian oracle to Hadrian's inquiry about the birthplace and parentage of Homer—'by dwelling he belongs to Ithaca, and Telemachus was his father, and Epicaste, the daughter of Nestor, his mother, who bore him most omniscient among men', *Anth. Graec.* xiv, 102—implies imperial favour towards Homer and Ulysses. In the *Contest of Homer and Hesiod* 314 this is taken as the explanation of Homer's praise of Ulysses.

² Alexandrian efforts to remove indecorous features from Odysseus's character and conduct are discussed by M. H. van der Valk, *Textual criticism of the Odyssey* (Leiden, 1949): see especially p. 115 (Aristarchus tries to avoid accepting the fact that Odysseus was skilled at scything grass, as stated in *Od.* 18, 367); p. 121 (attempts to explain away Odysseus's nakedness in *Od.* 22, 1, and his distrust of Calypso in 5, 171); p. 189 (the athetizing of fabulous elements in Odysseus's wanderings, due to Aristarchus's 'prosaic mentality and too punctual matter-of-factness'); p. 260 (objection to *Od.* 11, 524, because it seemed, indecorously, to make Odysseus play the part of a janitor in the Wooden Horse). His discussion of Alexandrian failure to comprehend many aspects of archaic morality (pp. 199–216) is specially illuminating. On the athetizing of *Od.* 14, 503–6, by Aristarchus and Athenocles he aptly emphasizes (p. 207) that archaic man was much freer in revealing egotism than the more sophisticated later Greeks. This fact explains why the Alexandrians took exception to remarks like Nausicaa's in *Od.* 6, 244–5, and Alcinous's in 7, 313 (on which a scholiast remarks 'this is bad form and unkingly').

³ Gladstone, *Studies on Homer* ii, 513 ff.; cf. my note on *Od.* 3, 464. One may ask why then did Odysseus not allow Nausicaa's handmaidens to bathe him? Not from exceptional modesty, but because there is a difference between being bathed by girls as an honoured (and presumably presentable) guest in a palace and being washed as a complete stranger when covered with the brine of long immersion in the sea. In matters of this kind it is the conventional circumstances that create the freedom from embarrassment. The branch which Odysseus plucked as a covering before he first approaches Nausicaa is best explained in the same way.

⁴ For strictures on Odysseus's appetite see chapter five.

⁵ The remarks of Rapin, Le Bossu, and Fénelon on Ulysses's manners are discussed in *Studies in Philology* 1 (1953), 451–55.

⁶ For the surviving fragments of Zeno's five books on Homeric problems see von Arnim, *Stoicorum veterum fragmenta*, 1, 66–7. Dio of Prusa (*Discourses* 53, 4) states that Zeno did not find fault with any of Homer's work, but taught that sometimes the poet wrote according to opinion, sometimes according to established truth, which explained his apparent self-contradictions. This argument, Dio adds, had been used by Antisthenes, but he had not worked it out in such detail as Zeno. For references to Homer among Zeno's successors see von Arnim 1, 118, 121, 124, 133; 2, 241, 251–4, 292–4; 3, 118–19, 192–3. Plutarch's essay on the life and poetry of Homer probably incorporates many of the appreciative remarks of earlier Stoics. For some further references to Odysseus by Stoics and Cynics see L. Castiglioni in *Acme* i (1948), 31–43.

⁷ Epictetus refers to Odysseus in *Discourses* 1, 12, 3 (his piety); 2, 24, 26 (his treatment by Achilles in the Embassy); 3, 24, 13 (his travels); 3, 24, 18–20 (Homer may have misrepresented Odysseus by making him so tearful, for 'if he wept and wailed he was not a good man'); 3, 26, 33–4 (his self-reliance when cast naked on the shores of Phaeacia); fr. 11, 26 (his manliness as apparent in beggar's rags as in a princely robe).

⁸ 'Wise (or philosophical)': *sapiens*. The semantic range of this word (from 'having common sense' to 'being a philosopher') contrasts significantly with the much wider range of the Greek σοφός which extends much further into the merely 'clever'.

⁹ Odysseus weeps when yearning for home in Ogygia (*Od.* 5, 157); when the Phaeacian bard sings about events at Troy (8, 86, 522); when the Cyclops devours some of the Companions (9, 294); when Circe tells him of his visit to the Land of Ghosts (10, 496); when they set out on their way to it (10, 570); when he first sees the ghosts of Elpenor, his mother, Agamemnon (11, 55, 87, 397, 465); when Elpenor is being cremated (12, 12); when he first reveals himself to Telemachus (16, 191) and embraces him (16, 216); when he sees the neglected state of his dog Argos (17, 304); when he first converses with Penelope (19, 212) and when he finally embraces her (23, 232). In each of the second references to his sorrow

with Telemachus and Penelope the strong word κλαίω, implying tearful lamentations, is used (as in the incidents with the Cyclops and Circe): in all the others the term used implies only that tears fell from his eyes (except in 5, 157, where the abundance of his tears and groanings and agonies of spirit are described, to emphasize the sorrow of his home-sickness). The Venetus B scholia on *Il.* 1, 349, quote a proverb, 'noble men are abundant in tears'; cf. Menelaus's remark in Euripides, *Helena* 950–1, and Eustathius on *Od.* 17, 304. For extremities of grief in the *Iliad* see, e.g., 18, 23–5; 24, 16.

¹⁰ Dryden in the Dedication to his translation of Virgil's *Aeneid*.

¹¹ Some attempts to claim Ulysses as an Epicurean in the more disparaging sense will be found in Athenaeus 412ʙ, 513ᴀ. Lucian, *De parasito* 10, chides Odysseus for his remarks in *Od.* 9, 5 ff., for not having been a better Stoic; cf. the reference to Crates in next note. A more serious-minded Epicurean, Philodemus of Gadara, who influenced Horace and Virgil, seems to have admired Odysseus to judge from the fragmentary references in his treatise *On the Good King according to Homer* (see index to Olivieri's edn., Leipzig, 1909). Cf. end of the next note.

¹² In *Odes* 1, 6, 7, Horace calls Ulysses 'two-faced' (*duplex*: I cannot agree with Page's view that this is simply a humorous depreciation of the epic *polytropos*), and in 4, 6, 12–15, he refers disparagingly to the stratagem of the Wooden Horse, implying that Achilles would have been a less deceitful (but not less ruthless) conqueror of Troy. Admiration for Ulysses is perhaps implied by borrowings from his Homeric speeches in *Odes* 1, 7, 30 ff. and 1, 13, 17 ff. His description as *inclitus* in *Satires* 2, 3, 197, is conventional. In *Epistles* 1, 6, 62 ff., Horace contrasts the weakness of Ulysses's crew (*remigium vitiosum*) who preferred forbidden pleasure (presumably the Lotus and the meat of the Sun-cattle) to their *patria*. In *Epodes* 16, 60, and 17, 60, Ulysses is called 'toilful' (*laboriosus*) and in *Epistles* 1, 7, 40, 'enduring' (*patiens*), both apparently in a sympathetic and appreciative sense—but here the influence of the early Greek lyrists (see chapter six) may be as strong as that of the Stoics. The dialogue in *Satires* 2, 5, may be intended as a criticism of Ulysses's eagerness to get wealth and a symptom of late-Cynic reaction against the Antisthenic conception of Ulysses as the proto-Cynic. This is Martorana's view (pp. 75–80): she quotes the letter attributed to Crates (Hercher, *Epistolographi Graeci*, p. 211) in which Ulysses is denounced as soft, pleasure-loving, self-indulgent, over-pious, mendicant, and self-seeking—and most unworthy to be called the Father of the Cynic School. Her reference to *meus Ulixes* as a synonym for an unscrupulous parasite in Plautus, *Menaechmi* 902, is also apt. But I take leave to doubt that Horace intends any serious criticism of the traditional Ulysses. Horace may simply have chosen the interview between Ulysses and Teiresias in *Od.* 11 as a convenient mythological framework for an entirely Roman dialogue in which the two Greeks are merely lay figures for contemporary satire. In other words Horace's intention was not to say 'Homer's Ulysses was really an avaricious pander like this' (Teiresias advises him to offer Penelope to some rich adulterer—advice which he actually follows in Nicholas Rowe's play as mentioned in chapter thirteen), but rather 'If Ulysses and Tiresias had been Romans of our time, this is how they would have talked'.

¹³ Some other points in Cicero's references to Ulysses: in *Tusc. Disput.* 5, 16, 46, he refers to Ulysses's *lenitudo orationis* and *mollitudo corporis* as described in Pacuvius's version of the *Niptra*. In *De oratore* 1, 44, 196, he notes Ulysses's love of his native land, an observation often made by patriotic Romans about Ulysses (cf. Horace in n. 12 above, and Martorana pp. 111 ff.). Naturally Cicero also admired Ulysses's oratorical powers. He defends Ulysses from imputations of cowardice based on his attempt to evade conscription (*De off.* 3, 26, 97 and on his pretended desertion to the enemy (*De invent.* 2, 58, 176). As Martorana (p. 115 notes Cesareo was wrong in taking the passage in *De invent.* 1, 49, 92, as implying disparagement of Ulysses by Cicero personally: it is simply a piece of advice on rhetorical technique Cicero observes in praise of Ulysses that he alone, and not Ajax or Achilles, is called 'city destroyer' by Homer. But here his admiration seems to outrun the facts: Homer in our text applies the epithet to Achilles four times (but see Tyrrell and Purser *ad loc.*).

¹⁴ For the many other references to Ulysses in Seneca's prose works see the index to Haase' edn. (Leipzig, 1897). They are generally appreciatory. The contrasting tone of Seneca in his plays is discussed in chapter eleven.

¹⁵ See n. 15 to chapter twelve.

¹⁶ Marcus Aurelius implies admiration of Ulysses in *Meditations* 5, 31 (his blameless conduct cf. *Od.* 4, 690), 11, 31 (his inner exultation, cf. *Od.* 9, 413).

¹⁷ For studies on Homeric allegories see the works cited in Pauly s.v. *Odysseus* col. 1914 especially Wehrli. Post-classical developments are discussed by H. Rahner, *Griechisch*

Mythen in christlicher Deutung (Zurich, 1945), and also *Hermathena* lxxvii (1951), 52 ff. The Latin poets of the *Priapea* used allegory *sensu obscaeno* in connection with Ulysses, e.g. in 68, where the Moly is explained as the *mentula* and Ulysses's stringing of the Bow as *nervum tendere*.

[18] Cited from F. Oelmann, *Heracliti Quaestiones Homericae* (Leipzig, 1910): some parallels to Heraclitus's allegories are cited on p. xliii.

[19] Apollonius, *Homeric Lexicon* on μῶλυ. Eustathius on *Od.* 1, 20, 51, 73, 105, mentions various other allegorical interpretations of Odyssean motifs.

[20] Servius on *Aeneid* 3, 636, on the Cyclops. His explanation of the position of Polyphemus's eye is curiously suggestive of spiritualists' views on the 'pineal eye'.

NOTES TO CHAPTER X

Martorana and Cesareo discuss most of the material used in this chapter. For comparisons between Virgil and Homer, and Aeneas and Ulysses, see especially W. F. J. Knight, *Roman Vergil* (London, 1944).

[1] For variations in the Greek and Trojan pedigrees of Latinus and the Roman kings see Roscher, Hartmann, Phillips, and Martorana. For the reputed founding of Rome by Ulysses (first attested in Hellanicus fr. 84, Jacoby) see W. Schur, 'Griechische Traditionen der Gründung Roms', *Klio* xvii (1921), 137 ff., and Phillips, pp. 57–8.

[2] Phillips discusses many other local Latin associations with Ulysses.

[3] With Lucan's admiration for Cato's loyalty to the losing side contrast the admiration of the Chorus in Aristophanes's *Frogs* (534 ff.) for the opportunistic Theramenes.

[4] Juvenal, *Satires* 3, 60 ff. He sums up his feeling about the Greeks in the scathing phrase— 'a nation of playboys' (*natio comoeda est*). For scorn of Ulysses's stories at the court of Alcinous see *Satires* 15, 13 ff. As further confirmation of Roman antipathy towards Greek cleverness, Martorana, pp. 43–56, notes that in Latin versions of the contest between Ajax and Ulysses all authors, including even Cicero, favour Ajax (with the exception of Ovid, as discussed in chapter eleven).

[5] *Alexandra* 344 and 658 (a reference to the stealing of the Palladium: the scholiast says that Stesichorus first gave Odysseus the emblem of a dolphin).

[6] For discussion of Lycophron's references to Ulysses and of their relationship to Timaeus and the earlier historical tradition see Phillips, pp. 58–61.

[7] In *Aen.* 6, 528–9, the ghost of Deiphobus refers to Ulysses as 'instigator of crimes' and 'scion of Aeolus' (a reference to his alleged descent from the crafty Sisyphus). In 9, 602, a Rutulian prince calls him *fandi fictor*, a phrase difficult to express in English, perhaps 'coiner of speeches'. Virgil's references to Ulysses outside the *Aeneid* are conventional. His summary of Ulysses's adventures in *Culex* 326 ff. is quaintly and effectively translated in Spenser's *Gnat*.

[8] Sellar, in the 3rd edn. of his *Roman poets of the Augustan age: Virgil*, p. 334, notes 'The bitterness of national animosity is especially apparent in his exhibition of the characters of Ulysses and Helen. The championship of the cause of Troy demanded an attitude of antagonism to her destroyer. . . . Virgil's mode of conceiving and delineating character is much nearer to that of Euripides than to that of Homer. The original error of Helen and the craft in dealing with his enemies, which is one of many qualities in the versatile humanity of Ulysses, gave to these later artists the germ in accordance with which the whole character was conceived. They did not adequately apprehend that the most interesting types of nobleness and beauty of character as imagined by the greatest artists are also the most complex, and the least capable of being squared with abstract conceptions of vices or virtues. The full truth of Homer's delineations of character was apparently not recognized by the most cultivated of his Roman readers'. I venture to disagree with the last sentence.

[9] This device of inventing a lost companion of Ulysses is also used by Ovid, *Metamorphoses* 14, 158 ff. For the curious belief about the ghost of one named Alybas see Phillips, p. 57.

[10] For Odyssean influences on the *Aeneid* cf. Sellar, op. cit. in n. 8 above, pp. 312 ff., and W. F. J. Knight, op. cit., pp. 95–9 and passim. R. S. Conway in *The Vergilian Age* remarks (p. 141): 'The books with odd numbers show what we may call the lighter or Odyssean type: the books with even numbers reflect the graver quality of the *Iliad*'. Phillips, p. 67, observes: '. . . it is clear that the *Aeneid* represents the final stage in the adoption for Aeneas and Rome of all that was impressive in the wanderings of Odysseus as located in Italy'.

[11] Sellar, op. cit., in n. 9 above, p. 397. See also pp. 398 ff. for further remarks on the strength and weakness of Aeneas's character in comparison with other heroes. The relative

merits of Homer's and Virgil's heroes were a constant source of controversy in the seventeenth century, e.g. in Rapin's *Discours académique* (1668), in which Aeneas is eulogized and Ulysses ridiculed.

[12] H. W. Garrod, p. 152, of *English literature and the classics*, ed. by G. S. Gordon (Oxford, 1912).

[13] Similar pro-Trojan bias is found in the French *grec* and German *Grieche*.

[14] But this kind of gloss goes back at least to the tenth century A.D., when Suidas in his Byzantine dictionary explains 'Οδύσσειος as denoting villainy and craft.

NOTES TO CHAPTER XI

Martorana discusses the following aspects of the Ulysses theme in Latin literature: Ulysses's ancestry, voyages, death; his role in the Judgment of Arms, the sacrifice of Iphigeneia, the deaths of Astyanax and Palamedes, and in the recall of Philoctetes; his descriptions in Horace, *Satires* 2, 5, and in the *Aeneid*; his wisdom and other virtues; allegorical interpretations; his popular reputation.

[1] A notable exception to this was John Gower in his Ovidian *Confessio Amantis* (1390): see chapter fourteen.

[2] The references to Ulysses in Propertius, Tibullus, and Martial are conventional. Catullus does not mention Ulysses directly; but some of his phrases suggest overtones from the *Odyssey*.

[3] For the treatment of Ulysses in early Latin drama see Warmington, *Remains of Old Latin* passim. The only novel feature is that mentioned in chapter nine. It is regrettable that so little is known of the *Latin Odyssey* of Livius Andronicus (not a mere translation, probably) and nothing of how Tuticanus (the friend of Ovid: cf. his *Epistles* 4, 12, 27) handled Ulysses's adventures in Phaeacia.

[4] But Lucilius's *Satires* (Book 17) and Varro's *Sesculixe* (*Ulysses-and-a-half*), now lost, may have shown a Ulysses in the manner of Epicharmus or Aristophanes.

[5] Praise of Ulysses's eloquence: e.g. Cicero, *Brutus* 40; Quintilian 11, 3, 158 and 12, 10, 64; Aulus Gellius 1, 15, 3 and 6, 14, 7. His style was held to be *magnificum* and *ubertum*, often with special reference to *Il.* 3, 216–24. Roman rhetoricians often chose episodes from his career, especially his contest with Ajax, for their exercises and displays (see S. F. Bonner, *Roman declamation*, Liverpool, 1949, pp. 15, 23, 25, 162).

[6] As well, of course, as such prosaic mythological compendia as are mentioned in n. 5 to chapter twelve.

[7] These exceptions are when Ovid calls Ulysses 'apt for thieving' in a patriotic passage in *Fasti* 6, 433, and when in *Metamorphoses* 13, 712, he adopts a Virgilian attitude in describing how Aeneas sailed past the *regnum fallacis Ulixis*.

[8] According to the scholiast on *Od.* 8, 75, this controversy about the relative merits of valour and prudence (ἀνδρεία and φρόνησις) goes back to the quarrel between Achilles and Ulysses as described there. The same motif recurs in the treatment of the Ajax-Ulysses contest by fifth-century sophists as described in chapter seven. It was a favourite controversy in Renaissance times. A late Greek reference (cited to me by Dr. van der Valk) is in Georgius Pisides, *De exped. Persica* 1, 71–5. For a comparison of several Latin versions of the contest between Ajax and Ulysses see Martorana, pp. 43–56.

[9] I am conscious that my suggestion of some slight sympathy towards Ulysses's predicament in Seneca's *Troades* runs counter to the general view as expressed, e.g., by Martorana (p. 62): *Ulisse nella tragedia di Seneca è semplicemente odioso* (once more the nemesis of Autolycus). In Seneca's *Agamemnon* Ulysses is called *subdolus* by the Chorus (v. 636) and he 'envies' Ajax in v. 513.

[10] For Senecan influences on sixteenth- and seventeenth-century French plays concerning Ulysses see *Studies in Philology* 1 (1953), 448–50.

[11] A noteworthy proof of the prevailing hostility of Latin writers towards Ulysses is to be found in the Supplement to Roscher where J. B. Carter has listed the epithets applied to Ulysses in classical Latin poetry, sixty-one in all. About twenty of these merely describe his ancestry or status without any ethical implication. Of the remainder twenty are derogatory (*aptus furtis, artifex scelerum, commentor fraudis, dirus, duplex, durus, fallax, fictor, gravis ultor, infidus, inimicus, inventor scelerum, machinator fraudis, minister sortis durae, pellax, proditus, saevus, sollers, subdolus, varius*). About twelve are appreciatory, most of them being conventional

references to his fame, courage, endurance, patience, eloquence, and foresight—*acer, aerum-nosus, decus Argolicum, facundus, illustris, heros, inclutus, magnus, patiens, potens, sapiens, vigil.* Obviously the derogatory list is more emphatic than the other. To it should be added *hortator scelerum Aeolides* in *Aen.* 6, 529.

NOTES TO CHAPTER XII

Wüst, Roscher, and Cesareo quote most of the significant references for this period. Highet, chapter three, surveys the literary background. Allen, pp. 137 ff., discusses the testimonia for the later anti-Homeric writers.

[1] Theocritus complains about Homer's monopoly of the reading public in *Idyll* 16, 20–21.

[2] For Ptolemy Chennos's epic entitled *The Anti-Homer* (*c.* A.D. 100) and for other writers claiming knowledge superior to Homer's about the Troy tale see Allen, p. 146, and Schmid-Stählin 2, 1, 364–5 and 421–2. Cf. n. 15 to chapter seven. It is arguable that the circumstantial stories told by these anti-Homeric forgers to authenticate their versions of the Troy tale were merely a literary device not meant to be taken seriously. But the other view seems to fit the general tone of their writings better (though the sophisticated Philostratus is the most inscrutable on this point). In any case the historical fact remains that the spurious claims of Dares and Dictys, at least, were believed by medieval and Renaissance writers generally until the sixteenth century.

[3] For Dio on Homer, Odysseus, and Autolycus, as liars, see § 17 of the *Trojan Discourse* (11). Allen, p. 165, notes that Dio virtually confesses that his version of the Trojan war is false (§ 124), and that his motive for writing it may have been anti-Greek feeling as he was an Asiatic by birth (p. 169).

[4] Dio praises Odysseus elsewhere as an exemplary ruler (2, 20 ff.), as resembling Diogenes (9, 9; cf. 14, 22; 33, 15), as a lover of his native land (17, 6; cf. 33, 19), and in general for his intelligence, versatility, adaptability, wisdom, tact, and manual dexterity: see the index to de Budé's edn. (Teubner, Leipzig, 1919). In 2, 43, he finds a significant parallel between Homer's description of Odysseus's house in *Od.* 17, 266–8, and Odysseus's own character as an ἀσφαλὴς ἀνήρ. Dio is obviously influenced by the Cynics' admiration for Odysseus: cf n. 23 to chapter 7 above. But in 13, 4, Dio criticizes Odysseus's unmanly tearfulness in his exile with Calypso.

[5] Most notably for the Ulysses theme, *The Library* by Apollodorus (Greek A.D. i–ii) and *Fables* by Hyginus (Latin, perhaps A.D. ii). These mention some details not found elsewhere: see Wüst and Roscher.

[6] Ulysses is mentioned seven times in the *Ilias Latina*, once (v. 139) as 'illustrious in council', twice (vv. 527, 589) as a 'deviser of deceit'. For evidence that the Romans on the whole preferred the *Iliad* to the *Odyssey* see I. Tolkiehn, *De auctoritate Homeri in cotidiana Romanorum vita* (Leipzig, 1896).

[7] As the *Heroicus* is not a long work it is hardly necessary to give references to the passages cited. Highet, p. 575, cites authority for the view that Philostratus favoured Achilles to please Caracalla. I agree with his doubts on the paradoxical theory that Philostratus intended to justify Homer's against Dictys's version of the Trojan war.

[8] For references to Odysseus in Dictys and Dares see the index to Meister's edns. (Teubner, 1872 and 1873). For Dictys in general see Allen, chapter seven. I cannot agree with his view that Dictys's version contains genuine pre-Homeric material. Lang suggests (*W. of H.*, p. 190) that Dictys may have got some of his bias against Ulysses and in favour of Palamedes from the *Cypria*. This is possible but not, as the evidence now stands, provable.

[9] For the vast influence of Dares and Dictys on medieval European literature from Russia to Iceland see Meister's introductions, as well as N. E. Griffin, *Dares and Dictys* (Baltimore, 1907), and 'Un-homeric elements in the medieval story of Troy', *Journal of English and German Philology* vii (1907–8), 32 ff.; Highet, chapter three and pp. 574 ff.; and *Hermathena* lxxvii (1951), 52–64.

[10] Benoit de Sainte Maure in his *Roman de Troie* gives both versions of the death of Ajax without apology for the direct contradiction.

[11] Chaucer, *The House of Fame* iii, 386–8; cf. R. K. Root, 'Chaucer's Dares', *Modern Philology* xv (1917), 1 ff. The allegation that Homer favoured the Greeks is not, of course, entirely untrue, and it originates much earlier than Dares and Dictys: see Schmid-Stählin 2, 1, 365, n. 1, for Daphidas and the Homeric scholia on this topic, and cf. Geddes, pp. 324–7, for instances in the Homeric poems.

[12] Perizonius's edn. of Dares and Dictys in 1702 finally demolished their pretensions. But as late as 1945 a writer in a learned journal could still be deceived. See Highet, p. 576.

[13] In *Hermathena* lxxvii (1951), 52–64; two further appreciatory references to Ulysses in this period are quoted by J. Adhémar in·*Influences antiques dans l'art du moyen age français* (London, 1939), p. 22.

[14] I have not thought it worth while to discuss the minute variations in the Ulysses tradition which are to be found in the Greek authors of the late classical and Byzantine period, as their influence on the main tradition was slight. Details will be found in Pauly, Roscher, and Cesareo, pp. 29 ff.; see also A. Ludwich, *Zwei byzantinische Odysseuslegenden* (Koenigsburg, 1898).

[15] For Plutarch's appreciation of Odysseus see, e.g., *Quomodo adulator* 66F (Odysseus's frankness based on public spirit in *Il.* 14, 82 ff.), *Conjug. praecepta* 139 (his prudence), *De vit. poes. Homeri* 2, 4 (his moral courage, nobility). Other references will be found in the index to Bernardakis's edn. of the *Moralia* (Teubner, Leipzig, 1896). The strictures in *Brut. anim. ratione uti* (*Gryllus*) 987c are, of course, not typical of Plutarch's attitude. It is Plutarch, *De audiendis poetis* 8, who records the curious Etruscan tradition of a sleepy and unapproachable Ulysses: cf. Phillips, p. 65. For Plutarch's influence on the later tradition see chapter thirteen.

NOTES TO CHAPTER XIII

For the general background to this chapter see especially Finsler, Highet, and, for the English tradition, the invaluable studies by Douglas Bush, *Mythology and the renaissance tradition in English poetry* (Minneapolis and London, 1932) and *Mythology and the romantic tradition in English poetry* (Cambridge, Mass., 1937). For citations by author's name only see the general list of books.

[1] For scattered references to Ulysses by Petrarch and Boccaccio see *Hermathena* lxxviii (1951), 82. Bush (*Myth. and renaissance trad.*, pp. 31–2) describes influential mythological handbooks of the renaissance period. That of Natalis Comes (1551) is notably appreciative of Ulysses (*Hermathena* loc. cit.), but in Ravisius Textor's popular *Officina* (1532) he is placed among the *Astuti et fraudulenti*.

[2] Elyot's views are discussed at greater length in *Hermathena* lxxix (1952), 34–7.

[3] Henri Quatre was also devoted to Plutarch. For further remarks on Ulysses in sixteenth- and seventeenth-century France see *Studies in Philology* l (1953), 446–56. Chapman's admiration for Homer and Ulysses is discussed by Phyllis B. Bartlett, *Review of English Studies* xvii (1941), 257–80, and in *Hermathena* lxxxi (1953), 43–5.

[4] For other influences working against Ulysses in the seventeenth century see *Hermathena* lxxxi. Some examples of burlesque and anti-heroic treatments of the Ulysses theme are cited there.

[5] Rapin in his *Comparaison entre Virgile et Homère* (publ. 1668) stigmatized Ulysses as a drunkard, adulterer, vulgarian, liar and self-seeker. Here Ulysses is partly a victim to the Battle of the Books (as in Perrault's reference to the incongruity of his qualities of prudence and trickery, heroism and baseness). Le Bossu's defence is mainly conventional, in the Stoic and Horatian manner. Fénelon, having the licence of a novelist in his *Télémaque*, defends Ulysses partly by making Philoctetes deliver a remarkable recantation of his tirades against Ulysses in Sophocles's *Philoctetes* and partly by making Ulysses into a figure of aloof, impressive *hauteur*. See *Studies in Philology* loc. cit. for fuller references.

[6] Fénelon describes Ulysses as having 'an air majestic but subdued'; 'his heart is like a deep well: no one can fathom its secret. He loves truth and says nothing to do it harm. But he only speaks the truth when it serves a good purpose. His wisdom, like a seal, keeps his life ever closed against useless words'. For further defence of Ulysses's powers of dissimulation see the note on *Od.* 13, 338, in Pope's version: Ulysses is 'artful' but not criminal. For Pope's view of Ulysses in general see Douglas Knight, *Pope and the heroic tradition* (New Haven, 1951). The notes to Pope's *Homer* contain much of interest on Ulysses.

[7] See further in Warren Ramsey, 'Voltaire and Homer', *PMLA* lxvi (1951), 182–96, a valuable study for the whole Augustan period.

[8] For the general neglect of the *Odyssey* in the eighteenth century see Clarke, op. cit. in n. 16 to chap. xiv, pp. 142–3.

[9] Details of the characterization of Ulysses in the medieval Troy tale and bibliographical references are given in *Hermathena* lxxviii (1951), 67–83.

[10] The idiom and outlook of the medieval Troy tale were revived in the nineteenth century by William Morris (especially in his *Scenes from the fall of Troy*: for Ulysses see *The descent from the Wooden Horse*) and by others. Ulysses usually played an inferior part in these revivals. (But John Masefield in *A tale of Troy*, 1932, gave him credit for wisdom, courage, vigilance, and initiative, in the episode of the Wooden Horse.) In general the romanticism of the medieval style (with its emphasis on languishing lovers and elusive ladies) was foreign to the Ulysses-type with its practical common sense and its conjugal fidelity. The dim Troilus suited this atmosphere far better. Hence Boccaccio, Chaucer, and others said nothing of Ulysses in their versions of the Troy tale. Shakespeare was the first to give Ulysses a prominent part in the Troilus and Cressida story: see K. Young, *The origin and development of the story of Troilus and Criseyde* (London, 1908).

[11] A favourable description of Ulysses (as depicted in Ovid's *Metamorphoses*) is given by Dryden in his preface to *Troilus and Cressida*. Contrast Shirley's *Contention of Ajax and Ulysses* as cited in *Hermathena* lxxxi.

[12] The variorum edition of *Troilus and Cressida* by H. N. Hillebrand and T. W. Baldwin (Philadelphia and London, 1953) summarizes the chief opinions on these problems. For Shakespeare's sources see pp. 419–49, also J. A. K. Thomson, *Shakespeare and the Classics* (London, 1952), pp. 141–5. A general acquaintance with the *Iliad* (and probably with Chapman's version of Books 1–2, 7–11, and 18, published in 1598) is indicated. Chambers, as cited there, suggests also some knowledge of the Sophoclean presentation of Ajax (which implies Ulysses's portrait in *Ajax* as well). For various performances in England of Sophoclean and Euripidean plays connected with the Ulysses theme between 1564 and 1596 see E. K. Chambers, *The Elizabethan stage* (Oxford, 1923) i, 127–8, 130, 233, and iv, 87, 146.

[13] The references to the passages quoted in this paragraph are (in the same order) as follows (with the abridgement 'S.' and *T. and C.*): S. A. Tannenbaum, '*S.'s T. and C.*; a concise bibliography (New York, 1943), p. ix; R. Grant White, *Studies in S.* (London, 1885), pp. 40–1; George Brandes, *William S., a critical study* (translated New York, 1898) ii, 213; Barker, p. 64; Julius Bab, *S. Wesen und Werke* (Stuttgart, 1925), p. 287; B. Dobrée, *T, and C.* (edited: London, 1938, p. xxi; H. C. Goddard, *The meaning of S.* (Chicago, 1951), p. 401; E. Dowden, *S.—his mind and art* (12th edn., London, 1901), p. viii (cf. his *Introduction to S.*, p. 73); E. M. W. Tillyard, *S.'s problem plays* (London, 1950), pp. 72 ff.; James Joyce in Frank Budgen's *James Joyce and the making of Ulysses* (London, 1934), p. 169. Other (mainly favourable views) will be found in C. Williams, '*T. and C.* and *Hamlet*' (*Shakespeare criticism*, 1919–35, ed. Anne Bradby, Oxford, 1935), p. 189; H. B. Charlton, *Shakesperean comedy* (London, 1937), p. 227; G. B. Harrison, *S.'s tragedies* (London, 1951), p. 118. Goddard (op. cit.), the most recent critic I have quoted, has much more to say in support of his conviction that Ulysses is a cold-blooded master-villain.

[14] Hillebrand, op. cit., pp. 389–410, examines views on the 'degree' speech and concludes that Ulysses's speech in *Iliad* Two (via Chapman) prompted it, though much may be derived from other sources ranging from Plato to Elyot.

[15] To use Aristotelian terms Ulysses insists that what matters both for character and reputation is virtue in action (*energeia*), not completed deeds of virtue (*erga*): a profoundly Ulyssean philosophy.

[16] I find this ominous note (suggesting the more sinister aspect of Tudor statecraft with its spies and the Star Chamber) in vv. 204 ff., beginning:

> The providence that's in a watchfull State,
> Knowes almost every graine of Plutoes gold, etc.

(Despite certain editors 'State' here must surely mean the body politic.) One is reminded of Ulysses's success as a spy in the Homeric tradition: but here he speaks more as the spider at the centre of a web of espionage. Note also vv. 210 ff. on the 'divine operation' of the 'mysterie in the soule of State'—a foreshadowing of woes to come in European politics. Baconists may well see Ulysses as the mouthpiece of his author here.

[17] For Shakespeare's references to the other Homeric heroes, and his probable sources, see R. K. Root, *Classical mythology in Shakespeare* (*Yale Studies in English*, 1903), and E. K. Chambers, *William Shakespeare: facts and problems* (Oxford, 1930) i, 447–9.

[18] For recent views on Shakespeare's attitude to 'honest Troyan' (*Love's labour lost*, 5, 2, 681) and 'cogging Greeks' (*T. and C.* 5, 6, 11) see G. Wilson Knight, *The wheel of fire* (4th edn., London, 1949), pp. 47 and 59, and E. M. W. Tillyard, *Shakespeare's problem plays* (London, 1950), pp. 9, 85, 87–8. In general the view that Shakespeare was anti-Greek in *T. and C.* seems to prevail. I hope to answer this more fully elsewhere.

[19] The possibility of veiled allusions to contemporary Elizabethan figures in *T. and C.* is discussed in Hillebrand, pp. 375–88. The case seems strongest for seeing something of Essex in Achilles. One critic (p. 381) sees Ulysses as a 'shrewd old puritan' and Troilus as a 'heart-broken young cavalier'; another (p. 382) identifies Ulysses with Cecil. Chapman did not publish his *Odysses* with its address to the Earl of Somerset and his 'Ulyssean patience' until 1616. His identification of Achilles with Essex appeared in 1598. Essex was executed for high treason in 1601; so it might have been dangerous for Shakespeare to portray Achilles favourably.

[20] Hillebrand, p. 179, notes: 'Ulysses's speeches evidently concerned him a great deal and he worked at them with more than ordinary care'; cf. p. 381. Shakespeare's other references to Ulysses are to be found in *The rape of Lucrece*, vv. 1394–1400 (quoted in chapter twelve above); 3 *Henry VI*, 3, 2, 188–90, 'Deceive more slily than Ulysses could' (cf. ibidem 4, 2, 19–21), *Coriolanus* 1, 3, 91 ff. (the only reference to an Odyssean aspect of Ulysses), and *Titus Andronicus*, 1, 1, 379–81 (a reference to Ulysses's magnanimous role in the burying of Ajax). The only definitely disparaging reference is the second; the others are appreciatory or neutral. A. M. Pizzagalli, 'Riflessi omerici in Shakespeare', *Il Mondo Classico*, 1932, pp. 459–63, thinks it possible that S. had the story of Ulysses and Nausicaa in mind when portraying Miranda in the *Tempest*, but admits that the resemblances may be accidental. Shakespeare could have learned to admire the *Odyssey* from Ascham's *Scholemaster* (see next chapter); but no English translation was available until Chapman's in 1616.

[21] For the influence of Seneca on neo-classical French dramatists see Léon Hermann, *Le théâtre de Sénèque* (Paris, 1924), and other works cited in *Studies in Philology* 1 (1953), 449.

[22] The Ulysses of Racine's immediate model, *Iphigénie in Aulide* by Rotrou (1642), seems to me to be a rather nobler figure: e.g. in Act 3, sc. 3; Act 5, sc. 5. For an unquestionably favourable portrait of Ulysses in the Iphigeneia incident see André Obey's *Une fille pour du vent* (Paris, 1953): he opposes the sacrifice compassionately and nobly.

[23] For Racine's comments on the *Odyssey* see G. E. Broche, *Examen des remarques de Racine sur l'Odyssée d'Homère* (Paris, 1946), and R.-C. Knight, *Racine et la Grèce* (Paris, 1951).

[24] I am indebted to Dr. M. H. van der Valk for information about Vondel's play.

[25] For plays about Ulysses in seventeenth- and eighteenth-century French drama see H. C. Lancaster's standard surveys. In the *Ajax* of Poinsinet de Sivry (1762) he appears as a *philosophe* tinged with religious scepticism but prepared to use religion as a means of quelling popular insubordination: the soldiery, he says, would revolt *si par le Fanatisme il n'est plus enchainé* (Act 2, sc. 1).

[26] Lord de Tabley, *Collected poems* (London, 1903), p. 184. In contrast, André Gide's play, *Philoctète* (1899) is much less biased against Ulysses. Gide obviously admired (no doubt mainly for personal reasons) the lonely integrity of Philoctetes more than Ulysses's social utilitarianism. But his Ulysses is no blackguard or knave: he is sad at having to deceive a friend, but *'la patrie n'est elle pas plus qu'un seul?'*—which is a genuinely Ulyssean attitude.

NOTES TO CHAPTER XIV

For the general background see the works cited for chapter thirteen.

[1] For example Heine in *Nordsee-Dichtungen* 1, 4 (with a pleasantly ironical touch of self-depreciation) and Foscolo, more obliquely, in his sonnet *A Zacintho*.

[2] Homeric touches are in the phrase *plein d'usage et raison* (cf. *Od.* 1, 3) and the reference to the chimney-smoke of his home (cf. p. 50 above), which is repeated in *Les regrets* cxxx, 3. The last line, perhaps less deliberately, suggests 'the mild death off the sea' which Teiresias had prophesied for Ulysses in *Od.* 11. For other references to Ulysses in du Bellay see *Les regrets* xxvi, xl, lxxxviii, cxxx.

[3] Seferis, *Poemata 1924–46* (Athens, 1950), pp. 95–7: the quotations given are mainly from a translation by Mr. George Savidis. Seferis also makes use of Ulysses as a symbol in his poems *Kikhle* and *Mythistorema* in the same collection.

[4] The most readable medieval version of Ulysses's last wanderings is that at the end of Lydgate's *Troy tale* V, 1781 ff. (cf. *Hermathena* lxxviii, 1951, 67 ff.). For the unique Irish narrative, *Merugud Uilix Maicc Leirtis*, with its additional folk-motifs, see R. T. Meyer in *Modern Philology* 1 (1952), 73–8. Parallels have been suggested between Ulysses's adventures and those of Beowulf, Loki, St. Brendan, Maelduin, and other early figures, but they are slight.

[5] No satisfactory source has been found for this innovation of making Ulysses go from Circe to his death. Perhaps Dante had heard some confused account of Ulysses's voyage to the Land of Ghosts after leaving Circe (as described in *Od.* 11). He could, perhaps, have got some notion of the story of the *Odyssey* from travellers, crusaders, or pilgrims, who had been in contact with Byzantine Greeks. Ulysses's voyage in the Atlantic may have been suggested to Dante by the legends of Maelduin and St. Brendan, as Dorothy Sayers notes.

[6] Cf. the quotation from Barker on p. 75 above and see the whole of Barker's essay for Dante's Ulysses (a symbol of the Aristotelian *intellectus agens* in conflict with *fides*). I have added some further comments in 'Dante's conception of Ulysses', *The Cambridge Journal* vi (1953), 239–47. My views on Dante's Ulysses have been criticized by Dr. Mario M. Rossi in *Italica* xxx (1953), 193–202.

[7] *Cambridge Journal* loc. cit., where Croce is cited for the remark, 'No one was more deeply moved than Dante by the passion to know all that is knowable, and nowhere else has he given expression to that noble passion as in the great figure of Ulysses': cf. W. H. Auden, *The enchafèd flood* (London, 1951), p. 21.

[8] See St. Augustine's strictures on *curiositas* in *Confessions* 10, 35, and St. Thomas Aquinas, *De curiositate* (*Summa Theologica* 2, 2, 167): and further in 'Modern literary scholarship as reflected in Dante criticism' (*Comparative Literature* iii, 1951, 289–309), by H. Hatzfeld, who criticizes the view that Ulysses is a kind of tragic hero, remarking 'The principle at issue is this: divine justice punishes the misguided will, the root of the action; the action itself may contain elements open to human pity'. But is Dante's justice to be equated with God's justice? And did not Calderon, an equally orthodox theologian, find a means of salvation for Ulysses on his departure from Circe? And does not Dante condemn Ulysses for an action which is entirely his, Dante's, own invention?

[9] Some further remarks on Ascham's views on Ulysses and other contemporary opinions are given in *Hermathena* lxxix (1952), 38 ff., notably those of Sidney, Spenser, and Golding in his version of Ovid's *Metamorphoses*.

[10] For Chapman's Ulysses see further in n. 3 to chapter thirteen, and for his 'mysticism' see *Envoy* v (1951), 62–9. For other seventeenth-century English versions of scenes from the *Odyssey* (by Samuel Daniel, William Browne, and, in burlesque, James Smith) see *Hermathena* lxxxi (1953), 41 ff.

[11] Some Odyssean influence has been traced in *Gulliver's Travels* by G. McCracken in *The Classical Journal* xxix (1934), 535–8, but it is slight.

[12] Vico is cited from the translation of *The new science* by T. G. Bergin and M. H. Fisch (Ithaca, N.Y., 1948). The passages quoted are §§ 38, 654, 648. For further illustrations of the scientific attitude to Homer and his heroes see *Hermathena* lxxxi (1953), 50–1. Some twentieth-century writers have also tried to find scientific symbolisms in the *Odyssey*: according, for instance, to H. G. Baynes, *Mythology of the soul* (London, 1940), p. 369, the connection between the anima and the mother-complex is illustrated in Ulysses relations with Calypso and Nausicaa.

[13] *Letters*, ed. E. V. Lucas, vi, 386.

[14] For further discussion of Lamb's attitude to Ulysses and its influence on James Joyce see *Envoy* loc. cit. and *The Listener* for July 19, 1951, p. 99. Lamb also influenced Samuel Butler's oratorio *Ulysses*: see H. Festing Jones, *Samuel Butler: a memoir* (London, 1919), ii, 104–5 (a reference which I owe, with others, to Prof. L. J. D. Richardson).

[15] In what follows here I have relied on the translation of Calderon's two plays by D. F. MacCarthy (London, 1861) recommended to me by Dr. A. E. Sloman. For other remarkable contributions to the Ulysses theme see Julio Palli Bonet, *Homero en España* (Barcelona, 1953), pp. 97 ff.: on pp. 141 ff. he describes the *Polifemo* of Juan Pérez de Montalbán in which Ulysses is equated with Christ, an analogy severely criticized by Quevedo. Portugese contributions are discussed by A. Loiseau, La légende d'Ulysse dans la littérature portugaise', *Révue de la société des études historiques*, li (1885), 469–74. Naturally Camoens was specially interested in him: see Mary L. Trowbridge, 'The influence of the classics on Camões' *Lusíadas*', *Classical studies in honour of W. A. Oldfather* (Urbana, 1943), pp. 190 ff.

[16] The descriptions of Ulysses's influence on Goethe in this and the following paragraphs are mainly taken from Humphry Trevelyan, *Goethe and the Greeks* (Cambridge, 1941), pp. 64 ff, 104 ff., and E. M. Butler, *The tyranny of Greece over Germany* (Cambridge, 1935), pp. 94–5. Goethe was familiar with Ulysses in Calderon and Shakespeare as well as in Homer. For a notable judgment of his on *Troilus and Cressida* see J. E. Spingarn, *Goethe's literary essays* (London, 1921). Goethe may have derived his conception of Ulysses as a *Naturmensch* from Blackwell's very influential *Enquiry into the life and writings of Homer* (1735) through Herder: see M. L. Clarke, *Greek studies in England* 1700–1830 (Cambridge, 1945), p. 130.

[17] Trevelyan, op. cit., p. 165. For the play in general see *Goethe-Handbuch* (ed. by Julius Zeitler, Stuttgart, 1916–18) iii, 18–20, and G. Kettner, *Goethes Nausikaa* (Berlin, 1912).

[18] Butler, op. cit., p. 113.

[19] For efforts by Bungert, Viehoff, Schreyer, and von Geibel to complete Goethe's play see *Goethe-Handbuch* iii, 20, and Gaude.

[20] For post-Goethean interpretations of Ulysses in German literature see Gaude and Matzig. For a general survey of classicism in Germany (with bibliography) see Highet, pp. 367–90 and 661–70.

[21] For the general implications of this term see B. H. Stern, *The rise of romantic Hellenism in English literature* (Menasha, Wisconsin, 1940). He cites, with other evidence for the prevailing sense of renewal, the final lyric in Shelley's *Hellas*—'A new Ulysses leaves once more / Calypso for his native shore'.

[22] In Bush's list of poems on classical themes published in England 1786–1936 (*Myth. and the romantic tradn.*, pp. 540–92), by far the majority since 1840 on the Ulysses legend concern his experiences with Circe, Calypso, Nausicaa, and the Sirens.

[23] e.g. William Gager in his Latin play *Ulysses redux* (1591–2). See *Hermathena* lxxix (1952), 45–6.

[24] For this and other specimens of seventeenth- and eighteenth-century allegorizations of Homeric themes see Finsler, Cesareo, and *Hermathena* lxxxi (1953), p. 52. Writers in England and the Netherlands chiefly dwelt on parallels between the *Odyssey* and the Old Testament.

[25] I owe my information about Bilderdyk's play to Dr. M. H. van der Valk.

[26] Phillips includes episodes from earlier parts of the *Odyssey*. His Ulysses is noticeably more subservient to feminine influence than in most of the tradition, and there is a good deal of Yellow Book eroticism in some scenes. But his love of Ithaca is expressed in a fine speech to Calypso, and he speaks with characteristic strength after his return to Ithaca. It seems as if Phillips, tired himself of the languorous airs of the 1890's, could appreciate Ulysses's desire to leave Calypso's amorous, violet-perfumed grot for 'gaunt Ithaca'. Contrast Pascoli's attitude, as described later in this chapter.

[27] See A. Laudien, 'Gerhart Hauptmanns Bogen des Odysseus', *Neue Jährbucher f. d. klass. Altertum* xlvii (1921), 215–23, also Gaude and Matzig. Matzig emphasizes the *Naturgewalt* aspects of Hauptmann's Odysseus. For Hauptmann's attitude to the Homeric hero Gaude cites his *Griechischer Frühling* (1912), p. 13: 'Allerlei Vorgänge der Odyssee, die ich wieder gelesen habe, beschäftigen meine Phantasie. Der schlaue Lugner der selbst Pallas Athene belügt, gibt manches zu denken', and p. 121, 'Ich bin durchaus homerisch gestimmt'.

[28] As Matzig notes this quality was previously expressed in Hauptmann's novel, *Emmanuel Quint, der Narr in Christo*, four years before (1910).

[29] In discussing Eyvind Johnson's novel I have relied on the French and English translations, *Heureux Ulysse* by E. and P. de Man (Paris, 1950) and *Return to Ithaca* by M. A. Michael (London, 1952). The former includes a short critical preface discussing aspects of Johnson's Ulysses and Penelope.

[30] See chapter six above. The legend that Ulysses died in Etruria inspired one notable English poem—*The Last of Ulysses* by W. S. Landor (published in *Hellenics*, 1847): he had previously published a Latin version in 1830. For his sources see Stephen Wheeler, *The complete works of W. S. Landor* (London, 1933), xiii, p. 382. Some references to Ulysses will also be found in Landor's dialogue between Homer, Laertes, and Agatha, in *Heroic Idylls* (1863). The Odysseus referred to in *Imaginary conversations: miscellaneous dialogues* xv is not the Ithacan but the contemporary Greek Klepht whom Byron and Trelawney also admired.

[31] Hallam Tennyson, *Alfred Lord Tennyson* (London, 1897), i, 196.

[32] W. H. Auden, *Tennyson: an introduction and selection* (London, 1946), p. xix.

[33] For Tennyson's early adoration of Byron note especially his conduct after the news of Byron's death in 1824 as described by Sir Charles Tennyson, op. cit., in n. 34, p. 33. Byron describes his chronic *taedium vitae* in a letter of January 1, 1821: 'What is the reason that I have been, all my lifetime, more or less ennuyé . . .? I . . . presume it is constitutional,—as well as the waking in low spirits, which I have invariably done for many years. Temperance and exercise, which I have practised at times, and for a long time together vigorously and violently, made little or no difference. Violent passions did—when under their immediate influence—it is odd, but—I was agitated, but *not* in depressed spirits.'

[34] Cf. Tennyson's remark, cited by Sir James Knowles in 'Aspects of Tennyson', *Nineteenth Century* xxxiii (1893), 182: 'There is more about myself in "Ulysses" (sc. than in *In Memoriam*), which was written under the sense of loss and all that had gone by, but that still life must be

fought out to the end. It was more written with the feeling of his loss upon me than many poems in "In Memoriam".'

[35] Tennyson had been familiar with the *Divine Comedy* from his boyhood: see Paget J. Toynbee, *A British tribute to Dante* (1921), p. 59. Boyd's and Cary's translations had recently stimulated English interest. The library in Tennyson's home contained a copy of Boyd's *Inferno*. See further in *Alfred Tennyson* by Sir Charles Tennyson (London, 1949) for this and for the poet's early interest in Homer, Shakespeare, and Byron.

[36] Tennyson, like Dante, Goethe, Joyce, and many other writers on Ulysses, had an eager scientific curiosity; cf. Sir Charles Tennyson, op. cit., pp. 57 and 149, and especially his youthful verse: 'Would I could pile fresh life on life and dull / The sharp desire of knowledge still with knowing. / Art, Science, Nature, everything is full / As my own soul is full to overflowing'.

[37] Another possible echo from *Troilus and Cressida* may be heard in Tennyson's phrase 'Death closes all', cf. *T. and C.* 4, 5, 223, 'The end crowns all'.

[38] With Ulysses's veiled contempt for Telemachus here cf. E. M. W. Tillyard on romantic individualism in *Five poems* (London, 1948), p. 85: 'At his worst the self-propelled wanderer expressed a kind of snobbery of pessimism: only the inferior and insensitive find repose: the best people are like Io, driven about the world by the gadfly of remorse or of hypertrophied sensibilities.' Cf. also Melville in *Moby Dick*: 'In landlessness alone lies the highest truth, indefinite as God.'

[39] Bush, pp. 208–11, makes some valuable observations on *Ulysses*, among them: 'Out of his (the poet's) grief and philosophic bewilderment the poem was born, and it expounds no ready-made moral lesson; the forces of order and courage win hard victory over the dark mood of chaos and defeat'; 'Both in spirit and in many details the poem is quite un-Greek'; 'In the process of modernization Ulysses naturally loses his notable guile, and is endowed with a nineteenth-century elegiac sensibility and magnanimous reflectiveness, a capacity for not only seeking experience but interpreting it' But, without my entirely agreeing with Auden's view, I find rather less 'Doric strength' and much less magnanimity (especially in Ulysses's scornful reference to Penelope, Telemachus and the Ithacans) in the poem. For what amounts to a recantation of the spirit of restlessness in *Ulysses* see Tennyson's later poem *To Ulysses* (meaning W. G. Palgrave), especially v. 8.

[40] A detailed comparison between Dante's and Pascoli's Ulysses, together with a discussion of Dante's influence on other Italian poets is given by Bertoni.

[41] Other notable poems by Pascoli on the Ulysses legend are *Anticlo* and *Il sonno di Odisseo*, but they are less philosophical than *L'ultimo viaggio* and add nothing noteworthy to the characterization of Ulysses.

[42] *Maia* 31–3. The first phrase is, of course, a direct quotation from *Inferno* 26, 94. Cf. Bertoni, p. 29, for d'Annunzio's use of Dante's Ulysses.

[43] *Laus vitae* xvii (*L'heroe senza compagno*). In this poem Ulysses becomes a supreme pattern for modern heroes. The description of Ulysses's appearance in *Laus vitae* iv is stylistically vivid but commonplace in conception: compare the livelier vignette by Matthew Arnold in *The strayed reveller* (1849): 'This spare dark-featured, / Quick-eyed stranger / Ah, and I see too / His sailor's bonnet, / His short coat, travel-tarnish'd, / With one arm bare!' It is regrettable that Arnold attempted no full characterization of Ulysses.

[44] *Laus vitae* iv.

[45] Emile Gebhart, *Les dernières aventures du divin Ulysse* (in *D'Ulysse à Panurge: contes héroï-comiques*, Paris, 1902): a sardonic study in sensuality, cruelty and disaster, curiously like Pascoli's *Last voyage* in the outline of its narrative, but utterly different in its harsh, embittered tone. When Ulysses in the end revisits the ruins of Troy he is filled with remorse for his part in the death of Astyanax. Eventually Telegonus, his son by Circe, a sinister, sadistic youth, kills him under a mass of tottering masonry.

[46] *The world's desire* by H. Rider Haggard and Andrew Lang (1890): Ulysses seeks the supreme manifestation of spiritual beauty in Helen, who is 'the world's desire'. Among other remarkable experiences he meets Moses and the Children of Israel, and becomes involved with the Spirit of Primeval Evil, before he finally triumphs at his death. As in Phillips's *Ulysses* feminine influences (here of the Haggardian mystical variety) predominate. Nothing significant is added to Ulysses's character, except a vague yearning for half-spiritual, half-erotic revelations.

[47] Arturo Graf, *L'ultimo viaggio di Ulisse* (published in *Le Danaidi*, 2nd edn., Turin, 1905): a narrative poem in about 300 lines; its chief novelty is that in the end Ulysses catches a glimpse of the New World before being overwhelmed by a hurricane, a novelty which

Graf apparently owed to V. Finali's *Cristoforo Colombo e il viaggio di Ulisse nel poema di Dante* (1895). Graf also refers to Tennyson, Pascoli, and some classical sources. See further in Bertoni, p. 28.

[48] Sentimental: e.g. J. W. Mackail in *Love's looking glass* (London, 1891) as quoted in chapter four, and L. S. Amery's story, *The last voyage of Ulysses* (in *The Stranger of the Ulysses*, London, 1934). Cynical: e.g. Gebhart in n. 44 above and Lion Feuchtwanger in *Odysseus and the Sirens* (London, 1949) on Nausicaa. Hedonistic: e.g. *Ulysses* by Robert Graves (*Collected poems*, 1914–47). Giraudoux's *Elpénor* (Paris, 1938) presents Ulysses's adventures with the Cyclops and the Sirens, together with a travesty of the Nausicaa episode, in a mocking, witty, fanciful style. The Cyclops, for example, lives in 'the world of ideas' and is overcome by a tissue of disconcerting philosophic parodoxes produced by Ulysses (much in the manner of Euripides's *Cyclops*); and Ulysses does not hear the Sirens because the Companions talk so much: the frivolous approach.

ADDITIONAL NOTE. H. Hunger in his *Lexikon der griechischen und römischen Mythologie* (Vienna, 1953) s.v. *Odysseus* mentions some versions of the Ulysses theme in modern literature (mostly French and German) not referred to by me: also some musical renderings (to which add Butler's oratorio cited in n. 14 above), most notably Monteverdi's *Il ritorno d'Ulisse in patria* (1641) with libretto by Giacomo Badaro.

NOTES TO CHAPTER XV

In the section on James Joyce I am chiefly indebted to the following: Budgen, op. cit:, E. R. Curtius, *James Joyce und sein Ulysses* (Zurich, 1929), Stuart Gilbert, *James Joyce's 'Ulysses'*, (2nd edn., London, 1952), Herbert Gorman, *James Joyce: a definitive biography* (London, 1941), Seon Givens (editor), *james joyce: two decades of criticism* (New York, 1948), Harry Levin, *James Joyce: a critical introduction* (London, 1944), Richard M. Kain, *Fabulous voyager: James Joyce's 'Ulysses'* (Chicago, 1947). Citations from *Ulysses* refer to the Bodley Head edn., London, 1947. Some other aspects of Bloom's Odyssean characteristics are suggested in my article in *Comparative Literature* v (1953), 125–36, and cf. n. 14 to chapter fourteen.

[1] *Ulysses* contains 260,430 words (according to Hanley's index as cited by Levin, p. 70), Kazantzakis's *Odyssey* 33,333 lines averaging about six words a line (=200,000 words, approximately), Homer's *Iliad* and *Odyssey* 15,692 + 12,109 lines, say 195,000 words (but *Ulysses* is out of sight in much of the *Iliad*).

[2] For the epic quality of *Ulysses* see Hugh Kenner, Joyce's *Ulysses*: Homer and Hamlet', *Essays in criticism* ii (1952), 85–104, and cf. Shelley's remarks on Dante as an epic poet as cited by A. J. Symonds, *Introduction to the study of Dante*, chapter four: 'Homer was the first and Dante was the second epic poet: that is, the second poet, the series of whose creations bore a defined and intelligible relation to the knowledge and sentiment of the age in which he lived, and of the ages which followed it. . . .' And (after a reference to Milton): 'Besides these three poets there is none who, in the form of a continuous work of art, has succeeded in fixing any moment so specific and representative in the history of thought as these. . . . Were *Don Quixote* a poem Cervantes might take his stand with Homer, Dante, and Milton, with a better right than Ariosto'.

[3] See Kain, p. 38, Levin, pp. 59–60, for analyses of the time, place, and Homeric parallels, of the episodes in *Ulysses*; and cf. Gilbert in general for some extraordinarily minute analogies to Homeric details. In Joyce's MS. each episode was headed by its Homeric description, but these sub-titles were removed before the book went to press.

[4] Kain, p. 37, prefers to see the four levels of *Ulysses* as: the classical (Homeric), the medieval (symbolic), the naturalistic (time and place), and the poetic (tonal). But this seems to confuse categories of form, meaning, and setting; and it is misleading to identify the symbolical with the medieval.

[5] Cf. Kenner, loc. cit., p. 88: 'much of Bloom's ignobility is a function of the ignoble material with which his prudence, charity, temperance, fortitude, justice, etc., are engaged'.

[6] Professor Stanislaus Joyce has kindly informed me that his brother had studied the following writers on Ulysses: Virgil, Ovid, Dante, Shakespeare, Racine, Fénelon, Tennyson, Phillips, d'Annunzio, and Hauptmann, as well as Samuel Butler's *The Authoress of the Odyssey* and Bérard's *Les Phéniciens et l'Odyssée*, and the translations by Butler and Cowper.

[7] When set an essay on the subject 'My favourite hero' at school when he was thirteen, Joyce wrote on Ulysses. For a reference to Ulysses in a letter of his dated February 2, 1907,

see Gorman, p. 176. Levin and C. Shattuck (in Givens, pp. 47–94) give an analysis of the many Ulyssean traits in Joyce's *Dubliners* (1914), noting amongst others the following motifs: exile owing to the wrath of a god, longing for home, a sense of wonder, caution, grief, loneliness, amorousness, and (more specifically) a scarred leg, the return of the wanderer, and reunion with his wife. These critics also identify several characters in *Dubliners* with Ulysses. But there is no sustained identification. For Joyce's interest in the many-sidedness of Ulysses's character see Budgen passim, especially pp. 16–17, where Joyce contrasts Ulysses favourably with Faust and Hamlet as a 'complete all-round character' (and cf. 'Conversations with James Joyce' by Georges Borach, translated by Joseph Prescott in *College English* xv (1954), 325–7, which adds references to Don Quixote and Dante). C. G. Jung (in *Nimbus*, as cited in n. 8 to chapter sixteen) has remarked (p. 18), 'Ulysses stands to the man Joyce as Faust to Goethe, or as Zarathustra to Nietzsche'.

⁸ Cf. Curtius, pp. 27–8.

⁹ The identification of the Cyclops with furious nationalism recalls Vico's political allegories. Cf. also T. S. Eliot's comparison of Sweeny (presumably an Irishman) with Polyphemus in *Sweeny erect* (1920).

¹⁰ Professor Stanislaus Joyce has informed me that Joyce made a special study of schoolgirl journals to get an authentically novelettish flavour for his Nausicaa episode.

¹¹ For Joyce's views on the Slaughter of the Suitors see Budgen, pp. 262–3, and cf. *Ulysses* p. 635 for Bloom's reluctance to shed human blood 'even when the end justified the means'.

¹² The recurrence of the word 'parallax' as a motif in Bloom's thoughts indicates a special interest in astronomy—a traditional quality mentioned by Homer, Dante, and Gower.

¹³ For the extraordinary range of Bloom's intellectual curiosity see Kain, p. 246.

¹⁴ Joyce had academic authority for making his Ulysses partly Jewish. Bérard's theories had pointed to strong Semitic influences on the *Odyssey*, and Cesareo had described him as *una specie d'Ebreo errante del mondo greco*. Cf. Budgen, p. 174, where Joyce remarks 'There's a lot to be said for the theory that the *Odyssey* is a Semitic poem'. Joyce had many Jewish friends when writing Ulysses and admired their domestic virtues (see Jolas in Givens, op. cit., p. 23).

¹⁵ The variation 'Darkinbad the Brightdayler' in Bloom's final thoughts (*Ulysses*, pp. 697–8) may be a reference to the theory, popularized by Max Müller, that Odysseus was a solar figure. F. L. Lucas, *The decline and fall of the romantic ideal* (2nd edn., 1948), pp. 120 ff., discusses Ulysses and the Ancient Mariner in romantic literature: on the whole the more 'gothic' Mariner was preferred as a symbol of the wanderer in the nineteenth century. For recent discussions of the modern sea-wanderer motif see E. M. W. Tillyard, *Five poems* (London, 1948), p. 71 (the Ancient Mariner represents 'the small but persisting class of mental adventurers who are not content with the appearances surrounding them but who attempt to get behind'), and W. H. Auden, *The enchafèd flood* (London, 1951).

¹⁶ The last section of *Ulysses*, not discussed here, consists in the soliloquy of Bloom's wife. There is some similarity between her allegorical aspects (she is described on p. 697 as being 'in the attitude of Gea-Tellus') and the Calypso of the last scene in Pascoli's *Ultimo viaggio*.

Mr. Edmund Epstein has kindly shown me two further Homeric analogies in the closing scenes. Bloom lights a cone of incense in the bedroom; this corresponds to the fumigation of the hall by Odysseus after the slaughter of the Suitors (*Odyssey* 22,481 ff.). Bloom finds that the bed has been much moved about in his absence: this provides an ironic contrast to the impossibility of moving the nuptial bed as described in *Odyssey* 23,183 ff.

¹⁷ See Arthur Power, *From the old Waterford house* (London, n.d.), p. 67, quoted by Joseph Prescott in P.M.L.A. lxviii (1953), 1223.

¹⁸ For evidence that Kazantzakis to some extent identified himself with his hero see his *Toda-Raba*, p. 113 cited in French by O. Merlier in his edition of Kazantzakis's *Ascèse: salvatores dei*, Athens, 1951, p. 24 (my translation): 'You know my personal leader is not one of the three leaders of human spirits: neither Faust, nor Hamlet, nor Don Quixote: but Don Ulysses! It was on his sailing-ship that I arrived in the U.S.S.R. I have not the insatiable thirst of the occidental mind, nor do I sway between yes and no to end in immobility, nor do I any longer possess the sublimely ludicrous urge of the noble windmill-slayer. I am a mariner of Ulysses with heart afire but with mind ruthless and clear: not, however, of the Ulysses who returned to Ithaca, but of the other Ulysses who returned, killed his enemies, and, stifled in his native land, put out to sea again.' He goes on to say how, like Ulysses, he heard the siren-voice of Russia (*la sirène slave*) but kept his soul intact. Cf. *Ascèse*, p. 71:

'Nous sommes une humble lettre, une syllable, un mot de l'immense Odyssée. Abîmés dans un chant gigantesque nous luisons comme luisent les humbles cailloux tant qu'ils sont au fond de la mer.' The sections entitled *Moi*, *la Race*, *l'Humanité*, and *la Terre* in *Ascèse* correspond to some extent with the four main phases of his *Odyssey*.

¹⁹ The following summary of Kazantzakis's *Odyssey* (Athens, 1938) has had to be based almost entirely on translations and synopses, as in my own efforts to grapple with the text (which was accessible to me only in Oxford and Athens) I found the style too obscure for my knowledge of modern Greek. (Apparently even Greeks have also found it difficult, despite the glossary of some 2,000 words appended to the first edition.) In such circumstances I would not have ventured to discuss the book at all if I had not been convinced by Robert Levesque's survey in *Domaine Grec* 1930–46 (Paris, 1947) that it was one of the two chief contributions to the Ulysses myth in modern times. In what follows I am very greatly indebted to Mr. George Savidis who provided me with a supplement to Levesque's synopsis (which ends at the Foundation of the City) as well as with many valuable references to Kazantzakis's other works. I am also grateful to Sir Maurice Bowra, Professor Phaidon Koukoules of Athens, Mr. Philip Sherrard, and Professor C. A. Trypanis, for help and information. I hope that my derivative study of Kazantzakis's book despite its inadequacy may stimulate further study of this remarkable work in English-speaking lands. But I trust that no one will build on my remarks without checking them with the text.

²⁰ *Nea Hestia* xxxiv, 389 (15 Aug., 1943).

²¹ See *Helen* in Index.

²² There is a Homeric parallel to this solitary communion with God by Kazantzakis's hero. In *Odyssey* 12, 333–4, Odysseus on the island of Thrinakia went away from the Companions to pray to the gods to see if one of them would show him a way of escaping from his difficulties. The destruction of the Companions soon followed.

²³ In *Ascèse* (p. 50) Kazantzakis exclaims: 'I am the wonder-working fakir, seated motionless at the crossroads of the senses to watch the birth and disappearance of the world, to watch the crowd move and shout on the multicoloured pathways of this universe of vanity'. For previous comparisons between Ulysses and Indian religious figures see Fries and Carnoy.

²⁴ Kazantzakis had translated Dante's *Divine Comedy* in 1934.

²⁵ *Nea Hestia*, loc. cit.; cf. *Ascèse*, pp. 36–40.

²⁶ *Voyage to Mount Sinai*, p. 238 (as quoted in *Ascèse*, p. 36; cf. p. 43 ff.). For more on Kazantzakis's conception of Crete see *Ascèse*, pp. 13, 16, 34 (where he hopes he has some Bedouin blood in his veins). On p. 27 he is quoted as regarding Crete as intermediary between Europe and Asia (rather than Africa), a shift of emphasis.

²⁷ *Nea Hestia*, loc. cit., pp. 1028–9. Besides his epic *Odyssey* Kazantzakis has produced a drama *Odysseas* (Athens, 1928) based on the return of Odysseus as described in the second half of Homer's *Odyssey* (like Hauptmann's *Bow of Odysseus*). Two novels of his have been recently translated into English, *Zorba the Greek* (K. ranks this rascally, lovable Greek figure with Nietzsche, Bergson, and Homer, as a dominant influence in his spiritual evolution: see *Ascèse*, pp. 21 and 23, where Buddha, Mahomet, Confucius, and Dante are also suggested), and *Christ re-crucified* (a tragic conflict between Greek asceticism and Greek hedonism as personified in an Orthodox community).

ADDITIONAL NOTE. I regret that linguistic difficulties have prevented me from following the Ulysses theme further in modern Greek literature. For Seferis's *On a foreign line* see chapter fifteen. Another poem on a similar theme in *Ithaca* by C. P. Kavafy, translated by John Mavrogordato in *The poems of C. P. Kavafy* (London, 1951), pp. 47–8: for suggested influences see T. Melanos, *Mythologia tes Kavafikes Politeias*, Alexandria, 1943, pp. 30–1. I owe this reference to Mr. George Savidis, who has also told me of a remarkable version of the Iphigeneia incident written in 1720 by Petros Katzaïtes, a Cephallonian, for local performance (edited by E. Kriaras, *Collection de l'Institut Français* 43, Athens, 1950). In it Odysseus is portrayed in a favourable light with his traditional characteristics of cunning, wisdom, eloquence, and valour, embodied in an Ionian nobleman under Venetian rule.

NOTES TO CHAPTER XVI

¹ The effects of historical assimilation on mythological figures could also, of course, be traced in the graphic arts, ancient and modern. But this is beyond my scope. Some material will be found in the following: F. Inghirami, *Galleria Omerica* (Fiesole, 1831–6) as indicated at *Ulisse* in the indexes; A. Baumeister, *Denkmäler des klassischen Altertums* (Munich, 1889) ii,

1035–46; F. Müller, *Die antiker Odyssee-Illustrationen* (Berlin, 1912); K. Bulas, *Les illustrations antiques de l'Iliade* (Lwów, 1929), and in *American Journal of Archaeology* liv (1950), 112–18; and Jane Harrison (see Book list). Medieval conceptions are to be found, e.g., in the Manchester MS. of Lydgate's *Troy Tale* (John Rylands Library), pp. 153, 155, 162, 168. (Mr. L. D. Ettlinger of the Warburg Institute has kindly informed me that a monograph by Professor Saxl on medieval illustrations to the Troy Romance will appear soon.) Among painters and draughtsmen who have treated the Ulysses theme are: Pintoricchio, Castello, Rubens, Claude Lorrain, Ingres, Fuseli, Turner, Garnier, Preller, Doucet, Samuel Palmer, and Russell Flint. Hunger (see additional note to chapter fourteen) adds: van Balen, Boecklin, Caracci.

² On the use of myths for self-discovery and self-understanding see Snell, p. 204.

³ T. S. Eliot, *The three voices of poetry* (London, 1953), p. 13, notes that in the dramatic monologue 'what we normally hear . . . is the voice of the poet, who has put on the costume and make-up either of some historical character, or of one out of fiction', and 'the author is just as likely to identify the character with himself, as himself with the character'. (He goes on to note a contrast with true drama where several characters contend.) On the basis of this distinction one might say that d'Annunzio, for example, tended to identify Ulysses with himself and Tennyson rather more to identify himself with (mainly the Dantesque) Ulysses. My view that Dante 'put something of himself' into his Ulysses receives some support from Dr. Eliot's interpretation of the dramatic monologue; for Ulysses's speech in *Inferno* 26 is essentially of that genre.

⁴ Cf. T. S. Eliot, op. cit., pp. 10–11: 'I can't see, myself, any way to make a character live except to have a profound sympathy with that character. . . . It seems to me that what happens, when an author creates a vital character, is a sort of give-and-take. The author may put into that character, besides its other attributes, some trait of his own, some strength or weakness, some tendency to violence or to indecision, some eccentricity even, that he has found in himself. . . Some bit of himself that the author gives to a character may be the germ from which the life of that character starts. On the other hand, a character which succeeds in interesting its author may elicit from the author latent potentialities of his own being'. Similarly Byron (Letter to Moore, March 4, 1822): 'My ideas of a character run away with me: like all imaginative men, I, of course, embody myself with the character while I *draw* it . . .'.

⁵ There is a *reductio ad absurdum* of the personal fallacy about the authorship of the Homeric poems in the curious work by 'Constantin Koliades' (a pseudonym for J. B. Lechevalier) entitled *Ulysse-Homère, ou du véritable auteur de l'Iliade et de l'Odyssée* (Paris, 1829) in which it is argued that Ulysses must have written both poems himself. His view had been previously suggested by Jacob Bryant in his *Dissertation concerning the war of Troy* (2nd edn., London, 1799): '. . . I am led to think that in the history of Ulysses, we may trace the life and adventures of Homer. The sufferings of the one were copied from what the other had experienced; and all the sorrow and anguish displayed, and all those melancholy emotions, originated in the poet's breast'. On this fallacy see also the remarks by J. Dover Wilson in *The fortunes of Falstaff* (Cambridge, 1943), p. 9.

⁶ Compare the degeneration in the meaning of the German word *List*, from 'wisdom' to 'trickery'.

⁷ See the books by Butler and Austen cited in the notes to chapter one.

⁸ Jung's theory of archetypes seems, within my very slight knowledge, to offer some possible explanations for the use of Ulysses as a personal symbol. Cf., as a mere sample, the following remarks from *The psychology of C. G. Jung* by J. Jacobi (5th edn., London, 1951), pp. 56 ff.: 'Themes of a mythological nature whose symbolism illustrates universal human history . . .'; 'When the archetype clothes itself in corresponding symbols . . . it puts the subject into a state of profound emotion, whose consequences may be unpredictable'; 'The archetype . . . has inherent in its bipolar structure the dark side as well as the light' (compare the Autolycus-Athene antithesis in Ulysses); and p. 113: 'These symbols from the unconscious, whether they make their appearance as dreams, visions, or fantasies, represent a kind of "individual mythology" that has its closest analogies in the typical figures of mythology, sagas, and fairy tales'. See also Jung, *Modern man in search of a soul* (London, 1933), p. 189, on the theme 'It is therefore to be expected of the poet that he will resort to mythology in order to give his experience its most fitting expression'. Miss Maud Bodkin, in her Jungian interpretation of literature, *Archetypal patterns in poetry* (London, 1934), p. 245, remarks: 'The archetypal hero-figure stands poised between height and depth, between the Divine and the Devilish, swung forward and upward in reflection of imagination's universal range, hurled

T

backward and downward in expression of individual limitation and the restraining censure of the whole upon the part'. This certainly is paralleled in the ambivalence of the Ulysses figure.

So far as I have found from a brief search, Jung does not seem to have considered Ulysses specially in his theory of archetypal figures. (But in his monologue on Joyce's *Ulysses* in *Nimbus* ii, 1 (June–August, 1953), 7–20, he notes 'an archetypal background' to Joyce's book: 'Behind Dedalus and Bloom there stand, no doubt, the eternal figures of spiritual and carnal man'. I am grateful to my colleague, Dr. E. G. Bennet, for this reference.) However, on p. 64 of *The psychology of G. C. Jung* Prometheus and Hercules are mentioned: so also in more general terms the Mage and the Wise Man. Perhaps, then, Ulysses's popularity as a personal symbol could be explained on the grounds that his character, as Homer fulfilled it, contained some of these dynamic archetypal forms (not, I think, that Ulysses exclusively represented any single one of these forms). I must leave it to others, if they wish, to explore this aspect of the Ulysses theme.

BOOKS AND ARTICLES CITED BY AUTHORS' NAMES

Allen, T. W., *Homer, the origins and transmission*. Oxford, 1924.
Altenberg, F. W., *Ulixes qualis ab Homero in Odyssea descriptus*. Schleusingen, 1837.
Barker, Sir Ernest, *Traditions of civility*. Cambridge, 1948.
Bérard, V., *Les Phéniciens et l'Odyssée*. Paris, 1902.
Bertoni, G., 'Ulisse nella "Divina Commedia" e nei poeti moderni'. *Arcadia* xiv,
    vol. v–vi N.S. (1931), 19–31.
Bethe, E., *Homer* iii: *Die sage vom troischen Kriege*. Leipzig, 1927.
Budgen, Frank, *James Joyce and the making of 'Ulysses'*. London, 1934.
Carpenter, Rhys, *Folk tale, fiction, and saga in the Homeric epics*. Berkeley, 1946.
Carnoy, A., 'Les mythes Indiens de Mātariçvan-Agni et ceux d'Ulysse en Grèce'.
    Museon xliv (1931), 319–34.
Cesareo, P., 'L'evoluzione storica del carattere d'Ulisse'. *Rivista di Storia Antica* iii
    (1898), 75–102, and iv (1899), 17–38, 383–412.
Chaignet, A.-Ed., *Les Héros et les héroines d'Homère*. Paris, 1894.
Croiset, M., 'Observations sur la légende primitive d'Ulysse'. *Mémoires de
    l'Institut National de France, Académie des inscriptions et belles-lettres*, xxxviii, 2
    (1911), 171–214.
Crooke, W., 'The wooing of Penelope'. *Folklore* ix (1898), 97–133.
    'Some notes on Homeric folklore'. *Folklore* xix (1908), 52–77, 153–89.
Davaux, Jean, *Etudes sur le personnage d'Ulysse dans la littérature grecque, d'Homère
    à Sophocle*. Unpublished thesis, Louvain, 1946.
Delebecque, Edouard, *Euripide et la guerre du Péloponnèse*. Paris, 1951.
Frazer, J. G., *Apollodorus*, 2 vols., Oxford, 1921.
Fries, C., *Studien zur Odyssee*. 1. *Das Zagmukfest auf Scheria*. 2. *Odysseus der
    bhikshu*. Leipzig, 1910, 1911.
Garassino, A., 'Ulisse nel teatro greco'. *Atene e Roma* x (1930), 219–51.
Gaude, P., *Das Odysseusthema in der neuen deutschen Literatur, besonders bei Haupt-
    mann und Lienhard*. Halle, 1916.
Geddes, W. D., *The problem of the Homeric poems*. London, 1878.
Goosens, R., review of Grégoire op. cit. *L'Antiquité Classique* iii (1934–5), 321 ff.
Grégoire, H., 'Euripide, Ulysse et Alcibiade'. *Bulletin de la classe des lettres, Acad.
    Roy. Belgique* xix (1933), 83–106.
Gruppe, O., *Griechische Mythologie und Religionsgeschichte* i (Munich, 1906).
Guthrie, W. K. C., 'Odysseus in the Ajax'. *Greece and Rome* xlviii (1947), 115–19.
Harrison, Jane, *Myths of the Odyssey in art and literature*. London, 1882.
Hart, W. M., 'High comedy in the Odyssey'. *University of California Publications
    in Classical Philology* xii (1943), 263–8.
Hartmann, A., *Untersuchungen über die Sage von Tod des Odysseus*. Munich, 1917.
Highet, Gilbert, *The classical tradition*. Oxford, 1949.
Hole, R., *An essay on the character of Ulysses as delineated by Homer*. London, 1807.
Houben, J. A., *Qualem Homerus in Odyssea finxerit Ulixem*. Trier, 1856.
    Qualem Homerus in Iliade finxerit Ulixem. Trier, 1869.
Jaeger, Werner, *Paideia*. English edn., vol. i. Oxford, 1939.
Kretschmar, O., *Beiträge zur Charakteristik des homerischen Odysseus*. Trier, 1903.

Lang, A., *Homer and the Epic*. London, 1893.

　The world of Homer. London, 1910.

Lang, A., ed., *Anthropology and the classics*. Oxford, 1908.

Lesky, A., 'Hethitische Texte und griechischer Mythos'. *Anzeiger der Osterreich. Akad. der Wissensch. Phil.-hist. Klasse*, Vienna, 1950, 137–59.

Levy, G. R., *The sword from the rock*. London, 1953.

Mahaffy, J. P., 'The degradation of Odysseus in Greek Literature'. *Hermathena* i (1873–4), 265–75.

Marcowitz, G., *Ulixis ingenium quale et Homerus finxerit et tragici*. Düsseldorf, 1854. Not seen.

Martorana, Michelina, *Ulisse nella letteratura Latina*. Palermo and Rome, 1926.

Masqueray, P., 'Agamemnon, Ménélas, Ulysse dans Euripide'. *Revue des Etudes Anciennes* vi (1904), 171–204.

Matzig, R. B., *Odysseus, Studie zu antiken stoffen in der modernen Literatur, besonders im Drama*. St. Gallen, 1949.

Menrad, J., *Der Urmythus der Odyssee und seine dichterische Erneuerung*. Lindau, 1910.

Meyer, E., 'Der Ursprung des Odysseus mythus'. *Hermes* xxx (1895), 241–73.

Müller, H., *Odysseus, Mann, Seele und Schicksal*. 2nd edn. Chemnitz Brunner, 1932.

Murray, Gilbert, *The Rise of the Greek epic*. 4th edn., Oxford, 1934.

Osterwald, K. W., *Hermes-Odysseus*. Halle, 1853.

Patroni, G., *Commenti mediterranei all Odiseo di Omero*. Milan, 1950.

Pauly, Wissowa, Kroll, *Real-Encyclopädie der classischen Altertumswissenschaft*. Stuttgart.

Philippson, Paula, 'Die vorhomerische und die homerische Gestalt des Odysseus', *Museum Helveticum* iv (1949), 8–22.

Phillips, E. D., 'Odysseus in Italy'. *Journal of Hellenic Studies* lxxiii (1953), 53–67.

Radermacher, L., 'Die Erzählungen der Odyssee'. *Sitzungsberichte d. Kaiserlich Akad. in Wien, phil.-hist. Kl.* clxxviii (1916), 3–59.

Robert, C., *Die griechische Heldensage*, vol. iii, part 2. Berlin, 1923.

Roscher, W. H., *Ausführliches Lexicon der Griechischen und Römischen Mythologie*, vol. iii, Leipzig, 1897–1902, s. v. *Odysseus* (by J. Schmidt).

Severyns, A., *Le cycle épique dans l'école d'Aristarque*. Liége, 1928.

Schmid, W., and Stählin, O., *Geschichte der Griechischen Literatur*. Munich, various dates.

Schmidt, Johannes, 'Ulixes Posthomericus'. *Berliner Studien* ii (1885), 403–90.

　'De Ulixis in fabulis satyricis persona'. *Commentationes Ribbeckianae* (Leipzig, 1888), 99–114.

　'Ulixes Comicus.' *Jahrbücher fur Class. Phil.* Suppl. vol. 1888, 361 ff.

　Article on Odysseus in Roscher's lexicon (see above), cited as 'Roscher'.

Seeck, O., *Die Quellen der Odyssee*. Berlin, 1887.

Sheppard, J. T., 'Great-hearted Odysseus'. *Journal of Hellenic Studies* lxvi (1936), 36–47.

Shewan, Alexander, *The lay of Dolon*. London, 1911.

Snell, Bruno, *The discovery of mind*. English translation by T. C. Rosenmeyer. Oxford, 1953.

Svoronos, J. N., 'Ulysse chez les Arcadiens et la Télégonie d'Eugammon'. *Gazette Archéologique* xiii (1888), 257–80.

Thomson, J. A. K., *Studies in the Odyssey*. Oxford, 1911.

Tolstoi, J., 'Einige Märchenparallelen zur Heimkehr des Odysseus'. *Philologus* lxxxix (1933), 261–74.

Vikentiev, V., 'Le retour d'Ulysse du point de vue égyptologique et folklorique'. *Bull. de l'Institut d'Egypte* xxix (1948), 183–241.

Wehrli, Fritz, *Zur Geschichte der allegorischen Deutung Homers in Altertum*. Leipzig, 1928.

Wilamowitz-Moellendorff, U. von, *Die Heimkehr des Odysseus*. Berlin, 1927.

Woodhouse, W. J., *The composition of Homer's Odyssey*. Oxford, 1930.

Wüst, Ernst, *Odysseus*, in Pauly (see above), xxxiii, 1937.

GENERAL INDEX

285

INDEX OF GREEK AND LATIN WORDS DISCUSSED